THE PAVERS

THE PAVERS

Dana Hoff

ISBN 978-1-7334411-0-0 (E-book)
ISBN 978-1-7334411-1-7 (Paperback)
ISBN 978-1-7334411-2-4 (Hardback)

This book is a work of fiction. Any references to historical events, real people, or real places are used fictitiously. Other names, characters, places and events are products of the author's imagination, and any resemblance to actual events, places or persons, living or dead, is entirely coincidental.

Front Cover Design by Pintado.
Developmental and Copy Editing by One Love Editing.
Proofreading by Karen Mueller.
Interior Design by Pressbooks.

Printed by Ingram Spark in the United States of America.

First printing edition 2020.

Dana Hoff
O'Fallon, Missouri

danahoffauthor.wixsite.com/books

To my husband, for always being my knight in shining armor. Thank you for your love, and encouraging me no matter where our paths take us. To my parents and my family for raising me with a high dose of creativity.

CONTENTS

THE RECKONING

"Heart rate's dropping!" a nurse shouted as she helped lift a woman onto a steel operating table. *Angels are among us* was tattooed at the base of the nurse's neck in beautiful flourished lettering. *God, I hope so,* I thought. *Looks like she needs some angels right about now.* I stepped closer and peered over the nurse's shoulder at the woman, her strawberry-blonde hair tangled and matted to her pale, ivory skin. Her face was badly bruised with dark swollen welts lining the left side of her face. From the looks of it, she was pretty, in her early twenties, but I couldn't tell from all the damage.

Her body was limp as they cut away her blood-soaked shirt. Her lower body was completely naked as they threw a blue medical towel over her. Blood seeped out of an angry-looking gash on the side of her stomach while a nurse placed an oxygen mask on the lifeless patient. Almost as soon as it was fastened, a defeated, ominous tone rang out in the corner. The heart rate monitor was flatlining. My breath caught in my throat as I stared at the poor woman, wondering if her family knew she was dying. I wondered if she had dreams that she hadn't accomplished yet, or if she'd told the people she loved the most how she felt about them. Did she even have anyone that would miss her?

"Fight hard! We're gonna need you to push through this!" the nurse with the tattoo demanded at her lifeless patient. The monitor continued to sound its alarm in resounding protest, ignoring the nurse's pleas as I looked on helplessly.

"Doesn't look good, does it?" a calm voice chimed in next to me.

Startled, I turned to find a charming young man smiling indignantly back at me with gentle, pale blue eyes. A black vintage hat with a peacock feather at the rim framed his kind face, which seemed completely oblivious to the tragedy unfolding before us. He was a little overly dressed to be in an operating room, his dark navy blue suit tailored perfectly to fit his slender build. All I could manage to do was stare. Where did he come from? He seemed so out of place, yet no one seemed bothered he was there. No one seemed bothered I was there either, for that matter. All their attention was dedicated to the life they were losing, the woman who seemed too young to die. There was too much blood—I couldn't make out her broken form as the medical team surrounded her. I had a sinking suspicion that her life would be lost tonight. There was no way she could be saved now.

"Yeah, I don't think she's going to make it." I looked back over at the mad rush of surgical scrubs dashing around the room, trying to resuscitate her.

I wondered who would have let the strange man in during all the chaos. Everyone was focused, doing everything they were trained to do. There wasn't a moment to spare to open the door. Did he just let himself in? I could feel his eyes still trained on me as the monitor continued to ring out. I found it so strange that he wasn't doing anything to help. He didn't even give the woman a second glance. I wasn't sure if I wanted to ask him what he wanted or to tell him to leave.

I finally settled with "Are you a doctor?" as I smiled politely up at him. I didn't have it in me to be rude—it wasn't my nature—but sometimes I wished I could be more forward. I was the kind of girl who said "sorry" after I bumped into a pole at a grocery store.

The man's blue eyes danced under his tilted hat, as if he were laughing at my presumption. A bright energy seemed to glow around him, but there was no true source. Even his brown oxford shoes glistened from a fresh polish under the hospital fluorescents.

"My sincerest apologies, Georgia. My name is Jerry Carter, and might I say it is a pleasure to finally make your acquaintance." He eagerly extended a hand as he inspected me from head to toe and nodded as if he approved. I squinted back up at him. How did he know my name?

I cautiously reached out to grab his hand and was shocked by his warmth as his long fingers curled around mine. His smile deepened, and gorgeous laugh lines crinkled at both of his temples.

"And no, I'm not a doctor. I'm here on official business… I'm here for *you*." His lips quirked upward .

Me? But why?

"Now, I don't mean to alarm you, but there's two gentlemen that are here to meet you. They're in the lobby down the hall, and I'm afraid it's rather urgent." His kind face grew serious as his eyes wandered over toward the dying woman. I awkwardly dropped my hand from his grip.

"What's it about?" I asked with a suspicious glare as I watched him check his golden Gucci watch.

He nodded toward the poor soul bleeding out on the table. "It's a matter of life and death. Now if you wouldn't mind following me?" He stepped toward the door leading out to the hallway, beckoning me forward. "We don't have much time."

I watched his tall frame disappear as he left the room. My gaze returned to the woman on the table as a nurse brought over the defibrillator while another performed CPR. What could be that urgent? I didn't know how I felt reconvening with a strange man and his mysterious visitors, but maybe I should at least leave the room. I didn't feel I should be there anymore. No one needed me, and I wasn't doing the girl any good by just standing there.

I headed toward the door and peeked down the dimly lit hallway. The corridor was empty but was somehow filled with a buzzing energy I couldn't quite pin down. One would think that hospitals would have more people walking around. *Where is everyone?* I looked down toward the end of the vacant hallway, the strange man nowhere to be seen.

I turned back as the monitor's alarm continued to resonate, echoing down the vast, empty hallway. A wave of nausea coursed through me, my heart sinking even deeper for the mysterious patient. I felt a deep pull away from her, and a more distinct push toward Jerry. A beckoning, a calling. I finally gave in, shooting one last glance at the heartbreaking scene before I continued out the door.

"Jerry?" I shouted, hoping he hadn't gone too far. My voice sounded unfamiliar and flat, like I was in a small, soundproof room. Loneliness and fear started to creep in as my eyes scanned the desolate passage for any sign of life. Suddenly, he poked his head around the corner.

"We don't have all day, Georgia!" he called out at me and disappeared again with a distant chuckle. Despite the fact Jerry was a stranger...and a little odd, for some reason, I was grateful he was there. I quickly jogged down the hall and rounded the corner, where he stood waiting. He grinned at me, his laugh lines crinkling at the corners of his eyes again, and pointed to his left at a seemingly vacant waiting room. I scanned the rows of sterile blue chairs until I noticed two people sitting together, waiting in the corner.

"Go on in, sweetie, and find yourself a seat so we can begin." He waved me in, clapping his hands with unhinged excitement.

At the end of the last row sat an uncharacteristically handsome man. His legs bounced anxiously as his hands ran through his short, light brown hair. Both of his sleeves were rolled up to his elbows, and my eyes widened as I caught sight of a large tattoo on his left forearm. He was too caught up in his own worries to notice I'd joined them as he concentrated on the busy hospital floor. To his left sat a young boy around ten years old with his hands stuffed under his legs, kicking his feet against the floor. He grinned up at me as I picked the empty seat next to him.

"The name's Jack," he greeted, the boy's grin widening as he surveyed me with deep black pools for eyes. "Glad you're here. Dude's been freaking out since we got here." The boy jerked his chin at the man next to him, who immediately stopped bouncing his legs and snapped his eyes up at us.

He was breathless as he seemed to take in his surroundings for the first time. He stilled as he squinted over at Jack, and then his stormy gaze locked with mine. I froze under his glare; his eyes were like stone-cold *steel*. I could feel my mouth dry as he took me in, his eyes slowly trailing across my face, his firm jawline hardening.

"I-I'm Georgia," I sputtered out with a slight smile, unable to break eye contact with him. He didn't return the gesture. Instead, he studied me with careful, watchful eyes, scanning me from head to toe like I was a welcome threat.

"Graham," he grunted, his voice hard as he gripped the armrest on his chair.

I raised my eyebrows at his name. Graham seemed like a strong but gentle name, the kind of name the boy next door would have, and nothing about the man in front of me looked gentle. He glanced out toward the lobby and then turned back to me, eyeing me suspiciously.

4

"Do you know where we are?" he whispered.

A chill went up my spine. His voice was soft but demanding. I imagined he was quite the charmer in a less...mysterious context. My eyes shifted to his tattoo again, which sat proudly on top of a well-defined muscle. At this angle, I could make out the thick, bold words.

Semper Fi.

My dad had a poster in his office with the saying hanging above his desk. It meant *always faithful*. He lived by that mantra. He worked with veterans to help them find jobs and housing. He'd helped servicemen and women from every military branch, especially the Marine Corps. Hot Semper Fi guy was probably in the Marine Corps—it was their motto. It would make sense. His body looked like a weapon, handcrafted by a militant and rigorous workout regimen. He was built for fighting and protecting. His face was strong, with harsh lines, and his gaze was penetrating, dangerous even. He sure as hell wasn't apologizing to inanimate objects at the grocery store. He cocked an eyebrow up, clearly noticing I had just peeked at his muscles. I could feel warmth spread across my cheeks as I straightened up, pulling my shoulders back.

"We're in a...hospital," I retorted, trying to recover from my blatant stare. "What I want to know is *why* we are here? Where is everyone?"

I tore my eyes away from him to scan the empty room, dumbfounded. It was almost Christmas, and the holidays are always the busiest time for hospitals. Everyone is trying to cook things they've never made, getting sick or losing their minds to the stresses of the season. How could *no one* be here?

Jack shook his head and rolled his eyes. "He wouldn't tell us anything. He just told us to sit here until he went and got you." Jack nodded over toward Jerry as he took a seat in the row across from us, exhaling dramatically. His expression darkened as he watched us, his fingers tapping on his knee.

"Jack, Graham, Georgia," Jerry said, his tone unnervingly calm, "I'll just cut right to it, then, because time is of the essence." He adjusted his suit jacket and leaned forward like he was about to share the latest office gossip.

"Your hearts have stopped beating, and your souls have left your bodies." He paused and looked at each of us, his blue eyes ablaze. All I could manage to do was stare stupidly back at him.

"Excuse me?" I coughed out.

Jerry snapped his gaze over toward me, raising his eyebrows as if he were surprised I had spoken first.

"You heard me right, Georgia. You are dead, but not for much longer." He nodded matter-of-factly and glanced down at his watch again. "I suspect you'll need to return in a few minutes, but until then I need to deliver a very important message."

I blinked, trying to process everything he'd just said. He couldn't have just told us that we were...*dead.*

"As I've mentioned, my name is Jerry Carter, and I am your Light...or spirit guide for that matter. I'm here to talk you through a few things before you return to your bodies." He held up his index finger.

"First, welcome to your Reckoning. A Reckoning is sort of like a summoning, or spiritual bond between souls who have never met during their time on Earth. For whatever reason, your souls have decided to link together in the afterlife." He stood up abruptly and made his way across the aisle.

"When a Reckoning occurs, every spiritual bond has an Anchor. The Anchor is the soul that casts out the link that brings souls together." He glanced down at me, his eyes bright with anticipation. "For this bond, that's you."

To my horror, he leaned over and gently patted my knee. I could feel Jack and Graham's eyes burning a hole into the side of my face as I shook my head vehemently.

"You...must be mistaken. I...I honestly didn't mean to cast a link...or whatever you just said." I grabbed the edge of my chair, forcing myself to stay seated when all I wanted to do was escape this nightmare. Jerry's face fell as he watched me.

"Georgia, honey, you didn't do anything wrong. This is divine work in the making. In our business, there is no such thing as a coincidence or a mistake. God works in mysterious ways, and the first step toward accepting your new role is to own that."

My new *role?*

Jerry began pacing in front of us as he ticked his middle finger.

"Second, you all are here because it appears you've been selected to join our Paving ranks. We as Pavers operate as a secret society, but our work is essential for humankind."

A silent snicker interrupted Jerry's rant, and I turned to catch Jack shaking his head with a contemptuous smirk.

"The hell is he talking about?" he muttered under his breath. God how I wish I knew.

Jerry eyed Jack with a calculating stare before continuing. "Call us angels on earth, guides, whatever you want. We are creatures hand-picked by God himself to help our fellow man. That's what we do, and that's what we've always done, since the beginning of time until the day we are no more." He peered down at his watch again, his voice growing fervent.

"And last, but certainly not least, once you return to your bodies, you'll need to find each other. You have a sacred, unbreakable bond now, that no human soul can disrupt. Listen to it. Listen to your instincts, your very hearts. They will help you find each other." He clasped his hands together and peered down at us beneath his hat.

"Although I am your Light, I cannot help you find each other. It is your right of passage, and your duty, to find each other and yours alone. Once you have located one another, I will be able to commence your official training and initiation. Until then, the rest is up to you."

I snuck a look at Graham, his jaw twitching and his shoulders tensing like he was ready for a fight. My eyes flicked to Jack, who stared wide-eyed, his deep black pools narrowing at Jerry.

"I have got to say," Jerry continued with an untimely smile, "I've been observing Reckonings for a few months now, and I've never seen three people connect. It's always just been two...until now. Perhaps God has something extra special planned for you." Then he *winked*, like we should be so lucky.

Jack let out an annoyed laugh. "Dude, are you for real right now? This isn't some punk-ass TV prank show, right?"

I startled from his abrasiveness; I had to do a double take to make sure he was as young as I thought. Yup, he was definitely no older than eleven years old. I frowned at that thought. He was just a kid...yet here he was. *Dead.* Like me...

Jerry's intent gaze fell on the young boy, his mouth dipping to an unnerving frown. "Yes, as serious as a heart attack. As we speak, you don't have a pulse, and you're losing oxygen to your brain every second we stay here," Jerry stated as he stepped forward. He checked his watch one last time before he clapped his hands together, rubbing them excitedly.

"Speaking of which, it's showtime."

I cringed at the way his eyes dazzled. Flashes of the broken and bruised body down the hallway filled my thoughts.

And then, it hit me. That was me. That broken and bruised tragedy was *me*.

And I was going back...

"Returning is beyond painful, without comparison. Not to mention, each of you died...rather violently, so there's that..." Jerry sighed as he glanced over at us. "But know this, and know it well: God is with you every step of the way." Jerry beamed back at us like that was somehow reassuring.

"Now, once you return to your bodies, you might experience...strange phenomenon you'd otherwise explain away with a tired mind. Feel things that seem...incredible. Maybe even *impossible*." He stopped in his tracks, turning toward us with a fierce urgency.

"Make no mistake, listen to your instincts. People tend to write off things so quickly, especially if it doesn't fit into their rational clean-cut box. It's unfortunate, because those are the things they need to see and hear the most."

I felt Jack tense next to me as Jerry glided over toward him.

"All right, kid. You're first." He extended a hand out to Jack, who immediately crossed his arms.

Jack's defiant angle made him seem much thinner than I had noticed before. His eyes were sunken in, and his baggy clothes seemed to shroud his frail frame. His face was scuffed and dirty, and his black hair was unkempt. God, what had happened to him?

"Fuck no," Jack spat. For a second, I swear I saw Graham's lips curve up into a smirk.

Jerry didn't even flinch at the boy's protest. Instead, he proceeded to remove his hat with genuine and stylish ease and knelt before him.

"I can assure you, you've got quite an adventure waiting on the other side for you. An adventure that can't begin until you go back with *them*." Jerry waved at Graham and me on either side of him.

Jack peeked up at us, not impressed in the slightest.

"Not to mention, I don't like to get forceful, but I will if I have to. Staying here longer than intended can have some...unpleasant consequences," Jerry warned, standing back up and replacing his hat defiantly at the same perfect angle.

Jack rolled his eyes and groaned in an epic display of preteen attitude.

"*Fine*. Be quick with whatever you're gonna do," he barked.

Without any warning, Jerry pressed a hand to Jack's chest and his small, slender body vanished into thin air.

The hell?

A frenzy of movement whirled around me before I felt Graham's strong hands gripping my hips, his hard back pressing into me.

"I will give you five seconds to tell me where the hell you put him," he growled at Jerry, his broad shoulders nearly blocking my view of him.

Jerry's eyes flashed with what appeared to be respect as he took a step forward. "Graham, I must repeat that this is a time-sensitive matter. Recovery is easier for us, but I can't stress enough that it may have lasting effects if you stay longer than intended."

"I won't ask again," he seethed, his grip tightening around my waist.

Jerry's piercing eyes flicked over to me before resting back on the hulking man in front of him. His voice lowered into a whisper, so low I could barely hear him.

"She's going to need you on the other side, you know. If you want to protect them, you both need to be *alive*." Jerry's voice was fiercely calm as he fastened the top button of his suit jacket. He must have been crazy brave or just plain stupid as he began to approach Graham's unwavering form.

I sincerely worried for his well-being as his hand clapped Graham on his shoulder, pulling him in to his chest. Graham froze, his jaw working the whole time as Jerry whispered something inaudible in his ear. I leaned in, but Jerry spoke so softly, it was no use. Finally, he released his grip and leaned back, both of them seemingly communicating without speaking. And just like that, Graham's shielding form disappeared, leaving Jerry and me alone.

Terror gripped me, and I considered running away for a moment. What did he just tell Graham that I wasn't supposed to hear? My eyes darted to the nearest exit, and I did a quick calculation of how many steps it would take to get from here to there. Fifteen, maybe twenty? I didn't know if I was ready to go back, especially to that terrifying scene down the hall. I eyed Jerry's stance, which was still utterly composed, but his gaze remained fixed on me. He would outrun me. He said himself he'd get forceful if he had to. I exhaled deeply and fell back into the chair behind me, surrendering.

"Are you ready?"

I flinched as he raised his hand toward me.

"Wait!" I cried.

He froze, his hand inches from my chest.

"How do I find them? Please just tell me. At least give me their last names?" I started to go into panic mode, just thinking about going back inside the bruised, lifeless body that I watched flatline moments before. A tremor ran through me as I wondered how I'd died. My body looked like it had been thrown into a blender. Had I been in a car accident? Had I fallen off a building? I would probably be in the hospital for months recovering. This was going to be a living hell.

Jerry shook his head, his eyes softening. "No can do, Georgia. The journey to find your Reckoning partner is sacred. Not to mention, it's essential in developing your *Aftereffects*. Speaking of which, I left one thing out. The Anchor is typically the only one that can locate the others, considering you cast the link. Sorry to say, but it looks like it'll be up to you, and you alone."

I groaned at the impossible task and the strange words he kept using. He broke out into one of those untimely smiles again.

"I said *typically*, Georgia. Something about you and your boys there don't appear to be typical in the slightest." He inched closer as I leaned away, pressing into the chair behind me.

"You'll be fine. Maybe we'll meet for coffee later—you like mocha lattes, right?"

His baffling comment floored me, leaving me speechless. Before I could fumble out any form of a response, he slammed his hand onto my chest, jolting me with a painful blow.

My eyes shot open, as I inhaled a sharp raspy breath. Agonizing pain coursed through every inch of my body. Bright, merciless lights glared down at me as I blinked furiously, trying to understand what was happening. Several muffled voices shouted as blurred figures danced around me. A long face with a thin nose and intense brown eyes came in and out of focus. He was saying something, but I couldn't understand him. I watched his mouth move, trying to grapple with all the unfamiliar sounds he was making. Intense nausea surged through my body in aching waves. I turned my head to vomit but didn't have enough energy to heave. My head pounded as the stale stench of blood and sterile chemicals filled the air.

And the world started to fade. Fast.

Until there was nothing.

2

THE DOCTOR IS IN

My eyes fluttered open as bright sunlight flooded in, blinding me. *Where the hell am I?* I tried to call out for help but coughed, my throat too dry to speak.

"Nurse!" a familiar voice called out, as hurried footsteps ran to my side. A rustle of noise seemed to surround me as a beautiful figure appeared, sunlight creating a halo effect around her auburn hair.

"Hi, baby girl." A sob escaped from her lips. Before she was even finished speaking, I recognized the inconsolable woman.

"Mom?" I whispered groggily as she faded in and out of focus.

Strong hands grabbed my shoulders and pulled me into a tight squeeze. I inhaled the familiar scent of sweet perfume and coffee, but a stronger clinical smell of rubbing alcohol assaulted all my senses. I tried to return her embrace but was stopped short with various cords hooked to my arms. She finally pulled back, and her red-rimmed eyes settled on mine. I could feel my own eyes fill up with tears as I traced her loving and tender features. I knew from her weighted expression that something terrible had happened.

"Oh, thank God you're alive, I thought you'd..." She broke down before she could finish.

Thank God I'm alive?

I turned my attention to the IV in my arm and the monitor sitting to my right, reading all my vitals. A low murmur of beeps and steady whirs came from the machine as it seemed to register an influx of activity as I awoke. I turned to scan the room where sage-green cabinets lined the walls, and on a counter nearest to my bed sat various jars of medical supplies.

I was in a hospital. But why? What happened to me?

I could feel the onset of a panic attack forming as my heart began to race. I pinched the bridge of my nose, a small headache beginning to rear its ugly head. The fluorescent lights above, mixed with the bright daylight outside, sent a wave of nausea over me. I closed my eyes and started to breathe, trying to dig for any helpful memories, any answers. What was I doing yesterday, or better yet, what day was it? I started to run through a series of questions in my head when a chipper voice broke the silence.

"Good morning, G—" The nurse's singsong trill suddenly stopped as she stood, gawking at me, her eyes glazed over in shock.

"Nurse...?" my mom probed softly.

The nurse stared for a few more unsettling moments before she snapped herself out of her trance. She shook her head in disbelief, unable to pull her horrified look from me.

"Your *face*..." she breathed as if she had never been trained on bedside manner a day in her life.

I had a sinking suspicion that her reaction had nothing to do with her lack of training, but something deeper. I didn't want to think about why I'd shocked a medical professional. I wanted to hide and fall back into oblivion. I wasn't ready for this reality yet.

As if she seemed to realize her unprofessional reaction, she checked her watch hanging from her scrubs shirt pocket and returned her shaky gaze to me.

"I've called Dr. Cobbs; he'll be in soon," she announced as she straightened up and seemed to remember she was a nurse and not a shocked onlooker. She cleared her throat nervously before she approached my bedside.

"Vitals are...ahem...looking good. Let's take a look at your wound," she uttered as she skittered toward the cabinets on the far wall.

I could feel the color drain from my face as I tried to make sure I'd heard her right.

My *wound?*

I was at a complete loss. Just the effort alone to process what was happening had me wanting to sleep for a week. I didn't remember anything, or how I got here, and I knew I wasn't ready to see this "wound" she was referring to. I almost began to ask if I could rest when a tattoo, barely visible at the nape of her neck, caught my eye. Something about it made my stomach sink all the way to the floor.

"Excuse me, but what does the tattoo on your neck say?"

She paused and turned back toward me in surprise. She locked her eyes with mine and seemed to finally regard me as a person instead of a cryptic medical case. A faint smile crossed her lips, and she sighed, letting out any tension she might have felt before.

"It says 'Angels are among us.' I got it after a sixteen-hour shift when an organ donor saved seven different lives. The donor died from what some would call a freak accident, but I'm a firm believer that everything happens for a reason." She reached up and closed the cabinets, turning back with a handful of medical supplies. Her face was pinched with scrutiny, as if she were trying to decide whether to say something or not.

"You know, in the middle of all the horrible things we see here, we also get to see a lot of miracles. Miracles like *you*." Her eyes trailed along my face again before she headed back over to my bed.

She snapped on a pair of latex gloves and gave me one last nervous glance. "Anyway, let's just have a look." She sat opposite my mom and carefully lifted my covers, pulling back my gown. I gasped in a raspy breath as I saw the bandage that was still taped to my abdomen. Spots of blood had soaked through the thick hospital-grade bandage. I could feel another panic attack bubble up inside me, before a soft reassuring voice called out to me.

"It's okay, Georgia."

I exhaled as I looked up at the nurse, who managed to give a tight smile.

"If you want, just close your eyes and it'll just take a minute," she reassured, her rigid face softening.

I looked back over at my mom, and she reached out to squeeze my hand. I gladly took the out. I usually couldn't stomach violent scenes in movies, and I feared that if I caught so much as a glimpse of my own flesh wound, I would pass out. Maybe that wouldn't be so bad, though. I screwed my eyes shut and felt the sickening pull of dried blood and skin as she removed the bandage.

My mom's hand pulled away, and a pair of sharp gasps hissed next to me.

My eyes shot open to find the nurse staring at my abdomen, horrified in all sense of the word.

"I-Impossible!" the nurse stammered as I watched her back away.

I peeked back down at my stomach nervously, not sure if I really wanted to see what she saw.

A raised pink line of nearly healed tissue stared back at us. It was a simple but fresh scar, certainly not a battle wound like the blood-soaked bandage had suggested. I carefully lifted my hand and grazed the line with my fingertips.

Completely painless.

Is this a joke?

I looked back up at the nurse, confused. Her eyes widened as they darted from the scar to my face. Without another word, she ran out of the room, leaving us in her terrified wake.

"Georgia...?" My mom broke the silence as she stared nervously at my scar.

I didn't have any answers to give. I searched her face, hoping she could give *me* something, anything. All she could do was stare back in the same confused state.

Suddenly, all I could think about was that nurse's tattoo. It was like a divine, cosmic shift shot through me, and despite everything, that tattoo seemed to be the only thing worth worrying about. I let the calming words fill my mind.

Angels are among us.

Why is it so important?

A surge of unwelcome images flooded through me as I fisted my hands into the sheets of my hospital cot.

Broken and bruised body. Pale blue eyes. Peacock feather. Hospital Lobby. Jack. Graham.

Angels are among us.

Jerry.

I hurriedly started ripping the cords from my body as the monitor rang out. My mom let out a bewildered shriek as she watched me claw my way free.

"Baby, leave those on!" she yelled desperately.

Ignoring the alarms and my mom, I grabbed my IV stand and half sprinted, half stumbled to the bathroom mirror. When I reached the sink, I stared at my reflection. My face had been an absolute train wreck. My whole body had been covered with scratches and bruises. Most importantly, that pink scar was an undeniable confirmation that I was bleeding out on a table. I had died, and I experienced the impossible while I was dead. But was it all real...? Were Graham, Jack and Jerry...*real*?

"Georgia, please tell me what's happening," my mom's voice quaked as she approached me. She stopped a few feet away, as though she sensed I needed some space as I processed everything.

I gawked at my healed reflection in the mirror as the alarms continued to bounce around the room. Brilliant green eyes stared back, long strawberry-blonde hair fell to my waist in golden waves. I turned my face to see just a few residual gray-green bruises, but my ivory skin was nearly flawless.

"How long have I been here?" I cried out as I continued to stare at my reflection.

"Just for a night, baby wh—"

"Holy *shit!*" I shouted, nearly sending my mom through the ceiling. "Mom, did they tell you what happened to me?" I asked, imploring for the worst, as I turned to look at her.

"They haven't told us anything." Her voice trembled as she stared at my horror-struck face, her eyes brimming with tears.

She ran to me and reached for my shoulder, squeezing it tightly. "Do you remember anything?"

A knock at the door interrupted us.

"Good morning, ladies." A familiar man with a white coat entered, stopping abruptly as the alarms continued to sound. He gazed curiously at me for a moment and proceeded into the room, unfazed by our worried faces. He linked his arm with mine, and my mom followed suit, grabbing the other and leading me back to my bed. They both helped me in, and the man began returning the monitors to their appropriate places, quieting the screeching sounds from the machines. My mom found a seat in a nearby armchair and plopped down, drained and exhausted. Silence filled the room, and the man's warm but intense brown eyes stared down at me. His silence continued until he grabbed a stool next to the far wall.

"I'm Dr. Cobbs. I'm just going to run through a few routine questions with you," he said as he rolled the stool over to my bedside and sat down.

His intense gaze trailed across my face and down to my neck, taking in the lack of bruising. His eyes flickered with something unreadable before he began with his first question.

"Can you please give me your full name, age, and your employer?" he asked as he continued to gape at me.

"My name is Georgia Lee Scott, I'm twenty-six years old, and I work at O'Fallon Paving Incorporated."

No, that couldn't be right. Strange how it just came out so naturally, like I was firing out facts. I knew my name was Georgia Lee Scott, and I knew I had just turned twenty-six a few months ago, but I had no recollection of working at a paving company. Even the sound of it seemed so strange rolling off the tongue.

My mom's eyes widened, a terrified look creeping up her face as Dr. Cobbs pulled open a drawer and pulled out a tablet. He was checking my file. His brow furrowed as he scrolled and looked back up at me, confused.

"Your emergency contacts and records say you've worked at Whitman's Staffing Solutions as a recruitment specialist for the last three years. When did you start working at O'Fallon Paving?"

My mind raced as I tried to remember working at Whitman's Staffing Solutions. That sounded unfamiliar too. I shook my head fearfully, my hands knotting through my hair as I tried to remember. *Oh, God, please remember.*

He pulled out a stylus and noted something on the tablet. His eyebrows arched as he peered back up at me, fascination flashing across his face. He continued to run through a series of extensive questions: whether I knew who the president was, what year it was, the names of my family members, and so on. Apparently, it was December twelfth, just a few weeks before Christmas. I didn't even remember doing any shopping, or planning, but I was sure I was running around checking off my perpetual to-do list like I always did.

Dr. Cobbs cleared his throat and peered down at me. "I'm just going to take a quick look," he said as he sat back on the stool.

His cold forefinger and thumb grasped my jaw and turned my head left and then right, analyzing every angle. He paused a moment and then reached in his pocket. He clicked on a small flashlight and shined it into my eyes. His cool breath hit my face as he clicked it back off.

"Interesting," he said under his breath.

He then slowly lifted the covers and pulled my gown aside. I looked over at my mom nervously. She shrugged and crossed her arms as she watched him. He gaped at the miraculously healed wound for several moments before bringing his curious gaze back up to my face.

"Very interesting," he repeated and let out a deep sigh as he glanced toward my mom.

"Mrs. Scott, would you mind waiting outside in the lobby for a moment? I need to speak with your daughter alone." He nodded toward the door as a different nurse came in, smiling warmly at her.

"I've got some paperwork I need to be filled out up at the front, and then I'll show you where the cafeteria is," the nurse instructed. Before my mom could protest, the nurse escorted her out, shutting the door behind them.

I shifted uncomfortably on the bed as I sat under Dr. Cobbs's suspicious stare.

"Georgia, honestly I'm amazed at your recovery. You about scared Nurse Calloway half to death, and rightly so. I'm curious, do you remember anything from the attack?"

Attack.

Time seemed to stop as I concentrated on the word. I was *attacked*? That must have been a mistake—my body had basically been mauled. There's no way that another human being would hurt someone that bad. I stared back up at Dr. Cobbs, trying to hold back a sob.

"I don't remember," I whimpered, closing my eyes, desperately searching for any other details I might have forgotten.

Nothing. Absolutely nothing.

"I see." He frowned back at me, clasping his hands together. "Well, let me give you the basic rundown. Two of your ribs were fractured, you had a minor concussion, and you lost nearly eight liters of blood." His eyes lowered to the pale pink scar that was still exposed. I quickly pulled the covers over the ugly line, a sickening thought filling my head. Who would have done that? What could I have done to deserve that?

"Apart from your possible retrograde amnesia, you appear to be perfectly healthy. Your concussion, your bones, and your skin seem to have repaired itself in record time." He lifted his chin, squinting down at me...almost like he knew a secret that I didn't.

"You know, your heart stopped beating for about four minutes." He crossed his arms expectantly, as if he were waiting for me to explain myself. I stared back at him blankly, not sure if I was imagining his reaction.

After a few moments of silence, he dropped his gaze, his jaw tightening.

"Georgia, when you were brought in last night, you had some bruising that implied sexual assault."

I felt the color drain from my face, ice freezing through my veins. A sob caught in my chest as I stared at him. His penetrating but regretful brown eyes locked with mine.

"We ran a rape kit, but the few DNA traces we found appear to be untraceable."

I flinched at the ugly words.

"A rape kit?" My voice broke, tears pricking at the corners of my eyes. He nodded, taking a slow breath as he watched my world crumble beneath my feet.

I couldn't handle this—I wasn't strong enough. I had survived the apparent attack, but I didn't know if I could survive the shock of knowing what had happened. The room started to shrink as the walls closed in, and my lungs began to collapse. Then, a vivid thought seemed to push all the darkness away, bringing light into focus.

The hospital lobby scene floated around in my mind as I saw Jack's small body and goofy grin. Graham's protective stance and steely regard. Jerry's kind face beneath that crazy hat eased its way to the forefront of my thoughts, and suddenly I felt like I could breathe again. I inhaled and exhaled several times before I peered back up at Dr. Cobbs.

"You said no...traceable DNA?" I repeated, as I held back a tremor.

"I'm afraid not."

I pulled my knees to my chest, trying to ground myself.

"I know this is very difficult, but there is a detective on their way that would like to speak to you regarding the attack," he said, his face growing more serious.

I had no idea what I would tell them, considering I couldn't even remember who my employer was. I would likely be just as helpful as a pile of rocks to their investigation. I played out the awkward conversation in my head. He would come in, introduce himself, and listen to me stammer my way through several "I don't remembers" before sidestepping his way out. I had nothing to offer. Everything inside me wished otherwise, but the truth sat strong and steady, unrelenting.

"Ms. Scott, I believe this particular detective will be an asset to finding your attacker. I've worked with her before, and she's got an eye for this kind of thing." His eyes seemed to laugh as he spoke, as if he were sharing an inside joke with me.

Maybe I imagined that last bit, but maybe he was right. I was also impressed that he mentioned the detective was a woman. That lessened the other fear I had. I wasn't interested in discussing any intimate details of my attack with a man. I thought it over in silence before I nodded up at him slowly.

"All right, I'll speak with her," I agreed reluctantly, wrenching my hands together.

Dr. Cobbs smiled, then sat up straight, his deep brown eyes boring right through my soul.

"Now, last but not least, I'm curious if you remember the name of the Light that sent you?"

I stared at him, dumbfounded, as I repeated the question in my head. Did Dr. Cobbs just ask me who my *Light* was?

"I'm not sure what you mean..." I muttered, hugging my knees even tighter now.

He frowned and eyed me warily. "My apologies, Georgia. I know this might seem rather unorthodox, considering the circumstances," Dr. Cobbs rambled as I stared with my mouth ajar. "But based on your miraculous recovery...and the energy that surrounds you, I can already tell you just came back from a Reckoning."

I held back a gasp as a dizzying wave of nausea rolled through me again. Did he just say *Reckoning*?

"Dr. Cobbs..." I fretted nervously.

He shifted as he watched me. "In most cases, the Light explains all of this during the Reckoning. Do you remember the name of the person who sent you back?"

Yup, he most certainly said the word "Reckoning."

I blinked a few times, as if that would help me hear better. His frown deepened as he surveyed my hysterical expression. He crossed his arms over his chest and narrowed his eyes.

"If you're trying to rationalize any of it, just stop now. Don't you find it peculiar that you mentioned you work at O'Fallon Paving Incorporated? When in fact, you work at Whitman's Staffing?"

Dr. Cobbs's expression remained calm but completely solemn. I shook my head at him, trying to fight the terror that began to fill me. He couldn't possibly know anything about what I may or may not have experienced after I died. Even if all of this was real, it would be ill-advised to talk about anything paranormal with a doctor. Oh, you were talking to some guy with a peacock-feathered hat while you were dead? He told you to find a little boy and some really hot guy? Surely that would be my one-way ticket to the psych ward. Dr. Cobbs seemed to sense my confusion, or reluctance for that matter, as he cleared his throat.

"Never mind, Georgia. We'll discuss this later. I understand you've got much bigger things to worry about now," he said, watching me carefully. "I'll send the detective in when she arrives." He stood, taking a beat before heading toward the door.

"Wait." I exhaled the word before I could stop myself.

Jerry's sparkling blue eyes etched into my brain, as if he were urging me to speak his name.

"Jerry," I whispered, just loud enough for him to hear.

Why did I just say that? This was impossible. All of it. Graham, Jack, my miraculous recovery, the fact I was...*raped*. I shuddered just thinking about it. There's no way he would know what I meant when I said Jerry.

Dr. Cobbs stared down at his watch, his lips thinning as he nodded.

"Let's keep this between us, shall we?" He tapped his watch and left the room with haste, his white coat flapping behind him.

3

SCARLET SNOW

I stared at the door that Dr. Cobbs just fled from as I tried to grapple with the truths he'd laid down.

Someone raped me, and he hadn't left any traceable evidence. I felt a single tear stray down my cheek. Not only had he raped me—he had *killed* me.

And...Dr. Cobbs somehow knew what I'd experienced while I was supposed to be dead. The words *Reckoning* and *Light* definitely escaped his lips. He knew something about the mysteries that clouded my mind...maybe he knew everything.

Don't you find it peculiar that you mentioned you work at O'Fallon Paving Incorporated? When in fact you work at Whitman's Staffing?

Why, yes, Dr. Cobbs. I find it downright unsettling.

I wrapped my hospital gown tightly around me, a shiver running up my spine. I closed my eyes and exhaled, trying to calm my nerves. I needed to think about something more peaceful, less impossible. I didn't want to think about anything Dr. Cobbs said anymore. The Reckoning...the attack. *The rape.* My shaky gaze traveled to the window, which featured a cloudy sky. A few remaining hopeful rays of sunshine peeked through, but I could tell that something a little more threatening was headed our way. The clouds were moving quickly, almost like they felt the shift in the wind and they themselves wanted to seek shelter.

I gathered the mountain of cords attached to my arms and chest. I wanted to see the outside world, while mine was crashing and burning in here. I needed to know that there was something solid and real still. My feet hit the cold hospital floor, and I took a minute to stretch, making sure all the wires remained in place. I carefully dragged the mobile monitor with me, along with my IV stand, toward the vast window. For a hospital room, it had a surprisingly beautiful view of downtown St. Charles, Missouri. The shops and boutiques below lined the cobblestone streets where shoppers weaved in and out with various boxes and colorful packages. The lampposts and window displays were covered with pine wreaths and red ribbon. Carolers dressed in period clothing serenaded the passersby. Snow frosted the ground, but the dark clouds rolling through certainly threatened for more.

A woman in a bright red jacket caught my eye as she flaunted her way through the holiday bustle. People moved out of her way as she passed, not the other way around. For a second, it almost seemed like her chin was tilted upward and she was watching me. We were watching each other. I let out a dry, humorless laugh as I shook my head, contemplating the probability of that. There had to have been hundreds of windows looking out into the historic street. Out of all of them, she of course would choose my window of all windows. The woman in red suddenly disappeared among a throng of shoppers, or maybe she simply vanished. I couldn't tell, but I wouldn't put it past all the other impossible things going on around here. Jerry had warned that I should trust any strange phenomenon for what it was before he sent us back. I didn't know what was real and what wasn't at this point anyway. A cold numbness was beginning to take hold of me that I wasn't so sure I wanted to fight.

Another bout of commotion captured my attention in a nearby courtyard. Several kids were throwing snowballs at each other while their parents chatted around the park benches. A particularly large boy threw a snowball with all his might at a much smaller girl in a bright pink scarf. The snow smashed across her little face, and she crumpled to the ground as he doubled over in laughter. Immediately, a bout of heated rage replaced the numbness I felt as I watched the girl lying in the cold snow. God, I wanted to give him a swift kick in his...

Before I could finish that thought, another boy several feet away rushed to her aid, brushing the snow from her face and shoulders. It looked like she had started to cry when he reached to help her up. At first, she froze midsob as she took in the tall boy in front of her. He seemed to sense her unease as she leaned away from him, untrusting. He was twice her size, after all.

23

He slowly stood up, and for a second I thought he was going to leave her. He took a step back, but before he turned away, he started to dance. I could tell she was fighting back a smile as he traipsed around, uncaring of anyone watching. Finally, he finished and bowed at her feet in theatrical splendor, as she erupted into a fit of giggles. He reached out again, and this time she accepted, shooting him an adoring smile. He gently pulled her to her feet and helped her gather some snow, shielding her from any future blows. Once she had a decent assortment of arctic ammunition, they both attacked the other boy, flinging lobs of snow at him without mercy. The larger boy's arms flew up in an immediate sign of surrender, but Mr. Knight in Shining Armor shot one last snowball right to the boy's face, feigning ignorance as the little girl held back a laugh. I couldn't help but let out a chuckle myself as the boy ran to his mother's side, pointing his accusing finger at the pair behind her.

Well then. Chivalry did exist. I crossed my arms and smirked as the mother patted her son dismissively.

"Wow." A cheerful voice filled the quiet room. I whirled around to see a beautiful young woman with a swooping dark brown bob at the door, grinning from ear to ear.

"Your recovery is quite remarkable." Her red heels clicked against the tile as she glided into the suite.

I didn't even remember hearing the door open. Goose bumps ran up my arms as I caught sight of a bright red jacket thrown over her arm. Nope. She couldn't possibly be the same woman I saw on the street, cat walking her way through the crowd.

She flashed a brilliant smile with perfectly painted red lips, as if she were saying "I wouldn't be so sure." Her teeth were just as white as her pressed suit. I stared at her with wide eyes, silently cringing at the hideous hospital gown I was wearing next to her powerhouse attire. I was apparently staring a little too long because she shook her head and laughed.

"I'm Detective Weiss, but you can call me Scar. It's short for Scarlett," she added enthusiastically, her cheeks still pink from the cold outside.

I ogled the red briefcase she placed at her feet and her freshly manicured fingernails painted a deep scarlet red.

I would have never guessed.

She let out a chuckle as if she heard me, but her smile faded as she took me in. It was like she was...assessing me. *Reading me*. I couldn't help but to look back at the door to see if she had a partner, but it seemed she was alone. She appeared to be even younger than me, but there was a confidence within her that took years to own. A confidence that I envied, especially now in the middle of this personal hell.

"Y-You're so...young," I stuttered.

I immediately regretted pointing it out; it came off a little condescending. She had to be good if they sent her alone, especially for a case like mine. She laughed, her deep brown eyes sparkling. Her laugh seemed musical and carefree, like she wasn't here to interview an assault victim in a hospital. Her genuine manner put me at ease, and just for a moment, I felt normal again.

"Yeah, I'm a bit of a spectacle down at the station. At first, they hired me to keep things organized. I think they keep me around, though, because there is absolutely nothing like a woman's intuition." Her eyes sparkled as her lips curled into a ruby smile.

"Shall we head back into bed, then?" she asked in a singsong way as she sauntered over toward me with that same modelesque stride. I didn't answer, but she helped me amble my way back into bed anyway. She took extra care with my IV stand and monitors, keeping them in close range. She lifted the covers and helped me climb into bed. I watched in awe as she surprisingly began tucking me in. Once my pillow was fluffed and all the corners were tucked in just right, she grabbed her briefcase and turned to sit in the armchair nearest to the bed, her deep espresso eyes fixed on me.

I smiled at her nurturing spirit. Somehow, she made me feel just a little bit better about the awkward conversation that was yet to come. I imagined how she was with the rest of the police force. They had to be wrapped around her perfectly polished finger. I stared at her a moment longer before I realized she was waiting for me to speak first. I paused, not even sure what to say before finally deciding on the only thing I knew for sure.

"Detective Weiss, I wish I could tell you what I remember, but I just don't know what to tell you. I can't seem to remember much of anything."

I pulled my knees to my chest, wishing we could talk about anything else. Maybe like why she carried a briefcase. It was so retro-vintage. It fit her so well, though, like it was an extension of her personality. Maybe she just had an old soul like me. The kind of soul that sits alone in her apartment on a Friday night reading or researching storage solutions on Pinterest. Her face lit up into a bright smile, as if my answer was reassuring to her in some way.

"Please, Georgia, just call me Scar. Memory loss is common after a traumatic experience, but it is important you share anything you can grab ahold of. Perhaps we can start with the last thing you remember even if it was from two weeks ago." She spoke with a soothing and graceful eloquence that matched the rest of her sophisticated style. She took her time with each word and seemed to measure my reaction as she spoke.

A flurry of movement caught my attention in the corner of my eye, and I turned toward the window looking out at the street again. Several large snowflakes were whirling in every direction. The dark, threatening clouds had rolled in, and the sun seemed to have made its last debut of the day. Scar sighed nostalgically as she stared at the white snowfall outside.

"Don't you just love white Christmases?" she said with another quirk of her scarlet lips.

There was something in the way she was beaming back at me, or perhaps it was what she said, that seemed to trigger a series of strange memories.

Beautiful tree lights dancing in the corner of my apartment. A Christmas movie playing in the background. Christmas cookies.

A knock at the door?

Scar perked up, as if she sensed I had something helpful to share. She clasped her hands over her knee as she waited for me. I doubted any of those random visions would help the case, but the heck with it. She did say anything could be helpful after all.

"I don't know if I just remembered something or not..." I trailed off and peeked up at her.

She nodded with an encouraging grin, but something unsettling was behind her gaze. It reminded me of Dr. Cobbs's and Jerry's piercing but kind eyes, like they could see so much more than the natural world. I shook the strange feeling off and chewed on my bottom lip, trying to figure out the best way to explain the vague memories.

"I think I was sitting in my apartment baking some cookies...and watching TV. I think the Hallmark Channel was playing a Christmas movie marathon." I stared in shock as Scar's face split into a wide smile.

"Ooh, I love those!" Scar's eyes lit up like Christmas morning. I slowly returned her smile and nodded. "And there was no one with you, correct? You were alone?"

Scar's innocent words cut a little deeper than I expected. I rarely hung out with people these days, except for the sweet older couple next door. I used to be more social...more available. But that was when I left my heart out there, wide open for anyone to break. Before...Braxton. Before I found out he was cheating on me. Since then, I just stuck to what was comfortable—my apartment and myself. No Mr. Knight in Shining Armor for me.

"Yes, I was alone." I nodded. "The Hallmark Channel makes for great company on a Friday night, don't you think?" I shrugged lamely.

Really, Georgia? God, I need more friends.

"Me too, girl, me too. I mean, what is wrong with the male population that none of them have proposed to two good-looking girls like us?" Scar shook her head in disappointment.

I doubted she had any trouble finding interested men, but I loved how easy it was to talk with her. It was nice to be myself with someone that was around my age again. I had lost touch with friends from college for years now, and I tended to keep everyone at an arm's length anyway. I found that getting too close to people usually resulted in disappointment. You could only trust someone for so long before they went and broke your heart.

"I'm sorry to say, but I can't remember anything else. I don't even remember where I work, so I don't know if I'll be of much help. I told Dr. Cobbs I worked at some paving company," I snorted as I threw my hands up in the air.

Scar's smile faltered just a bit, her eyes flickering dangerously. Before I could read more into it, the nurse with the tattoo on her neck bustled into the room with a large cart. She seemed to have recovered from the horror she had experienced earlier from my immaculate recovery. I couldn't blame her. I would likely have behaved the exact same way. Nothing in a medical textbook could prepare you for...*this.*

She blinked back at us, her gaze lingering on Scar. "Sorry to interrupt, but I just need to take a few blood samples for testing." She then turned to look at me, her face remorseful and embarrassed, surely from earlier.

"I told your parents that you're speaking with Detective Weiss, and I think your mom said that they'll be in the cafeteria until you're through," she added as she attached a vial to my IV.

My parents, plural. My dad was here. I was shocked my dad hadn't stormed the castle yet; I could picture him now much like Graham had been in the hospital lobby. Anxious. Terrified. My thoughts were interrupted as the nurse handed me a large tumbler filled to the brim with ice water.

"Drink up, Georgia. Even with the IV, we want you hydrated. You lost a lot of blood," she commanded.

I cringed at her last comment but was suddenly elated to feel the coolness from the cup against my hands. God, I was parched. My throat felt like sandpaper as I licked my cracked lips. As I swallowed down a few desperate gulps, Scar reached toward her briefcase on the floor and pulled it to her lap. It looked handcrafted with the red leather casing stretched to the sides with dazzling antique brass latches on top. She drummed on the briefcase as she glanced up at me and then unlatched the bolts. She slid a pair of thick-framed glasses with the same deep red frame on her nose and proceeded to shuffle through several papers hidden in the case.

"All done!" the nurse announced as she pulled off her latex gloves, smiling back at me.

I looked down at her cart, where several vials of my blood lay ready for testing. I frowned as I wondered what they could be testing me for. Sexually transmitted diseases? If all my organs were working? If I were an alien life force with rapid healing powers?

"I'll put these through the lab, and they should be done sometime tonight." She frowned over at Scar, who was still rummaging through her papers, and then turned back toward me. "Dr. Cobbs might have you going home tomorrow morning if everything comes back normal." She smiled faintly again, but her tone was doubtful. Of course she didn't think my tests would come back normal. Nothing about this was normal.

She leaned over and checked the monitor near the bed one more time before leaving the room, closing the door behind her.

"God works in mysterious ways, they say." Scar's gentle voice brought my attention back to her. The red briefcase was back at her feet, a thick file lying in her lap.

Blood flushed my cheeks as I played her words over again in my head. What a strange thing to say in these circumstances. I faintly recalled Jerry saying something similar as he was explaining my new role...

My new role as a...

God, I couldn't remember what he'd said. What had he called us? Something about an angel on earth...

As if on cue, Scar leaned forward with an impressive smile.

"Your neighbor, Mrs. Taylor, was your godsend. She was the one that notified the police. She said she and her husband were leaving for vacation, but she forgot the plane tickets in her apartment. On her way back up, she heard you screaming, so she called the police. Without that call, the first responders would have never arrived on time."

Mrs. Taylor's kind face filled my mind. She and her husband were always so sweet and kept an eye on things when I wasn't there. They always seemed to remember my birthday and gave me a Christmas card every year. In fact, I think I was baking Mrs. Taylor's Christmas cookie recipe when I was attacked. My heart sank as I thought about her being anywhere near the monster that hurt me. She had been talking for weeks about this trip. It was going to be the first time in a decade that they were able to get away as a couple. I was so grateful she had been there when she had, but I hated thinking that she heard me screaming. What was he doing to me when she heard those screams? Scar's demeanor grew serious as her grip tightened on the file in her lap.

"I have a few photos I want you to review. They're going to be difficult to see, but I'm curious if you notice anything out of place—besides the obvious damage." She sighed and then handed me the file, its weight menacing in my hands.

The obvious damage? Oh, God.

I carefully opened the file and inhaled a sharp breath as my eyes fell on the first picture. My apartment, or the remnants of what was left, was in complete shambles. A Christmas tree lay toppled over the coffee table in the living room, and drops of blood were splattered across the floor. My shaking hands shuffled to the next photo. My bathroom. The mirror was broken, and several bloodied shards of glass covered the sink. My stomach turned as

I considered whose blood that was. My heart sank as I rested on the fact that it had to be mine. I looked back up at Scar, searching for an explanation.

"When the first responders came on scene, they said that the TV was still on and burnt cookies were in the oven. Your memory seems to align with the...conditions of your apartment." Scar's brow furrowed, her eyes narrowing at me. She leaned over at the edge of her seat, placing her fist under her chin thoughtfully.

"There were no signs of a break-in. It's possible you let your attacker in willingly, but it's hard to say. Does anyone else have a key to your apartment?" Scar's gaze seemed to bore into my soul, as if she were searching for the answers I couldn't give myself. I shrugged uncomfortably.

"I want to say that I would have checked who it was first, but I'm not so sure. Like I said, I don't even remember where I work, so I just don't know." I sighed as I looked back at the photos, anger boiling deep inside me. Maybe I really did let him in and this was all my fault. Maybe I knew who he was. I probably let the bastard inside and welcomed him with open arms. I might have even offered him cookies and milk before he—

"Georgia don't do that." Scar stared at me pointedly, like she had heard every word of my inner pity party.

"Do what?" I asked, confused.

Did I say that out loud? No, I was certainly having a monologue in my own dreadful mind. I supposed she could tell I was beating myself up for not being more proactive with my security. It didn't take a detective to know I was running through all the what-ifs and could-haves. She shot me a stern look but decided to move on.

"Whoever he was, he specifically came for you. Your jewelry box, your electronics, and anything else of value appears left untouched. Of course, whenever you're ready, I'll need you to confirm any missing personal items."

I shuddered thinking of walking into that dark and violated apartment. God help me, that was the last place I wanted to go. I met Scar's eyes as I sat on what I really wanted to ask. I needed answers. My parents would need answers, but I wanted them first.

"Scar, can you please tell me what *you* think happened?" I pleaded, as I placed the heavy file on the edge of the bed.

She exhaled and tapped her fingers on the armchair, twisting her mouth as if she were deciding how or if she wanted to tell me. Her face finally relaxed, as if she settled on something, leaning closer, at the edge of her seat.

"Are you sure you're ready to hear it all?" she whispered.

I nodded and I prayed for the first time in what seemed like forever.

Oh, God, please give me strength.

4

A VISION IN WHITE

She held up a finger instructing me to wait as she grabbed a water bottle out of her briefcase. She unscrewed the cap, and I watched in silence as she sucked down the entire bottle in deep, desperate gulps. I couldn't help but stare as she finished and wiped her mouth hungrily.

Okay...I guess a girl's got to stay hydrated?

Something about the way she was acting, like she was preparing herself for a triathlon, was beginning to make me rethink everything. Maybe it was best I didn't know what she thought happened. I watched her as she put the water bottle back in her briefcase, when I refocused my attention to the file on the bed, the photos strewn about in an unsettling display. A particularly gruesome picture with scratch marks and blood lining the hallway shook me to my core. I shuddered as I considered what he did to make me bleed so much. My stomach clenched as I followed the path of blood...down to the bedroom.

Nope. I'm not strong enough for this.

Before I could tell Scar I changed my mind, her warm hand gripped my arm, nearly sending me out of my own skin. I looked up at Scar, her face rigid with what looked like intense pain. Her pale skin was taut as the color drained from it, and she winced like she was avoiding a blow to the head. I wanted to call out to her, to see if she was okay, but the words caught in my throat as I focused on her eyes. They were some of the deepest brown eyes I had ever seen, but now...

Her eyes had taken a bright iridescent honey-golden shade, with silver flecks that moved as she concentrated on me. Even though she was staring right at me, it seemed her line of sight was out of focus, like she was looking at something off in the distance. Her face contorted into a pained grimace now, a whimper escaping from her lips. A tremor ran through her as her grip tightened. Without warning, she withdrew her hand and stumbled away from me. She fell back into her chair, visibly shaking, wrapping her arms around her middle.

Maybe this was a blood sugar thing? A blood sugar thing that changed your eye color...? I eyed the call button next to my bed, and my hand twitched toward it as I watched her helplessly.

"Scar...?" I whispered as panic began to fill me again. Great, I managed to break the detective after only being with her for five minutes.

She groaned as another shudder ran through her. A sick feeling overcame me as I watched her hands ball into nervous fists, her knuckles going white from her grasp.

"Scar...are you okay?" I repeated, my breath hitching. It didn't appear she heard me, as she continued to stare at her feet. My eyes darted to the call button again, and I started to reach for it when she caught my wrist, her fingers ice-cold.

"Sorry if I...frightened you, Georgia," she said in a raspy voice, so unlike the cheerful one she spoke with moments before. "Sometimes, I get these terrible...stomachaches," she continued in the most unconvincing way possible.

One thing my ex taught me was how to pay attention to my body when someone lies to me. Like the way my stomach knotted in my chest after he told me he'd be studying late and to not wait up. Like how the hurt had started to bubble underneath the surface, even though I knew I had no evidence otherwise. But this...*this* was a little more concrete. Scar was probably one hell of a detective, but she was a terrible liar. Stomachache, my ass.

She patted a bead of sweat on her forehead away with her wrist and shot me a weak smile. Scar took a deep breath and focused all her attention on the file that was on the bed beside me. She slowly reached over with shaky hands and shuffled through the stack of photos. She plucked a black-and-white one from the bottom and handed it to me, her face pale with terror...or perhaps revulsion.

"This is a picture of our perp," she explained in a low voice, as her hands fell back into her lap.

I squinted down at the photo, letting my eyes adjust to the fuzzy quality of the surveillance camera shot. I felt bile rise in my throat as my gaze settled on a tall figure captured in midstride. He was turned away from the camera, but he was dressed head to toe in black, and it looked like he was wearing a ski mask. I brought the photo closer, squinting at his mountainous form. He didn't seem familiar, but that didn't really say much considering he was covered like a coward. The time stamp said 8:14 p.m. December 11. Strange, it felt like such a casual time and date. But it was so much more than that. It was the pivotal moment before my entire life changed.

8:14 p.m.

In that exact moment, he could have turned away, he could have left, but instead he kept walking, likely anticipating all the things he was going to do. I clenched my hands at my sides, my stomach turning as I considered the kind of person he was. Did he have a family? Someone who loved him? Was he even capable of love? His frame was massive; his back and shoulders were thick and wide. He could have used his strength to protect, to build, to love and cherish. Instead, he used it to steal everything from me. A little piece of my heart broke just then, and I slowly turned my head away, toward the window where the snow fell in sad, wistful waves. The snow had lost a piece of its magic, and now it just seemed cold and unyielding.

Like *him*.

Scar cleared her throat, startling me. I had almost forgotten she was there. The color in her cheeks had returned, but her eyes were still worried and sad. Scared. She raised her eyebrows and tapped on the fuzzy surveillance photo.

"You see his gloves and jacket? That's leather, and it looks like he strapped his jacket cuffs and pant legs with black duct tape. He was careful—he was trying to minimize any traces of his DNA. Tape and leather are harder to tear through."

I stared hard back at Scar, trying to process what she said. He *taped* his clothes to his gloves and shoes? That man—no, that *monster*—came ready for the world of hurt he was about to put on me. He was trying to protect himself. Protect himself from *me*, a small twenty-six-year-old who was baking cookies and watching Christmas movies down the hall.

"He knocked at the door. It was an innocent one, polite even. You unlocked the door with your guard down. I think you expected your neighbor, Mrs. Taylor. As soon as he heard that latch unlock, pure evil walked into your apartment, Georgia." I caught her shudder in the corner of my eye, and I quickly turned back toward her. A deep, sickening pull tightened in my belly as I watched her. Her gaze was out of focus, and she spoke so confidently in a strange prophetic eloquence like she were there herself, watching and narrating everything as it happened.

"Once you realized it wasn't her, you reacted quickly—you tried to get away. He chased you to your living area, where he tackled you to the ground. Your Christmas tree fell over during the scuffle which distracted him just long enough for you to escape." A loud gasp sounded in the room, before I realized it was mine. Scar frowned as she seemed to snap from her trance, her eyebrows knitting together in concern.

"Georgia, do you...want me to continue?" she prodded.

I had to be brave. I survived him, I could survive this too. I had to. I turned back toward Scar and nodded nervously.

She paused as she looked me over and shot me a tight but reluctant smile.

"Okay," she sighed as she grabbed a photo of my apartment floor plan and trailed her finger from the living room to the bathroom.

"The struggle moved here where you tried to get away and lock the door. Unfortunately, the small space gave him an advantage." She pointed to the picture with the broken bathroom mirror.

"He threw you against the sink and got in a few jabs to your head. The mirror crashed all over you, and the brunt force left you unconscious." She swallowed, her eyes darkening.

"He picked you up and dragged you to where he ultimately wanted you, your...bedroom." Her face twisted into a scowl, disgusted as if she were seeing it before her eyes. But then, the corners of her lips curved up into a vicious sneer.

"When he threw you on the bed, you regained consciousness. You fought like hell, Georgia. You kicked, scratched, punched, and screamed."

My gaze fell on the picture of my bloodied bedsheets, and my heart sank.

35

"Is that where he..." I couldn't bring myself to say the words. Did I really want to know what he did to me on that bed? At first, I couldn't even look at Scar, afraid of her answer, afraid of the truth. I inhaled a deep, shaky breath, bracing myself. I couldn't run away from this—I needed to own my reality. Scar pursed her lips together, her gaze faltering.

"He...managed to force himself on you...and he began...to assault you." She paused and locked eyes with me. "It appears he used a condom."

I bit my lip as I began to tremble. I didn't want to hear any more, but Scar persisted.

"Your cookie timer went off...along with the fire alarm."

"The fire alarm?" I repeated, confused.

She nodded. "Strangely enough, it was an electrical malfunction. There was no fire, but it was just enough of a distraction to give him pause. That moment of grace allowed you to push him away, but by then he was tired of fighting you. He needed to subdue you somehow, so that's when he pulled out his knife." She took out a few additional pictures of my bedsheets.

"You entered survival mode, and girl, you were unrelenting. I imagine he wasn't expecting such a fight from you. I believe the knife was supposed to be more of a scare tactic than a weapon. But before he could stop himself, he plunged the knife in your stomach. You bled out quickly, too quickly..." she said, her eyes widening. "All the blood...it...it spooked him, so he decided to flee."

I stared in shock as she finished, before I sputtered out a laugh that must have seemed hysterical. The poor guy got scared as I started to bleed out in my own apartment...after he raped and stabbed me. Must have been oh so *horrifying* for him.

Scar raised her eyebrows curiously, and her eyes dropped to my hand. "Do you wear a ring on your left hand?" she demanded.

I peered down at my hands again which were gripping the bedsheets so tightly my knuckles were white. A thin, pale indent on my left ring finger stared back in place of what once was my commitment ring. I hated calling it a "purity ring," but for lack of better words, that's what it was. I wasn't a virgin. My ex and I had put that to rest several years ago. I hated thinking I'd given him my everything when he abused it so easily. Even his name annoyed me now. His name was Braxton, but he insisted on being called

Brax. At first, I loved his name. It was sporty and outgoing, just like him, and I found it adorable. Now all I could think when I heard that name was lies and deception. I should have known it would end in disaster the moment it fell from his lying lips the night we met.

We were at a party when his eyes locked on mine from across the room. He glided over confidently, like he had handpicked me from the crowd. He offered his hand and asked me to dance and proceeded to sway me slowly to an upbeat hip-hop song. I remember laughing as he dipped me, and from that moment, he had me hooked. My heart had been set ablaze. Weeks went by, and he treated me like nothing but a princess. I remember finally feeling beautiful, like someone had taken notice of me for the first time. He was a year older than me and was the kind of handsome that could make any girl swoon.

Oh, and they did.

The next couple years were fun, at first. Until they weren't. My parents hadn't been too fond of him, which drove a deeper wedge between me and my family. He was flirty, and girls responded, especially at parties. I had always hated parties, but I went with him anyway to appease him. I just never felt like I belonged at them. Even after I joined a sorority, I still tended to flock toward my introverted sisters and focus on school. Soon, he started to focus more on school too. I was so proud of him at first, as it seemed he was finally starting to take more initiative with his academics. Over time, he would need to "focus on school" more and more, until I realized he was focusing on everything but. He was a master at talking his way out of his lies, and even better at making me feel guilty for questioning him.

After I walked in on Brax and the girl that lived down the hall, all I could manage to do was laugh. Not at him and the hideous, compromising position I found them in, but at myself. I laughed at the victim I had become with him, and how even now I was being haunted by his actions. He had the balls to crawl back the next day and beg for me to take him back. He even cried as he tried to give me some cheap bracelet with my initials on it. Oh, he was good—good at being an ass. I broke up with him in so many words and asked him to have even an ounce of honor as a man and leave me alone. Surprisingly, he left with his tail between his legs. Turns out the girl down the hall had the same initials as me, because I saw that same bracelet clasped around her wrist a week later.

The. Audacity.

After that, I stomped myself over to the local jewelry store. I bought the simplest white-gold band they had and made a vow. I promised myself I wouldn't let another man near me until he'd proven his character, love, and commitment. I had it engraved with the words "Truth. Love. Honor." in the inside of the ring. They were the three values that I desired in a man. The three values that seemed impossible to find nowadays in the middle of hookup culture. Deep down, I wanted the faith and loyalty that came with marriage, the kind that I'd grown up watching with my parents. Was it so bad that I wanted a traditional love story? Didn't every girl deserve a knight who protected her and cherished her?

"Yes," I croaked, a lump forming in my throat as I answered Scar's question. "I never take the ring off, so I don't know where it could be," I whispered.

Scar's frown deepened as she squinted down at my left hand.

"I spoke with Dr. Cobbs before I came in and he mentioned there were no confiscated jewelry pieces when you were brought in. None of your valuables seemed out of place, but I'll have the guys double-check with your jewelry. What troubles me is that the nature of your attack was incredibly personal. He came for you. He knew where you lived and that you'd be home. Most perps would have fled after even half of the fight you gave. But he stayed, not willing to give you up." She looked back down at my naked ring finger.

"Sometimes sick perps take trophies," she added quietly.

Trophies? My stomach twisted with that thought. Trophies were earned, not stolen.

"You mentioned an ex-boyfriend, uh...Braxton, was it? When was the last time you saw him?"

My body tensed at her words. I mentioned an ex-boyfriend? I tried to recall everything we spoke about, but I don't remember saying anything about Brax, out loud anyway. But...maybe I did. Everything seemed to mix together at this point. I couldn't tell what was real and what wasn't anymore.

I didn't like where she was going with that either. He had hurt me, but I didn't think he had it in him to rape and kill me. I shook my head at Scar.

"He was a class A jerk, don't get me wrong, but he was never physical with me." I stared at the bloody display of photos strewn all over my hospital bed. He simply was not capable of *that*.

Scar sat in deep thought as she stared at the flurry of white outside.

"I've seen many kind, normal, well-meaning men do some terrible, awful things. There's no such thing as a killing 'type.' Circumstances and deep-rooted intentions are the real killers."

I frowned at that notion. It made the task of finding my attacker that much more impossible. But, impossible things seemed to be happening more often than not lately.

"Were there any surveillance videos of him leaving, or any witnesses? Did Mrs. Taylor see him?" I asked nervously. She shook her head.

"Unfortunately, your apartment building hadn't finished installing all the cameras, so there is no footage of him entering or leaving the residence. Mrs. Taylor said she ran back to her car, where she and her husband stayed until the cops came," she sighed.

I rubbed my temples as a headache began to form behind my eyes. How could she even begin to find the man that did this?

Scar seemed to sense I had hit my breaking point, so she slowly stood and began gathering the photos. She placed them inside the file and stuffed it in her briefcase again. Her eyes crinkled at the corners as she smiled down at me.

"Georgia, I can't tell you how helpful you've been. I think it's better if I leave you to rest for now. I'll let Dr. Cobbs know that you'll be resting and to not allow visitors while you sleep." She paused and took a step back to get a better look at me.

"Your apartment has been screened as a crime scene, so you won't be able to go home until further notice. Do you have somewhere you can stay until then?" she asked in a nurturing tone.

I thought for a moment, considering my options on where I could stay. My parents lived several hours away, and I wasn't sure when I needed to go back to work. I let out a sigh. I had no idea what a recruitment specialist did, and I didn't even know where Whitman's Staffing Solutions was. How was I supposed to explain all of this to my boss?

My battered body on the operating table flashed through my thoughts again as the alarm rang out like a final ballad of death. I should be a little more grateful that I was alive and I actually had a job to go to after everything. I needed to stop sweating the small things.

I was *alive*.

I peered back up at Scar, her patient gaze fixed on me, still waiting for an answer.

"I'll probably just stay with my parents," I said with a hopeful shrug.

Her face split into a gorgeous reassuring smile, and she nodded back at me. Even though I wasn't confident in my answer at all, somehow the way she was beaming gave me all the confidence in the world.

"We're also combing through all your personal effects including your phone to determine any unusual chain of communication. We took your phone chip and replaced it with a new one for now. I'll put your phone here whenever you're ready." She took out a small bag from her briefcase and placed it on the table next to the bed. Despite the unfortunate news, she continued to beam at me as if something exciting was about to happen.

"I suspect we'll see each other soon, Georgia. Until then, please don't hesitate to call me if you remember anything else." She reached into her pocket and pulled out a small business card. I reached to take it, but she pulled it back with a frown.

"You know, it's rare that criminals become repeat offenders to the same victim, but this case is unsettling for me. Too close for comfort. I'm going to do everything in my power to find him, but just be vigilant," she warned.

Her warm, scarlet smile returned, and she extended her card to me graciously. Chills went up my spine from her warning, but for some reason, I trusted her with my whole being. I knew it was a question of when, not if, she was going to find my attacker. I smiled back and wrapped my fingers around the card.

Time seemed to freeze the moment our fingers touched. I heard the clock on the wall tick in slow motion as my gaze flicked back up to Scar, her eyes turning honey gold again. A strange black, murky fog swirled around me in dense onyx wisps, Scar's smiling face vanishing from sight. Suddenly, an incredible brightness filled the room, and nothing but white light surrounded me. A gust of terrible wind rushed past, tearing my hand from Scar's grasp.

Peace. Simple and calm peace.

Soft sunlight hit my face as a rooster crowed off in the distance. My eyes fell on a stunning two-story farmhouse with a magnificent front porch, the sun glistening off its metal roof. It was perched so perfectly on the top of the hill, almost like a Christmas card. Tall trees surrounded the clearing, and a nearby gravel road winded off down a hill toward a wooden barn. My eyes darted across the horizon, searching for Scar, for any evidence that I wasn't losing my damn mind.

A soft breeze blew through my hair as nearby birds chirped in the rustling trees. Smoke puffed from the chimney, and a wonderful aroma of herbs and spices filled the air. I inhaled slowly, a feeble attempt to steady my rapid heartbeat. My heartbeat! *My heart is still beating, so I must be alive...or do hearts beat in heaven?* I looked around again at my serene surroundings. If I had died again and if this was heaven, I guess I didn't mind as much. I looked down to find my bright green hospital gown still shrouding my small frame. Maybe this was all a dream and I was still trying to cope with the trauma of my attack.

"He doesn't have much time," a firm voice warned behind me.

I turned on my heel to find a beautiful woman with gorgeous brown skin and thick braids that fell to her waist. She stared back with a piercing urgency as the breeze picked up, the wind blowing through her long flowing white dress. Maybe she was an angel. She was just so beautiful, so intense.

"Who doesn't have time?" I shouted as the wind began to pick up. Dust swirled around me as my hair blew in my face, blinding me.

"Find them," she demanded, ignoring my question.

"Find who?" I yelled, but I couldn't tell if she heard me. She just stared back at me, unrelenting, as the wind roared. I almost asked again before Jack and Graham's faces swam vividly in my head.

"*Them*," she repeated in a fierce whisper, but her lips never moved. Her voice echoed as if it was in my head, shaking me to my core.

"How?" I cried out through the wind. *Please tell me*, please.

She lifted her chin with a strange pride as a soft smile tugged at the corner

41

of her mouth. Before she could answer, the dense, black fog surrounded me again, shadowing me in complete darkness.

The wind softened to a whistle, and I felt myself being lulled to sleep from the noise. Before I knew it, I was being rocked away into a world of knights in shining armor and angels caked in snow.

5

THE CROOKED PATH

"Good morning, Georgia," a soft voice whispered in my ear, stirring me from one of the best sleeps I'd had in years. My eyes fluttered open, and a nurse with a kind face smiled back at me as she started to pull out my IV. I winced as pain shot up my arm. My eyes widened as I stared at the length of the needle, and I shuddered. *Well, if I wasn't up before, I sure am now.*

"Sorry, sweetie. I try and get the worst of it done first, so now all that's left are these sticky pads. Dr. Cobbs is planning on discharging you today, but he wants to speak with you first before you leave. He won't be done with his rounds until about an hour, so he prescribed a hearty breakfast for you while you wait. Doctor's orders." She chuckled as she began removing the other monitor pads from my chest.

"How long was I asleep?" I coughed as I sat up to stretch, noting the sunlight pouring in from the window.

"You slept for quite a while, almost sixteen hours, but I think you needed it. Rest only improves the healing process!" She fluffed my pillow, and a curious look crossed her face as she studied me with narrowed eyes.

"You know, you healed mighty fast. Unheard of really... All the nurses are talking," she said in a hushed, hopeful tone, as if she were waiting for an explanation.

All I could manage to do was stare back at her with wide eyes, hoping she'd understand I was just as innocent in the matter. She seemed to realize I wasn't going to give her anything, and her lips drooped into a disappointed frown.

"I suppose miracles happen every now and then...especially around *here*," she huffed.

I raised my eyebrows at her unnerving comment. Especially around *here*? I continued to stare in silence, not sure how to move the conversation forward. I never knew how to do that anyway. I was too much of an introvert to manage small talk like normal people. My go-to topic when things got awkward was typically the variations between different types of chocolate. I would sometimes get an enthusiastic chocoholic like me, but most of the time I would get polite nods and smiles before they "found" someone across the room.

"Did you know that the Aztecs used to use chocolate as currency, and some even used to put cocoa beans in their dowries?" I word vomited before I could stop myself. The nurse paused for a moment and looked me over before she responded.

"No, I didn't know that. How...interesting!" She let out a small laugh and shrugged as that infamous polite smile appeared. "You've got some visitors that want to see you. They got here just a few minutes ago, just in time for visiting hours. Dr. Cobbs sent them home last night, and I bet they're sure happy to finally see you."

Damn. Guilt filled me as I thought about my parents. They were both waiting in the cafeteria last I heard, but I just couldn't stay awake anymore. I was with Scar and then...

Without warning, my stomach growled angrily, demanding even. The nurse raised her eyebrows, then handed me a hospital menu with a click of her tongue.

"Sounds like you need something a little more filling than this power juice right here," she said as she thumped my IV bag.

A gorgeous picture of pancakes doused in syrup caught my eye as I perused the menu, and before I knew it, my mouth started to water. Hospital food or not, I was starving.

"Now order whatever you want, and I'll make sure it comes up right away. Would you like me to send your parents in now?" she asked as she headed toward the door.

I nodded back at her as my stomach growled again. I was eager to see my parents, but I was not looking forward to their questions. They would surely ask the things I wasn't ready to tell.

After I called in the order, I sat in silence, considering my time with Scar.

The memory of her visit was foggy, but the strange things I'd experienced were undeniable. Her eyes, her uncanny intuition, the way she seemed to know the impossible. I couldn't even remember saying goodbye. All I remembered was I had that strange vision of the farmhouse, or perhaps it was a dream. I wanted to believe that I was just so tired that I had managed to pass out, mid-handshake. But I knew better. It had to have been just another impossible thing I couldn't explain away.

A glimmer caught my eye, just below my line of sight. I looked down toward the nearby end table where a small piece of paper stood perfectly propped against a lamp. Intrigue gripped me as I slowly picked it up, studying the heavy cardstock between my fingers. The paper was thick and professional with golden embossed, letter-pressed typeface. It was the business card that Scar had left me before...

Color drained from my face as I stared at the top line of the card, and confusion mixed with incredible fear swept over me.

O'FALLON PAVING INC.

Scarlett Weiss

Logistics Coordinator

O'Fallon, Missouri

1000 Golden Path Road

This was the straw. The final straw that broke my back and every other fragile bone in my body. Was this all just some test to see how many curveballs they could throw my way before I broke? I imagined a team of scientists behind a one-way mirror taking notes as they observed me, sniveling over their latest find: Girl loses her shit when handed too much.

Why was my detective's name under the same exact company I told Dr. Cobbs I worked for? Why didn't she say anything when I told her I worked there? I stared at the card, tracing the words with shaky fingers. I couldn't be losing my mind. This card was evidence. There really was a paving company, and Scar was a representing employee.

I stared at the address: 1000 Golden Path Road. Why would a business only provide an address but not a phone number? Scar specifically told me to call her if I remembered anything. How was I supposed to do that now?

There wasn't even a website, no social media...just an address. Scar seemed like she did well for herself—surely they could fork some funds over to brand themselves a little better. I picked the card up and continued to stare at it, as muddled questions and theories crowded every thought.

Why would a paving company need a logistics coordinator that acts as a detective, especially one like Scar? Why would they care about an assault victim like me? Why leave a business card at all? What did Dr. Cobbs know? How was he involved in all of this?

A stifling headache began to creep up as my stomach lurched from hunger. I was going to drive myself crazy with all these unanswered questions. I didn't know if I could wait until Dr. Cobbs finished his rounds. I needed to talk to him now.

I jumped as the bag next to my nightstand started vibrating. The same bag Scar had left with my phone in it before she handed me her card. I slowly reached for it and pulled my phone out. Mia Swanson flashed across the front, a name that sent a wave of guilt over me. She was my best friend, and my sorority sister from college. Mia was my rock during my breakup, and a significant light part of my life when there was only darkness.

Mia: *Hey girl, I've been thinking about you lately. You want to have a girl's night soon? We haven't had one in a while and I miss you.*

A while was an understatement. We hadn't seen each other in a few years, and God, I missed her too. Mia had been my rock through my terrible breakup with Braxton, and she'd reassured me countless times that I'd find another. And what did I do in return? Apparently, I drowned myself in work at Whitman's Staffing Solutions...or O'Fallon Paving. Or wherever the hell I worked. I wanted to tell her everything. She had a special ear for people in pain, but I sure as hell wasn't going to unload on her in a text message.

Me: *Mia, that would be amazing. I'm doing some renovations on my apartment, so I don't know if tonight would work, but maybe tomorrow?*

I hated to throw some fake excuse at her, but it was all I could think to say. I for sure wasn't going to tell her I was stuck in a hospital because someone had raped and killed me. I wanted to go and let loose with Mia this very instant, but I had no idea if or when I was ever going to get discharged or not. Before I put the phone down, it dinged with a response.

Mia: *Come on, stay with me tonight! It'll be just like college again. I need a girl's night, and you know you can't fight the power of this face...*

Her beautiful face popped up underneath her text and I couldn't help but gasp at her beauty. She had always been a knock-out, but the years had certainly treated her well. Her gorgeous blonde hair fell over her shoulders and her bright hazel eyes glittered with demand. Her lower lip was puckered into a pout and by God she was right. I could never say no to that face.

Me: *First of all, don't put your fancy witchcraft on me. Second of all, I miss you too. Like a LOT. Okay. I'll text you later tonight?*
Mia: *Fine, I guess. I've got a ton of papers to grade, anyway, so I'll just be waiting. Alone. Missing my best friend I haven't seen in forever.*

I was so happy for her. She did what she had always wanted to do—teach. She was so creative and personable, and I loved that she had found her calling. At least one of us had followed their dreams.

Me: *Can't wait to pick up where we left off, Mia. See you soon.*
Mia: *Alright, but be careful, I heard snow is moving in!*

"Gee-Gee?" One of my favorite voices shook my concentration, tearing my focus from my phone.

My dad's sweet face smiled back at me, my mom right behind him. I could tell they hadn't slept at all, as the bags under both of their eyes ran deep against their pale faces. This was the first time I'd seen my mom without makeup in years. And my dad...

Tears threatened to spill over as I stared back at them, the weight of everything crashing down all at once. I couldn't even speak. All I could do was spread my arms and motion for them to come in for a hug. My dad slowly approached me, as if he were worried I would break into a million pieces right in front of him. I was grateful because deep down I thought I just might. He reached for me, and once I felt his safe, strong arms wrap around me, I lost it. It was like my face exploded with tears and incomprehensible sobbing all at once. I hated how this was the first time in weeks I'd seen them both together. They were so busy, and they lived hours away, not to mention I had my own job to worry about. My excuse list was long for not taking the time to visit. I never took the time to call them either, to tell them how grateful I was for everything they did for me. Why hadn't I loved harder and cared deeper?

"Baby, what happened? What did the detective tell you? Do you remember anything?" my dad whispered softly, as my mom started to shudder with silent sobs.

I was glad that Dr. Cobbs and Scar had kept my situation confidential, even though I hated the fact they had probably mulled over every worst-case scenario in spite of it. I squeezed my lips together, not sure I wanted to disclose everything to them. How could I even begin to explain my experience with Scar, the farmhouse, Jerry, and especially my attack? Where to start—what did they need to know the most?

"A man broke into my apartment. He attacked me, stabbed me, and then got away. The detective thinks I know him, but I don't remember anything," I rambled. I swallowed painfully as I stared back at them, hoping that was all I had to say. Their outraged faces said otherwise, so I continued, more slowly.

"He's...still out there. They don't know who he is. They're going through my apartment now, and they said they're not sure when it will be available again. If they discharge me tonight, I'll probably stay with Mia for the night. You guys remember Mia, right?"

I knew they remembered her. They were so happy when I introduced her to them during our sorority parent day. Before then, I'm sure they were terrified I would just waste away friendless and marry the boy they never approved of. Trust me, I feared the same thing. My mom crossed her arms and frowned.

"Honey, are you sure? I mean, you were just attacked. You need time to heal. Why don't you just come home with us. I'll call off work and—" She reached for her phone before I grabbed her arm. I hated thinking that my attack was going to halt their lives like it was doing for mine. I knew the holidays were the busiest time for both of them. I wanted to move on from this, not hide away like I always had.

"Mom, I know you're worried...I'm scared too, but I can't live in constant fear. That's not what I need right now, and I think it'll be good to hang out with a friend. She lives just a few minutes away, and I'm sure it will be fine," I pleaded, trying my best to stay calm.

I could tell my mom was considering it. Ever since my breakup, they both watched helplessly as I isolated myself from others. I was never good at making friends in the first place, despite their encouraging efforts. I think they just worried for me, particularly after I moved away and started living alone. Apparently for good reason, considering I was in a hospital. Because someone attacked me...while I was home. Alone. My mom twisted her mouth as she considered it.

"Baby, we just want you safe. As long as you're not by yourself, I think that's best," my dad intervened, and my mom finally nodded in unenthusiastic agreement.

Thank God for Mia. She was my ride or die. Somehow, she made me feel like I was normal, but loved that I was different all the same. I wished I had kept in contact and tried harder after we graduated. I wished I had done a lot of things. The whole nearly dying thing really started to put things into perspective.

Last week, I was sure I was completely enthralled in my shopping and to-do lists for the holidays. Running a million miles a minute seemed so trivial now. What was I really doing with my life other than working at some random company I didn't even remember?

I'd lived a life of checking off boxes. I went to college, got my degree, got an apartment, maintained my independence, but had I *lived*? When was the last time I tried something crazy, went somewhere else besides my apartment after work, said "I love you" and meant it? What had I been doing this whole time? I sat back and took a moment to look at my parents' faces. They had watched me grow and urged me to get out of my comfort zone. They were experts at that, and I think that's why they were so successful.

My mom, Audrey Scott, was a true entrepreneur. She had started her own fashion business when she was twenty-one and named it Georgia Lee's after me. When she was younger, she would create sketches and handcraft her own designs using old fabrics she found. She had designed her own homecoming dress from curtains hanging in her room. She saw beautiful designs and patterns everywhere she went and lived loud and proud like any creative professional. Now she had a staff of 250 employees and was on the board at a local university. When I turned twenty-one, the hardest decision I had to make was which wine I wanted to try. I still had no idea what I wanted to do with my life—how was she so sure? How did she just take the leap and have faith that things would work out?

And then, there was my dad, Frank Scott. He was an airman in the United States Air Force. He worked with local companies on how to recruit veterans for their business needs. He worked with some of the finest men and women our country had to offer and put them into the positions they were made for. He always said that military veterans were some of the most underutilized resources in our country. They were coachable leaders, survivors, warriors, problem solvers. He was amazing at it too. He was able to branch his company out across the state, but lately, he'd been working on growing it nationally.

My parents were both so successful and happy. They'd met when they were young and never looked back. I'd never even tried to date since my breakup, too terrified to try again, too scared of the raw state that love left me in. They sought after their dreams and were always unapologetically *them*. Why couldn't I do that for myself?

"I feel like I'm not doing it right," I sputtered out on a gargled sob, my face crumpling again helplessly. I knew I was putting the term "ugly cry" to shame.

My mom's lips trembled as tears stained her shirt, but then a soft smile broke free.

"If you're talking about crying, I think you're managing just fine," she chuckled as she blotted my tears away with a tissue. I shook my head.

"No, Mom, I'm talking about life. I feel like I haven't done anything remarkable. Like I've just been sitting in this safe glass box and watching everyone else move on in their lives. I mean, I was attacked in my apartment because I was alone on a Friday night...because I shut out everyone in my life. Maybe if I'd had a friend over..." My voice trailed off in a whimper.

"Honey, this is not your fault. Just because you were alone in your apartment does not justify being attacked," she urged. She shook her head as she wiped away my tears. "You *have* lived, Georgia. Not everyone can say they graduated from college with honors. Not everyone gets that opportunity, and if they do, not everyone succeeds. Not to mention, you're working for a competitive corporation. You've accomplished a lot in your young life!" she reassured, brushing my hair back behind my ear.

"That's exactly it, Mom. I've *accomplished* things, but is that what life is all about? Have I made a difference at all?" I sobbed, wondering if I could sound any more pathetic. I could already hear the smallest violin playing for all the privileges I had taken for granted.

"Gee-Gee, I get it. Doc said you almost died, so this is a great time to reevaluate and self-reflect. But honey, you help people all the time. You find them jobs and help them put food on the table," my dad added softly.

I helped people find jobs? Is that what I did as a recruiter? I supposed that made sense considering it was a staffing solutions company. Of course, I was spending time helping others find their dreams, and neglecting my own. Was I even good at helping others find their path? And then I thought the eight thousandth frustrating thought of the day. Were any of my recruits *fulfilled* in their jobs or were they just "putting food on the table" like I had been doing?

"Speaking of food!" the nurse sang as she briskly walked in with a tray of all the hospital cafeteria delicacies a girl could ask for. "I brought you a few extra cookies and ice cream." Her face fell a little as she noticed my tears. "Dr. Cobbs will be in soon, honey. Mr. and Mrs. Scott, you're welcome to stay until then, but he was specific about speaking to her alone." She smiled, but her words were more of a command than a request.

"Thank you, Nurse. Once Dr. Cobbs comes back, we'll see ourselves out." My mom smiled back at her, but it didn't meet her eyes. The nurse carried on as she checked my monitor again. My numbers seemed to satisfy her, and she shot me a wink and left me alone with my parents.

The delicious scents from the tray wafted over to me, and my stomach grumbled loudly in protest. I smiled down at the tray the nurse left on the bed. In addition to the pancakes, eggs, and coffee I ordered, she'd filled the tray to the brim with brownies and chocolate chip cookies. I guess my awkward chocolate fact resonated with her more than she let on.

Without a moment to waste, I dove into the pancakes, and God help me, they were the best pancakes I'd ever had in my life. Well, this new life anyway. Where nothing was taken for granted, and I found the beauty in the things I hadn't before. My dad reached out and squeezed my shoulder.

"Gee-Gee, you are a brave woman, and I am so proud and blessed that you survived. They've been saying you're a miracle around here. Even Doc seemed like he needed a stiff drink after handling you." His tired eyes glimmered with a laugh. "But remember, you're alive and you've been given a second chance to do something that makes your heart happy. Don't waste the gifts you were given." He kissed my cheek and pulled me in for another hug.

"Couldn't have said it better myself." Dr. Cobbs's boisterous voice filled the room as he walked in.

My eyes narrowed at him, and his mouth perked up into a slight smile, as if he'd been expecting this reaction. He turned to my parents, ignoring my glare.

"Mr. and Mrs. Scott, would you mind giving us a moment? I'd like to discharge your daughter, but I need to go over a few things with her first," he said, his grin widening. My parents gladly shuffled out, kissing me on the cheek as they left.

And finally, we were alone.

6

THE PAVERS

"I suspect you have...questions from our last encounter?" Dr. Cobbs asked as he pulled the stool to my bedside, staring at me intently.

I regarded him for a few uncomfortable heartbeats as frustration pulsed through me. His face was calm but confident. A doctor's face, no doubt. He was going to make *me* do all the asking.

I swallowed my mouthful of pancakes and pushed the tray of food away. I didn't care about going to the psych ward anymore. If that's where they put me, then I would smile as I put my own straightjacket on. Knowing the truth mattered more to me than anything else at this point.

"What do you know about...a *Reckoning*? And...how did you know to ask me who my *Light* was?" I frowned at him, wondering what his next move was. His mouth twitched, as if what I said had touched a nerve, but he dropped his gaze from mine and crossed his arms over his chest.

"Yes...I shouldn't have asked you those things, especially right after you'd woken. I understand this is already traumatic, given the circumstances of your death." He stared at my stomach, as if he could still see the mocking scar forever branded on my body. I stared at him blankly before he let out a deep sigh.

"I...asked you about the Light because I...wanted to see if you had the same one as me." His eyes drifted back up to me, with an intensity that shot chills up my arms.

"What do you mean?" I whispered.

"I died from a heart attack, several years ago. I was finishing up my residency when it happened. It was sudden." He shifted on his seat, his expression darkening. "Life is quite fleeting, as I imagine you're discovering for yourself."

I nodded slowly, settling back toward my pillow. "Please...go on."

He frowned and scanned the room as if he were nervous that someone was listening. After a thorough search, he turned back toward me, satisfied, and rubbed his hands against his thighs.

"They didn't write about what we experienced in my medical textbooks." A silent, incredulous laugh escaped his lips. "What I remember most were the colors. Colors so vivid and clear, it was as if they were from a spectrum that doesn't exist on this planet. High definition doesn't even begin to cover the beauty. I was in a field with some of the greenest grass and the most beautiful flowers I had ever seen in my life." His smile grew even wider as he looked off into the distance, letting the image take him over.

"And then, I saw them." He blew out a short breath, as his expression settled into a dreamy awestruck daze.

"There were two women. The first woman was terrified and shaking. I remember thinking that it was strange she was so scared. I didn't know where we were, but wherever it was, we were bathing in peace. It felt like pain and suffering didn't exist there. I wanted to tell her she was safe, that we were both safe, but the other woman took her hand and soothed her. She introduced herself as our Light. She said her name was Maria." He peered up at me curiously.

"You said your Light's name was Jerry, right?"

"Yes...Jerry Carter." I nodded.

Dr. Cobbs grasped his chin and sat in thought for a moment before he shook it away dismissively.

"From what I've gathered over the years, I've learned that every Reckoning is different. I'm guessing you weren't in a field like me?" he continued, leaning forward, fascinated as he watched me. I shook my head up at him.

"No...I met Jerry down the hall in the hospital lobby." I shrugged awkwardly. He perked up at my answer and let out a startling chuckle.

"Is that so? Interesting. Did you catch your Reckoning partner's name? Who did your Light say was the Anchor?" Light. Reckoning. Anchor. I couldn't believe this conversation was happening.

"Jerry told me I was the Anchor, and there was a man and a little boy, Graham and Jack." Warmth filled me as I said their names out loud. I felt so protective of them, and a sudden urge to leave and go find them filled me.

"Wait... You had...*two* Reckoning partners?" Dr. Cobbs pulled my focus back to him. His grin was quickly replaced with a deep frown, his face filled with concern and confusion. I shrugged back at him, not sure what else to say.

"Jerry was a little shocked himself that there were three of us. He said he'd never seen it before."

Dr. Cobbs blew out a puff of air, his eyebrows arched in disbelief.

"I was a Paver for several years, and I've never heard of a Reckoning...trio." He shook his head, dumbfounded.

Paver.

That's what Jerry had called us. Of course! O'Fallon Paving Incorporated.

"Paver?" I repeated, crossing my arms and frowning back at him. "Jerry tried to explain during the Reckoning...but the memory is foggy. He rushed through the facts, and none of them made any sense. Can you please explain?"

His face sobered as he pondered on my question for a moment, choosing his words carefully.

"I'm afraid it's against protocol to discuss anything before you've found your Reckoning...trio." He trailed off. I glared at him, completely annoyed now. No, I wasn't annoyed. I was furious.

"Excuse me? So, you're really not going to tell me anything else?" I demanded, my chest growing tight. I was not planning on punching a doctor today, but I was afraid my fists might fly if he didn't give.

"Well, to be honest, I haven't kept in touch with the local Pavers in years. You see...I left the organization a few years back. It's a taboo thing in the Paving community, to abandon your God-given role, but life is already hard enough as it is. Paving tends to...consume you. It comes with tremendous responsibility and discipline. So does the medical field. It became...too much to manage." He skittered his gaze around the room again, his complexion paling. I knitted my brows together, confused.

"Why do you keep looking around the room? There's no one else in here."

His nervous eyes snapped over to me as he shook his head.

"As Jerry probably mentioned to you, Pavers run a highly covert operation. They require complete privacy and have to be very careful to keep their business secure. It would be an international disaster if anyone...discovered them." He shuddered at the thought. "They have eyes everywhere."

"You mean like...cameras?" I squinted up at him, not sure what to make of anything he was saying. He let out a quick humorless laugh.

"No, they don't work like that. They have...much more up close and personal technology." His eyes flashed as he spoke.

"You see, they live by a very strict code of conduct. There are consequences if you go against protocol. It's not a society to be taken very lightly." His voice quavered like he was scared of something. He peered around the room again nervously. I scanned the room with him, but it remained empty, apart from us.

For God's sake.

"Dr. Cobbs, I couldn't give two shits about the code of conduct. I want to know what you know." I lifted my chin with confidence, but I was appalled at my newfound rudeness. His eyes narrowed at me, assessing me. Calculating me, as if he were trying to see if I was worth it or not. He finally lowered his head in silent surrender.

"Fine. The only reason I'm about to disclose this information to you is because you're my patient. Your blood pressure was a little too high for my liking, so I'm just alleviating any stress-causing factors." His eyes flitted around the room again. "You must not repeat that I told you anything, though, are we clear?"

"Clear," I responded, sitting up straight. "Now tell me what you know."

He leaned forward, his face a few inches from mine as his voice dipped into a whisper.

"You, me, Scar, we're Pavers. There's a small but strong network of us in every city on the planet."

A faint smile crossed his lips as he caught sight of Scar's business card on the bed. I had probably thrown it on the covers when my parents came in. He reached for it and picked it up, running his thumb across the top.

"I haven't seen one of these in quite some time," Dr. Cobbs chuckled, turning the card over in his hands. "You see, to anyone else, this just looks like a blank piece of paper, but to a Paver, we can see the words. I asked them about a million times how they did it. My guess is it has something to do with our brain chemistry. You know brain chemistry tends to change after one has a near-death experience."

I blinked back at him, my brain clouding with all this new puzzling, fascinating information.

"Scar is quite talented, for such a rookie. She's only been a Paver for about six months now, but she's incredible. She can read minds, if you haven't figured that out already. Comes quite in handy in her field."

Realization settled around me. Of course she could read minds. It was like she knew exactly what I was thinking. She had even said Braxton's name out loud when I knew I hadn't said it yet.

"It's her gift, or *Aftereffect* as they like to call them. We all have at least one. As for me, I can determine medical conditions just by touching someone. I suspect you'll be noticing your Aftereffects soon. They tend to develop within a few weeks after the Reckoning. They typically work in a field that's relevant to their gifts. It's strange how it works out that way, but it does."

A regretful expression crossed his face as he stared at the card. "Scar's the only Paver that still talks to me. But she kind of has to, considering she collaborates with the hospital on special cases like yours."

"So...is Scar even a real detective? I mean...is she going to find the guy that hurt me?" I could feel hot tears threatening to spill as a lump formed in my throat. He froze for a second, his face grave with earnestness.

"Scar is a real detective, and I can assure you she will not rest until she finds your attacker. As I said before, she's got an eye for this kind of thing." He squinted up at me nervously. "I'm guessing she touched you...to see what happened to you?"

I thought about the way Scar's eyes changed before she told me what she thought happened. But I had never imagined that she was...

"When she touched me, do you think she felt everything...like I felt it?" I remembered the way she wrapped her arms around her middle, the way she looked defeated and broken afterward. Probably a lot how I looked...

Dr. Cobbs's jaw hardened. "I'm afraid so ."

Incredible guilt surged through me as I thought about another human being going through the same pain, the same torture I'd experienced. Certainly not Scar. I didn't have any memory of what happened, aside from what she told me. And even just hearing about it was too...horrible. Too evil.

"I had no idea that when I asked her to tell me what happened, that she'd feel *everything*." I felt tears well in my eyes, my vision blurring as I fought back a sob. That monster had not only hurt me...he'd hurt Scar too.

"Ms. Scott, she was well aware of what she was doing. Paving is a selfless trade, let me assure you. She was willing to endure it in hopes of finding him."

I gasped. She knew very well what happened to me. She'd seen the crime scene photos, the rape kit. She had sacrificed herself, for *me*. That wasn't just selfless, that was laying yourself out for slaughter. And all to help a complete stranger?

Dr. Cobbs gently placed the business card back on the bed and tapped it.

"Keep this safe. You'll want to remember that address."

I peered down at the business card still shining in the light, almost like a beacon in the dark. I didn't imagine I'd forget, but what happened when I touched the paper left an unsettling feeling inside me. The vision of the farmhouse rooted at the forefront of my thoughts, now.

"When she gave this to me, I saw a farmhouse. There was a lady—she said 'he doesn't have much time.' She also said to find Graham and Jack, but I have no idea how to do that. I don't even know their last names, or where they live."

"A farmhouse?" Dr. Cobbs repeated in a hushed, shocked tone.

"Yeah, it was beautiful really—wraparound porch, metal roof, the whole rustic package. The lady, she was wearing all white. I thought she was an angel. She had braids, and—"

"Braids?" he said even quieter than before. I stared at him for a moment, slightly disturbed by how shocked he seemed at everything I was saying.

"Yes," I whispered, squinting back up at him. He bit his lip and dropped his gaze toward the ground.

"That's our...ahem...*their* headquarters. Well, O'Fallon's anyway. Every city has a headquarters. O'Fallon Paving is based in a farmhouse. Some of their Pavers live there, but it's just so...strange that you saw it. It's not even on a map, and they don't let new recruits near it until they've received their first training."

I just gawked back at him as I inhaled every word. He let out a breath, letting his shoulders sag in defeat.

"The woman that you saw, the one in white. That's Harlow, she's...my Reckoning partner. She was the woman that was shaking and scared in the field. She and I were..." A hint of a smile crossed his lips before it disappeared. "She's O'Fallon's managing agent. She's...your supervisor." He shifted on the stool as he scanned the room again.

"And regarding you finding Graham and Jack...I'm sorry to say, that's a sacred journey that no one can interfere with. Even if I knew where they were, I couldn't help you find them. They'd have my head."

"But why?" I yelled.

Harlow's foreboding warning filled my head.

He doesn't have much time.

If she was referring to Jack or Graham, I needed to know. I needed to find them, to save them. It was surely below freezing outside as the flurry of snow swirled around. What if Jack was out there in the freezing cold, alone.

Dr. Cobbs shot me a stern look.

"Paving is so deeply intertwined with the human instinct. You must develop your sense of self and your relationship with the world. You must go on the journey alone and find your Reckoning team on your own. It's so you can develop your instincts and trust them with your life. With *their* lives." He shook his head as he dropped his gaze to my abdomen.

"You know, this kind of thing doesn't happen with every near-death experience."

"What doesn't happen?" I demanded.

"*This.* Being chosen to become a Paver. It's quite rare. Near-death experiences happen more frequently than you'd imagine. Only a small fraction of them are chosen to become part of the Paving community. To this day, we don't know why we are chosen. And to think...you have a Reckoning *team*. I mean the probability of that is...like picking a star in the night's sky." His wonder-filled eyes locked with mine. "Must be something special planned for you three."

I thought about that for a second, an uneasy feeling knotting in my chest.

"So...how did you know I was a Paver?" I whispered. His face broke out into a wide grin.

"Well, your miraculous healing was a good start, but the fact you said you worked at O'Fallon Paving confirmed it for me . In fact, I thought it most unusual that you mentioned the name. Most Pavers just have the memory of their Reckoning to carry them through their journey. It's so rare to know your home base, much less say it out loud. It's prohibited to speak about it with normal citizens. It's another way to keep our...I mean, *their* business secure. The fact that you knew the name is...very curious." He considered that for a moment before pressing on.

"You can spot a Paver a few different ways if you're paying attention. Sometimes you just feel this static energy around them, this feeling you just can't kick. And you, Ms. Scott, have a particularly strong energy about you. Pavers also tend to change eye color the moment they begin to use their gifts. Civilians can't see the color change, but we are hyperaware of the environment around us." He made another nervous flick of his eyes around the room.

"They tend to carry around briefcases and wear watches. It's a time-sensitive thing. As Pavers, they need to have the right supplies and have impeccable timing." Scar's bright red leather briefcase popped into my head, and Jerry's golden Gucci watch. Funny, I never imagined my spirit guide rocking Gucci.

"They need to be able to blend into a crowd but be noticed all in the same breath. So, the briefcases are a unique way to capture attention."

"For what, though? What do Pavers *do*?" I demanded, my tone drenched with impatience.

"They help people stay on the right path."

I just blinked at him as he frowned at the corner next to the window. He stared at it a few more moments, his face paling again as if he saw a ghost.

"Dr. Cobbs...?"

His penetrating stare snapped toward me as a pool of sweat beaded on his upper lip.

"You know those pivotal moments in time where you feel like the world is turning for you? Maybe you found a long-lost friend in another country during a last-minute trip? Perhaps you were let go from a job, but it finally gives you the excuse to start the business you always wanted? Maybe you get in your car, but the engine won't start. At first, you wonder if anyone is on your team looking out for you. Little do you know, that's *them*, making sure you don't get into a fatal accident on your route to work that morning," he whispered, his eyes snapping over to the empty corner again.

"What are you talking about?" I whispered as I glanced over at the corner myself. It remained empty, but a strange feeling came over me in that moment. Like someone was watching. *Listening.*

"That's them, Georgia. They help pave the way to help people find their destiny." He locked eyes with me, his intense gaze burning into me.

"Do you believe in destiny, Ms. Scott?" he shot back, raising his eyebrows.

Honestly, I never thought about this kind of thing before. So far, my life had been a game of finish lines and staying in my comfort zone. I stayed focused, my eyes were always on the prize, but I still felt like something was missing. I didn't have any mojo in my dating life, I couldn't even remember where I worked or what I did, and here I was in a hospital, recovering from an assault. Was he trying to suggest that I had landed myself here because it was my destiny?

"Please don't tell me I was raped because it was written in the stars," I seethed, anger bubbling inside me.

"Ms. Scott, pain is never one's destiny. Pavers do everything in their power to help keep people safe, to lead them in the right direction, but every road to destiny is a two-way street. They help pave the way, but people still have to choose to take the roads that were created for them. It's called free will." He watched me for a moment, understanding and resentment growing in his dark eyes.

"Did Scar happen to tell you about any things that happened during your attack that may have distracted your attacker? Perhaps someone helped save you?"

I hated going over the things that happened to me again, but something Scar mentioned stood out. Mrs. Taylor had called the police just in time because she *forgot* her plane tickets. Mrs. Taylor was not the forgetful type in all the years I'd known her. She was the most organized person I'd ever met in my life. In addition to that, the fire alarm went off. I didn't even think I had put batteries in it. My hair began to stand on end as Jerry's words floated through my mind.

In our business, there is no such thing as a coincidence or a mistake.

I peered up at Dr. Cobbs and bobbed my head nervously.

"She said my neighbor had forgotten her plane tickets. She had come back to get them when she heard me screaming."

"Ah, yes. Sounds like a projection to me. Anything else?" I stared at him, dumbfounded.

"What is a projection?" I demanded, crossing my arms.

"Pavers can project an idea or a thought into a civilian's mind, only if it helps them follow through with their destiny. Or if it helps save a life," he added pointedly.

I blinked back at him, my mouth hanging open.

"Anything else?" he repeated, ignoring my blatant confusion. I cleared my throat and continued.

"She mentioned the fire alarm went off while he was..." I stopped before I let the words fall out of my mouth. Dreadful realization filtered across his gaze, and he turned away from me, to stare out the window at the cold gray sky.

"I'm sorry that you were hurt like that, Ms. Scott. I know it's not fair, and although they are powerful, they are not all encompassing. Pavers are only equipped with so much energy when they're working outside the body." I raised my eyebrows at him.

"*Outside* the body?" I repeated. He quickly scanned the room again and clamped his fist over his mouth.

"I'm sorry, Ms. Scott, I really have said too much. It's not my job to train you on what a Paver does. They prefer you discover it all on your own...after you find your team."

"So... Graham and Jack? They might not know everything that I know?" I started to panic as I thought about Jack. He was just a kid.

"I'm afraid not. Most Pavers wake up with the only the memory of their Reckoning, and the responsibility of locating the others rests with the Anchor."

I could already feel my body begin to buckle underneath the pressure.

"But what if I never find them?"

"You will, I have a good feeling about you." He sighed, as he took me in.

"I wish I could give you more answers. I know you must be so curious. Hell, I'm still curious and I was a Paver for years. All I know is that you're here and you're *alive*. And you're going home today." He smiled once again as he handed me a thick packet of discharge papers.

"I sent in your medical leave papers to Whitman's Staffing. Don't worry, I didn't include any specifics, but I requested a minimum of two weeks while you adjust to everything. Your Human Resources department said they won't expect you until after the holidays. Hopefully this will give you enough time to figure things out." His grin widened, and I hated the sick feeling in my stomach as I thought about what "figuring things out" looked like. I stared at the plate of food, still piled high, barely touched. But I had lost my appetite.

"Thanks" was all I could muster, as my mind ran wild with everything.

"I have a feeling we'll see each other again, Ms. Scott. Just sign that packet at the bottom and leave the papers on the bed." He nodded toward the medical novel in my hands. He turned to leave but paused just before he got to the door.

"Oh, and...uh, maybe on your way out, stop by Trish's Café down the street. I've heard they have a world-class mocha latte." He winked and before I could stop him, he turned on his heel and left me alone, drowning in my own questions.

7

MOCHA LATTES

I closed my eyes and sucked in a big breath, trying to steady my nerves again. *Okay, get it together. All I need to do is just wander around aimlessly, while I follow my heart and hope that I find Graham and Jack. And as I'm doing that, I also need to remember what I do at Whitman's Staffing, while I also try to figure out what I do as a Paver. Oh, and don't forget a murderous rapist is still on the loose. So just don't forget to stay alive. It's fine, totally doable.*

"I hear my baby girl gets to go home today!" My dad's enthusiastic voice boomed across the room.

My eyes fluttered open, and I couldn't help but laugh when I saw my parents' eager faces. My dad had a bouquet of gift-shop daisies, and my mom was holding a large duffel bag.

"We bought you some essentials for your stay with Mia, given that your apartment is off-limits. It's just the basics, but we can get more if you need anything else," she announced proudly as she dumped the contents of the bag out onto the bed.

The perk of having a mom that designed clothes for a living was that my wardrobe was always on trend. Her boutique was a number one online seller in the United States. She knew exactly what women wanted. I always felt empowered when I wore her clothes, like I could take on anything the world threw at me.

Among a few trendy printed shirts, jeans, and flats, she was also thoughtful enough to include some comfortable clothes. A hoodie, some basic T-shirts, sweatpants, a hat, tennis shoes, a jacket, and some toiletries lined the bed. I gawked at the treasure trove in front of me, then back to my parents, speechless.

I couldn't believe they did all of this for me. I was always grateful for the things they did, but this. *This.* Everything just pulled at me in all the right ways, I couldn't help but to let the water-gates open again. I never liked crying in front of people, not even my family. I remember judging people for crying in public, wishing they would wait until they were alone. I hated how I judged people so easily. I let the stigma of showing any emotion keep me from embracing humanity. My mom looked me over, her brow creasing in concern.

"What's wrong, baby?"

She started to brush my hair behind my ears like she always did, before I pulled her into a tight squeeze. I was not prepared for all the raw, uninhibited emotions that came with nearly dying. I tried to say "I love you" through thick sobs, but it came out more like inaudible gurgling.

"I love you too, but maybe you should take a shower before you leave?"

My mom pulled away and laughed as she scrunched her nose from my apparent stench.

"Dang, Mom, we were having a moment!"

I put my hand on my chest, feigning deep hurt as I wiped away the river I just cried. She laughed, but I caught a whiff of my sheets. Okay, so nearly dying and staying in a hospital doesn't smell like a bed of roses. My dad cleared his throat, gracefully stealing our attention from my hygiene. We both stared as he lifted a small bag over the bed and dumped a few more things on top of all the clothes.

"I got you a few things as well. You need to be able to defend yourself, and...well..." He trailed off as we all scanned the array of vicious-looking gadgets on the bed.

They seemed so out of place mixed with all the bright colors and floral patterns from my mom's boutique. I zeroed in on one particular item in the center and picked it up.

"Nunchucks, Dad? Really?"

I held back a laugh as I stared at my dad's serious expression.

"I'm actually not a hundred percent sure how those got in there, but that's not the point. You said your attacker is still out there. I want you protected."

A murderous glint flashed across his face, and I shivered as reality set back in. He picked up a rectangular object and held it out in front of me.

"This is a stun gun. All you do is hold it like this, shove the end here on your target, press the button...and *bam!*"

My mom and I jumped back as he whooped and hollered, flailing his arms about like he was being electrocuted. After a few moments, he stilled and raised his eyebrows as if he were asking "Did you catch that?"

"And here, you got your mace, an attack baton, spike rings..."

His voice fell as he watched me pull out the attack baton and try a practice hit on the side of the bed. I think the blow hurt me more than the bed because an unwelcome pain shot up my arm in mocking protest.

"Thanks, Dad... That is so...sweet of you." I smiled weakly again as I put away the baton and rubbed my arm.

"I think that'll be enough, dear," my mom said gently, but he frowned back at me. He didn't say anything, just tenderly wrapped his arms around me.

"We just want you safe. Nobody messes with my baby girl. We'll just get this all packed up for you while you go take that shower."

He pulled away and looked at me, his nose scrunched up just like my mom's. I let out a weak laugh.

"All right, all right, I get it. I smell like literal death."

I grabbed a stack of clothes and toiletries my mom brought and ran to the bathroom. Finally, I was alone again. Alone in my thoughts, fears, and that glorious-looking shower. There is something so sanctifying and religious about taking a shower. Hot water, soap, steam, washing away the day's dirt and grime. Or dried blood and iodine from your almost murder. Or all of the places where you were touched without consent. I guess showers can't wash away everything. After I finished, I put on some minimal makeup and chose a light-gray hoodie and black leggings.

As I came back into the hospital suite, my dad was teaching my mom a trick with his nunchucks as she looked on unenthused. While he made various stunt sounds, I went through the discharge papers in depth to make sure there were no more hidden clues or instructions on what to do next. I was tempted to start shouting incantations at it in hopes it would reveal something...anything, but I fought the urge. Instead, I left the papers signed on my bed and tucked Scar's business card neatly in my bag. As we left, I tried to hunt down Dr. Cobbs, but the nurses said he'd left for the day. Of *course* he had.

Finally, I walked out toward the main entrance with my parents, passing the infamous lobby as we left. The waiting room was packed this time, filled with worried families as I predicted. I stared at the corner where Jack, Graham, and I had sat. The same corner Jerry told us our lives were ending but really just beginning. I turned away uneasily. The heaviness of everything I needed to do was resting on my shoulders, and I didn't know how much longer I could take it.

"What do you say we take you to get a real breakfast? Something a little less hospital cafeteria?" my mom asked. "What about...Trish's Café down the street?"

I stopped midstep as I replayed my mom's inherent suggestion in my head. Dr. Cobbs recommended I get mocha lattes at Trish's Café too. And I faintly remembered Jerry even mentioning mocha lattes before he sent me back. I half expected the heavens above to open up and God himself would come down and hand me a chocolatey coffee concoction.

"Yeah, that sounds great." I forced a smile back at my mom as she linked her arm with my elbow. *All right, Jerry, what do you have up your sleeve?*

We arrived on Main Street as soft, wet snowflakes fell on my hair and face while we crunched our way down the sidewalk. I took a moment to relish in the peace of the snow. The world was so much quieter during a good snowfall. It was like a gentle hand on my shoulder whispering for me to slow down a little and enjoy the ride. The distant sound of hooves clapping against the pavement echoed across the brick cobblestone lining the street. I caught a glimpse of a pair of beautiful white horses leading a buggy behind it. The carriage was decked with stunning red ribbons, and it had a snuggled-up couple in tow, covered with a blanket. This was the kind of stuff every romance novel was written for. Graham's intense face and soft gray eyes surged through my mind as I watched the couple pull each other closer. Something about the way he'd held me away from Jerry so fiercely made my heart do a quick somersault before I shook the thought away. I reached toward my ring finger to twist my commitment ring, but I was quickly reminded it was gone. *He* had taken it. He had *killed* for it.

"It's just up there, I think," my mom said as she pointed ahead into a sheet of white.

It was hard to see much farther than a few businesses ahead with all the snow. For a moment, I considered telling my parents to just go home so they could avoid the slick roads. I imagined that conversation going south very quickly, and frankly, I didn't want to leave my parents just yet. I wanted to be with them and talk like we used to.

As we neared the corner, a cute decorative wooden sign with "Trish's Café" painted on the front caught our eye. As we got closer, it appeared the bistro was full of holiday shoppers and breakfast lovers. I eagerly pushed the door open and walked in, a bell ringing as we entered and busy chatter buzzed through the warm room. A swarm of delicious aromas filled the air. Cakes, pies, holiday specialties, breakfast sandwiches, and anything else I could have wanted lined the display shelves.

I frowned as I caught sight of the girl behind the counter. She seemed like she had been working there too long. Indifference and unenthusiastic vibes flowed around her as she stared out the window at the snow.

"Hi, what can we make for you?" she asked half-heartedly, avoiding eye contact as another horse-drawn carriage passed by outside.

Something about the way she looked felt familiar. The lost look in her eye, like she wasn't sure of what path to choose. It was as if she had worked there too long and demanding customers had left her cup a little empty.

"I'll have a mocha latte and something from the shelf. Surprise me." I smiled at her as she rang in the order.

"I too like to live dangerously. We'll have it right out," she droned as I handed her some cash.

Everything seemed to sway in slow motion as our fingers grazed. It was like our souls linked and everything she felt, desired, who she was to her very core filled me. Images of brilliant art, classical music, paint strokes and splatters, bright primaries, soft palettes, her life itself took my breath away. She was creativity, soul, and bold blues. She lived for art. She *was* art. My eyes dropped to her name tag hanging on her tattered apron. Jessie.

"Jessie, you're a painter, right? Have you ever thought about hanging your work up and selling it here?" I asked before I could stop myself.

Where the hell did that come from? She looked up at me for the first time, surveying me, surprise crossing her face. I probably looked just as shocked because she let herself smile for what felt like the first time in quite a while.

"How...did you know I paint?" she demanded.

Her tone was guarded as she glanced over at my parents behind me. Panic started to set in before something caught my eye. Flecks of white and blue paint were spattered on her wrist, and I let out a sigh of relief. Classic artist. Maybe I saw the paint and just assumed...

"You've got some paint on your arm." I pointed at her forearm.

She continued to study me as she walked over and grabbed a giant slice of chocolate cake labeled "Holy Moly Chocolate Godiva Cake." She plated it and handed it to me as her mouth curved upward.

"I guess I never really thought about that. I mean, what's more cultured than art and coffee?"

A spark of life seemed to ignite behind those subdued eyes. And there it was. I forgot how much one tiny comment could break just as much as build. Sometimes it just takes one person, one solitary action, to light up the way.

After we got our mocha lattes and food, my parents and I ended up talking for hours about anything and everything. Our successes, hopes, struggles, plans, whatever came to mind. Even though my attack and my rapid healing was at the forefront of our thoughts, we kept those topics out of the equation. I forgot how wonderful it was to have family time. I missed just talking and being together. As my mom laughed about my dad's ridiculous array of self-defense tools, I took a moment to enjoy the gorgeous view of downtown St. Charles.

A light dreamlike haze surrounded everything as I looked out toward the street window as the snow began to accumulate. Here, we were in our own little snow globe as a few pockets of white swirled and danced to their own winter waltz. No one seemed to be paying attention to the wonderland outside, the loud bustle of chatter and noise booming in the shop. What a pity—they were missing God's greatest show. My eyes traveled across the room at each face, casually talking about their plans as Sunday morning began.

The distinct sensation that someone was watching me crept up my spine. The hairs on the back of my neck began to stand on end, so I continued to scan the shop. A particularly active flurry of snow captured my attention back to the window, or so I thought as I peered across the street. Through the blanket of white, a pair of piercing pale blue eyes locked with mine. Across the way, sitting on a bench with his legs crossed, sat Jerry. His iconic hat and tailored suit seemed to shine through the chilling wind that billowed around him. A brilliant smile crossed his face as he lifted his hat and tipped it toward me in a gentle, knowing gesture. I flung my hands against the glass and pressed my face against the window. I squinted through the snow to get a better view, when a hand squeezed my shoulder.

"Georgia, are you okay? We were asking you when you were planning on meeting up with Mia ," my mom asked, worry creasing her brow.

"I'm sorry...I...thought I saw something," I breathed as I turned back to search the street.

The bench was empty, and Jerry had seemingly vanished without a trace. There was barely any foot traffic outside, but he couldn't have gone that far. I turned back toward my parents, who were both looking outside now in the direction of the bench. A pang of guilt filled me as I considered how crazy I just seemed. They didn't need to worry about me going insane in addition to knowing my attacker was still out there. Before I could reassure them I was okay, the sound of the bell at the door rang out. A beautiful woman with long flowing blonde hair pulled back into a ponytail entered. I knew that pretty smile and the way she seemed to light up the entire room.

"Holy geez!" she laughed heartily as she stomped her polka dot boots against the floor.

"Mia?" I stood up, already certain it was her. No one could mistake the warmth and love she spread wherever she went.

"Georgia!" Mia's face was radiating with joy as it always was. She ran over to me and pulled me into a warm embrace. Time never seemed to stop with Mia. It was as if we had only seen each other yesterday and she was ready to pick right back up.

"Damn, girl, it's not fair that you make a hoodie look sexy. When I wear hoodies, I just look homeless," she giggled as she looked around at my parents. "Frank and Audrey, what are you doing in town? Are you helping Georgia with her apartment renovations?"

I cringed and prayed that my parents wouldn't say anything, knowing full well I wasn't renovating my apartment. I rocked back and forth on my heels before I let out an awkward, high-pitched laugh.

"Yup, they braved the weather to help me. Aren't they just amazing?" I plastered on a smile, even though I could feel my mom's penetrating glare boring into my skull. "Anyway, what are you doing here?"

"I don't know if it's the papers I'm grading or the fact it's almost Christmas, but I needed Trish's famous mocha."

Of course she needed a mocha latte. I fought the urge to search the shop for Oprah, who was surely ready to announce to the whole room that she was buying a round of mocha lattes for everyone.

"Anyway, now that you're here, do you want to join me? I was just gonna pop down to a few shops before I head home. I wanted to get my students a little something for Christmas."

Somehow, her smile made me forget that I had died thirty-six hours ago. Another rush of guilt and regret bubbled up inside as I remembered not reaching out to her more often. She was like a ball of walking sunshine and positivity that I needed more of in my life. I looked over at my parents hesitantly. The weather was getting a little out of hand, and they had quite a drive home. My mom reached out and squeezed my shoulder, shooting me a watery wink.

"I suppose it's time for us to head back home, anyway. It looks like the snow isn't going to be calming down anytime soon, so you girls be careful. Don't stay out too long!"

My mom was doing her best not to cry as she swallowed back her tears and pulled me into a tight hug. I was barely able to fight back sobs of my own as I thanked her and my dad for everything.

After we got my luggage into Mia's car, we began to say our goodbyes. My dad even pulled me to the side and offered me his gun he kept in his glove compartment. Given I already had a hefty collection of defense tools, and guns scared the heck out of me, I refused. We continued to chat for several minutes in the frigid air and hugged a dozen more times before they finally left. Not even the cold ice and snow could deter a classic Midwestern goodbye.

Main Street was famous for its boutiques, restaurants, and gift shops; we simply couldn't help ourselves. The shop windows were so cheerfully displayed with Christmas ferns and lights, and the snow added a magical, frosted glow to the evening. I couldn't remember laughing as hard as I did when I was with Mia. She knew how to have a good time even in the middle of a blizzard. We ventured our way to each shop, getting to know the local business owners, chatting with other shoppers, and buying our fill of Christmas gifts, scented candles, and décor. Mia was the type of human being who knew how to make people feel like they'd known her for years, even though she'd just met them. With her, she made me forget about all the trivial things in the world like time, being murdered, and the fact that a full out ice storm was blowing outside. We made our way down the strip just in time before businesses started to close down one by one. I squinted through the storm, trying to scan the street, but it appeared vacant. I supposed most of the shoppers had gone home long before we had finished. I looked down at all of the packages we were carrying and the half-mile trek we had left to get back to her car.

"Georgia, do you mind if I leave the bags with you while I run and get the car? I promise I'll be quick, I just don't think we can make it carrying all of this," Mia asked as she peered down at the ridiculous mound of purchases in our hands. The wind whipped around us angrily as I put my bags at my feet, crossing my arms.

"Of course. I'll just be right here, freezing my ass off," I shouted through the wind.

She laughed but took off her scarf and wrapped it around me, securing it under my chin.

"I will be right back! I'll run the whole way there!" she yelled.

I frowned at her but gave her a quiet nod. Before I knew it, she disappeared into the wintery white arctic. The snow kept falling in my eyes; it was getting harder and harder to see even a few feet ahead of me. The wind and snow were chilling right down to the bone, and I prayed that Mia would make it for both our sakes. I didn't want to be buried alive next to all these packages, days after I had been murdered. I mean, did I really need five scented candles? Well, yes. I think I actually did, but I wasn't ready to *die* for them. A strange sound echoed behind me, and I quickly turned to find nothing but more snow and an empty sidewalk. The wind was howling like crazy. It was impossible to tell if it was the wind or something else. Maybe

Jerry had found me again... I *knew* I'd seen him outside on the bench. Maybe he wanted to catch me before Mia came back to give me more instructions? To keep me safe while I waited...alone?

"Jerry?" I yelled into the abyss, but a strong gust of wind carried my voice away.

If Jerry had responded, I would have never known because it sounded like nothing but an angry train rolling through. My belly tightened as I sensed someone near me, my blood going cold as my eyes darted across the street. I left all of the defense tools my Dad gave me in Mia's car. What I wouldn't do to have those nunchucks with me now. Every alarm bell in my head was screaming at me to run. I quickly began to gather the bags at my feet as another chilling gust of wind rushed toward me.

Without warning, a brick wall slammed into me, or maybe I slammed into it from the wind, I couldn't tell. The bags I was carrying flew to the floor, and I could hear one of my scented candles break. No, wait—the wall was moving on top of me. My blood ran cold, and I instantly froze as I realized the brick wall above me was a *person*. I could barely make out the shape of a man, his dark form pinning me against the wet, cold grave below. I tried to scream, but I couldn't. My mouth seemed to be frozen solid. All I could think to do was fight as adrenaline pumped through my veins. I tried to buck him off, but he was too strong. Solid hands squeezed my wrists and shoved them hard above my head against the pavement. I tried to wriggle free, but the snow was too slick. His free hand found his way around my throat and pushed down, leaving me with just enough airway to plead.

"Please, don't hurt me," I gasped out.

Before I could finish my sentence, he removed his tight grip from around my throat. I took a chance while I had it and turned my head to see if anyone was around to help. The white sheet of snow swirled around us, limiting any visibility. I turned back to the dark figure, still pinning me mercilessly to the cold, hard ground. He seemed frozen on top of me, as blood rushed to my ears, my whole body shaking. He slowly leaned down, closing the distance between our mouths. This was it. He was going to kill me right here, and they wouldn't find me until my body was frozen solid tomorrow morning. Steel-gray eyes peered down at me underneath a dark hoodie.

"Georgia?" His gruff voice growled in my ear, a familiar but pleasant sound.

I peered back up, getting a better look at his uncharacteristically handsome face.

Graham?

8

PISTOLS & POLKA DOTS

The snow clouded around us as he stilled above me. My chest rose and fell in thick bated breaths, wondering what his next move was. The man was clearly out for blood; his attack was murderous and filled with intent. Yet, here he was, studying me with that familiar careful gaze he had in the hospital lobby. He almost looked confused, perhaps even bewildered as he looked up, searching the street. Maybe he was looking for witnesses before he finally killed me. Without warning, he scrambled off me, snow flurrying around us even harder now. I used this as an opportunity to scout out any escape routes when his strong hands wrapped around my waist, pulling me to my feet. I wiggled from his grasp and stepped backward, my back hitting the real brick wall behind me.

I pressed my hands against the icy surface as I tried to sidestep away from him. I braved a quick peek at him and was baffled by his worried expression. Was he just trying to watch me squirm before he decided to pounce again? God, I prayed that Mia was on her way, wishing anyone could help me. I refused to be a victim again. I couldn't even imagine explaining this to my parents after everything. Maybe I'd never even get the chance.

A much gentler grasp fell on my shoulder. I flinched and screwed my eyes shut as I held my hands out in front of my face, waiting for the inevitable blow. The hand quickly withdrew, but I kept my eyes shut for a few more heartbeats, knowing he was just biding his time. I slowly opened my eyes to see Graham's jaw was tight, his gray eyes terrified. His hand was brushing through his hair, pulling at the roots as he stared at a place above my eye.

"Georgia, are you okay? I...swear... I thought..." He trailed off, his voice cut short through the snow and the wind. His voice was less controlled than the one I remembered from the hospital lobby. It was filled with concern, his face contorted with torture as he watched me.

"Georgia?" Graham repeated.

I flinched again, pressing farther into the wall away from him. His eyes snapped back up to my forehead, which started to throb with my pulse. He reached for my face, but I pulled away from him with a yelp.

"Please don't touch me!" I whimpered, leaning farther away. He retracted his hand immediately and lifted his hands in surrender.

"I'm not going to hurt you, okay?" he shouted through the wind. "I'm just going to get something."

I followed his hand as he dug it into his jacket pocket. As he pulled it back out, a shiny glint reflected off a nearby streetlight, and I stared, frozen as he pulled out a knife. An aggressive-looking knife with a thick blade. A guttural sound escaped my lips as my body went numb.

"No, Georgia, I promise I'm not going to hurt you. I want you to take it." His eyes softened as he flipped the blade and extended it toward me with the handle out. "If you feel at any moment like you're in danger, I want you to just plunge this sucker right in me." He took a slight step forward, offering me the knife.

I studied his calm but shocked expression. My instinct told me he was being truthful, but I wasn't sure if I should trust him. Just because he was supposed to be one of my Reckoning partners, didn't mean a damn thing, especially now. I nodded and reached out for the knife with an unsteady hand. Once my fingers closed around the handle, he let go of the blade and took a step back, giving me space.

"Explain yourself," I yelled as I gripped the knife, the snow continuing to fall relentlessly.

I laughed at my empty threat. Honestly, I would never be able to stab him, even if he came at me again. What if he didn't explain himself well enough? Was I going to scold him? As he just demonstrated, he could easily hurt me, so why did I feel the need to listen to what he had to say. His jaw clenched, and then he nodded in surrender.

"I had this...dream that you were..." He stopped and looked at me carefully before he continued. "I had a dream that someone was hurting you. I saw you outside in the snow, in this exact place. I saw the street name, and the time and everything, and I just knew I had to come. When I parked, I heard a woman screaming, so I ran toward the sound." His eyes grew wide with fear. *He was scared? Scared of what?*

"As I got closer, I saw you and...him. Whoever he was, he was pushing himself on you. Like he was..." He looked away, his hands running through his hair again.

"Well, there wasn't anyone on me! Sounds a lot like you're just rehashing everything you just did to me," I retorted, as my grip on the knife tightened.

"Listen, I know it sounds insane, but it's the truth," he urged, his voice almost desperate.

His eyes trailed up to my forehead again, concern etched on every part of his face. I watched him, taking in his familiar protective stance. Graham was a *Marine*. Marines protected; they defended. They didn't assault women, right? Dr. Cobbs said that being a Paver was all about following your heart and listening to your instincts. Everything about Graham radiated safety and security...despite the fact he just tackled me. My heart, my instincts were yearning for me to trust him. I started to shiver as I looked around at the bags scattered across the sidewalk.

"Where's your car? I'll carry these for you," he said, his intense gaze still fixed on my forehead.

I watched his warm breath cloud around him in the cold air as he continued to stare at me. The way those dangerous lines had softened, and his steel eyes had turned to a sad stormy gray. He was disgusted with himself that he hurt me. A sick thought filled my head: maybe he really *had* seen someone...

At that exact moment, Mia pulled up to the curb and swiftly got out, stumbling through the snow as she swerved around her car.

"Georgia!" she shrieked as she approached us.

Graham and I both watched as she skidded to a halt and assessed the knife in my hand and the throbbing place above my eye. I had to do a double take as Mia firmly planted her feet and pointed a small handgun at Graham's chest. Her face was scrunched with pure malicious focus as she cocked the gun. Graham slowly put his hands up as they stared each other down. I hadn't seen Mia in a few years, but this was a side of her I'd never known. Mia was kind and loving, not to mention a petite five-foot-two sorority sister. This Mia was cold and calculated, ready to take the shot if she had to. This Mia was a straight badass.

"Georgia, get in the car," she demanded, her concentrated eyes never leaving his.

I hesitated as I watched them both in shock. Graham's shoulders stiffened before he turned back toward me.

"Do as she says, Georgia," he called out.

"Shut up! Don't look at her. Keep your eyes on me," Mia yelled, her voice breaking slightly as she reached out to pull me closer.

I grabbed her hand as I looked back over at Graham, my whole body screaming to stay with him, to end this madness.

"Mia, he's not going to hurt us. He was trying to...protect me," I quavered as I reached for her to lower the gun.

"Isn't that right, *Graham?*" I shot back over at him, demanding that I wasn't going crazy.

"Wait...you know this guy?" Mia commanded.

Just then, hurried footsteps crunched behind us a few feet away. Both Mia and I whipped around to see nothing but darkness behind us. Mia's arms were still out with the gun pointed into the winter storm as the wind howled ruthlessly. The footsteps had stopped, but that same sinking instinct crept up my spine that someone else was there. The sun had set, and the street was darker now, except for the dwindling streetlamps burning low in the middle of the blizzard. Adrenaline surged through me, as my eyes tried to adjust to the growing darkness.

"Who's there?" Mia yelled, but the wind continued to whistle, as if it were screaming for us to run.

"Get in and lock the doors!" Graham's deep voice cut through behind us.

Before I could protest, he grabbed my arm and pushed me into the passenger seat, slamming the door behind me. My ears rang from the silence in the car, and I watched in horror as Mia stood with her gun pointed back at Graham. Then, it appeared she heard something again and whirled around toward the darkness creeping in. She backed up as she zeroed in on whatever hid themselves in the dark. The unknown, hiding like a coward. I heard a muffled exchange of voices before Graham and Mia shuffled around the car and hopped in, Mia back in the driver's seat and Graham taking the back seat. The pile of all our specialty shop goodies remained scattered on the ground outside.

Mia locked the doors and started the car as she pulled out into the treacherous wave of ice, wind, and snow. As we passed a small alley in between shops, my stomach dropped to the floor. A dark hooded figure emerged as large beady eyes stared back. The terrifying surveillance shot of my attacker filled my mind, and I quickly turned away, trying to catch my breath. Our heavy panting filled the vehicle as Mia drove, adrenaline still coursing through us. She drove a few more blocks in silence, before her windshield wipers froze midswipe. She quickly pulled over and threw the car into park. After a moment of ear-ringing silence, she turned back toward Graham, her hand still on her gun.

"Start talking. Who are you? What happened?" she sneered at Graham accusingly.

He raised his eyebrows and swallowed. Flashbacks of the hospital lobby scene pulsed through me. Underneath all those muscles, Graham was scared. Perhaps he was intimidated by Mia, something that made me like him just a twinge more. I still wasn't sure how to read Graham, or Mia for that matter. It seemed I didn't know either of them at all. Mia was apparently a badass gunslinger from a zombie apocalypse movie, and Graham was just...a complete mystery.

"Mia...that's your name, right?" His jaw ticked as he waited, but Mia just stared back, unmoving.

"Someone was going to hurt Georgia, okay? I thought I saw him on her, so I dove in and grabbed him. Unfortunately, I...tackled Georgia instead." His regretful gaze trailed over to me before he snapped it back to Mia.

"You tried to tackle him, but you tackled her instead?" Mia repeated coldly. Graham's hardened gaze faltered before he regained his confidence.

"You know there was something out there with us. You heard footsteps. I don't know how, but I knew they were there to hurt her." He let out a slow breath and looked out the window for a second, in deep thought.

"Listen, the snow is too thick to keep driving, and it's probably going to get worse. I know I just tackled your friend, but I live just up the street with my Marine buddies. They're good guys, and Georgia needs to get that cut looked at. I've got a fireplace, and an extra room for you both." He eyed Mia, her hand still gripping tightly around her pistol. "You've got your gun, and Georgia has my knife. I know if you feel like you're in danger, you won't hesitate to shoot."

Mia's eyes darted over to the knife in my hand and then looked up at me. Whatever she saw made her grimace. After a beat, she returned her glare back to Graham. She stared hard at him, studying him as if she were making a thousand decisions all at once, before finally finding some resolve.

"How do you know this guy, Georgia?" she whispered, narrowing her eyes.

I looked over at Graham, and my heart seemed to skip a beat as I traced his familiar face. My eyes fell to his left arm where his Semper Fi tattoo was surely hidden beneath his hoodie. I trailed down to his hand, which was balled into a fist at his side. I couldn't believe he was here, in this car with me, when I had only met him in the afterlife. Something tied me to him, an unbreakable bond that seemed to flow through my veins. Even though he didn't make a very good first impression, I couldn't lose him. This was the very definition of a miracle, and I needed to see this out.

I remembered the strange sensations that I felt when I touched the barista's hand at Trish's Café. I seemed to feel the essence of who she was as a person, her life, her personality, her dreams. Maybe...just maybe I could try the same thing with Graham. The fact he was here with me was crazy enough, and the impossible was becoming more probable with every moment that passed. Then, I did the unthinkable. I slowly reached my hand out for him, motioning for him to take it. His brow furrowed as he glanced back over at Mia and then at me, not sure if this was the most appropriate time to try holding hands.

"Georgia, what'reyoudoin?" Mia sputtered, her voice comically high.

"I...I just want to try something," I whispered, eyeing Graham carefully.

Mia let out a frustrated huff, her fingers tensing around her gun, but Graham didn't seem to care. His stormy eyes dropped to my outreached hand, and after a few moments of awkward silence, he cleared his throat and reached out toward me.

A welcome surge of warmth and safety filled me as I felt his strong grip and fingers intertwine with mine. All of his intentions, desires, and dreams surrounded me. Graham was hazy front porch sunrises. He was strong hands, unwavering courage, and boundless honor. He was warm summer rain, and hurricanes and hail. Heroic scenes filtered in my mind's eye as Graham ran toward the danger, never away. He was dedicated service, protection, and unfailing loyalty. Of all the emotions and feelings I got from Graham, the strongest of them was pure love. Not necessarily romantic love, but the love you have for your fellow man, your brothers and sisters. This man cared deeply for the person standing next to him, stranger or not.

"We have...history," I whispered as I withdrew my hand, avoiding Graham's confused stare.

Instead, I peered over at Mia, the throbbing above my temple increasing. Mia chewed on her cheek as her gaze shot between us.

"Okay, but if you even for a second make any sudden movement, I'm shooting." She bit down on her lip, trying to conceal a contemptuous smirk.

I could feel Graham's penetrating gaze linger on my face a few more beats before he finally turned back to Mia.

"Sounds like a plan. Georgia, you just make sure your friend keeps her hand on that trigger," he whispered, a hint of amusement riding on his tone.

I couldn't help myself. The sound of my name on his lips made me glance back up at him. For the first time, his face split into a gorgeous smile I simply wasn't prepared for. His harsh, dangerous lines softened, and a kind, younger man emerged as he grabbed the car door handle. There was that warm summer rain in the middle of an ice storm.

Mia and I both followed suit and got out of the car. Wind and icy snow roared into my face and ears. I was completely blind to anything and everything around me. Before I could think or do anything, a strong grasp fell on my upper arm, pulling me into the wintry abyss. I was putting all my faith in a man I had only met an hour ago. A man that had tackled me and pinned me to the floor. *Here's to breaking free from my safe glass box.*

I couldn't even see my feet as we walked; all I could concentrate on was Graham's charging form in front of me, Mia close behind. Finally, I could see what appeared to be a narrow walkway, which led upward into an icy stairway. Graham carefully helped us climb the stairs, his strong arms keeping us steady. As we approached a door, I could hear loud male voices on the other end as Graham pulled a key out from his pants pocket. He opened the door and ushered us in first. Warm heat greeted me as several fierce and silent faces turned and stared back up at us. My eyes darted to each aggressive face, war raging behind each pair of eyes. Each man stood slowly, a few of them staring at Mia's gun, several others at my knife and throbbing temple. Graham stepped in front of us and turned to the men closest to me.

"Bennett, I need the first aid. Davis, can you start the fire for them? They've had a hell of a night," Graham's deep voice instructed.

Immediately, the two jumped into action, while the others continued to gape at us curiously.

"Boys, we've got guests tonight. The weather isn't letting up, so they'll be staying upstairs." He turned toward us, and I couldn't help but to gasp as his tall, massive form towered over us.

"And if you don't mind, I'll show you both to your room." Graham smiled that same charming smile as he walked toward a rickety staircase.

Mia and I both stood frozen to the spot, unable to move as we gawked back at the men in silence. Seven men, including Graham. That was seven men too many, and the look on their faces suggested they could do some serious harm if they wanted.

"They can have my room!" a short, stocky man in the back called up to Graham as he ascended the staircase. A goofy smirk crept across his face as he winked at us both, when another elbowed him in the ribs.

"Don't worry, Tex, that was already the plan!" Graham called back down at him, as a laugh rumbled between the crew.

"Come on, let's go," Mia whispered as she nudged me toward the staircase, pulling me from my trance. My gaze fell to the floor, avoiding their evasive stares as we rushed after Graham.

Once we climbed in silence to the top, he led us down a long, narrow hall lined with beautiful tall doorways. He ushered us in to the one at the end, with a couch, a queen-sized bed, and its very own bathroom. It appeared he had given us the master suite. The furniture and the house itself were in disrepair, but there were hints of stunning architecture and detailed design all over. The house was Victorian and was probably the most prized house on the street in its heyday, but it had certainly seen better days.

The beautiful hardwood floors were warped and eroding, the sheets and furniture tattered. My heart fell as I remembered that Graham said he lived here with his fellow Marines. Even though they were terrifying, those men had fought and defended their country, and when they should be treated like kings, they were living in decay.

"I know it's not much, but I hope it'll do for tonight. I'll bring you both some warm clothes and tow—" Graham stopped short, his hand shamelessly reaching up to my face.

I sucked in a breath as his hand cupped my chin, lifting it toward him. His mouth pulled back into a thin line as he stared, as if whatever he was seeing offended him deeply. Heavy footfalls sounded behind him, and we all turned to see the man he called Bennett with the first aid kit in tow.

"What happened, Keaton?" Bennett asked as he stared up at my eye and then over at Graham.

Keaton? Who the hell is Keaton?

"Thanks, *Keaton*. We've got it from here," Mia seethed as she tugged the first aid kit from Bennett's grasp and pulled me into the room, slamming the door behind her.

"Georgia, I saw the way you looked when he said his name. You don't *really* know him, do you?" Mia asked as she assembled the first aid supplies and tended to my eye.

I stared at her, not sure where to even begin with explaining. She huffed, resentment and fear crossing her face. I wanted to tell her. No, I *needed* to tell her, but how could I explain things that didn't even make sense to me?

"You just let me know whenever you figure out what's going on," she stewed, rolling her eyes. "And don't for a second think that you skated by with not explaining the weird hand-holding in the car thing," she continued as she placed a bandage above my temple. Before I could respond, a loud knock at the door made us both jump.

"Georgia? It's Graham. I brought you guys some clothes."

Mia shot me a pointed look, shaking her head.

"Well, go ahead. Open the door for *Keaton*," she seethed, clearly still heated.

No, that warm summer rain was about to tell me why Bennett called him Keaton. I needed to be sure that Mia and I were safe tonight, in a house full of strange men. I at least needed to know their real names if this was going to work. I stomped over to the door and flung it open. Before I could get any angry accusations out, I stopped and looked at a very shirtless Graham...or Keaton standing casually in the doorway. He was packing heat, and then some. His body was exactly as I had imagined it would look like. It was hard edges, clean-cut lines, and could easily be a shield or a dangerous weapon. I trailed down his sculpted abdomen, but I couldn't help but linger over a few faint dark scars on his shoulders and chest. Graham had died like me, but how? How did he get those scars? He cleared his throat, and I startled, snapping my lustful gaze back up to him.

"Georgia...I'm so sorry I hurt you. I thought I was protecting you—that's all I wanted to do. I *swear* I saw a man trying to force himself on you..." Graham shook his head in disgust like he was seeing it all over again.

I could hear Mia snorting angrily behind me, making her disapproval evident. I shook my head at him, dismissing his apology.

"Why did your friend call you Keaton?" I demanded, crossing my arms.

He arched an eyebrow, as he took me in.

"'Oh, um...that's my last name. The men I served with know me as Keaton," he answered softly, recognizing the mistrust in my eyes. Of course it was that simple. He let out a deep breath and handed me a few towels and some clothes. "I understand if you don't trust me, but I want to be very clear with you. You are safe here," he said, his focus returning to my temple. His face hardened again, and a muscle popped in his jaw.

"I want you to know, I have never raised a hand to a woman in my life. I would *never*—"

I held up a hand, cutting him off. I leaned closer to him as the heat from his body radiated toward me, and I lowered my voice to a whisper.

"Graham, it's okay. I believe you had that dream, and I believe you saw me get attacked. I...saw a man as we drove away. He was out there, waiting and watching in the dark. Not to mention, I've had my fair share of strange visions and experiences myself since the...Reckoning," I whispered, as Mia stomped into the bathroom behind me. I flinched as she slammed the door. "I haven't told Mia anything...but I'm going to. Can you just tell me what your friends know downstairs?"

"I told them pretty much everything...they're more like brothers than friends," he whispered.

I arched my eyebrows up at him.

87

"*Everything?* And they believed you?" I repeated, creasing my brow.

I heard Mia throw the bathroom door back open, and Graham backed away from me immediately, as if he realized we were standing too close.

"When you guys are dressed, we'll have a hot fire and some food waiting if you feel up to it," he said sheepishly, his eyes dropping to the floor.

It felt like he wanted to say something else, but he pursed his lips and turned, disappearing down the hall and down the stairs. Strangely, I missed his warmth, but I shut the door and turned back toward Mia, finally ready to share with her what happened to me. I was ready to share everything. Mia was my sister too, and she didn't deserve for me to keep secrets, especially now as we stayed in a house full of strangers.

Big, beastly strangers.

"Mia...I'm not renovating my apartment," I confessed, shrinking my shoulders in front of her. She froze and looked up at me with widened eyes.

"Someone...attacked me." I continued, as I tried to find the right words. Over the next few hours I replayed everything that happened. I told her about the Reckoning, my strange encounter with Scar, and her account of my attack. I brushed through Dr. Cobbs's explanation of Pavers and did my best to explain what happened with Graham out in the snow. She listened patiently the whole way through and only asked a few questions that I didn't have the answers to.

"Georgia...I'm so sorry that happened to you," she cried, as she threw her arms around my neck. "I'm even sorrier for yelling at you—I just didn't know what was going on !"

"Mia, you have nothing to apologize for. I would have been mad too. Now I just need to know what Graham knows. You think they're still up down there?" I whispered.

I wished I knew what he had told them. What exactly did Graham mean by *everything*? I distinctly remember Jerry leaning in and telling Graham something I couldn't hear when we were in the hospital lobby. He knew something that I wasn't supposed to know, and it was time to get to the bottom of it.

"Well, there's only one way to find out," she replied deviously, a smirk lifting the corner of her mouth. And with that, we silently tiptoed out into the hallway and descended the old staircase.

88

9

THE BROTHERHOOD

Once we reached the landing, we heard hushed voices whispering around the corner. Mia grabbed my arm and held a finger over her mouth. I nodded back at her, and we both leaned in, peeking around the wall to find all the men huddled at the table. A fire roared in the living room, and delicious aromas filled the air. My stomach lurched with hunger again, and I quickly wrapped my arms around my middle, hoping they wouldn't hear. It appeared they hadn't, because they continued talking in low voices, unfazed.

"Man, this is some freaky paranormal shit. You know, one time when I was twelve, I predicted the lottery numbers. I couldn't get a ticket, being that I was twelve and all, but man when I saw those numbers, I about pissed myself!"

"What's new, Tex?" One of the men slugged him on the arm as a laugh ripped across the table. Tex crossed his arms and slumped down into his chair shaking his head.

"So where's the kid, now?" a handsome blond asked in a quiet tone as the laughs died down.

They all stopped and stared at Graham, who seemed to be looking off into the distance, in deep thought. To my slight disappointment, he had finally found a shirt.

The kid. He was talking about Jack. His thin body and hollowed-out cheeks haunted me as his image filled my mind. I wondered if his parents knew everything he was going through and if he had someone he could talk to about all of this like we did.

"I don't know, but I've got a bad feeling about him. He reminded me of when we were younger. You know...he was aggressive, angry at the world. Makes me feel like he's had a rough go, and he might still be in danger. I'm gonna see if Georgia knows anything, but I think she needs her space right now, given the fact I fucking *tackled* her." Graham's frown deepened as he took a long pull from his beer and turned to watch the fire, the light dancing across his features dangerously.

"Keaton, we believe you saw someone hurting her. We can't explain any of this, but there's been a lot of weird shit going on since that thing happened in the bar. We know you're a good man." A large brawny man with beautiful ebony skin chimed in, patting him on the back.

The thing that happened in the bar?

"Yeah, I mean how else can we explain two hot babes sleeping in Tex's bed? Divine intervention?" Another man with thick curly hair winked as a resounding echo of agreement and laughing filled the room, a few of them clinking their glasses.

"Hey, boys, I've got plenty of game. I got girls fighting over me left and right," Tex defended as he dusted off his shoulders.

The curly headed man pushed Tex playfully. But Tex came back with a vengeance and knocked him to the floor, both of them rolling around in a brotherly scuffle. This appeared to be a regular occurrence because the rest of the men stayed put staring at the fire.

"Davis, you want to bring up your famous hot chocolate and soup for them? If I've learned anything growing up with sisters, women need access to food and chocolate during a crisis," one of the tallest men suggested, as the two scuffling on the floor bumped into a nightstand.

"For God's sake, boys. If you scuff up my Grandma's furniture—" the handsome blond called down at the two, who continued, uncaring in the slightest. He shook his head, then nodded.

"Yeah, I'll put together a tray."

"Oh! I want to bring it up! The hottie with the gun was totally checking me out earlier," Tex shouted as the other found him in a chokehold.

Mia's fingers dug into my arm, pulling me toward her in a panic.

"Come on, let's go back up before—"

Mia's mouth fell open as she stared in horror at something behind me. I whirled around to find deep black eyes and a square jawline staring back, his heavy masculine presence filling the stairwell. We both stared back at him in shocked silence, my back pressing into Mia as he stood watching us.

"Would you ladies like to join us?" he offered in a low, gruff tone, speaking just loud enough for us to hear. He was being kind, giving us an out if we wanted to remain unseen. I heard Mia gulp loudly, before I finally decided to grow a backbone.

"Yes, we would appreciate that," I said, surprised to hear my voice as steady as it was.

I could feel Mia tense behind me, her fingers still clenched around my wrist. His black eyes flashed with a hint of amusement, then over to Mia before nodding, shooting us a quiet, spirited smile. His large frame moved, giving us enough room to walk past him.

"Gentlemen, there are ladies in our presence," he announced in the same gruff tone to the room. The two men on the ground stopped mid-scuffle as every pair of eyes rested on us. I hated being the center of attention, especially now, with a flappy bandage over my temple and swimming in Graham's flannels twice my size. Mia's fingers dug deeper into my wrist, signaling me to do or say something.

There was a surge of commotion as the men straightened up, clearing the table and making enough space for us to sit. Graham and the handsome blond rushed over to pull out two chairs for us. Graham shot me a worried look, like a wounded animal, as I led Mia over to the table. I gave him the faintest of smiles as I sat down, allowing him to push his chair in for me. Once Mia was seated, the handsome blond rushed back over to the kitchen and continued putting together a tray of goodies, while another gathered a few blankets.

"I'm glad you decided to come down. You feeling okay? Are you dizzy or nauseous at all?" Graham whispered, his eyes darkening painfully.

I shook my head.

"Graham, I'm fine. Don't worry, okay?" I reassured him as I scanned the room.

Tex and his wrestling mate had found their way next to the table as they straightened their shirts, trying their best to look presentable. The others gathered around, all of them not really sure what to do except stand and stare.

A tray of steaming tomato soup, crackers, a block of cheese, and two mugs of hot chocolate were placed in front of us. I fought the urge to squirm as the seven of them stood, watching us expectantly in silence.

"Um, thank you, guys, for letting us crash here tonight, and...for all of this," I praised at the blond behind the kitchen counter. His cheeks reddened as he smiled back bashfully. For seven intimidating Marines, they were surprisingly kind of adorable.

I felt movement behind me, and I twisted around to find Tex leaning down between us with an overly eager grin.

"I'm Tex, born and raised in Houston, Texas." He leaned even closer, his grin widening. "And if you were wondering if the saying is true about everything being bigger in Texas...it is."

A series of groans floated around the room from his brazen comment.

"Jesus, Tex. Could you not terrify the only women that have ever been inside our house?" a tall lanky man chided, shaking his head. I couldn't help but to laugh as I took Tex in. He was shorter and Hispanic, his accent laced with Spanish spice and homegrown Texas all in one. He had a unique charm to him that made me feel like we were instant friends, despite the fact he was clearly hitting on us.

"Reed, speak for yourself, man. I've brought a girl here before, but none of you were home...so you wouldn't know." He smirked, raising his chin high.

"If you're referring to that one time you picked my sister up from the airport...you know the one that's married and has three kids? Then yes, you'd be correct."

Tex shook his head, muttering something about how she wasn't married that night under his breath. He turned back toward us, his eyes flashing with amusement.

"If you ladies need anything tonight, and I mean *anything*, I'll just be down the hall. Oh...and ignore whatever you find in the drawer next to my bed." He winked, a slight dimple forming on his left cheek. A heavy hand pulled him away from us where the man he had been scrimmaging with stood in his place.

"Sorry about my friend—the only big thing about him is his ego. The name's Andrews."

Andrews was boyishly handsome, his light brown hair curly and out of sorts in a sexy way. He eyed Mia curiously as he flashed a wide grin at her.

"I saw you packing some heat when you came in the door. You maybe want to take a trip to the shooting range sometime?" he asked as Mia stared at him, her mouth hanging open.

He didn't wait for an answer; instead he draped two blankets he was carrying over our shoulders. He seemed to be spending a little too much attention straightening out the blanket around Mia's neck before the tall man swatted his hand away.

"Ladies, please disregard those two. We strive to only *respect* women in this house, and I'll be sure to personally kick both of their asses later tonight. Until then, my name's Reed, and please know that you're safe from harm here." He eyed Graham and straightened his shoulders, somehow growing another three inches taller. "Keaton's been telling us about your adventure tonight, and I'm pleased to say you've got one of the most elite and well-trained militant response units in the country at your beck and call."

He leaned over and shook both of our hands with a strong grip. Reed was unusually tall, his head just a few inches away from the ceiling, and his limbs were lean but muscular. His pale face was kind, and his eyes were alarmingly blue, almost like Jerry's. Another man stepped forward, clapping Reed on the shoulder. It was Bennett, the man who had brought us the first aid kit. He was rugged and handsome with soft brown skin. He wore thick-framed academic glasses, and he had a gorgeous smile to match.

"Yeah, we're sorry you ran into some trouble earlier, but it looks like you've got that cut taken care of. Good choice using the double-duty bandages—that cut looked a little angry."

I could feel Graham's shoulders ripple with his words, but he didn't seem to notice. Instead, he stepped forward and shook both our hands adoringly, almost reverently, his massive hands swallowing ours whole.

"That's Bennett. He's our medic but also our self-proclaimed chaplain. He's...curious about the circumstances of how we met," Graham explained.

His gaze trailed over to Mia as he muddled through, choosing his words wisely, not sure how much she knew.

"It seems you've already met Cooper—he's one of our best hand-to-hand combat specialists."

I looked over toward Cooper, his body tense, his brooding demeanor focused unnervingly on me. He nodded, a twitch of a smile playing at the corner of his mouth before it disappeared. I smiled back at him. There seemed to be a lot going on behind those deep black eyes, but he kept his head down, not letting on that he was anything more than muscle.

Graham pointed over toward the blond who was busying himself in front of the stove.

"And that's Davis. He's our house cook. He can make a mean gourmet filet mignon, but he's also our sharpshooter. Let's just say he's got a great eye for things."

The handsome clean-cut blond beamed back at us as he waved.

"Please, eat up. My mom always said a good meal helps the body heal," Davis recited as he nodded toward the soup.

Mia and I both looked at each other hesitantly before digging in. A gourmet chef was by far the biggest understatement of the year. The soup was incredible, with hints of red pepper, and cheesy croutons floating at the top. Even the hot chocolate was homemade, most certainly not just a packet microwaveable drink. He had topped it off with whipped cream, nutmeg, and cinnamon, and even threw a mini candy cane in as a stir.

"This is *amazing*," Mia moaned in between spoonfuls. I bobbed enthusiastically up at Davis as he threw a hand towel over his shoulder proudly.

"My mom's recipe. I learned from the best," he said as he began cleaning up around the kitchen.

Mia and I ate uncomfortably while the men watched. After a few awkward moments of silence, Mia put her spoon down and narrowed her eyes at Graham.

"So...*Keaton*, how did you die?" Mia blurted out.

I gasped as I snapped my horrified expression toward her.

"Mia! You can't just...ask people how they *died*," I muttered over at her, nudging her with my elbow.

She shrugged as she took a sip of her hot chocolate, watching Graham expectantly.

"Well?" she urged, leaning back into her chair.

Graham raised his eyebrows at me before Tex let out a laugh.

"So you know that Graham and Georgia are like some freaky soul mates or some shit?" Tex grinned over at Mia, his eyes flashing excitedly.

She half laughed, half choked on the hot chocolate.

"That's one way to put it," she chided, crossing her arms.

I couldn't help but glance over at him too before dropping my gaze to the floor. I felt like death was such a personal detail of someone's life. Maybe Graham didn't want those facts shared with the room. I knew I didn't want to talk about how I died. Tex took a seat at the table next to Mia, planting his hands on the surface. It was almost like he was bracing himself for the story.

"Let me tell you, it was *epic*. We were all hanging out at a bar, when our boy Keaton notices some asshole spiking a girl's drink. So, when the girl got up to go to the bathroom, Keaton confronted him." Tex shot a proud grin at Graham, who had finally decided to take a seat at the table.

Those hard lines and rough edges had made their way back to his face as he watched me. His expression was pained, almost like he sensed my hesitation in talking about our deaths. He wasn't worried about him; it was almost like he was worried about *me*.

"He asked the jerk if he needed him to buy another drink, considering he ruined the other one. At first, the dude played it off like he was just giving her some medicine she forgot to take earlier. Like, why would you be dropping her meds in her beer when she wasn't looking?" Tex threw up his hands in disgust.

"*Then*, the dude starts getting angry, starts pushing Keaton, and by then all of us were up out of our chairs ready to beat his ass. Ain't nobody be messing with my little Graham Cracker, okay?" Tex stood up and strode over to Graham, pulling him lovingly into his chest as he stroked his hair.

Mia mouthed, "Graham Cracker?" over at me, and I couldn't help but giggle.

"All right, all right. I think they've heard enough, Tex," Graham admonished as he shook himself free of Tex's motherly embrace.

"No, they need to hear this, mi corazón," he threw back, patting him dismissively.

"So, the girl comes back from the bathroom, and Keaton tries to warn her. But before we knew it, dude swung a straight left hook into Keaton's jaw. He recovered quickly, though, because my man got these catlike reflexes, almost as good as mine. Anyway, Keaton popped him in his face—you know, gave him the ol' one-two. But then, the dude throws a shot at his chest. And man, I'd never seen a soldier go down that fast." Tex let out a slow whistle, like the sound of a rocket flying in. "You know this man's been shot four times for his country and got sliced open by some shrapnel from a grenade? But one left hook from drink spiking bastard and *boom*!"

Mia and I jumped as he belted out, his eyes widening in delight.

"Okay... I think that's enough," Graham repeated, his eyes still trained on me.

"I'm almost finished, Graham Cracker," Tex said as he waved him away. "*Apparently*, the guy slammed his fist so hard into Keaton's chest, his heart stopped beating. I know. Unbelievable, right? Surprisingly, this wasn't the first time I've seen it happen. Back home, when I played baseball, I saw a line drive shoot right into my teammate's chest. It dang near killed him, but someone gave him CPR and he made it. Our boy Bennett was quick thinking too and brought my little Graham Cracker back to life. And that's where you come in, sweet Georgia peach." Tex grinned at me, squeezing one of my shoulders. "Keaton says he met you and the boy and some James Bond–looking dude in your Recon or whatever it's called." He shook his head, amazed. "Sounds like you got a lot to figure out..." He shot me another goofy grin before his face grew curious.

"So, enough about mi patito over here. Georgia, what happened to y—"

I jumped as Graham stood up, fast as lightning. The sound of his chair scraping against the wood echoed across the room. A vein in his forehead had popped out, and his broad shoulders were like steel as he glared at Tex. The room grew painfully quiet as every pair of eyes locked on him.

"Graham, it's...it's okay." An uncomfortable laugh escaped my lips, but no one laughed along with me.

Instead, everyone's eyes fell on me, both concerned and curious all at once. I could feel blood rush across my cheeks and up my chest. Panic began to set in, but I quickly swallowed it back down. I peered up at him, pleading with my eyes for him to sit. A hard muscle twitched just above his tattoo. He gave Tex one more glare before he slowly sank back in his seat and dropped his enraged gaze to the table.

I cleared my throat as the heat from the fire began to engulf me. I tried to form the words in my head, but they became muddled and heavy in my mouth. I startled as I felt Mia's kind, encouraging hand soothe my back, and with that simple act of kindness, I was able to find my footing again.

"Someone...attacked me. And...whoever he was, I think he tried to come for me again tonight," I explained as I avoided their eyes.

I hated how vulnerable I felt. Even though I had given them minimal information, I felt naked and exposed in front of all of them. I glanced up through my eyelashes at Graham again, who appeared to be holding on to the table for dear life. It looked like he was rooting himself to the spot to keep him from hurting someone. Those harsh lines looked more terrifying than ever as the fire danced across his face. I needed to change the subject. I was afraid more questions would ensue, and there were more important matters at hand to discuss anyway. My heart clung to the topic that seemed most precious of all.

Jack.

I peered over at Graham again. His steely eyes were like ice as they stared off into a distant place far away from here.

"Graham...you don't know where Jack is, then?" I uttered quietly.

Graham seemed to shake from his angry trance and locked eyes with mine, sending a shiver through me. There was an untamable fire behind those eyes. A fire I would never want to get in the way of.

"No, I was hoping you knew," Graham whispered with a pained grimace.

Disappointment tore through me as Harlow's warning flashed through my thoughts again.

He doesn't have much time.

If it wasn't Graham whose time was slowly ticking away...then it must be Jack's. Knots formed in my stomach as his small frame filled my mind. Where could he be? How could we even begin to find him? Graham was the one that found me, so my locating skills were clearly underdeveloped. The task alone made me want a drink—something a little harder than hot chocolate .

I eyed the beer that Graham had been nursing on the table and snatched it before he could take another sip. I took several deep gulps and finished it, slamming the empty bottle down. Graham arched his eyebrows at me, his eyes dancing with amusement.

"Would you like another?" he asked, surprise and a hint of admiration coating his tone. I shook my head then thought better of it.

"Yes, actually I would love another one," I said with a quiet laugh.

"I'll have one too!" Mia chimed in, and Graham quickly got to his feet, heading toward the fridge.

"Yes, ma'am," he called back as he grabbed a few Bud Light beers and popped the caps off each one.

I stared at the fire as I thought about how Graham found me. Jerry had said I was the Anchor, but how did Graham find me first?

"Maybe Jerry was wrong about me being the Anchor," I whispered as he handed me my bottle. I took a few more deep gulps and smiled as the cold beer rushed down my throat.

Graham shook his head. "I don't think he was wrong. I think I found you because you were in danger...and I needed to protect you."

A rush of heat filled me as he said those last words. It might have been the beer, but I liked the way he felt like he needed to protect me. I took another swig, avoiding his burning stare.

"What about Jack?" I asked nervously, as the wind rattled the windowpanes next to the sink.

"It's not safe to be out there right now, and we wouldn't be doing him any favors if we got stuck in a ditch trying to find him. Once the weather clears, you and I are gonna go find him, though. Okay?" Graham reassured.

He reached for my arm to comfort me, and as his fingers grazed my elbow, a jolt of electricity seemed to spark between us. I pulled my arm away, but based on Graham's shocked expression, he felt it too.

"You know we're coming with you, right?"

We both turned to find the rest of the men sharing a popcorn bowl next to the fire. Somehow Mia had traipsed herself over with them as she snacked away on a mouthful, nodding enthusiastically.

"Yeah, Georgia, school's cancelled tomorrow, anyway," Mia muffled as she grabbed another handful.

"Oh, are you a teacher or something?" Andrews asked as he swept a lazy glance across her face. "I love teachers, although I'm afraid to say I was a very bad student back in my day," Andrews emphasized as he started to wrap his arm around Mia's shoulder. She smacked it away with an eye roll.

Graham ignored them and shifted back toward me. It almost felt like he was seeking approval. And for some reason, I wanted nothing else but to give it to him. I peered up at him through my eyelashes and blushed under his unrelenting stare.

"The more company, the better, I think. We need all the help we can get." I shrugged. Graham jerked his chin and turned toward the rest of the group.

"All right, then it's a plan. We'll have to confirm with your dad, Reed, but I want everyone's bags packed tonight just in case. Reed and Cooper, you've got shovel duty this time. I think the roads might be cleared by morning, if all the plows are working."

I held back a laugh as I watched them all jump up and down like they had just won the lottery. Graham caught my grin, and he smiled back, that gorgeous smile that took away years from his face. He sat back down next to me and took another sip from his beer. I took a drink as well, and as I pulled the neck of the bottle away, I swear I caught Graham's gaze lingering on my lips.

He leaned in closer and lowered his voice so only I could hear him. "We've been working at Reed's dad's auto shop for the last year, since we finished our contract with the Marine Corps. The work is steady, and it's awesome to get paid while hanging with these guys, but we miss the thrill of adventure." His eyes trailed up toward my bandage, his smile faltering a little.

I tensed as I considered my own employment dilemma.

"So, you remember where you work?" I asked as I took another drink.

Graham's brows drew together as he nodded.

"Yeah, why? You don't?"

I shook my head regretfully. "Apparently, I'm a recruitment specialist at Whitman's Staffing Solutions." I sucked on my lip as I stared at the fire. I was beginning to feel the numbing effects of the beer. "Weirdly enough, I told the doctor I worked at a company called O'Fallon Paving."

I giggled, which felt strange coming from me. I was never a serial giggler to begin with, but here I was in this man's house, drinking beer and talking about paving. I leaned in closer to him, the sweet smell from his breath crashing against me.

"Does that sound familiar to you? O'Fallon Paving Inc.?"

He tensed next to me as his eyes dipped downward to my lips again. Heat coursed through me from his hungry look, and my fingers flew instinctively to my ring finger. But I was cruelly reminded that it had been taken. *Again.* And whoever that monster was, was still out there. Exhaustion and anger rolled through me, and Graham's smile disappeared altogether.

"Georgia, you okay?" he prodded as he squinted down at my left hand.

"I'm sorry, Graham. I'm...not feeling very well. I...I think I'm going to go to bed," I said as I stood slowly.

The room seemed to shake as I rose. I was such a lightweight, I couldn't remember the last time I'd had a drink. I felt my body sway, dangerously close to Graham's before his hand shot out, gripping my wrist. I gasped as I felt the warmth from his hand steadying me. I eyed his hand and slowly trailed my gaze upward until I met his hardened face. His eyes were molten lava as an electric charge shot between us again. Mia was at my side in an instant, sensing something was wrong.

"I'll take her," Mia bit out at Graham as she wrapped her arm around my waist, hoisting me up. He hesitated before dropping his hand at his side, following my every move like a hawk.

"Good night, boys! Don't stay up too late—we've got a big day tomorrow!" Mia called behind her shoulder at the men.

A string of good nights flew after us, but I could feel Graham's eyes on me as we ascended the stairs, and somehow it calmed me. Graham's protectiveness was unyielding.

I let Mia have the bed, while I took the couch, despite her protests. I started to truly feel ill, and I worried I might get sick in the bed if I slept with Mia. As we lay in silence, the wind howled outside and my mind was plagued with a thousand and one different thoughts. I tried to channel my inner "Anchor," hoping that somehow Jack's location would make itself known. But to no avail. Even if we did find him, how would his parents handle all of this? I played out the awkward encounter in my head.

"Hi, Jack's parents... We, as in total complete strangers, would like to please meet your son so we can learn how to be Pavers and do strange paranormal things that we can't talk about with you. We'll have him home by seven, okay?"

Oh, God, honestly. What would we *say*?

I listened to the scratching of the trees against the windows and prayed that he was safe out there. Comforting images of him cozy and next to a fire somewhere soothed me and I let those images send me into a deep sleep.

———

Beautiful, soft white lights danced across my dimly lit apartment, as Christmas music and the smell of freshly baked cookies filled the air. A Christmas movie marathon was playing on the TV, my personal favorite cookie baking tradition. I leaned down to check on the cookies. They were already getting that golden-brown rise, the kind of color that I lived for.

A soft knock rapped on the door, and I whipped around to check the time. It was fifteen minutes past eight; I never had anyone over except Mrs. Taylor, and she religiously went to bed before then. No, wait, they were going on a trip this weekend. She said she was taking an evening flight—maybe she needed me to do something while they were gone. Maybe I could pack a few cookies for them before they headed off into paradise. It was her cookie recipe anyway; I was sure she would love a snack before they boarded the plane. I ran over to unlock the latch, then hurried back to get a bag.

"Door's unlocked, Mrs. Taylor! Come in!" I shouted as I bent down and shuffled through the cabinets. I heard the door open and close as a pair of footsteps trailed in through the kitchen.

"Hey, Mrs. Taylor! I'm just getting a bag for some cookies. Are you leaving soon?" I yelled over my shoulder.

Time stood still as a large but strong hand had curled around my hip. Another hand grabbed my upper arm, yanking my back against a hard chest. Pain rippled up my shoulder as their fingers dug into my skin.

"So innocent, so trusting," a sickening, low voice whispered against my neck as my heart hammered.

Rough fabric rubbed up against my cheek. Oh, God, he was wearing a mask. I slowly peeked down at his hands gripping my arm. He was wearing gloves too. Leather gloves. Bile rose in my throat as I contemplated why he might be wearing those formidable items.

His hand slid up from my hip and grazed past my navel up to my breast. A satisfied growl rumbled in his throat as he groped me, and I fought the urge to vomit right there on the floor. Maybe the fact he wasn't showing his face was a good sign. He was talking. Maybe, just maybe I could talk my way out of this.

"Listen, I have money. Lots of it. Let me just get it for you," I whimpered as his grip moved up toward my throat.

His long fingers tightened against my jaw, mashing my cheeks against my teeth. An unnerving laugh escaped his lips. I swallowed another lump of bile as his bitter breath drifted across my neck.

"You know that's not what I came here for, sweetheart," he whispered, before he jerked me around to face him.

I let out a cry as fat tears rolled down my cheeks.

"Now be a good girl and let me show you what I'm really here for."

He brushed his fingertips against my lips to silence me, but all I could manage to do was scream.

10

MAGNETIC & ELECTRIC

"Georgia!" a voice shouted, as strong hands gripped the sides of my face.

I tried to claw free from him, pulling at his thick arms, but it was useless. I slumped over, unwilling to fight anymore, and waited for him to do his worst.

Bright lights flicked on, and I snapped my eyes open with them. I looked up to find Graham staring fearfully down at me, while Cooper and Andrews felt for the locks on the doors and windows. Mia stared with wide eyes, her blanket pulled tightly in her grasp as she huddled in the corner.

"Clear!" Tex emerged from the bathroom, a gun in his hand, his boyish grin replaced with a malicious scowl that would put the fear of God in anyone.

"Windows and doors secure," Cooper announced as Andrews went over to calm Mia.

"Georgia, what happened? You were screaming," Graham urged in a hushed tone, his fingers grazing my face and shoulders, searching for any injuries.

I let out a quiet sob as I wiped my tears and shook my head. It was a dream. It was just a terrible, horrible dream.

But deep down...I knew it was a terrible, horrible memory.

"I'm so sorry..." I peered up at him, my eyes still brimming with tears.

Graham looked me over once more before movement at the doorway captured his attention. Reed, Bennett, and Davis were now gathered outside the door, peering in.

"Downstairs is clear," Davis said, holstering his gun.

Oh, God. So much for not being the center of attention.

"All right, boys, at ease." Graham turned toward the rest of the room. "Everybody's safe and accounted for. Let's go back to bed."

After a moment of quiet exchanged looks, everyone filtered out one by one, without a sound. My heart sunk in embarrassment as I watched them leave. I couldn't stop shaking from the terror from my nightmare. His voice, his hands, his intentions. I dropped my tear-filled gaze to the floor as my attacker's words echoed in my head.

So innocent. So trusting.

The bastard was right, and I hated it. I hadn't even taken a moment to check and see who it was. I was just as dumb as everyone that dies in every horror movie ever. I was the girl that everyone was yelling at in the movie theatre as she took a shower while the crazy clown killer hid in the closet. I froze as Graham grasped my chin and wiped away a few stray tears.

"You're safe, it was just a dream. No one's going to hurt you, okay?" He dropped his voice to a whisper. "Do you...want to talk about it?" he asked, his imploring eyes digging deeper.

Too deep.

Nope. Absolutely not. Graham or anyone else didn't need to hear about it. Instead, I just stared at him, still silently processing the memory. Mia and Graham exchanged a quiet look before he spoke again.

"Georgia, why don't you sleep in my room, and I'll take the couch downstairs. So you both can get some rest?" Graham asked, looking between us both.

I peeked around his broad shoulders over at Mia. Her expression was worried in every sense of the word, but there were bags under her eyes. She was exhausted. Maybe it would be better to let her have her own space tonight. We had a big day ahead of us tomorrow after all.

I shrugged at Mia and then nodded at Graham. She narrowed her eyes at me, as if she were saying "Are you sure?" but I had made up my mind. Graham helped me up, and I walked over to her, shooting her a weak smile.

"I'm sorry I—"

"Georgia, honestly, are you sure you're okay? Was the dream about...your attack?" Mia whispered tenderly. I blinked back at her and nodded, tears threatening again before she pulled me into a tight embrace.

"Girl, just stay here. I'm here for you," she urged while she rubbed my shoulders.

"Mia, maybe Graham's right. If Jack's out there, I want to make sure we give him our best. I want you to get your rest, okay?" I pleaded with watery eyes.

"All right, but don't you dare be afraid to wake me up again if you need me. Okay?" Her voice was strained and her eyes were widened with focus.

"You know I will," I reassured as Graham led me toward the door.

"Don't get any ideas, all right, *Graham Cracker*?" Mia called after us before he turned off the lights.

"Yes, ma'am. Now get some rest," Graham shot back with a casual salute, closing the door behind us.

Quiet rustling sounded behind the door, before I let the fact that Graham and I were alone set in. His careful gaze was fixed on me as he led me down the hall into a much smaller adjacent room.

It was minimalistic in design, with a small desk, chair, and a mattress on the floor. The white walls were blank, but he had two pictures resting on his desk. The first picture was of Graham and his Marine brothers dressed proudly in their uniforms. Graham was standing in the middle with his arm hanging around Tex, both of them laughing at something behind the camera. They all looked so young and adventurous; even Cooper's gruff demeanor was much more carefree. My focus gravitated toward the photo next to it. A beautiful woman with a gorgeous, white smile and a stunning pair of blue-gray eyes stared back. She was young, but something behind her sweeping gaze made her look much older, wiser. Did Graham have a girlfriend? She was so beautiful, and the picture was placed so intentionally, like whoever she was meant the world to him. How would she feel about another girl sleeping in his bed? Guilt rushed over me as my eyes lingered on the mattress.

"Listen...Graham. Let me just sleep downstairs on the couch. It's no big—"

"I won't have you sleeping downstairs; it's not as safe. Plus, it's noisy down there. Reed snores." He grinned back, but his face sobered as he caught my eyes flickering toward the mysterious woman's photo. He strode over and grabbed it like it was the most precious thing in the world.

"This was my mom. She died when I was eight."

"Oh," I replied stupidly, searching for something else to say. "What was she like?" I asked, stepping closer to see her face again. Now I started to see the resemblance. Her hair was the same color as Graham's, and she had that same breathtaking smile.

"I just remember she was always dancing and cooking. She seemed to always be moving to music even when there wasn't any playing," he answered with a laugh.

"And your dad?"

Graham raised his eyes up to me, his pupils dilating.

"I never knew him." He shrugged as he put the picture down and turned back toward me. Silence filled the room, and we both stared at each other as this magnetic electric charge danced between us.

"So...the bathroom is down the hall, and I'll be downstairs if you need me. Do you need anything? Maybe some water? A snack?"

His hair looked tousled and messy, and the way he was offering his bed, water, and food made me feel like a queen. I felt blood flush through my cheeks as I thought about him jumping into action after he'd heard me scream. The whole freaking house responded. Reed wasn't lying when he said we had one of the best response units under our roof.

"No...Graham. I'm okay. I'm...so sorry I woke you and your brothers up. I just—"

"Georgia, we're a house filled with ex-Marines. We're used to screams in the middle of the night." He said it so casually, like it was no big deal, but I felt the weight of his words crash over me. A slight sadness crossed his face before he shook it off and glanced back up at me.

"We won't let anyone hurt you or Mia. Whatever happened to you...whatever you dreamed about, that will *never* happen as long as you're with me, okay?"

Deep within my heart I knew he would protect me no matter what. I nodded at him and dropped my gaze to the floor as I felt the energy charge in the room. Jerry's kind face filled my thoughts, and I felt Graham's heat next to me as he stepped closer.

"Georgia...?" he whispered. "What's on your mind?"

I bit my lip as I peered up at him nervously. "Do you remember how Jerry called us Pavers?" I asked, digging my fingernails into my palms.

Graham's smile faltered before he turned to close the door. He hesitated and glanced back at me, leaving the door open by a few inches.

"Yes...what about it? Did you find out anything new?" he whispered as he pulled the desk chair out and took a seat.

I sighed as I considered how I could explain everything Dr. Cobbs told me. I could feel the weighted questions turning like clockwork in his head, so I pulled my wits together and went back to the very beginning. I went through the experience I had in the hospital with Dr. Cobbs and Scar, being careful to keep any personal information from the attack out of the equation.

"Dr. Cobbs was...nervous as he told me everything...like he was being watched. He said Pavers live by a very strict code of conduct and they have eyes and ears everywhere. I imagine they wouldn't be very happy that we've told everyone else in the house about the Reckoning."

He shrugged and sat in deep thought for a moment. His eyes were trained on the floor, and I couldn't help but stare at those hard edges lining his jaw.

"You said that he *left* the organization? Do you think we should be listening to someone who's no longer a part of it?"

I lifted my shoulders with a shrug. "I guess not, although he seemed so sad and...regretful, almost like he hated that he'd left."

"Why did he leave?" he whispered.

"He said that Paving...*consumes* you." A shiver ran up my spine from the way he'd said it. Graham tensed as he watched goose bumps rise along my arms.

"Are you cold? Do you want a blanket?" Without waiting for my answer, he quickly got up and opened his closet to pull an extra quilt from the top shelf.

I wasn't cold at all; in fact my skin was practically on fire. Every time I was near Graham, my skin felt flushed and feverish. I had my suspicions that perhaps it was just me reacting to his body, but there was something deeper about the sensations I felt. Something that had to do more with the Reckoning and the bond we had, whatever that was. He draped the blanket around my shoulders, rubbing my upper arms to warm me. I felt the sharp sting of an electric shock shoot through me again, and I jumped back, tripping on the mattress. I tried to find my balance but failed miserably. I tilted backward toward the bed. I felt the freefall, as Graham's hands wrapped around my wrists, trying to pull me back. Instead, he teetered and I jerked backward. Together, in a brilliant weightless collapse, we fell. His body was hard as it crashed against mine, my back hitting the soft, cool sheets below.

Graham froze as his body pressed into me from above, his hands still wrapped around my wrists.

"Jesus Christ, Georgia. Are you okay?" he breathed, his steely regard fixed on me. I shifted beneath him, and surprisingly I let out a small laugh that turned into a hysterical giggle.

"Graham...why does this keep happening?" I asked in between fits of laughter, which instantly halted as his hand reached up toward my forehead. I felt his thumb graze the place above my eye, which started to pound with my pulse.

"You're bleeding again," he whispered, his cool breath drifting across my neck.

His masculine scent of soap and the outdoors got caught in the mix, and I suddenly felt light-headed from the sensory overload. I peered up at his tender gaze, and I shifted underneath him again.

"Graham..." I uttered, as I twisted my wrist still firmly in his grasp.

His eyes snapped toward my wrist, and he immediately pushed himself off, rolling onto the other side of the bed.

"God, I'm so sorry..." He scrambled to his feet and rushed back over to his closet. He quickly pulled a small first aid kit from a bag and returned to the spot on the bed next to me.

"Do you mind if I...?" He gestured toward my forehead, and I nodded up at him. He slowly removed the bandage and took in a sharp breath as he caught sight of what was underneath.

"For fuck's sake," he breathed as he blotted my cut with a cotton ball. "Did I tell you I was sorry yet, because I...I am *so* sorry."

He shook his head as he tore away the bandage and prepared the new one. I reached toward his hand, and our fingers grazed past each other, once more. Front porch sunrises and warm summer rain filled my thoughts again.

The very essence of Graham cut right through me in every pleasant way possible. He jumped back and stared at me, his brows knitting together.

"Georgia, your *eyes*. They...they just changed color. They changed when we were in the car too, when you held my hand. I thought my mind was playing tricks, considering I had just tackled a woman..." He trailed off. "Mia didn't seem to notice either, but now I'm pretty sure I know what I saw," Graham continued, leaning forward, peering into my very soul.

I arched my eyebrows curiously at him. "What color did they change to?" I asked as I recalled the beautiful glow from Scar's eyes.

A wide grin spread across his face as he squinted over at me. "Well, they're normally this gorgeous green color, almost emerald."

I felt blood rush to my face, and at that moment, I was really starting to hate my traitorous ginger skin.

"But when they changed, they were this fiery yellow-gold color. It was pretty sick, actually," he said with a smirk.

I couldn't help but return his smile, as a burst of excitement ran through me.

"You know...when we held hands, I could...feel you," I whispered, as the wind howled outside, sending another shiver down my spine.

Graham peered down at me, a glint of amusement shining in his eyes.

"You *felt* me, huh?"

I could feel my skin burn as he repeated my words. Oh, God. I bit my lip and nodded up at him with wide eyes.

"What did you feel?" he asked as a guarded but hopeful expression crossed his face.

I couldn't hold his gaze any longer, and I looked toward the window as gusts of snow rattled against the glass.

"Well, I could feel that you're a...good man. You're a protector," I uttered, pulling my knees to my chest.

His eyes seemed to dance as I said the word. *Protector*. Like he was understood, and that I knew what he wanted me to know. He looked back up toward my cut as he finished replacing the bandage.

"How can you be so sure? I mean, it's not like I've tackled you twice in one day and marked up your face," he grunted, beckoning toward my temple remorsefully.

"My instincts are telling me so. Both Jerry and Dr. Cobbs said to pay attention to what...your heart tells you. You know, Dr. Cobbs mentioned Aftereffects too. He said they're like superpowers, or gifts that we develop after the Reckoning. I wonder if maybe that's your gift. Maybe you can see things that haven't happened yet. Or, you sense when people are in danger," I reassured, reaching up to pat his arm. As my fingers grazed his tattoo, that same electrical spark ignited between us, and I snatched my hand away. As I rubbed my hand, I watched Graham's eyes change just like Scar's, just like mine.

"Your eyes, they changed again!" Graham bolted to his feet, peering down at me. I pushed myself off the bed and stood up beaming.

"Your eyes changed too! It was like a golden flash, just a split second before they changed back. Did you feel that...shock?"

"Yeah, I did. I felt it at the table too, earlier tonight."

A sense of urgency overcame me to hold his hands again. Not just because I melted every time I felt his skin against mine, but because there was a compelling need deep within me.

"Take my hands," I demanded as I reached out in front of me. His brows drew together as his eyes darted from my face to my outstretched hands.

"Maybe I should take you out to dinner first? Don't want anyone getting the wrong idea about us..."

I blushed at his invitation before his face transformed into that gorgeous youthful man again. He reached for my hands, wrapping his fingers around my palms, his warmth consuming me. A soft tingling sensation shot up my arms, and I peered back up at Graham, his eyes turning that same beautiful golden shade as before.

Sharp images of a city skyline filled my mind. It was a romantic picturesque shot of tall buildings, gilded by a dazzling sunset. The St. Louis Gateway Arch glittered against the light, as the traffic weaved on through. Suddenly, the vision zeroed in on a beautiful copper sign bolted to a stone wall. The symbols and numbers were hard to read, as if they were backward or switched around. The word "Children's" was the only word that seemed legible in the mix. And just like that, the images disappeared, and all that was left was Graham and me, alone in a room, holding hands. I pulled my hands from his grip, rubbing them together as the electrical charge continued to run through me. The hot glow in Graham's eyes slowly diminished like an incinerator cooling down.

"Did...did you see that too?" I asked as I clenched and unclenched my fists, relaxing the joints. Whatever just happened left them numb and cold despite the warmth that Graham offered.

"I know that place." His voice was strained, distant, as if he wished he didn't. His face was pale, and beads of sweat rolled down his neck and forehead. "That sign, it's from the group home I grew up in," Graham whispered. He flicked his gaze back toward me, and concern began to darken his features. "You okay? You look like you're gonna be sick."

I shot him a weak grin. "I could say the same about you," I breathed as I wiped sweat from my own brow.

"What was the group home like?" I asked as I sat back down on the bed, crossing my legs. Graham's faint smile disappeared, and his eyes dropped to the floor. He shifted uneasily, the wooden floor creaking beneath him.

"After my mom died, I was put in foster care." His voice was cold and distant again.

My heart stuttered in my chest as I thought about a young Graham Keaton, bunkered up in a room all by himself, wondering about things that no child should worry about. Why his mother died, and how he would be cared for now that she was gone.

"When I arrived at the Gray House, it was..." This time Graham was the one who shuddered, and that sick feeling returned. "Let's just say...it was hard."

I sighed, slumping over as I silently reviewed all this new information. "There has to be a reason we saw that," I thought aloud, my mind racing with questions.

"Maybe that's where he is," Graham whispered.

"You mean Jack?" I demanded.

Graham nodded, his lips slackening from deep thought. Given I had no idea where to begin to find Jack, it was a good place to start. The windows shook again from the storm, and my breath hitched as I thought about the thin boy out there in this weather. All alone.

He doesn't have much time.

"Do you think he's okay? I mean, it's so cold outside. What if he got

112

caught in the snow and..." Tears started to well at the corners of my eyes as I considered the worst. Graham was next to me at lightning speed, his hands gripping my shoulders.

"Georgia, he's safe. I feel it in my bones. Don't you?" he whispered.

Deep down, I knew he was safe, just as Graham said. The strange electrical connection I felt with Graham seemed to taper off into the unknown, like it was connected to Jack somewhere out there. My link with Graham was just as strong as it was with Jack. He was out there, alive. He had to be.

"Yeah," I sighed.

Graham peered over at the photo of him and his brotherhood.

"The memories I have at the Gray House are rough, but not all of them were horrible. I met most of the guys there, way before we enlisted. That's where they became my brothers, my *family*." A sweet smile graced his lips as he let the memories run. "If he is there, they'll take good care of him. We will find him, so just rest easy, okay?"

He watched me for a few heartbeats and then walked over to the mattress on the floor. He leaned over, pulled the covers back, and motioned for me to climb in.

"Let's get to bed. We gotta give Jack our best chance, remember? We need some sleep." He beckoned me forward, but I remained rooted to the spot. One last question burned inside me, and I couldn't help but to give him pause as I remembered the Reckoning. Jerry had specifically told Graham something that I wasn't supposed to hear. Graham knew a secret, but we couldn't have those. I wanted to know what he knew.

"One more thing." I squinted up at him, hoping he would be forthcoming. "Jerry told you something, before he sent you back. He whispered it, like I wasn't supposed to hear." I studied him as his body tensed, his face hardening with those familiar harsh lines I was beginning to adore. "Can you please tell me what he said?"

Graham dropped his gaze, avoiding eye contact. He shifted uncomfortably again before his steel-gray eyes trailed up toward me, glassy and filled with dread.

"Jerry...told me what happened to you."

I froze as I let his words settle over me. An icy sensation floated over me, and suddenly my skin was hyperaware of the electrical charge still buzzing in the room.

"What do you mean, he told you what happened?" I whispered, already knowing full well what he meant.

He watched me carefully as he threw a hand behind his neck, like he needed to hold on to something, squeeze something.

"He told me someone raped you...and murdered you."

My breath caught in my throat, and I wrapped my arms around my waist. I stood there, motionless and shaking all in the same breath before him. Exposed. Naked. Graham knew all along. But Jerry knew what happened to me first. But how? If he had seen my attacker, maybe he could help me track him down. I watched Graham's hands clench at his sides, his careful eyes watching me. Waiting for me to say something.

"Did he...tell you his name? Something we could report to the police?" I looked up at him as I tried to keep my voice steady.

Anger flooded his expression, as if he were hoping it wasn't true. Oh, Graham...but it was. He shook his head and crossed his arms, his Semper Fi tattoo more notable than ever before.

"Georgia, if he'd given me his name, I wouldn't be standing here with you right now," he threatened as a vein popped in his forearm.

I choked out a sob as I felt the breath knock right out of my chest. The room began closing in as my knees shook, that faint feeling from before returning. I felt my knees give way, before Graham lurched forward, pulling me into his hard chest. I wanted to push him away, but instead, I melted into him, breathing in his calming, soothing scent. His tight embrace kept me grounded, at peace while the rest of the world seemed wild and out of control.

"I'm so sorry," he whispered into my hair. I felt him rest his chin on my head, his hands splayed across my back. I was shaking, not sure what to say, silently wishing that I'd never asked about this in the first place.

"Jerry said that he escaped, and that I needed to get back and find you. Find Jack. I think he told me so he could send me back without a fight." He pulled me closer to him, despite the fact that our bodies seemed welded together already.

"He knew I'd want to protect you both." His eyes washed over my face and up toward the bandage that still clung to my temple. I peered up at him with tearstained cheeks, as shame and humiliation filled me. I hated that he knew. I hated that Jerry told him, when it wasn't his story to tell.

"Georgia, as long as you're with me, I won't let anything ever happen to you again, do you understand me?" Graham growled with an intensity that set me on fire, but I believed every word with my whole heart.

Flashes of the little boy and girl in the snow filled my mind when I was in the hospital. How he knelt down and helped her back up and kept her safe. *Chivalry does exist.* Knights in shining armor exist. I nodded back at him, my lip trembling as he wiped away another tear.

"I'll stay with you until you fall asleep, if you want. I promise I'll leave as soon as I hear you snoring. Marine's honor." I let out a sob-ridden laugh as he led me toward the bed, helping me climb under the covers. After I was tucked in, he rounded the mattress and to my surprise took the chair next to the bed.

"You're not going to...lie next to me?" I asked, propping myself up on my elbows. He shook his head regretfully, no doubt.

"I'm afraid not, Georgia. Right now, I'm going to sit here and make sure you're safe until you fall asleep and that's it."

I stared at him, astounded. I hadn't met a single man that would turn down an opportunity to hop in bed, no matter what circumstances. But here Graham Keaton was, sitting in an uncomfortable office chair, keeping watch while I slept in *his* bed.

"Graham, for God's sake—"

"Georgia, trust me, this is the safest place for me to be right now."

I raised my eyebrows at his comment. Something in his tone seemed to suggest he thought it would be perhaps more dangerous if he slipped in bed with me. He hopped up and flipped the lights off, the only light flooding in from the streetlights outside. I startled as it hit his unrelenting stare.

"Now get some sleep. Jack will need us in the morning," he ordered through the dark as he sat back in his chair. I fought the urge to argue with him some more, but I knew he wouldn't give in. I imagined he'd endured much tougher things as a Marine than a stubborn girl in his bed.

"Good night, Georgia. Sweet dreams."

11

RIDE OR DIE

Hazy morning light poured in through the grand window above the bed, as loud metal scraping against pavement sounded outside. It took a second for me to remember where I was, before Graham's woodsy scent filled my senses. The events from last night came back in one tumultuous rush. Embarrassment and excitement burned within me as I contemplated everything that happened. I pushed myself up and quickly turned toward the chair Graham had sat in. Watching me. Protecting me. The chair was neatly pushed back under the desk. He was nowhere to be seen. I scrambled up on my hands and knees and peeked out the window at the roads down below.

The plows had done an excellent job at clearing the snow, and I was pleased to see Reed and Cooper shoveling the driveway and salting the walkways. It almost appeared like the snow was melting as the sun peeked across the rooftops and muddy patches of earth began to show against the blinding white. Missouri had its way of playing its way through at least eighteen seasons of weather...in one single day.

Loud laughter boomed downstairs, and I wondered if Mia was up yet. Her light, feminine trill flooded up through the air vents in the middle of the male bass voices downstairs, and I couldn't help but to laugh. That girl was fearless. I would never in a million years be able to just walk into a room crowded with hot guys by myself and just hang out like she could. Especially after the humiliating fiasco from last night, after I woke the entire house from my screaming.

"Andrews, what is wrong with you?" Mia's voice shouted playfully as it floated from the ductwork.

"What? It's just a little butter!" Andrews retorted with an echoing laugh.

"Yeah, if you mean little by enough to feed an entire nation for three months!" Mia was giggling hysterically at this point as I imagined an assortment of strange scenarios that tied to their intriguing conversation.

I hopped out of bed and found myself being pulled over toward Graham's closet door, just barely hanging ajar. I tiptoed over to it and eased it open, my cheeks reddening as I stared inside. I felt so mischievous for invading his privacy like this, but my curiosity overrode any guilt I felt. His closet was simple and organized. Just a few shirts and pants hanging on plastic hangers. His uniform hung proudly, separated from the other clothes; a military bag sat upright on the floor. I pulled a shirt from the rack and ran my fingers through the soft fabric. Before I could stop myself, I brought the fabric to my nose, inhaling that comforting scent that seemed to cradle me as it surrounded me. A loud roar of laughter sounded again from downstairs, and I jumped, hastily returning the shirt where I found it. *Georgia, my God, you can't be smelling his shirts and snooping through his things like this when he's letting you sleep in his room.*

I froze as I heard heavy footsteps ascend the stairs before they continued down the hall toward Graham's room. *My* room. A familiar electrical static charged through me as they stopped right at the door, a light shadow reflecting off the wood floors. It had to be Graham—who else would it be? I stared at the doorknob, waiting for the inevitable, so he could catch me red-handed, nose-deep in his deliciously clean laundry. I could hear him breathing on the other side of the door, the tension filling the room as if he were trying to decide whether to come in. After a few awkward heartbeats of silence, the footsteps turned back away, until they shuffled back downstairs. I let out a relieved sigh, laughing at myself for being such a creeper.

Graham probably had to pack for the trip, but he was being polite, letting me sleep in a little bit longer. The clock on the wall read a little after 8:00 a.m. It was time to get out of bed and get moving. We needed to find Jack, and I wasn't doing anyone any good, holed up in his room like this, not to mention reveling in his scent.

I opened the door, peeking my head outside to scan the hallway. No one appeared to be upstairs, as most of the noise was traveling from the kitchen on the first floor. I took a step forward when my foot fell on something soft on the ground. There at my feet were my clothes from last night, neatly folded and washed. I bent down and picked up the pile. I leaned forward and smelled the hoodie on top. The heavenly aroma of the detergent had Graham's refreshing scent saturated all over it. I could feel my face turn a bright shade of pink as my eyes fell on a Victoria's Secret sports bra and panties I had also been wearing last night. Graham had washed my clothes. For the love of all that was holy.

I frantically closed the door as quietly as possible. I needed to get changed and get down there so I could finally face everyone. I had to do it at some point, considering the last time I saw everyone, I was screaming at the top of my lungs in the middle of the night. I pressed my face into my newly washed laundry again, and a sense of calm soothed me. Even though I had a bag filled to the brim with trendy pieces from my mom's shop, all I wanted to wear were the clothes Graham had washed for me. They smelled like him, and something about it felt like home. I threw on the hoodie and leggings, before I slipped back out into the empty hallway toward the bathroom.

I stood in front of the sink as I assessed my face. The massive bandage over my eye had peeled back from a restless sleep, so I pulled it back, inhaling sharply at the gash hidden underneath. I guess my miraculous healing days were over, because the cut had bruised to a deep purple and dried blood formed an ugly black line above my brow. My heart thudded as I considered what Graham might have done if I hadn't spoken when I did. I tore the bandage off and washed my face, taking extra care around my eye. I brushed my fingers through my long, golden waves, covering my bruised temple, and finally headed down the hall. As I creaked down the old staircase, delicious smells of bacon, eggs, and waffles wafted through the air. Davis had to have been behind this, with those mad cooking skills of his. Hearty laughs and cheerful conversation echoed around the room as I met the landing and turned into the kitchen. The first face I spotted was Graham's, midbite into his toast.

God, he was handsome, it just wasn't fair. His hair was still messy, and unkempt, but it worked so well for him. He had on a dark gray hoodie and jeans that fit the shape of his body so perfectly. He shot me a welcoming grin, which I returned shyly. His face was reassuring and inviting as I approached the table, but his smile faltered as it landed on my eye.

"Good morning," I muttered to the table, as Mia reached over and cleared a spot for me next to her and Bennett.

A resounding "good morning" followed from everyone as Davis hopped up to prepare me a plate. Without warning, Bennett's hand cupped my chin and tugged it upward toward him.

"It's looking better today," he stated calmly, peering down at my forehead through his glasses .

I cracked a weak smile up at him, feeling Graham's eyes follow his every move. I cringed inwardly, wondering how bad it had to have been before.

"It'd probably be best to let the air heal it from now on. It'll heal faster that way." After a moment, he seemed satisfied, releasing his grip and forking his way through his plate again.

Graham rose to his feet, dusting off the crumbs from his hands, and headed over to the coffeepot.

"How do you like your coffee?" he called over to me.

I could tell he was trying to avoid my mocking eyesore above my temple.

"Cream and two sugars, please." I shot him a heartening smile as I dug into the plate Davis placed in front of me. Waffles, eggs, bacon, and a side of fruit. Damn, he was good.

"How did you know this is *exactly* what I wanted?" I winked over at Davis, and he chuckled.

"Who wouldn't want that, is what I want to know," he retorted as Graham handed me my coffee and squeezed my shoulder.

I stifled a smile at how easy it was to be around him. How easy it was to be around all of them. None of them seemed fazed in the slightest from the commotion I'd caused last night. I guess it was just another night for them.

"So, Georgia, Keaton says you guys are thinking Jack is staying at the group home we grew up in?" Bennett asked in between mouthfuls.

I glanced sheepishly over at Graham before I scanned the rest of their expectant faces. Several stopped chewing while a few others put their utensils down to focus on me. I stiffened at the attention but nodded back.

"Well...we're not sure, but it's worth a try." I shrugged over at Bennett and noted a few uncomfortable grimaces across the table.

I assumed they weren't happy with Jack's possible location, rather than my lack of knowing where he might be. Based on what Graham mentioned last night, it wasn't home sweet home for them. This was a trip down memory lane that perhaps they weren't so excited about.

"Graham says he met most of you at the home. And you've been brothers ever since," I said to the table while they ate. Graham smiled down at his plate and took another bite. Warmth shot through me as I noticed the way his lips curved whenever I said his name.

"Did all of you grow up in the home?" Mia asked, her knowing eyes narrowing at Graham and me like she sensed what I hoped my face wasn't telling.

"No. Reed, Davis, and I didn't meet this crazy bunch until the Marines, but it was love at first sight, let me tell you. We like to call ourselves the brotherhood when no one's around," Tex bragged as he wrapped his arm around Graham's shoulder.

"Dude, no one's around anyway," Bennett interjected, shaking his head.

I bit my lip to hold back a laugh. I had only known these guys for barely a day, and I already adored them.

"So, are you two sisters?" Andrews's voice broke through my thoughts as he eyed Mia and me.

"Yeah, kind of like how you guys are brothers," Mia answered, shooting me a wink.

"That's cool, that's cool." He nodded, shifting in his seat like he wanted to say something else. Mia and I both just stared as his ears began to turn a deep shade of scarlet.

"So...are you both single?" he murmured as he cast a hopeful glance over at Graham.

I peeked over at him too, to find him staring at his plate as he did his best to fight an ever-growing smile. My heart fluttered as a hint of color rushed up toward his neck. Interesting. Was Mr. Marine...*embarrassed?*

Mia put her fork down and turned to look at Andrews with narrowed eyes.

"What if I said that I was married and I had two kids back at home?" Mia demanded, before she sipped down some coffee.

Andrews just stared at her like he didn't really hear her. Instead, he broke out into a heart-stopping grin.

"I would probably go cry in my room later and mourn the loss of the six kids I want to have with you?" Andrews said in a quiet unrelenting tone.

"Six?" Mia shouted before a playful smirk crept across her face. "Well, I'm not married, and I don't have kids," Mia said sweetly before she picked her fork back up and poked at her food.

"Yet," Andrews whispered eagerly.

"And what about you, Georgia? Are you married with two kids?" Tex leaned forward excitedly.

"Tex," Graham warned, eyeing him carefully.

I cleared my throat and shook my head, waving Graham's protective glare away.

"Uh...no I'm...not seeing anyone." My ginger genes betrayed me yet again as blood rushed toward my face. Tex shot me that same goofy grin as he bounced his eyebrows up and down enthusiastically.

"You'll both be pleased to know that all of us are single as well. Every single goddamn one of us." Tex shook his head with regret. "So even though Andrews and Keaton might have staked their claim on you two, you can take your pick because you do get to have a say in the matter. Just because you and my little Graham Cracker have some freaky paranormal bond doesn't mean that this can't happen." He put on his best smolder as he waved his hand between us.

"Thanks, Tex. I'll keep that in mind," I said, trying not to laugh.

"Take that back—you can't pick Davis. My man over here likes to play for the other team, if you know what I mean." He reached over and grazed his fingers playfully across Davis's arm.

"Tex, we've already discussed this. You'll never be man enough for me." Davis pushed his hand away before Tex brought a fist to his chest, like he'd been shot.

"No matter how many times you push me away, I'll always love you," he cooed in his best Southern damsel voice, throwing a hand dramatically over his forehead.

I jumped as the front door opened. Reed and Cooper filed in as the cold air gusted in with them.

"Damn, it's cold!" Reed shouted as he unzipped his jacket and knocked his boots on the rug, Cooper following suit.

"The bikes are ready, and I've got the truck parked out in the driveway," Cooper announced as they both approached the table.

Reed squeezed Graham's shoulder as his eyes rested on Mia and me. "Glad to see you're both still here. Tex usually scares all the girls away before they even get here."

"I'm pretty sure Tex was just in the middle of doing that, before you both interrupted him," Davis pointed out with a chuckle. I caught Graham checking the clock on the wall before he cleared his throat and silence settled around the room.

"All right, I want to be on the road in about fifteen minutes. Can we do that?" Graham looked around at the table expectantly. Everyone nodded and before I knew it, we all jumped into action as one cohesive unit. I helped Andrews and Bennett in the kitchen while Mia and the others rushed to their rooms to gather everyone's luggage. Mia and I were about the same size, so I told her I'd share the clothes my mom packed with her. I loved watching the boys work together. Everyone had a job, and they knew exactly what to do. Within ten minutes, the dishes and kitchen were cleaned. Graham tore through the house for last-minute checks to make sure we didn't leave anything.

Once I got my jacket on, I walked outside to a scene straight from a movie. If I didn't know any better, there would have been some edgy hip-hop or rock-and-roll song playing as I approached the open garage. There, parked near the street, was a large black Chevy truck, steaming from the cold. Behind the truck in a perfect line were six stunning Kawasaki sports bikes in various colors. On each motorcycle was the rest of the crew, decked out in their helmets and jackets. I stared with my mouth open, as they all kick-started their engines, letting them roar as Mia made her way over toward me.

"I have been pleading with them to just drive with me in my car, but they insisted they ride their motorcycles," she said with an eye roll. I scanned the roads, which still looked slick despite the valiant efforts from the plow team. I caught sight of Graham jogging over toward us, an excited grin on his face as he neared.

"Don't worry, you two. You'll be in the truck with me." Graham's smile grew as he focused on my worried face.

"You all right?" he asked, his fingers brushing tenderly against my arm. Mia narrowed her eyes at the exchange, but I ignored her and shook my head.

"I'm more worried for *them*. Are you sure this is a good idea? What if—"

"Trust me, they *live* for this kind of thing. This is the only reason we keep working at the auto shop. We get to touch up bikes and trucks," he boasted as he turned toward the rest of his brothers. A few of them were revving their engines and whooping and hollering. It was literally 9:30 in the freaking morning, and the roads were still spotted with salt and sludge. Adrenaline junkies were a real thing. I don't think any of these guys lived a single day in a safe glass box.

"Where is your motorcycle?" I asked as I searched the empty garage. Graham shrugged as he shot me a wary look.

"I drove it to Main Street...after I had that dream. I knew it'd get me there faster than the truck, but it's probably plowed over by now." The welcome image of Graham riding through the snow filled my mind before I snapped out of it from another loud roar from the motorcycles.

Reel. It. In. Georgia.

"That's not important right now, anyway. What matters is we're going to find Jack. You guys ready for this?"

I glanced over at the six fearless men on their bikes, who were watching our exchange as a ridiculous smile crept across my face. Ride or die had a whole new meaning when it came to Mia, Graham, and his brotherhood.

"Hell yes," I smirked up at him before I headed toward the truck, waving at his brothers as I passed.

I couldn't tell which was which, as their helmets were tinted, but I assumed Tex was on the red one because he blew a kiss at me. Mia hopped in the back, and I took the passenger seat. I watched Graham lock up, securing each door before he jumped in the driver's seat.

"Here we go, ladies!" Graham shouted as he pulled out into the street.

I turned back to watch the rest of them follow behind. They all peeled out together in a tightly packed unit. I wanted to pinch myself, this all felt so surreal. Never in a million years did I imagine I would be throwing every caution to the wind like I was now. Here I was, with a great friend I hadn't talked to in a few years, a man I had physically met yesterday, with his crotch-rocket brigade brotherhood tailing behind us. And we were going on a road trip to find a little boy I'd only seen after I died, to a place that I'd seen in a vision.

My heart grew tenfold for the boundless faith that each of them had. I wasn't so sure I would be as willing to just hit the road, not knowing what would happen as they all were, especially in these dangerous conditions. All of them, Mia, the boys, Graham. They trusted each other. They trusted me, even though we all had just met yesterday. I knew that I would do everything in my power to maintain that trust.

The ride to St. Louis was scenic, and I couldn't help but feel like we were on this divine crusade. If only Jack could see us now, riding through the depths of winter, a team of fearless Marine-motorcyclists in tow to find him. We had a clear cause and mission, and that was to find him and make sure he was safe. With Mia and Graham's men, I knew nothing could stop us now. I couldn't help but wonder how each of the guys from the Gray House felt as they drove toward the place that they probably wished they'd forget. I'm sure they wished they had a team of courageous people on a mission to find them when they were there. Every kid deserves someone that would fight through hell to make sure they were okay.

Every single one.

As we approached the St. Louis Gateway Arch, I was in awe at how beautiful the city was. Even in the daylight, it was lit up with Christmas lights as people milled about cheerfully. Christmas was so beautiful in the city, and excitement poured through me as we neared our destination. We pulled into a parking garage a few blocks away and started our trek across the city. As we paraded the streets, it felt like everyone was staring at us, or more so, the brotherhood. We were a spectacle, that was for certain, as we passed packed restaurants and bars filled with shoppers. Tex was flirting shamelessly with any woman that walked by, shooting compliments left and right. My cheeks hurt more from laughing than from the cold, as we made our journey through the winter weather.

Without warning, a strange feeling overcame me. That same feeling that I had when I saw Jerry at Trish's Café. To my left, I saw a burst of sunlight catch on a sign just up ahead, and I immediately grabbed Graham's arm, electricity pulsing through me. Just ahead, several yards away, was that same beautiful copper sign I saw in my vision hanging on a pole. And there, beyond a short, wrought iron fence was a magnificent gray building lined with large windows. Groups of kids were playing outside in the snow, laughter filtering across the street.

"There it is, boys," Andrews whispered solemnly.

They all stood there, watching in awe before I brushed past them.

"What are you waiting for? Let's go!" I called back, walking more determined than ever before.

Jack was in there. I could feel it in my bones. I heard boots scuffle as they began to follow me, staying close behind. Silence consumed them as we walked up toward the gate. The kids playing in the yard looked refreshingly happy and healthy. A snowball fight was in full swing to our right, and another huddle of kids was sculpting igloos and snowmen to our left. A stern-looking woman with glasses met us at the entrance, her unimpressed gaze falling on me.

"Can I help you?" she droned as if our presence was a bitter inconvenience. Oh, God, I had no idea what to say. I was so eager to get to Jack I hadn't thought of the logistics of actually getting past the gate.

"Um, yes... We're here to speak with a boy that might be in your care. His name is Jack?" I made that last part a question. Well, that was so perfectly un-confident I half expected for her to shout at us to leave. Right after she would yell she'll get me and my little dog too. She assessed me, her eyes reaching up toward the cut on my brow, down to my clothes, her mouth pulling into a blatant grimace. An uncomfortable cough sounded behind me, her gaze snapping to the group at my back. I was afraid her eyes might pop out of her head. It was like we offended her for even breathing.

"What are your names?" she demanded, her voice drenched in disappointment.

"I'm Georgia Scott, and this is Graham, Mia, Bennett, Cooper, Davis, Tex, Reed, and Andrews." I turned and pointed each one out awkwardly as they stared back silently.

Tex lifted his hand in a casual wave. "Howdy, ma'am," he greeted with that sweet Texas drawl.

125

I almost slammed my palm into my forehead as her snakelike gaze flicked over toward him. God, not now, Tex. A surprising flicker of a smile crossed her face. It instantly disappeared as she turned back toward me. She gave me one last detesting once-over before nodding curtly.

"Meet me around the back," she instructed with a clipped tone. Then, she turned on her heel and headed in toward the building.

I slowly turned back to the group, a faint feeling overcoming me. Something about that woman made me question the very reason I lived.

"I think I just blacked out. What just happened?" I muttered. Graham laughed as he threw an arm around my shoulder, pulling me toward him.

"I think we just found Jack," he answered proudly as we ventured our way around to the back, my heart slamming against my chest.

"Oh," I breathed. That same ridiculous smile crept across my face as we crunched across the walkway.

We just found Jack.

12

OURS

The door in the back looked large and intimidating, laced with intricate gothic carving. It almost looked like a fortress door, impenetrable for both the outside world and the kids that lived inside. No one went in and no one came out. A loud buzz sounded, and I jumped. Large hands wrapped around my arms to steady me. I quickly twisted my head upward to find Graham at my back, his gaze hard as he slowly unfurled his fingers from my shoulders.

"Yeah, imagine living here," Andrews chuckled as Graham pulled the heavy door open.

We filed in one by one to find the same stern woman waiting impatiently inside. She peered down her thin nose at us with a disgruntled frown.

"My name is Ms. Raven."

She emphasized the "Ms.," and I couldn't tell if I imagined her eyeing Tex as she said it.

"Please, take a seat in our waiting area," she hissed and waved her hand toward the far corner.

She glared at us as we ambled our way over to the small lobby with a few comfy chairs. Besides Ms. Raven's oppressive presence, it was much lovelier inside than I had imagined. The hallways were decked with pictures of happy kids, artwork, and motivational quotes. A fresh lemony scent filled the room like it had just been cleaned, and light music drifted from around the corner down the hallway.

"Casey will be with you in a moment," Ms. Raven said, almost in a warning. She then turned and plopped into a puffy chair behind a desk, continuing her angry glare as we huddled together.

"That woman makes my insides squirm," Mia said, shivering as she stared down at the floor.

"Yeah, I don't remember her from when we were here, but I'm not sure if that's because I blocked her out of my memories," Andrews agreed.

"I feel like she wants to eat you for breakfast, Tex," Reed chuckled under his breath. I peered back over at her again, her gaze locked on Tex with an unnerving intensity.

"Good morning!" a cheerful voice squealed behind me, nearly sending me into cardiac arrest.

We all whirled around to find a short woman, no taller than four and a half feet, beaming back at us. She had long curly brown hair that fell to her chest, and she was wearing a plain black-and-white suit that seemed a little too big for her petite body.

"Graham and Georgia?" she asked, her smile widening as she bounced her gaze between me and Graham.

We rose to our feet, and heat rushed through me as I felt his hand at my back, nudging me forward. Her otherwise pleasant face frowned slightly as she grazed over the cut on my eye. Her eyes flashed, and her smile returned, bigger than ever.

"It's a pleasure to meet you. My name is Casey Spaulding, and it's great to put some faces with some names. Jack had a lot to say about you two," she praised, her curls bouncing as she talked.

I heard a small gasp behind us, as Casey peered over our shoulders at the crew we brought. The corner of her mouth quirked up into a slight smirk before she returned her watchful eyes to us.

"Looks like you brought a small army with you," she said, a laugh flickering behind her eyes.

"We're actually from the Marine Corps, ma'am," Tex announced proudly.

"I know." She grinned.

"Gentlemen...and lady." Casey nodded toward Mia. "I'm going to steal these two, and we'll likely be busy for a while. Might I suggest an afternoon out on the town? There's shops, restaurants, all kinds of things to do around here."

They all nodded at her, and I raised my eyebrows at her comment. *Busy for a while? What does she mean? What are we going to do?*

129

"Now, will you both please follow me?" she requested with a glint in her eye, turning toward the hallway to the right.

We both shot each other sideways glances, before Graham gently pushed me forward again. I waved at Mia before she disappeared as we rounded the corner. Casey turned her head to peek back at us.

"Don't worry about Ms. Raven. She loves those kids like her own. She's just very skeptical of anyone that passes through our doors, and I hate to say for good reason," she called over her shoulder.

"That's okay, she wasn't intimidating at all." I grimaced over at Graham as he held back a snicker.

We continued down the hall, following her in silence. We winded through various hallways, passing several rooms filled with books and games. I caught Graham smiling as he peeked in a few of them as we passed.

"This place really has changed," he whispered as we continued through the maze of corridors.

Finally, we were ushered into a quiet conference room with a long executive table. She closed the door and gestured for us to take a seat. She sat across from us and leaned back in her chair. My body tensed as I sat down, trying to prepare myself for the long list of questions I was sure she would ask. A subtle electrical charge seemed to dance in the room as we stared at each other. A slight ringing in my ears began to sound, and then without warning, it stopped as Casey's lips curved into a smile.

"I wasn't expecting you two quite so soon. I remember after my Reckoning it took me at least a month to find my partner," she praised.

I heard a laugh echo in the quiet room, before I realized it was my own. I shrugged at both of them and cleared my throat, avoiding their stares.

Of course. Casey was a *Paver*.

"Can I ask what happened to your eye?" she asked, unflinching as her eagle eyes grazed across my face.

Okay, here we go. Graham shifted uncomfortably in his chair and leaned forward as if he were about to explain.

"Graham was trying to protect me, but I got hurt in the scuffle," I interjected in my most confident voice. She raised her eyebrows at me, shooting her gaze between us, her knowing smile disappearing.

"So, you *hit* her?" she trailed off her eyes narrowing at Graham. I could feel his shoulders sag next to me before she reached her hand across the table.

"I believe we haven't shaken hands yet. How rude of me." She shrugged, a polite chuckle escaping as she reached her hand farther toward Graham.

He eyed her warily, before he grasped her tiny hand in his own. Her hazel eyes began to glow like raked-over coals as they shook. Graham moved to pull his hand away, but she clung to him, her mouth going slack as she stared off into the distance. His eyes remained his usual soft gray as he glanced over at me with a worried expression.

"Casey...?" he asked nervously, before she snatched her hand away and swayed as she tried to steady herself.

After a beat, she peered back up at him, her face pale as pockets of sweat beaded above her brow.

"You've seen a fair share of death in your life?" she croaked, her voice shaky. "You've even...killed before?"

Graham's muscles tensed in his neck as he frowned at her. His jaw tightened, avoiding my stare before he finally dipped his head in confirmation. I stifled a gasp as I considered what she might have seen. I certainly didn't see him *killing* anyone when I touched him.

Graham was after all a Marine. He had a dangerous, lethal side to him, like most warriors. But that didn't stop the hard truth from tearing its way deep inside me. Graham had *killed* someone.

Casey shuddered, before she flicked her gaze over at me with quiet curiosity.

"And you, my dear. Let me shake your hand."

I stared at her, not sure if that was a good idea. She looked like she was still recovering from whatever she saw when she touched Graham. I winced as I heard her clear her throat impatiently.

"Are you sure? I mean..."

"Give me your hand."

Her demanding voice was much less polite this time. It felt disconcerting coming from such a doll-like woman. I surrendered my hand to her grasp, which she claimed right away. As she clawed her fingers around mine, incredible clarity overcame me before the room faded away into total blackness.

In the depths of the darkness, images of broken hearts and broken children crowded my mind. Tears, anguish, trauma, abandonment. Broken bones, broken promises, starving hearts and stomachs. Every possible horror a human being can experience pulsed through me before unyielding sunlight drove the pain away. Incredible love, joy, and peace filled me as blinding, healing light coursed through each child. Their suffering was diminished, and light came through them. Children that were neglected and abused, trusted again. They loved again. Grace took hold of them and renewed them, giving them a fighting chance to change their fate. Without warning, I was sucked back into the conference room where Graham and Casey both stared back at me. A wide smile was plastered on Casey's face as she rested her chin on her palm, her eyes sparkling with curiosity.

"You saw something, didn't you? What did you see?" she asked as she rapped her long fingernails on the table.

I gripped the arms of my chair as I tried to process everything. Wait, wasn't she supposed to be the one to see something? A tear fell down my cheek, and I reached up to wipe it away, confused. I didn't even remember when I started crying.

"I saw...children. They were hurting...so...terribly," I whispered. "But then they were healed, and they could love and trust again."

I laughed through a sob, as my heart remembered the love that filled them. The glorious, unconditional love that washed away all of their pain. Her eyes flashed with intrigue as she leaned even farther forward.

"Interesting. I'm curious to see what kind of gift you're developing." She grinned, a very sisterly grin. The kind of smile that Mia would shoot me, after I tell her I'm crushing bad on Graham Keaton.

"Lately, I've been seeing beautiful things when I touch people's hands. Almost like I can see the goodness in their hearts. I don't know what it is. First, I saw art and creative vibes from this girl in a coffee shop. And with Graham..." I held back a smile as I remembered the love I felt when I touched him. "I saw...safety and protection. Bravery. He was always running towards the danger..." I explained as I felt Graham's heated gaze burn into me.

"I never saw death though..." I furrowed my brow at her quizzically.

"You only feel things when you touch someone's hands, right? Not their shoulder or face?" She squinted over at me. I thought about that for a second. I had hugged my parents and Mia, but I never saw anything then.

"I think so," I said with a slight nod.

"Interesting. Usually when your Aftereffect makes itself known with the touch of a hand, it has to do with their deeds, or their profession. I imagine because you saw specific images like artwork and running towards danger, you're seeing professional ambitions."

"Ambitions?"

"Yeah, you know. Like...the professional path that was intended for them. With me, you saw children healing, right?"

"Wait...can you...take people's pain away? You can heal them?" I asked timidly.

Casey laughed, throwing her head back as her curls bounced with her jerky movements.

"Oh, Georgia, if only that were my gift. That would save me and these kids a lot of trouble." She wiped a happy tear away. "I imagine you saw children healing because that's what I do professionally. I'm a social worker, so a lot of my work revolves around walking them through the things they've experienced." Her face darkened, an unnatural expression for the childlike creature she appeared to be.

"No, my Aftereffect is a little more sinister. I...see the worst in people, the darkest recesses of their minds. All the terrible things they've done, all the people they've hurt. I see their deepest, darkest secrets, the things that most people hide."

All I could manage to do was stare at her, scanning her small, fragile body. All the terror and pain I saw in just those few seconds was unbearable, unfathomable. It felt like I was being ripped in half, and all I could manage to do was hold my scream in. There was no possible way that this harmless pixie of a woman could handle all that agony. She worked in a home for neglected and abused children; how was she even standing upright? Then, I remembered she had held my hand, because she was likely searching for the darkest parts of me. The darkest parts of Graham.

"What...did you see with me?" I asked as I peered up at her.

She smirked as she leaned back in her chair.

"I definitely see darkness from the both of you, but nothing that worries me. Everyone has their fair share of evil inside them. It doesn't surprise me, though. Most Pavers I've met certainly have their demons, but they're usually good eggs, all things considered." She shot me a giddy wink, like we were talking about our favorite types of chocolate. God, how I wished that was what we were talking about.

"I was pleased to see your account of what happened to your eye was true. You saw someone hurting her, but there wasn't really anyone there...yet." She twisted her mouth as she eyed Graham like she was trying to solve a puzzle. "I suspect you might be developing the gift of foresight, Graham. My Reckoning partner, Jim, has that gift which comes quite in handy in his career as an EMT." Her gaze flickered over toward me, a slight smile tugging at the corners of her mouth.

"Although my gift of seeing people's worst is not for the faint of heart, I find it useful when I'm helping children heal from their past traumas. Most importantly, I find it helpful when I'm making decisions about adoptive and foster parents," she said as she pulled a thick file on the edge of the table toward her.

"Can you tell me how you both feel about becoming parents?" she asked, her sharp eagle eyes zeroing in on our faces.

"Excuse me?" I asked in an unfamiliar high-pitched voice.

She gaped back at me as she flipped the file open and turned it toward us. Jack's thin face stared back, a haunted half-smile twisting his expression into a peculiar glower. A shirt three sizes too big was swallowing him whole, and his hands were clenched into fists. Despite his brave face, his dark eyes looked terrified.

"This is the boy you saw in your Reckoning, correct? Jack Berkley?"

Both Graham and I leaned in closer to study his picture before I looked up and nodded. He was even smaller than I remembered. During the Reckoning, he was so full of life and sassy as all hell, but this picture read a different story.

"I asked how you feel about becoming parents," she repeated, shifting her birdlike gaze between us. I could feel Graham's body freeze, his expression almost tortured. I followed his gaze back down toward Jack's picture, and my stomach dropped as I realized where she was going with this.

"Are you asking this because of... Jack?" I whispered.

She nodded, a hint of amusement glimmering behind her eyes.

"Where are his parents?" I asked, my voice in a panicked soprano.

Casey's face grew startlingly angry, as pink rose across her flustered cheeks.

"To put it plainly, his mother is deceased, and his father is out for a warrant for his arrest. Max Berkley, his father, got mixed up in a drug deal gone wrong and gave his son to the dealer to pay off his debt." She frowned as she brushed her fingers through her hair, as if she didn't want to continue.

"The dealer shot Jack and threw him in a dumpster behind his apartment building," she said, her eyes glistening as she finished the last sentence. I sucked in a sharp breath as I grabbed Graham's forearm. He seemed to snap out of his trance as his steely eyes flicked up at Casey.

"He was *shot*?" he growled, his shoulders tensing.

I shuddered as I considered what kind of person would just kill a child? It was one thing to break into my home and try to rape me, but to shoot a *child*?

"Yes, I'm afraid so," Casey sniffed. "The dealer has a warrant for his arrest as well. At this point, the police are still searching for him."

My stomach dropped as I pictured Jack all alone, dying after he was betrayed by his own father. And then buried under trash and decay like he was nothing.

He was just a little kid.

"Let me make this very clear, you two. I understand neither of you asked to become Pavers, or parents for that matter. Pavers are granted the same basic rights as any human, of free will. Anything that is asked of us, anything that God demands from us, is merely a suggestion, not a requirement. You could easily say no right now and walk away. But please remember, Jack never asked for any of this either."

I choked out a sob as I caught sight of Jack's thin face on the table.

"But Graham and I...we don't live together. We've only known each other for like a day. I mean, we're not married..." I trailed off, blushing over the thought alone.

How did Casey expect this to work—was any of this even legal? Her lips thinned as she stared point-blank at me, as if she were staring into my soul.

"If you both decide to do so, we can license you to foster him with joint custody. You don't have to be married to foster or adopt." She darted her eyes between us, a deep crease forming between her brows.

She reached over and tapped Jack's picture with urgency.

"Let me paint this picture for you. If you both leave without Jack, you will be hindering the incredible beauty that comes with fulfilling your destiny. Not just yours, but Jack's as well. All three of you have a divine purpose to share your light, your gifts with the world as a team. Do you know how rare it is to have *three* Reckoning partners? That is unheard of in the Paving community. You should hear the talk..." She shifted in her seat almost like Dr. Cobbs had done, searching the room as if there were something...*someone* listening.

"There is something working here today that is so much bigger than each of you. Bigger than your doubts and your fears. You each survived death and are tied to each other whether you want to be or not. Don't you owe it to yourselves to see where this takes you ?"

Graham ran his hands through his hair, and flashbacks from the hospital lobby filled my mind. This was what he looked like when he was terrified.

"Can we...speak to him? I mean, how does *he* feel about all of this?" Graham's voice was shaky and uncertain. Casey's smile returned almost immediately as she peered up at him.

"Jack has expressed his interest in moving forward with you both," she said, her eyes filling with determination. "I know this is a lot to take on. I'm sure you both had expectations and dreams about your future." She glanced over at me particularly and then down at my naked left hand.

"Being a Paver alone comes with a tremendous amount of responsibility. To add parenting on top of that is something that many Pavers would find very difficult. It's a dangerous field with twists and turns, especially considering you have someone that might still be...stalking you." She softened her gaze as she stared down at me. Oh, God, of course she knew I had been attacked.

"Don't think I ask this of you lightly. I've done extensive research on the both of you, to ensure I'm recruiting quality foster parents here. I'm happy to say, I'm quite pleased with what I'm seeing, but as I mentioned it all lies with you two."

She knew the weight of what she was asking from us, the sacrifice that came with saying yes. Graham stood up and walked over toward a window looking out into a nearby courtyard. He watched in silence as those hard, dangerous lines took over.

"Jack has been through a deeper hell than I've ever been through. He will need our whole world, our dedication, our *everything*." He turned toward me, his gray gaze trapping me in place. "Are you really ready to be a mom?" Tenderness filled his tone, and my heart tugged forcefully as I considered his question.

"No." I laughed nervously, trying not to tremble. To be honest, I was scared shitless, and my brain almost started going into overload with the reality of our situation. I started to check off everything that he would need from us. Clothes, a stable home environment, food, love, and protection. I mean, damn, if I were pregnant, I would at least have a good nine months to prepare. I would have that time to get to know Graham better, and to trust that we could co-parent like champs. This was just a lot. I stood up, sending my chair tumbling backward, and I started to pace back and forth as Casey looked on.

"I mean...where will he sleep? My apartment was taped off because..." I peered up at Casey, avoiding Graham's pained expression. I continued my pacing, ticking off everything else.

"He'll need clothes, food...*safety*. Casey's right—he's out there still...watching."

Waiting.

"Georgia, Graham. You will be happy to know that every child fostered through our home receives an allowance for their food and clothes until they're eighteen. As far as his sleeping arrangement I imagine the Paving community will take care of that. God always provides what we need when we need it."

"Casey, have you heard a word I s—"

"I said God always provides."

Casey's eyes flickered with a dangerous fire that made me shut my mouth immediately. Her word was final, and I wasn't going to test it. I didn't care that she was only four and a half feet tall. I imagined her charging me at full force and wrapping her tiny hands around my neck if I said anything more.

I put the chair I overturned back in its upright position before I slumped down into it to mull things over. Yes, my attacker was still out there, but I had Scar out there looking for him. I had a woman who could read minds and experience the past just by touching someone. On top of that, Graham made me feel so safe and protected. He would surely watch out for Jack just as a father should. Just like his father should have been doing all along.

Casey seemed so confident, despite everything she knew about us, that we would be able to protect each other. She seemed to know without a doubt that we were the best choice for Jack. I also deliberated over the dreams that I had about my future. I mean, sure, I wanted that traditional romance. It was exactly why I'd stormed off and bought that stupid commitment ring in the first place. To remind myself that I was worthy of a much greater love. Of course, I always dreamed of settling down, getting married, and eventually starting a family. But Jack needed someone *now*. He needed us, and I was starting to believe that we needed him too.

I turned toward Graham, his soft gray eyes meeting mine. His face was hard with pain, and his shoulders were tense, but he seemed to breathe out any worry he had when he saw my expression.

"Graham, I think...she's right," I laughed as I shook my head in surrender. "Maybe we can do this."

I stared up at him, instantly feeling like a raging lunatic. I gripped the sides of my chair, preparing myself for a slew of "You're crazies" and "No ways." Instead, Graham walked over and squeezed my hand, a lingering sense of warm summer rain washing over me. Front porch sunrises and hazy evening sunsets flooded away all the worries I had.

"You know, when I was a kid, I used to sit next to that fence over there and watch as young happy couples walked by. I'd always wondered why none of them didn't just come in and take me away to be my family. Instead, they'd just walk on by and avoid eye contact, like we were plagued with an infectious disease. I used to make up stories for each couple as they passed. I would sit and daydream about it for hours, and imagine that they were actors or famous musicians that would travel the world with me. After a while, I started wishing for *anybody* to come and take me. You know, anyone that could just let me have a normal childhood. If they could afford groceries, keep the house clean, not hit me, let me have my own bed,"

Graham said, his voice breaking as he picked up Jack's picture from the file. "I needed somebody, just like he needs somebody. If you think we can do this, then I think so too. Let's make him ours."

Ours. An uninhibited sense of relief settled over me. I relished in the finality I felt as the weight of the decision crashed over me. I wondered if this was what God had intended for me all along. Was *this* my path? Graham? Jack? Excitement fluttered in my belly, and I wasn't sure if I should be concerned over my lack of fear. Was I just blind and plain stupid, or was this what following God's plan felt like?

"I never thought I'd have kids of my own, foster kids or otherwise," Graham whispered as he continued to stare at Jack's face. I watched as he grazed his thumb over his photo, and my heart erupted into a thousand pieces.

"But I always thought I'd be a good dad," he added with a humble shrug.

And somehow, I knew with every bone in my body he would be.

I stood up carefully, making sure not to knock the chair over this time.

"So...are we really doing this?" I asked, my whole body trembling.

He placed his hand gently on my shoulder and pulled me into him, stilling my body against his.

"I believe we are."

13

THE GATEWAY REUNION

We spent the next several hours filling out mountains of paperwork and running through all the formal procedures for foster care licensing. Graham had a sense of humor the entire way through and kept things positive, despite some of the outrageous questions in our paperwork. One of the questions asked what we would do if Jack started rubbing his fecal matter on the wall.

"I've actually seen that happen, right here in this building. Shit happens sometimes, I guess," Graham laughed as he scribbled "Clean it up" in the answer box. Once we finished with the mountain of awkward paperwork and background screenings for the state, Casey stood up, beaming at us.

"Are you ready to meet Jack?" she asked, clasping her hands together excitedly.

Graham and I exchanged looks, and I couldn't stop myself from blushing. Graham and I were about to have a child together—and we hadn't even kissed yet. How could I even begin to tell my parents that they were grandparents...to an eleven-year-old boy that I'd met during our *Reckoning*? How could I explain that I was adopting him with a man I had only met a few days ago? Not to mention, the last time we spoke was after I was released from the hospital. I had to be crazy. Society had traditions and norms for a reason, and nothing about what we were doing was normal. I could just picture my mother's horrified face now as she cried into my dad's shoulder about my lost potential. I shuddered as a gentle hand fell on my arm and squeezed it reassuringly. Graham's understanding, soft eyes met mine, and I was reminded that this was really happening. I was about to meet Jack. Our...*son.*

"Yes, I'm...ready," I stammered, clenching my hands into sweaty fists. Casey's glow dimmed, as she studied me with her watchful eyes.

"Just remember, there's no such thing as a perfect parent," she encouraged.

"I still can't believe you're trusting us to just walk away with him today. I mean..."

"Georgia, I felt your hearts. I saw your worst, and you both have exactly what it takes to help Jack heal. Plus, you three are Reckoning partners, and that's a divine assignment I'm not ready to get in between." She shivered at the thought. Her eyes grazed over me, and she cocked her head to the side curiously.

"Do you want to...pray?" Casey asked, her eyebrows arched up toward her hairline. I almost laughed but held it back as she continued to stare at me with those knowing wide eyes.

"Um..." I managed to say, as apprehension continued to knot through my chest. The last time I'd prayed with a group out loud was during Sunday school when I was in fourth grade. My parents had always dragged me to church, but I never truly felt connected there. I would try and pray on my own, but over time it felt more like I was talking to myself. When I did pray, it would be short and simple, nothing eloquent or thought out. I had stopped praying after I started dating Braxton, who always made fun of people who went to church. And now, in this moment, praying felt like something other people do during a crisis. Certainly not me.

"Listen, I was never really a religious or spiritual person before I became a Paver either. You don't have to, but can we consider the fact that all three of us are standing here, *alive*? Can we also consider how you just agreed to adopt a boy who you met while your hearts were flatlining?" She shifted on the balls of her feet as she stared up at us both. Okay, the woman had a point.

"I think you'll be quite surprised to find that you've got a room full of listeners every time you pray. In the Paving industry, it's best to keep the lines of communication open with the world around you."

She laughed again as we gawked at her uncomfortably. After a moment of silence, she rolled her eyes and sighed.

"Here, just hold my hands, and I'll do all the talking," she huffed as she stretched her hands out to both of us.

Graham shrugged over at me before they took ahold of each of my hands and we formed a small circle. Beautiful images of healing light and hazy afternoon sunsets filled my mind like before until they faded away into a peaceful, distant glimmer.

"Just breathe, you two, and open your hearts. God can see through all the bullshit, so when we pray, we give him our hearts, not our superficial desires." Casey bowed her head and closed her eyes, and silence filled the room, except for the light sounds of our breathing.

"God, Graham and Georgia have decided to follow through with what we can only guess is your plan for them. We ask for strength, grace, and your unconditional love to flow through them as they embark in this journey of parenthood, and Paverhood. Guide them with your unfailing light and love to help them pursue the things that you ask of them. Show them that you have provided everything that they need and protect them as they navigate the troubling waters ahead." She squeezed our hands tightly as she said the last part. She peeked up and grinned at the both of us.

"Do either of you want to add anything?" she asked quietly, her eyes darting between us. Honestly, I felt kind of dumb just talking to nothing in a room, but Graham cleared his throat and bowed his head like Casey did.

"Hey, God, or...Jesus. Or whoever you are... I've never prayed in my whole life. You probably know that by now if you're listening."

I bit my lip as I watched him. Even though I wasn't sure if I believed in God, even now with everything we'd experienced, Graham was praying. A man who had been through it all, had grown up in a group home, had lost his parents, fought on bloody battlefields, had just died...was *praying*.

"I figured I might as well tell you that I've always been confused and hurt by the cards you dealt me. I never felt like you were looking out for me, and you were just a presence that only cared about the rich and the churchgoers." He let out an uneasy chuckle as he squeezed my hand and shook his head.

The man was downright sexy when he spoke from his heart. Most men are so scared to be vulnerable and open up about their emotions, but

Graham Keaton stood here fearlessly, praying to a God who had seemingly forsaken him.

"I suppose I've been forced to reconsider that with the events from the last few days. For some unknown reason, you put me in the same path as Georgia." He peeked over at Casey, who was still bowing her head with her eyes closed. His soft gray eyes trailed over to me, before he quickly looked back down at the floor, color creeping up his neck again. I felt my lips quirk up into a smile before I finally bowed my head and closed my eyes with him. *Okay, Graham Keaton, keep talking because if God isn't listening, I sure am.*

"I never thought I'd be a father, and Georgia probably wasn't planning on being a mom anytime soon. But Jack is alone, and we want to be there for him. Casey says to speak with our hearts, so if you're up there and you can hear us now, please just help us. Help us to be the parents we are called to be, to help us understand what it means to be a Paver. Help me to understand what it means to be in a healthy, loving relationship with someone."

I could feel Graham's eyes on me again, but I kept mine shut tight as my heart fluttered with his words. We hadn't established any kind of relationship yet, aside from the fact that we were going to be Jack's parents together. But I knew he wasn't just talking about Jack. He was talking about me too.

A moment of silence passed before Graham and Casey let go of my hands. I met Graham's endearing gaze, which was beginning to feel more like home than anything, before Casey cleared her throat excitedly.

"All right, let's go get your boy," she sang as she opened the door and led us into the hallway.

I peered out the tall windows and frowned as thick clouds hovered in the distance. A flurry started to blow about again, almost in warning. It was getting dark outside too, and I was starting to think it would be better to get a hotel for the night instead of drive back through the snow. I wondered what Mia and the boys had been doing this whole time. Hopefully they'd escaped Ms. Raven's glare and were at least enjoying the city.

We followed her down the maze of hallways again, until we neared a corridor lined with bedrooms. Casey stopped in front of a closed door at the end of the hallway and rapped her knuckles against it.

"Jack? You have some visitors," she called through the crack.

A quick rustle of movement sounded behind the door, and I reached for Graham as the noise approached on the other side. The doorknob turned and the door flew open with a force that didn't feel appropriate for the small boy who stood staring back at us. His wide, sunken-in eyes peered up at me, and he slowly trailed across my face, stopping on the cut above my eye.

"What the fuck is that?" he seethed.

I glanced over at Graham, completely startled. Jack tore his gaze from me over to Graham, his face twisting into a heated scowl. He stepped forward, eyeing Graham angrily as he balled his hands into tiny fists.

"This motherfucker beating on you?" he spat as he continued to glare at him. My mouth fell open as I watched a malnourished eleven-year-old pick a fight with a fully sculpted ex-Marine. I could feel Casey shift her weight as she watched. The woman looked amused, as if she were entertained at this terrible first encounter.

"Sounds like you've got your cheeky mouth back," Graham retorted.

"Why does she have a bruise on her face?" he yelled, his voice echoing down the hallway.

"Graham was trying to protect me," I intervened, truly regretting not putting a bandage over it before we came.

"From what?" Jack demanded as he stayed trained on Graham, his fists still tightly clenched. Graham let out a sigh and nodded at Jack with defeat.

"I tackled her and—"

Jack lurched toward him like a lightning ball of energy. Tiny fists slammed against his rock-hard chest as he wailed with anger. Graham caught Jack's wrists as he heaved against him. I let out a sob as I watched them, praying Graham wouldn't accidentally hurt him. He seemed so small and fragile. So very breakable.

"I saw a man try and hurt her, Jack," Graham hissed back at him as he squirmed in his grasp. "I had a vision that he was going to do some very bad things to her."

Jack froze for a moment, and with incredible strength pulled his arms away from Graham, his shoulders heaving with quick, angry breaths.

"A vision?" he repeated. His eyes shot back up to my temple, and he shook his head in denial.

"I like that you want to protect her. You're a good man for it," Graham reassured, giving Jack some space. "I wanted to protect her too. I saw him hurting her, so I—"

"You *hit* her?" Jack barked, his dark eyes moving back toward Graham furiously. He quickly shook his head.

"I tackled her, and I almost did hit her."

I started to speak, but Graham held up his hand, willing to let him finish. Jack growled as he shifted his weight from one foot to the other, surely contemplating whether he wanted to dive toward him again.

"I thought I had the guy...but it was just a premonition. It hadn't happened yet, so I...hurt her instead, on accident." Graham watched Jack patiently as his breathing slowed. "The last thing I wanted to do was hurt her, okay?"

"Did you at least catch him?" Jack demanded.

"No. He got away," Graham relented, his tone filled with regret.

Jack glared up at Graham as mocking amusement played behind his eyes.

"You look like Superman, you know that? You might as well have an S on your chest. So heroic that you put a mark on a girl's face...while you were trying to save her." Jack spat on the floor, inches from Graham's feet. "Guess only Superman can catch the bad guys and save the girl." Graham froze at his words but gave him a quiet nod, and the silent one-sided standoff had finally ceased. Jack turned to look at me, his small body shrinking before me.

"I'm sorry I yelled. I...don't like it when I see bruises on girls' faces." Jack squinted up at me with a frown.

His face seemed so much older than I remembered. In the hospital lobby, he was energetic, almost carefree. He was just being a kid. Here, he was a kid who had experienced the pain of a thousand men that most adults never even experience in a lifetime.

"Jack, I'm okay. I truly think Graham saved me, still. I might not have been here if he hadn't have come when he did," I said gently.

Jack furrowed his brows at me, and I could tell he wanted to say something, but he pressed his lips together and dropped his gaze toward the floor. I took a step closer, and he startled, jumping back.

"I'm sorry...I just want to make sure you're okay," I assured.

His body stiffened as I scanned him for any injury, fully aware of the horrors that Casey said he'd faced. Besides his overly thin body, he looked like he had recovered from being shot. His dark black hair was ungroomed but clean. His clothes were unmatched and baggy, and his olive complexion was injury and scar-free. Casey cleared her throat and stepped forward, pulling our attention toward her.

"Jack, Georgia and Graham have been approved to adopt you as you've requested. You will be going home with them today," she gushed with a grin.

Panic started to set in as I watched his small face. I didn't think she'd just...tell him like that. I thought she'd at least talk to him privately, give him some space to think. Oh, God, what if he changed his mind? Our first interaction was not ideal in the slightest, and this was such a big decision for him. I wondered how much Casey and Jack had actually talked about this, and how much he knew about the whole process. I glanced over at her, and everything about her watchful gaze ensured me that she wasn't the type to leave things to chance. She was prepared, and she cared for these kids. No way would she leave Jack out in the dark.

Jack glared at Graham, sizing him up like everything was riding on this very moment.

"I'm not calling you Dad, *Superman*." The disdainful way he said the word sent ice through my veins, but Graham remained unfazed. To my surprise, I saw a flash of a smile creep across his face before it fell away completely.

"I imagine you and I will get along just fine," Graham confirmed casually.

"Okay, guys. Looks like I've got myself a happy family to send off," Casey sang, shooting me a wink.

Casey was certainly an interesting kind of person. I suppose you had to be a little off your rocker if you saw and felt the things she did. Especially if she worked in a place where they handled situations like Jack's.

"Jack, will you please pack all your belongings? I need to speak with Graham and Georgia for a moment." Casey waved Jack along, but he stood rooted to the spot, frowning up at us, unconvinced.

He stared in silence with weary, burdened eyes that were far too old for his age. I couldn't tell if he wanted to say something else, or if he was rethinking whether he wanted us as a family. After a few awkward beats, he turned back to his room and closed the door behind him. I blinked at the door a couple of times, trying to reel myself back to reality. My God, how could I—how could *we*—ever be enough for him? He had been hurt so badly before—how could I even begin to help him heal? How could he ever trust another adult again?

"Jack has just a few belongings, all of which were donations from the St. Louis Children's Division. Usually, adoptive parents have to fill out forms to get reimbursed for their purchases, but..." Casey reached into her pocket and handed me a folded envelope. "I have this emergency fund from the state now that can help cover some of his initial needs. You will still need to cover the rest until we can secure your official address."

I opened the envelope cautiously to find a stack of bills that would suit Jack for months.

"Well?" she asked, ushering for me to pocket the envelope.

"Casey...I don't feel comfortable..." I said as I stared down at the money.

"I'm afraid the correct response is 'thank you,'" she chided.

"Casey—"

"Take the damn money," Casey commanded, unwavering.

After another awkward moment of silence, I finally nodded and pushed the envelope into my back pocket. She smiled victoriously at me before the door flew open again. At first it looked like his hands were empty, but then I noticed a small trash bag clutched in his hand. Graham's face darkened as he stared at the bag, his jaw clenching.

"What's that?" I demanded, eyeing the bag skeptically.

"That's his stuff," Casey responded plainly, watching my face fall as I tried not to cry in front of all three of them. He didn't even have a suitcase? Or even a duffel bag?

"I guess not everything has changed," Graham whispered, shaking his head. Jack flicked his dark eyes over to him, and his brow creased as if he were trying to make sense of his comment.

"You been here before?" Jack demanded, his stance firmly planted in Graham's direction. Graham's steely regard returned as he nodded down at him.

"I grew up here," he said with a nod, a subtle smile curving at his mouth. Jack's black eyes widened as he studied him before I interrupted their staring contest with a sniffle.

"Do you have a coat in there? It's really cold outside," I said, my voice breaking slightly.

He furrowed his brow at me, before he dug in his trash bag and threw on a flimsy jacket with a few holes peeking through. Graham practically growled as he tore off his own jacket and handed it to him.

"You're wearing this," Graham said in a terrifyingly calm voice.

Jack laughed a dry, humorless laugh.

"You want to keep me warm, *Superman?*" Jack asked sarcastically.

"Yes, I do," Graham shot back, nodding for him to put the jacket on.

Jack glared at Graham before he finally threw the massive coat on with a defiant sneer. Something about the way Jack's small body swam in Graham's coat made my heart race a little faster. That familiar electrical charge shot through my chest, almost knocking me back as I took my new family in. They were mine. And I was theirs.

Kid, Mom, and Superman.

"It's getting late, and it looks like another snowstorm is coming in. It'll probably be safer if we find a place to stay before it gets too bad," Graham said in a low voice, his gaze trained on Jack's offensive bag of belongings.

Suddenly, Graham's phone dinged. He dug it out, and a gorgeous smile broke free, softening those deep, hard lines.

"The guys and Mia reserved a couple hotel rooms for us at the Best Western. They said they're at the hotel now and our keys are at the desk," he announced as he typed out a text on his phone.

"The guys...and Mia?" Jack repeated, peering up at me.

"Yeah. We brought company. They're our friends. Well, more like our family," I said with an overly enthusiastic smile.

Jack stared at me, just like Casey had. Like he was staring into my soul, and he knew all my deepest darkest secrets. I felt my muscles tense under his unrelenting gaze, which traced my temple again. He winced as he looked at the gash and shook his head angrily, blowing out a quick breath.

"Jack...what do you say we get some food?" I cocked my head at him, trying to change the subject. His eyes glazed over at the mention of food, and I could already tell just by the way he was gripping his bag he was starving.

Casey nodded, satisfied, before she led us through the maze of hallways.

We each hugged Casey—even Jack, who despite his small frame seemed to tower over her.

"Be good, Jack," she warned with a smile before she nodded over toward Graham and me with those watchful eagle eyes. "Take care, you two," she called as she shut the large fortress door behind us.

And then, just like that, we were alone.

———

The city sky was still and quiet as the snow continued to flurry around us. The streetlights were shining bright through the dark. I glanced nervously over at Jack, his pale face just barely visible. He clearly didn't have any decent belongings, and I wondered if we had enough time to get him some clothes. A loud horrible rumble filled the air, and I looked down at Jack, realizing it was his poor stomach.

"Jack, my God, you must be starving!" I exclaimed with widened eyes.

"No," he lied, clenching his trash bag in his fist with white knuckles.

"Um, you realize you just woke up the entire city of St. Louis with your stomach, right?" Graham retorted, raising his eyebrows at him. A hint of a smile crossed Jack's face before it disappeared.

"Okay, we're going to get you some food. There's a restaurant just down the street," I said as I pointed toward a lively looking bar-and-grill sign. Graham reached out toward Jack, offering to take his bag, but Jack clutched it to his chest, avoiding any eye contact with either of us. Fair enough, kid. That was all he had in the world, and he wasn't ready to trust us right now.

"This way," I said as I took the lead, passing in between them toward the restaurant. I could hear their footfalls crunch behind me as Jack's stomach growled again.

Inside the bar, we were seated toward the back, away from most of the noise and music. We perused the menu, which had all the basics from your typical bar food to some of St. Louis's famous delicacies.

"So, Jack. What kind of food do you like?" I asked, as he continued to cling to his belongings.

He shrugged and stared back at us with calculating eyes. The way he looked around the grill like a lost puppy made me feel like he had never been inside a restaurant before. *Tonight, that all changes. I'm going to put some meat on those bones, and my first mom move is getting him the best damn food St. Louis*

149

has to offer. We ordered a round of toasted ravioli, pizza topped with Provel cheese, and gooey butter cake for dessert. Jack ate in silence, taking huge bites and watching us both carefully, like he was trying to figure us out. I frowned as I saw him sneak a few pizza slices in his pockets, but I didn't say anything. He was worried he wouldn't eat again, hiding them away like a security blanket. In case another adult failed him.

Graham and I tried to ask a few basic questions about himself, but he just shrugged and gave us blank, uninterested stares. Neither of us took the conversation to the Reckoning. Tonight wasn't going to be tainted with the strange paranormal circumstances we'd met in. Tonight, it was about figuring out how to be a family.

After we all ate to our hearts' content, the streets had livened up with the nightlife crowd, despite the snow. It was getting late, and we really needed to get back to the hotel. Jack already looked so tired, and I felt like I was about to pass out from my own exhaustion. We walked in silence toward the parking garage with Jack squeezed in between us. An eerie feeling came over me as that same electrical charge pulsed through me, almost like a warning. In the distance, we saw two men approach us. Graham drew us behind him as they neared. One of them whispered something apparently hilarious as loud laughter echoed against the street. I fought the urge to squirm into Graham as one of them slowly dropped his gaze to my chest with a hungry look on his face. The stench of cigarettes, alcohol, and an excess of cologne nearly barreled me over as they brushed past us. Relief filled me as they rounded the corner and disappeared. Their maniacal laughter continued to bounce against the walls until it eventually faded away. Graham and Jack both scowled in their direction before they pushed forward, pulling me with them.

Once we got to the parking garage, it appeared to be desolate and not as well lit as I'd have liked it to be. Another shiver ran up my spine, but I feared that it wasn't because of the gripping cold from the snow. I had that familiar sensation that someone was watching. Perhaps Jerry was here to help us figure out what was next? Last time I saw Jerry, I found Graham...or more like Graham found me. But...we also almost ran into someone hiding in the dark...someone who didn't want to be seen. My eyes skated around the empty structure, but I couldn't make out a single soul. Graham seemed to sense my uneasiness and quickened his pace, hauling us with him toward the truck. Without warning, he halted, his broad shoulders tense, as he stood motionless. The truck was only a few paces away, but Graham remained rooted to the spot.

"Graham?" I whispered as I placed my hand on his rock-hard shoulder.

It rippled with my touch, and I gasped as I caught sight of his face. It was pained and terrified as if he were seeing something horrible play out in front of him. His eyes were glowing with that familiar honey-gold shade as before. He was having a vision.

"What the hell?" Jack demanded, pulling at Graham's shirt. He remained in what looked like a trance, his eyes blazing against the cold.

"Come on, Graham. Let's get in the truck," I urged, pushing him forward.

Immediately, he shook from his trance, his eyes returning to a steely gray as he scanned the garage.

"Let's go!" Graham commanded as he ushered us toward the truck. At this point, I was practically herding Jack, my hand clenched on the shoulder of his coat. Suddenly, a large hand wrapped around my wrist. I let out a whimper as the hand yanked me back against a tall, tense body. The hard sting of a sharp metal blade pressed into my neck, as warm bitter-smelling breath assaulted my senses.

"Dad!" Jack yelled in horror as Graham pulled him behind him forcefully. His face twisted into a ferocious, animalistic sneer as he held Jack away. I felt a man's hands knot in my hair and pull my neck taut against his blade.

"Dad, let her go!" Jack yelled from behind Graham as he held him in place.

Graham moved into action, backing Jack toward the truck as murderous rage flashed across his eyes.

"Give me my son, and you can have your bitch back," the man yelled over at Graham.

I watched as Graham pulled the truck door open and hoisted Jack inside effortlessly despite his desperate protests. Muffled high-pitched screams filtered through the door as he shut it after turning on the child locks.

"How about you let her go, and you get to fucking *live*?" Graham growled, malice drenched in every terrifying syllable as he slinked his way back toward us.

151

The man sliced his blade even farther into my throat before I felt a warm liquid trickle down my neck. I reached up and clawed at his arm, desperately trying to relieve the pressure from his knife.

"We just want to help Jack. We want him safe. He's just a little boy," I pleaded, my voice trembling. "Please, I only want to keep him safe." My stomach lurched as I caught Jack's horrified face in the truck window as tears streamed down his face.

He tightened his grip, the cold, serrated edge pushing into my neck again. His hot breath weighed against my throat as he whispered into my ear.

"He doesn't need a mother, bitch. He's made it this far without one, and you'd just teach him how to be weak and defenseless. Just like you." He pulled at my arm, and I was sure if he pulled any farther, he'd break it.

Graham's eyes snapped to my neck and then trailed back up to my assailant's eyes with a lethal-looking grin.

"You must be so fucking proud of yourself. *Father of the year.* Teaching your son how to be big and strong. How brave of you that you gave him to a scavenging bastard to settle your dirty debt," Graham seethed, taking a step closer.

The blade cut deeper into my neck, and I let out a cry that only infuriated him more. Graham had struck a nerve, and now he was going to pay.

"What the fuck do you know? You've got that pretty truck over there, nice fancy clothes."

The pain from his grip let up, but I felt the dinner I'd just eaten threaten to come up as I felt his hand squeeze my breast.

"You've got this piece of ass to come home to," he whispered, his lips pressing against my neck.

I let out a sob as white-hot pain shot across my neck from another slice of his blade. I tore at his grip, my fingers wrapping around his assaulting hand.

And before I could scream, I was plunged into a deep, unrelenting darkness.

14

ACT OF LOVE

Laughter and joyful voices echoed against the walls of a high school gym lined with tables and chairs. Hundreds of people with bleak and weary faces sat along the tables, eating what seemed to be the first hot meal they'd had in weeks. I scanned the vast dining hall, but no one seemed to pay me any attention. I jumped as loud laughter erupted from a group sitting in the corner. I squinted over at a familiar man, and I sucked in a gasp as his face turned toward me. A clean and healthy version of Jack's father stood proudly in the mix. I almost dove behind a table, but it appeared he didn't see me; he just looked right through me. His shirt was salmon colored, and I couldn't help but grin. I never would have pictured the man that was previously pushing a blade into my throat wearing anything in the pink color family.

He looked so different, so inviting and warm. His smile met his eyes, and I loved and hated how it reminded me so much of Jack. The man looked unnervingly like him, with the same olive complexion and black hair. Even his dark eyes resonated in deep black pools like his son. A beautiful dark-haired woman approached the table carrying a basket filled with what looked like hygiene kits and games.

"Max, baby, we've got more in the truck if you want to get those?" She smiled as she set the basket down and rubbed his shoulders.

"Yes, ma'am," he crooned, and there it was. Undeniable love and happiness that seemed so impossible before. He turned and headed out toward the back double doors when dark wisps of fog surrounded me, and the bright hall disappeared until I was engulfed by nothingness.

Without warning, I was sucked back into the dimly lit parking garage, as Max Berkley's knife tore against my flesh again. It felt like a flash of movement around me as Graham grabbed Max's hand and twisted it away from me. He pinned him against the parking garage wall and shoved his forearm into his throat. The knife clattered to the floor, echoing against the pavement as Graham trapped him in place.

"*Don't you ever* fucking touch her or Jack again, do you hear me?" he roared, his voice bouncing off the walls furiously. Berkley sputtered out a sob, his body shaking as Graham kept hold of him.

"Max is your name, right?" I called over Graham's shoulder as I wiped at my neck.

A little too much blood was beginning to flow from the fresh cut. Enough for it to need bandaging, and soon. Max's eyes widened as he took me in, as if he finally realized he'd hurt another human being. Graham slammed him into the wall with terrifying force.

"Answer her," Graham growled, his hands fisting into his grimy shirt.

"Y-yes. My name is Max," he stuttered, realizing Graham's strength.

I coughed, trying to keep my dinner down, as I wiped the blood on my pants and peered into Max's eyes. He was scared now that he wasn't in control anymore. And my heart burst into a million pieces as I recognized that fearful expression. It was the same one that Jack had. The same terrified look as his boy.

I cleared my throat and pulled back my shoulders. This man needed to hear what I saw. If Casey was right and I was seeing God's professional plan for people, then Max had a bright future. He could have a career helping others in the same situation he was in. He could save lives, and maybe he'd have a fighting chance.

"You made a mistake, didn't you?" I quavered. "You've probably made too many to count, and you'll make a thousand more, but that's what we do as humans. We try and we fail. We hurt, we struggle, and sometimes we do unspeakable things. Right now, you have a choice, Max. You see that little boy who's watching all of this unfold before him?"

I turned my head toward Jack, who had his hands pressed against the glass of the window, his lip trembling. I knew he saw his son because he immediately dropped his gaze to the floor and shook with silent sobs.

"God's not done with you, Max. This isn't it for you," I pleaded. This man was broken, but broken things can be mended. Broken things can always be made new.

"I've seen a life for you that is healthy, warm, filled with friendship, service, and love. A life that finds the magic in these cold winter nights, instead of fear and loneliness. You have a chance to walk away and give your baby a chance. You can give him life, and that will always be your legacy. Can you manage this act of love?" I urged.

His face was crusted with grime and smut from probably being on the streets, without the care he needed. He was thin, lost, and broken, all alone crying in a parking garage. And I wondered at what point had he strayed from his path. When did he stop listening to his true destiny?

"I didn't...th...think they'd hurt...him that bad..." he sobbed, his thin body caving into itself despite Graham's grip on him.

"I just thought..."

"What! What did you think?" Graham roared, his fist slamming against the concrete as he yelled, pressing his forearm farther into his throat. Max continued to sob, and I turned to catch a glimpse of Jack. He had his forehead pressed against the glass, tears gushing from those deep black pools and down his cheeks. Jack didn't need this.

I kicked the knife away and did the unthinkable.

I prayed. Out loud.

"God, please, please watch over us. We need so much guidance as we all strive for one thing, what's best for Jack. Please watch over us as we look to meet his needs, and to help him journey through this life, safe from harm. We ask for comfort, as we are all entering into a new chapter in our lives. Ease our transitions and help us pursue what's important. We pray for Jack, Mr. Berkley, and us. We pray for peace and understanding. We pray for growth, second, third, and a thousand chances, forgiveness, healing, trust. We pray that Jack knows that we are more than our actions, and that you give us all the grace of a new day."

Graham pushed away from Berkley in disgust as he crumpled to the floor. He kept his eyes trained on him as he backed up toward me, blocking my view of the broken man at his feet. I reached out and touched the hard place between his shoulder blades again, tension rolling off him.

"Graham, I want to give this to him," I whispered as I pulled out some cash in my back pocket from Casey's emergency money. Graham turned and stared at me for a good long minute, his brows drawing together like he had finally seen what an insane person looks like. His eyes were stone-cold steel, but a hint of light overcame them as he pulled himself out of the hate he felt toward Max. His gaze drifted over to Jack behind us, and based on the way his face fell, I knew Graham saw what I saw. He was hurting, and we were at the root of all the pain. His eyes flicked to me again, before he pulled the cash out of my hand and turned back toward Berkley. He leaned over, placed the money at his feet, and lowered his voice to a deadly whisper.

"I didn't have a dad growing up, but his absence taught me a lot, especially what it means to be there for your child. I can tell you one thing: I'm going to do my best to guide him in the right direction. I will protect him, love him, and have faith in him."

Max remained silent as he shook harder from his sobs. Graham practically growled as he backed away from Max and guided me back toward the truck.

"Let's go," Graham prodded.

Once I opened the door, Jack tried to wrestle his way past me to get to his dad, but I wrapped my arms tightly around him and held him to me. I had seen a beautiful future, or possibility with his father, but right now, he was still the man who'd left Jack for dead. I wasn't prepared to risk anything, especially Jack's life. Broken people will do incredible things because they have nothing left to lose, and he proved that. I climbed in with Jack pressed against me, and I locked the doors as Graham hopped in the driver's seat.

After several minutes of silence, besides Jack's silent cries and sniffles, his body fell limp against me. Jack, my son, had fallen asleep. His body couldn't take any more trauma and shut the world out. I gently pulled him in my lap and brushed his hair back just like my mom did, and he finally looked like he was at peace. This thin, broken child was beautiful in every way. But he wasn't broken—he had a beautiful future too, and Graham and I were going to make that a reality.

At rest, he actually looked his age. His eyes were closed, and his mouth wasn't pulled back into a scowl fit for a grumpy old man. Right now, Jack was just a child, sleeping on his mother's lap. Graham shifted the rearview mirror to me, and we locked eyes. Neither of us spoke, but we said everything in the silence that filled the cab. We were all safe, and we were going to figure it out. We had no other choice.

Graham's brothers and Mia met us both outside in the parking lot. Graham carried Jack into the hotel with Tex, Reed, and Davis while Bennett, Cooper, Andrews, and Mia stayed out in the car with me, tending to my cuts and scratches. I vaguely explained the horrors that we'd experienced, but they kept questions to a minimum, sensing I had met my limit for the night. Mia tried to convince me to call the police, but at that point, we had no idea where Max might have run off to. I had no interest in talking to the police or anyone for that matter. I just wanted to go to bed.

Mia and the boys reserved one room for Jack, Graham, and me together. Mia walked me to my room, linking her elbow with mine. The rest of the boys surrounded us, guarding us as we boarded the elevator.

"Georgia, I know what you guys experienced was terrifying, but I'm so glad you're safe. I just can't get over the fact that...he's real, and you found him. Jack is so beautiful." I seemed to snap from my trance as she said those words. And for the first time that night, I felt calm and at peace.

Yes, Mia. Jack is beautiful, isn't he?

I swiped the hotel key and the door unlocked. I kissed Mia on the cheek and waved at the boys before I walked into the room. The door closed behind me, but I was surprised to find the room completely dark. I let my eyes adjust to the blackness around me before I could make out a bed and Jack's sleeping silhouette. Everything was painted in murky shadows except for the dim lights that cascaded in from an outside street lamp. My heart froze as I caught sight of Graham sitting at the foot of the other bed, his intense gaze locked on me.

"Graham...?" I gasped.

He looked primal, tortured, with his jaw clenched and his shoulders heaving with each breath. Without warning, Graham was in front of me. He reached up toward my face and cupped my chin with a tender grip, scanning my neck in agonizing silence. He let out a slow breath, as if he were trying to calm himself. I melted against him as he pulled me into his chest, his strong arms wrapping around me. His heartbeat was racing as he buried his mouth and nose into my hair.

"I thought...he was going to kill you." His voice was pained as he stroked my hair, continuing to breathe me in.

I returned his embrace and wrapped my arms around his waist. Flashes of the terrifying moments when Max pressed his blade to my throat filled my mind. His breath, the pressure from his knife...it all twisted and turned with the attack in my apartment as memories shifted together. I shuddered, trying not to let all the fear consume me.

"We're safe, Graham," I whispered as I tried to convince myself.

His hands tangled in my hair, and he pulled me away from him to look at me again. His eyes trailed across my face down to my neck, then landed on my lips. A surprising burst of desire filled me as I felt his fingers trail down and press into my back. Before any other sensations could take hold, his hands dropped to his sides, and sudden disappointment raged through me.

"I saw him take Jack," he whispered, his voice so low I had to lean in closer to hear.

"What?" I gasped.

Graham stared at Jack in silence for a moment before lifting his steely gaze toward me.

"In my vision, I saw him take Jack from us, like it was the most effortless thing in the world." He let out a frustrated growl. "I never saw him take you, though. I can't tell what's real and what's not. It's like every time I have a vision, you end up getting hurt." His voice broke as his gaze snapped to my neck again.

"Graham, I saw something too when I touched Max's hand. I saw him helping out at a homeless shelter. He was so happy, and healthy. He was *clean*...and he had a girlfriend...maybe a wife? It was so vivid, so much more...real than any of the other visions I've had. Maybe our Aftereffects are still developing. Maybe they haven't matured yet—we just need to give it some time," I whispered.

A quiet rustle of movement sounded where Jack lay sleeping, and we both twisted around to see if he had woken. Jack had just changed positions, and he was now lying on his side. After a moment, his chest began to rise and fall again with each sweet breath. Graham cleared his throat and took a step back from me.

"We need to get some sleep," he said as he peered over at the empty bed.

"You take the bed, and I'll have the floor, okay?" Graham whispered as he grabbed a spare pillow and blanket from the closet. Oh hell no. The man had saved my life, while keeping Jack safe. And for God's sake, I wanted to feel him next to me on that mattress.

"No, Graham. You're going to sleep with me."

This time I was grateful that the lights were off because blood was surging across my face, and I didn't need Graham to know how ridiculous I looked right now. He stilled, and I could see his jaw tighten as he dropped the pillow on the floor.

"What?" he whispered.

"No...you know what I mean. You and I. We're just...going to share a bed." I cringed at how I always managed to make everything so awkward.

"Are...you sure?" he asked, his body hulking in the darkness.

All I could do was nod, and hope he understood. I felt my way around him toward the side closest to Jack and pulled the covers back. I climbed in and lay there unmoving as my lungs seemed to forget their basic function. *God, Georgia, grow up. You're fully clothed, you're twenty-six, and for holy shit's sake, you have a child now. You can sleep in the same bed as a member of the opposite sex. Even if he is now the father of your child. Even if his name is Graham Keaton. Even if his body looks like sculpted marble and you blush every time he looks at you.*

I stared up at the ceiling as I felt the jostling of the bed as he climbed in on the other side of me. I turned my head to check the digital clock. It was almost twelve a.m., and now all I could manage to think about was kissing my prince at the stroke of midnight. Graham's massive masculine presence and glorious woodsy scent spread across the pillow, floating through the air.

"You sure this is okay?" Graham muttered as he turned toward me. "You sure you don't want me to take the floor?"

"Yeah," I shot back as I pulled the covers up to my neck.

I could feel his heat from underneath the sheets, and I knew he was thinking the same crazy things I was thinking. Despite the fact I had been violated a few days ago, and Graham had tackled me, I wanted him. I *needed* him. Something about the way he made me feel safe, protected, cherished. Graham was the picture of faith and honor. He was the kind of man that I had waited for. I felt his body move closer to me, barely a few inches away from me.

"Georgia will you let me...hold you? I would feel better if I knew you were in my arms tonight," he whispered.

My God.

"Okay," I breathed, and before I knew it, his warmth was pressed against me. His firm, calloused hand had gripped the side of my hip, pulling me closer to him, and his nose nuzzled into my neck. Shivers ran all the way through me as my heart slammed against my chest. Even though my body was melting with lust, the way Graham's arms nestled around me made me feel treasured. In these arms, nothing could harm me, and I knew he would honor me and protect me tonight. The events from the evening suddenly seemed to took a massive toll on me, and I felt the energy drain from my body. I couldn't even think anymore, just breathe and be, in Graham's arms. And with Jack and Graham's even breathing and my slowing heartbeat, I was gently lulled to sleep.

Until a handsome man with a navy blue suit and a peacock-feathered hat prodded me awake.

15

THE NETWORK

I bolted upright and blinked up at a fabulously dressed Jerry Carter, who stood tall and proper with his arms folded across his chest.

"About took you long enough to fall asleep," Jerry said with his infamous grin, his piercing blue eyes sparkling evocatively.

I blinked again before movement in the corner of the room caught my eye. Graham and Jack were standing huddled together, watching our exchange silently. Despite the darkness in the hotel suite, all three of them emitted a bright aura that outlined their silhouette and made their skin seem opaque and milky white. I reached to turn on the lamp by the bed, but to my dismay, my hand swished directly through it, a cold, icy feeling shooting up my arm.

"The hell?" I yelled as I flailed myself out of bed, only to discover something even more terrifying than my hand passing through solid objects. A lump formed in my throat as I stared at my body snuggled up safely next to Graham's.

I whipped around, my focus tearing back to the very awake and alive figures of Jack and Graham behind me.

"Ohmygod, are we dead? *Again?*" I screamed as I ran over toward Jack, searching his face and body to make sure he was okay. Graham reached for my upper arm and nodded.

"We're okay, Georgia. Jerry said we're alive..." He shot a careful glance over at Jerry to confirm, who was beaming back at us proudly.

"Yes, you're all as fit as a fiddle. You're just sleeping and are experiencing what is commonly known as an out-of-body experience," he continued. "I couldn't be prouder of you three. You've located each other in record time. And my oh my, you two. I was amazed at how you have taken so quickly

162

to your Aftereffects…it's unbelievable." His eyes flashed with wonder as he grinned at us.

"All right, Jerry. Enough. What are we doing here?" Graham demanded, his jaw tightening with impatience. Jerry frowned at Graham's tone but sniffed it away as he crossed his arms.

"Well, it's your first training, Graham. You've located each other, and now it's time to train you on how to pave ." He peeked down at his watch and bit his lip with anticipation. "I've got quite an exciting appointment for you to attend that I think will be—"

"You've been watching us this whole time?" I cried, ignoring his surprised expression. I needed to know what he knew before he took us anywhere. My stomach twisted as I thought about Jerry watching with those excited baby blues as Jack's father attacked us. As he tried to take him…after what he did to his own son. My chest heaved with anger as I pictured him watching me stand alone in the snow, before Graham tackled me. Jerry's brows furrowed as his calming gaze settled on me.

"Yes, I've been watching you. You've handled every obstacle quite nic—"

"*No!*" I shouted, and all eyes fell on me.

I was enraged. I was so furious I felt like I would explode. He was supposed to be our spirit guide. Why had he watched Jack's father attack us? Not to mention, Jerry knew I had been raped. At this point, I didn't know if he'd stood by idly as a monster hurt me, as he *killed* me. Perhaps he had also watched on as someone murdered Jack and threw him in a dumpster to rot. I needed to know how he knew what happened to me. Why he hadn't tried to intervene if he'd known. Why hadn't he tried to warn us or clue us in on what was going to happen?

"We're not going anywhere until you tell us why you didn't help us," I said with narrowed eyes, lifting my chin defiantly. I wanted answers. I wanted someone to pay for the crimes against me. Against my *family*.

"Did you know how Jack would die? Graham? Have you just been casually observing us as all the evil in the world rained down on us?"

Jerry shook his head, taking a step toward me. "Georgia, I understand you're upset. You've been through a lot in such a small time frame. All of you have, but I can assure you, the Paving community has done everything in their power, as they always have, to help you and keep you safe.

"Safe? We *died*, Jerry!" I cried, as the tears began to spill. "Did you just sit there when Graham was attacked in the bar...when that girl's drink was spiked?" I took a step closer as a sob rattled through me.

"Tell me, did you stand by as a man shot an innocent child and cast him aside like he was *trash*?" And with that I sank to my knees, racking with hysterical sobs. "Were you there when that monster pushed me onto my bed and *raped* me?"

Jerry crossed the room in two swift steps, his arms wrapping around me, catching me as I fell. I tried to push him off me, beating on his chest, but he kept hold of me, comforting me.

"Georgia, I know how disappointing all of this is...trust me," he soothed.

I cried into his shoulder as he rocked me. I felt so ashamed. Ashamed of what happened, and how I was crying on the floor in front of everyone.

"When a Reckoning occurs, a Light is pulled towards the Anchor as they near death. So yes...I was there with you," Jerry whispered into my hair. His chest stilled as he said the words, and I fell limp against him, exhausted and so humiliated. Infuriated beyond belief.

"And no, I was not there when Graham or Jack died. The Light only gets snapshots of the other Reckoning partners' deaths. I saw what happened, but only after each of you arrived at the hospital." He turned back toward me and offered me the kerchief from his breast pocket. I took it but didn't use it. I just held on to it for dear life.

"Georgia, the most important and often the most frustrating part of Paving is we can never make a decision for someone. It is their God-given right and privilege. Free will, the oldest trick of the trade. I couldn't force him to change his mind; all I could do was try to influence his decisions. No matter how horrible."

"Wait...you just watched him...?" Graham growled.

I looked up to find Graham's face both disgusted and filled with rage as he pushed Jack behind him.

"A man can force himself on her, but you can't stop him because of an *ethics* code?" he demanded. Jack's deep black pools of eyes were watery in the dark as he watched me. I couldn't quite tell, but I had a sense that he was crying too. Jerry shook his head defensively.

"No, absolutely not. I tried to distract him, to reason with him, to help him remember the good he had inside himself. He wouldn't listen. So, I did the next best thing, I made sure all external resources were engaged."

I peered up at him confused as I wiped away a string of tears.

"External...*resources?*"

He nodded fervently, gripping my shoulders.

"It is outside our power to force a decision on someone. No matter how much I wanted him to stop hurting you, I couldn't make him. Of all the impossible things you've witnessed, that is the most impossible one—to contradict one's free will. When our traditional tactics don't work, we engage external resources to hopefully spark an influence."

I nearly laughed as I considered what he was saying.

"You're trying to tell me that you tried to *reason* with him? What? Did you just...*talk* to him?"

Jerry nodded solemnly. "I tried to show him the good inside him. The light that is in everyone. But he decided to let the dark consume him..."

"But I didn't see you! Where were you?" I demanded, heat rising in my chest again.

"Right in that room with you...next to you. Just like now. No one can see us when we're outside the body. Even other Pavers can't really see us, they can just...sense us. You know that voice you hear in your head? That ringing in your ear like there's been a shift in the environment? That's us, guiding you from outside the body. Hoping that you'll listen."

I'd heard that voice inside my head hundreds of times. That voice spoke to me when I broke up with Braxton. When I decided to go over and introduce myself to Mia for the first time. When I decided to become foster parents with Graham.

"*You're* the voice inside my head? You've been guiding me...all along?" I squinted up at him incredulously.

"No, not quite. I'm just your Light. I'm here to help you learn how to pave , how to transition you from your civilian life. That voice you've heard could have been dozens of Pavers. They receive missions every day to help a number of people. They aren't assigned to specific individuals like Lights are. They serve as needed, wherever they're called."

I blinked back at him, dumbfounded.

"So, what were these external *resources...?*" I mocked, crossing my arms across my chest.

Jerry surveyed me with a loving tenderness and pulled away from me, giving me space. "Pavers and Lights have the ability to manipulate certain things. We can infiltrate thoughts, dreams, and electrical machines to our advantage with our energies. So...I made your neighbor think she forgot her plane tickets so she would come up and call the police. I also made the fire alarm go off..."

"You invaded her mind to make her think something, but you didn't tell him to stop raping me?" I seethed, my chest heaving. "How is that not a breach of your stupid code of conduct?"

"We can only influence, never make a decision for someone. Trust me, I tried to influence him in every way I knew how. I made him think the police were barricading the doors. I even tried to make him think he was ill. It was like he just couldn't hear me; I'd never seen anything like it."

"Jesus, Jerry," Graham snarled. "Did you at least get any important identifying information? His name, any quirks, tattoos? You know...so we could try to bring Georgia some *justice?*"

Jerry frowned and shook his head. "I'm afraid not, Graham. He was covered head to toe, and there was something about him that almost barricaded me from him." He stood back up and offered me a hand, his eyes pleading with me. "Georgia, would you please just give me a chance. Let me show you how it all works before you turn your back on it."

I peered up at Graham to see what he thought, but to my surprise, Jack flew around him and ran into my arms, nearly knocking me over. He threw his slender arms around my neck, and he pressed his forehead against mine, his dark eyes sweeping across my face.

"I'm...so sorry my dad hurt you...touched you like that. Especially after you'd been..." he trailed off. Oh, God, I was so stupid. So selfish for dropping that bomb on him in the middle of all the trauma he was already dealing with. It hadn't even been a full day yet, and I was already failing at being a mom. I reached for him, gripping his bony shoulders.

"No, Jack! Oh my God, I shouldn't have said that. Not in front of you. It's *my* job to protect you, not the other way around." I bit my lip as his rage-filled eyes locked with mine.

"What? You shouldn't have said you were *raped*?" I trembled at the ugly way the word sounded on his sweet voice, tainting it. I shook my head, pleading with him.

"Jack—"

"Just because I'm a kid, doesn't mean I can't protect my...foster mom." A single tear fell down his cheek, and I quickly wiped it away with the back of my hand. "I never knew my mom. Never knew what it's like to even have one."

My heart broke at his words, another stream of tears springing down my cheeks.

"But now I got one. You can protect me all you want to, but you're mine too. I'm your...son, and I will protect you. With me, and Superman, anyone that ever lays a hand on you is so fucked."

I let out a shaky breath, narrowing my eyes at him.

"Jack, you really need to stop cussing," I sniffed as I shot him a weak smile.

"No promises." He shrugged with a smirk. Graham's strong hand gripped Jack's shoulder and helped pull him up to his feet. To both of our surprise, he pulled him into his chest.

"You're a good man, Jack," Graham whispered to him through the dark.

At first Jack froze as if he'd never been hugged a day in his life. But then, he came to, clapping Graham on the back with a loud thud.

"All right, Superman. That's enough." He wriggled free from Graham, and they both stretched their arms toward me, helping me up to my feet. I turned to face Jerry, who was standing calm as ever, carefully observing us beneath that perfectly cocked hat.

"Well?" he asked with arched eyebrows. He peeked down at that beautiful Gucci watch again expectantly. "We have an appointment soon that I don't want you to miss. I want you to see the good side of Paving. The side that keeps me coming back for more."

"What do you boys think?" I asked, shooting a look at my family. If Jack didn't feel comfortable, then I was ready to call it quits right then and there. Instead, he nodded, his olive complexion glowing just like it had in the hospital lobby when we first met.

"As long as you think it's okay, I think it'll be fine." Jack shrugged up at me. Graham's hard lines were still darkening his features, but he nodded toward me reluctantly.

"Jerry, if we don't want to continue at any time, you will take us back to our bodies. And that will be the end of it. No more contacting us, watching us, or anything like that. Do you understand?" Graham warned, his shoulders flexing with the threat.

Jerry's eyes flashed dangerously at Graham in a silent standoff. "Graham, I don't think you—"

"I said do you *understand?*" He took a step forward in front of me. Jerry was tall, but Graham was massive. I wasn't so sure that would be an advantage in the weird spirit world we were in, though. Jerry pursed his lips together, before he nodded curtly at Graham.

"Now if you wouldn't mind?" Jerry's eyes lit ablaze with excitement as he stretched his right hand out in the middle of our huddle.

"Pavers on three?" Jerry asked daringly. I shot Graham and Jack one more look before we all piled our hands on top of each other awkwardly.

"One, two..."

A deep pull shot through my stomach, as a dizzying collection of bright colors, off-key melodies, and voices filtered all around us. It felt like an out of control merry-go-round that was moments away from flying off its wheel and rolling away into the darkness. Suddenly, everything was still as we stood on the corner of a street in downtown St. Louis. I nearly fell as the shaky feeling began to wear off, but Graham's strong hands reached out to steady me. I squinted over at Jerry, who was unnervingly calm. He watched us with bright eyes, his form still and quiet in the dark.

"Is anyone hungry? I'm famished," Jerry sighed as he turned and crossed the street without looking.

Without any warning, a car sped right through him, but Jerry continued unperturbed toward a diner on the corner of the block. I couldn't help but to look three or four times as I kept hold of Jack's collar before we crossed. Once we got to the front door, Jerry walked through the glass with effortless grace, as if it weren't even there. I stared in shock as he continued toward a table and took a seat, uncaring whether we followed him or not. I peered in through the glass to see if he was going to help us, but instead he casually perused a menu. I huffed and started to walk through the glass, before Graham caught my wrist and shook his head.

"Let me go first," he instructed as his warm hand released me and reached toward the glass. We watched anxiously as his hand sliced right through it as if it weren't there, just like Jerry had.

"It's...fine, it just feels weird...like ice." He shivered as he withdrew his hand. "Wait for me to give you the go-ahead, okay?"

Jack and I nodded before he breezed through the glass with ease. He stood still for a moment on the other side as he scanned the diner. His body was stiff as he took in his surroundings. For a second, it looked like he was about to call the whole thing off. Something about the way he stood, like he was frozen in fear, made me want to take Jack and run. I started to reach for Jack when Graham turned toward us, waving us in. His eyes were wide, almost in...amazement. I passed through first, and it felt like ice-cold water rushing through my entire body. I felt Jack follow close behind, but I stopped short next to Graham as something bright flashed in the corner of my eye. I inhaled a sharp gasp as my eyes settled on one of the most beautifully terrifying sights I'd ever seen.

A stunning silver-white string of light that seemed to be flowing with energy branched in every direction across the restaurant. As I looked closer, it appeared to be connecting everyone in some strange glowing web, as each thread ended abruptly into each person's chest. No one seemed to bother with the fact that they were being impaled with a glowing string of light. Instead, they were casually chatting about their days or enjoying the peace of eating alone. An older woman in a bright yellow uniform walked over to a table with a pot of coffee. The string of light followed her every movement as she poured a fresh brew into their cups and continued to trail after her as she walked back behind the counter.

"What is that?" I managed to cough out.

No one in the restaurant was the least bit fazed that we'd just entered, and I didn't think it had anything to do with lackluster customer service. They just couldn't see us.

"It's only the most brilliant engineering feat ever, designed by the master architect himself. It connects us all. Every single human soul is tied to this intricate design, all around the world," Jerry explained as he continued to busy himself with his menu.

"The master architect?" Graham repeated as he stepped in front of me and leaned over to inspect the bright light nearest to us.

"God," Jerry answered with a nonchalant shrug.

Graham threw his hand through the light, and it passed through with ease. He peered back over his shoulder at me and beckoned me forward, reaching for my hand. I took it and let his warmth settle my nerves. I leaned forward to get a closer look, and a barely audible high-note frequency seemed to emit from it. My fingers trailed over the cord as warmth shot through my hand like flames licking at my fingertips.

"What does it do?" Jack whispered in awe. He was a little more fearless than me, as he waved his hand back and forth through the light, watching it pass through each time.

"It helps Pavers do their work." Jerry grinned as he watched us inspect the thread.

Suddenly, my eyes fell on a woman who emitted a beautiful shade of gold from her web. The light was pulling us toward it, like a moth to a flame, and we were powerless to its shine.

"Why is her string gold when everyone else's is silver?" Jack asked as he approached her.

I jumped as the uniformed waitress passed through me. A wave of warmth shook through me as I watched her place a steaming plate of waffles in front of the woman.

"Thanks, Paula," she mumbled as she unwrapped her silverware.

Paula nodded kindly and turned to grab some more plates. I dodged out of her way as she turned to head back down the aisle.

"Ah, so you've noticed the *orb*." Jerry patted the seat next to him and beckoned us forward with a glint in his eye.

The pull of the golden light was strong, and it was nearly impossible to turn away, but each of us headed over and took our seats in the booth with him.

"You see, when that gold light shines, that's what we call an orb. It signifies that they have a purpose to be fulfilled, and they need our help. When you're awake and in your body, you'll see a bright light hovering over someone. But here in the Paving Realm , *this* is what you see." He waved his arm toward the lights.

"What do you mean by a *purpose?*" A line in between Jack's eyebrows creased as he looked over at Jerry, puzzled.

"Well, most people have anywhere from thirty to a hundred purposes to fulfill by the end of the day." He sighed as he placed his chin on his hand, looking over at the woman as her orb glowed around her.

"Purposes can be anything from smiling at someone, to saying something to giving or receiving a gift. Most of the time, people will complete their purposes by the end of the day if they're listening intently...with their hearts. Those that stray from their path...or those that might have an overdue purpose...well, their orb shines bright like a beacon to Pavers."

"What are we supposed to do with them?" I demanded, still gawking at the bright light.

"Not every orb should be tended to when you see them. You see, timing is everything when it comes to this kind of thing. You only manage the orbs that you receive instructions for." He peeked down at his watch again and grinned up at us.

"A mission will come to you like a rush of images in your mind. You'll receive a time, a place, and you might get a picture of the face...or faces you'll be helping. Usually the images include specific instructions, but not always," Jerry said as he twisted around, peering outside the window.

"Ah, our second guest is right on time!" Jerry sang out as he tapped his watch. I squinted, trying to get a better look before a small golden light bobbed and weaved through the darkness, growing brighter as someone neared. I could barely make out an elderly man as he limped his way toward the front door of the diner. His clothes were tattered, and his breath puffed out into misty clouds around him from the bitter cold. His white hair peeked out underneath his frayed cap, and his face was worn and tired like he hadn't rested in days, maybe even weeks.

He paused just outside of the front entrance, before he finally came in and ambled his way toward a table in the corner, avoiding eye contact from the other guests. We watched with wide eyes as the thread that protruded from the middle of his chest glowed a bright gold, just like the woman's, and both lights stretched across the room, meeting each other in the middle.

"What does that mean, when it connects like that?" Jack gasped, his eyes watering from the blinding light filtering across the restaurant.

"When it links to another person with that gold color, they are supposed to meet each other," Jerry answered, his joy and excitement bursting at the seams.

"You know, I'd bet my hat that those two have passed each other a thousand times without speaking. We're a last resort, you know. God encourages us in many ways before he uses Pavers. Positive recurring thoughts, dreams, feelings, or strange impossible coincidences—you know, that sort of thing. God communicates in abstract ways, but when the message isn't heard or understood, our ranks move in. Sometimes it just takes a little bit of human encouragement to fulfill their calling!" Jerry said, clapping his hands together in delight.

"Now tell me this. What do you see when you look at them?" Jerry leaned forward with animated curiosity, resting his chin on his hand again.

"A bright light?" Graham suggested as he shielded his eyes.

Jerry shook his head.

"No, no. Really look at them, see if you can get a reading off the orbs. What do you *feel*?"

I sat in silence for a moment, listening to the hum of the lights above and the familiar clinking sound of silverware hitting plates. As I squinted over at them, a sudden rush of insatiable hunger, emptiness, loneliness, mixed with the undeniable need for love ached all the way through to my bones. It was like the wall and burden of isolation was crumbling around me, and I was moments away from shutting down. Desperation and fear crawled through my veins, gripping my very soul as if it would never let go. Before the dark feelings swallowed me whole, it was like a record player switched its discs, and a different set of images started to play across my mind's eye.

Words in different languages floated around, and the sounds of various voices filled my head. It was brief, almost like a whisper before the voices faded and wavered away. I blinked my eyes open, and Jack and Graham both frowned over at the man and woman, their expressions solemn and distraught. The emotional charge from the readings still hung in the air, clinging with aftershocks of sorrow.

"Well?" Jerry urged, before Jack turned around, his eyes brimming with tears.

"He's hungry, and lonely. He needs...love." And right then, my heart ripped open with anger and a need for vengeance. I knew Jack could relate, and he was no stranger to the terrible darkness that still swam through me from the orb reading.

"Jack, I simply couldn't have said it better myself," Jerry praised, as his own eyes glimmered with pain. "Now...did any of you get a reading from *her*, then?" Jerry beckoned over at the woman who continued to eat in silence.

"Maybe?" I shrugged as I thought about the words and voices I heard in different languages. Jerry perked up with pleasant surprise written on his face.

"That's wonderful! Some have much stronger readings than others, but sometimes you have to dig a little deeper to get an accurate feeling." Jerry pursed his lips and nodded expectantly, as if he were asking me to share with the rest of the class. "Well, go on. What did you feel?"

"I saw different languages...different voices. Maybe she's a public speaker, or she's an interpreter?" I shrugged.

Jerry's face brightened considerably like I had just discovered a city of gold.

"I think you're onto something, Georgia. Now, how do you presume you would connect these two?" he challenged, his eyes darting between us.

"Do...we just ask them?" Jack chimed in, shrugging.

"*Yes!*" Jerry yelled as he stood up and reached across the table, pulling Jack into an awkward hug and kissing him on the forehead. Jack grunted as he pushed Jerry away in disgust.

"Dude...that's enough of this touchy feely sh—I mean stuff..." Jack whined, trying to rub the kiss off his head, eyeing me sheepishly from his almost curse word slipup. Jerry chuckled and shrugged.

"Sorry, it's just no one ever gets it right on the first try," Jerry said as he adjusted his suit jacket and sat back down.

"So...who wants to see a purpose fulfilled?" he asked with a smile that shone brighter than the golden string of lights combined.

16

THE CALLING

"Jack, would you like to do the honors?" Jerry peered down at him underneath his hat expectantly.

"What...do I do?" he asked as he stared at the woman nervously.

Jerry grinned at him for a moment as he leaned forward. "I think you already know. It's all based on instinct, anyway. Just do what you think you're supposed to do."

Jack continued to stare at her for a few brief moments. Finally, he got up and took a seat across from the woman in the booth.

"Um, excuse me..." Jack said, peering up at her as she remained fixated on the plate in front of her. She immediately tensed, her fork freezing at mid bite, as if she heard him.

"I...I don't mean to bother you, but I was wondering if you'd like to go over and...meet that man over there. I think...he's hungry." Jack's voice was soft, almost tender and nurturing. Far from the angry, distant Jack we'd met yesterday.

He looked on at the woman, his eyes bright with wonder. A moment passed before she put her fork down and turned to look at the man. The cord glowed brighter than ever as she stared at him. I let out a gasp as we watched her slide out of her booth, and stride over to him. We all gawked as she stopped in front of his table and rocked back and forth on her heels.

"Sir," the woman whispered as the man shivered, sliding himself further into the seat, away from her.

"Sir, would you...like a meal?"

For a moment, the man trembled, shielding his weary face from hers. Finally, he surrendered, and he lifted his nervous gaze, his hands knotting underneath the table, as if he were still trying to warm himself from the relentless cold outside. His silence spoke volumes, but the pleading in his eyes resonated from across the room, hitting me hard in the gut.

"Sir, I asked if you would like a meal," she repeated, lowering her voice impossibly low.

A few more moments of uneasy silence passed between them, before she shot him a reassuring smile. Suddenly, the woman started to move her hands in quick, excited movements. The man gasped, his posture straightening as he leaned forward and grabbed her hands excitedly. His smile was brilliant from ear to ear, before he repeated the same hand movements in quick succession. The woman let out a musical laugh that filled the room, as the light around them grew even brighter. Soon they were both deep in a beautifully choreographed dance of a conversation in sign language, but somehow, we could still understand what they were saying. I suppose love was a universal language after all.

"I want to get you some food, what do you like?" she asked again. His hands shook as he reached into his pocket and pulled out two worn out dollars. The woman immediately pushed his hand away.

"Absolutely, not. Tonight, I'm taking care of you," she huffed, and turned on her heel, gliding over to the counter on a mission. She leaned over so the woman in the yellow uniform could hear her.

"Paula, can we get a number four and some hot coffee out for him?" The woman slid some cash across the bar. Paula nodded, with a kind smile that met her eyes, as she started to prepare the order. We watched in astonishment as the woman sat back down next to the man and started a conversation. His face had transformed into a much happier man, as he signed back to her gratefully.

An incredible glimmer of bright white light flashed across the restaurant, in a glorious display. It bounced in a rhythm-like movement through everyone's cord, pulsing until it fizzled out into the normal silver glow like a firework.

"What the hell was that?" Graham asked, as he stared open mouthed at the dimming light of the web. Jerry reached up to wipe a tear away before he answered.

"That, my loves, is what happens when a purpose is fulfilled. You see, even though it was *their* purpose, the act of fulfilling it resonates through the entire network. That one small act of kindness will be felt from across the world before dawn. Isn't it just beautiful?" Jerry sniffled and wiped away another tear.

My heart broke thinking of the man, isolated, unable to talk to anyone or share his day. Did he have anyone that would listen before this? Well now, he certainly had someone.

"I love seeing purposes fulfilled," Jerry said, as he dabbed his cheeks.

"Can they hear everything we say?" Graham asked in a low voice, almost a whisper as he watched the pair in awe.

"No, they only hear what we intend for them to hear. We just need to be intentional with what we say, and how we say it," Jerry instructed as he tucked his kerchief back into his pocket.

"What if she didn't want to listen," I demanded, as I pictured Jerry begging and pleading for my attacker to stop hurting me. *And he didn't.*

Jerry nodded, his lips pressing together with regret.

"When someone refuses to listen to their calling, their orb simply continues to shine on, until perhaps there comes a day when they are ready to pursue it." Jerry sighed as he tapped his fingers on the table in deep thought.

Disappointment crushed me as I let it sink in. I frowned as I glanced over at Jack. He was still watching in awe at the couple, and suddenly hope filled me again. If Jack could find wonder in something after he'd experienced the depths of hell, then perhaps there was hope yet. Maybe the man who hurt me still could fulfill a good life, he just needed to find the light again. I peered over at Graham, but was taken aback by his intense stare, his beautiful gray eyes fixed on me and it almost felt like gravity was shifting around me. His throat bobbed with a tight swallow, as if he were trying to gain some composure before his gaze dropped to his lap. My heart squeezed and fluttered as I wondered what he was thinking.

"I have one last part of the training I'd like to commence. Is it okay to continue on?" Jerry asked, his baby blues shining with intention again as he looked around at us. I peered over at Graham again, but he was looking at me, waiting for *me* to make the call.

"Okay, but just this last thing," I warned.

Jerry bowed his head respectfully, tipping his hat in a grateful gesture. "I want to explore your Aftereffects, now that you are showing...signs."

"Yeah, what is an Aftereffect?" Jack interrupted, his face scrunched up with confusion.

"Ah, excellent question! They are the gifts that you use to help people. Every Paver has at least one, and they are unique to each person." He turned his gaze towards me and tapped his forefinger against his lips suspiciously.

"Casey was right on the money with you, Georgia. It appears you can determine professional plans for civilians." He glanced over at Graham. "And you most certainly have the gift of foresight. I'm shocked that your gifts have developed so quickly. It seems you three are a force to be reckoned with..."

"What's *my* Aftereffect?" Jack asked with quiet curiosity, wringing his hands together in anticipation.

"That is what I intend to find out." Jerry turned to me, as he reached out and touched my shoulder. "Georgia, if you would be so kind?"

"What can I do?" I hesitated. Jerry cocked an eyebrow upwards knowingly.

"Hold his hand and tell us what you see. Your gift of insight should also be able determine to what a Paver's Aftereffect will be. After all, paving is a profession just as any other field."

Jack's guarded eyes locked with mine as he nodded up at me, extending his hand towards me. I reached for it, my fingers curling around his.

Instantly, an incredible surge of physical pain coursed through me, cutting and slicing through my very core. The cut from my neck and forehead stung relentlessly, and I doubled over from the dizzying pain. I wanted so bad to let go of his hand, from all the agony, but I held tight hoping there might be something else, anything else that I could feel. Before the pain had started, it lifted, a healing sense of peace filling the void from the pain, like medicine healing my wounds. Jack snatched his hand away like he had been burned.

"Oh my God! Jack! Did I... hurt you?" I demanded, suddenly terrified that he felt the same pain I felt. He shook his head, his dark eyes wide with either fear or excitement.

"Well?" Jerry asked placing his hand on my shoulder.

"I felt...pain, but then it was gone," I breathed as I continued to watch Jack stare at his hands. He was lying. The way he pulled his hand away was instinctual, and sudden like a hand on a hot stove.

"Was it like you felt with Casey? Like an emotional healer?" Jerry urged.

I shook my head. "No, it was more like physical pain. Like he was healing my bruises and cuts." Jerry's grin fell before he leaned back into the booth and crossed his arms.

"Jack, did you feel anything when you touched her?" Jerry asked with a stern edge to his voice. Jack stilled before he finally nodded, avoiding eye contact with me.

"And...?" Jerry continued, his foot tapping on the floor underneath the table. Damn, Jerry had a better mom voice than me.

"It was nothing, just a little sting, like a paper cut." Jack shrugged and looked around at the man and woman still talking enthusiastically behind him. Almost like he was looking for a distraction, an out.

"Jack! Why didn't you tell me? I never meant to—"

Graham grabbed my hand and I immediately shut my mouth. He beckoned towards Jack who was now looking down at his hands, his ears reddening.

"My dad hurt you, Georgia," he whispered, keeping his eyes trained on his fists in his lap. "I said I'm going to protect you..." Jack let out a deep breath, shaking his head. Graham leaned forward almost like he was going to hug Jack again, but he reached for me instead, his pupils dilating.

"Georgia...your neck!" He gestured towards my throat. Jack startled, lifting his widened eyes up to my jaw line.

"What does that mean?" Graham demanded, peering over at Jerry.

"It appears..." Jerry was just as perplexed as Graham, shocked even.

"It appears he is exhibiting physical healing powers. Not to mention, he did it... intentionally." Jerry shook his head in disbelief. "I've only met one other Paver that could heal physical wounds, but they have since... passed on. How interesting..." Jerry's eyes sparkled brighter than I'd ever seen before like it was Christmas morning. He continued to stare in awe for a few more minutes before he shook himself from the trance, peering back down at his watch again.

"I suppose it's time for you to return to your bodies, now. Lesson one completed and... passed with flying colors, mind you." He winked at us as he motioned for us to stand. "Until you've been issued your brief cases and watches at headquarters, almost all of your paving work will be done while you're in your physical bodies. Until then, just keep your heart and your mind open for any additional missions," Jerry instructed like it was as simple as breathing.

"You still have the address for headquarters, right?" Jerry asked, shooting me a wary look. I let out an exasperated laugh. How could I forget that address?

"1000 Golden Path Road in O'Fallon," I recited with a smug look. Jerry nodded, satisfied.

"So...what do we do at headquarters?" Graham asked, intrigued.

"It's where we reconvene, gather notes about our projects of the day, get guidance and trainings. You know, just like any other business because that's exactly what we are. Even though we operate in secret, we still operate like your run of the mill homegrown business."

His eyes danced dangerously under his hat. "I can't wait for you to meet the team."

"How many other Pavers are in O'Fallon? Are there other kids?" Jack was fully invested now, his eyes brightening with excitement.

"Yes, it's rare to have kid Pavers, but there is a girl, her name's Rachel. She's twelve."

Jack seemed to think on that a little too much, so Graham clapped him on the shoulder, nearly sending him forward.

"Sounds like you might have a friend?" Graham beamed down at him.

"With you three, we now have thirteen Pavers altogether. Some don't come by at all though," Jerry said, lowering his voice his expression slightly annoyed.

"What do you mean?" I asked dropping my voice to a whisper like Jerry did, even though I knew no one could hear us.

"Well...being a Paver is a tricky business and it runs many of us dry. Some deny the calling altogether and stick to being...normal." Jerry let out a heavy sigh as he stared out the window as a light snow started to fall. I thought about the way Dr. Cobbs had explained why he left.

Paving...consumes you.

I shuddered as the weight of the responsibility fell on me. On *Jack*, an eleven-year-old boy. We were apparently now responsible for guiding people towards their God-given destiny. How could we even begin to do that, when I wasn't even sure about my own.

"Don't think I didn't overhear your conversation with Dr. Cobbs, Georgia." Jerry added, arching his eyebrows.

"What?" I asked, startled.

"Yup, I know you talked to him about some of our trade secrets. Ex-Paver or not though, he told you the truth. Paving is selfless and can be very draining. It's a burden we take for the sake of the greater good," Jerry said with pursed lips.

"When you're called to be a Paver, it's expected that you embrace the role for what it is. It's the ultimate insult to not accept your own destiny to help others with theirs. I mean, imagine if Madonna had decided to play it safe and sing children's songs." Jerry cringed at the thought and I bit my lip as I tried to hold back a laugh. In the corner of my eye, I caught Jack's face scrunch up with confusion. I imagined he wasn't confused about the choice to become a Paver... but rather he was trying to figure out who Madonna was.

"I hope you three will find that paving is some of the most meaningful work a human being can be called to. People need us, and we were chosen for a higher purpose. Sometimes people just need a little extra push to make beautiful things happen." He waved his hand at the couple behind us, still in deep conversation, as the man finished his meal.

"You did that, Jack. You helped them." Jack glowed as a subtle smile crossed his face. A deep sense of pride filled me as I watched him find joy in helping others.

"Behind every beautiful and amazing thing in the world, you can bet that a Paver was behind it," Jerry proclaimed as he popped out his arm and peered down at his golden Gucci watch again, surprise shining across his face.

"My goodness, you need to get going. You know in your hearts where headquarters is. Just trust your gut and you'll find us," Jerry said with a wink before he jutted his hand out into the middle of the table.

"Pavers on three?"

17

THE GIFT

A soft tapping noise gently lulled me awake, as warmth spread throughout my body. It took a second to register where I was, as I scanned the dark room. I squinted over toward the window where a bit of light shed from the curtains of the hotel suite. I followed the light as it flooded toward Jack's sleeping silhouette. Small, sweet breaths sounded from across the room, and my heart fluttered with excitement. I pondered the fact that this was going to be the first whole day I had of being a mom. Is this what motherhood felt like for everyone? Pure joy and utter terror? I could feel Graham behind me, his chin nestled into the back of my neck, his hard body pressed against me in all the right places. One of his thick arms was thrown over my stomach, his Semper Fi tattoo bold and resilient, even in the dark.

Another soft sound rapped on the door, and Graham began to stir, his warm body moving away from me. I missed his heat and twisted around to look at him. His smile was somehow ten times sexier with morning stubble as his bedroom eyes settled on mine. His focus lowered to my neck, and he reached for it gently, his fingertips grazing the tender skin underneath my jaw, sending shivers throughout my body.

"They're really gone," he whispered, his eyes fervent and focused.

At first, I wasn't sure what he was referring to, given that his fingers were tracing my throat, setting my whole body on fire. He could have been telling me we were on the moon for all I knew, as I melted under his touch.

"Your cuts, they're gone," he repeated in his steady, careful voice.

Suddenly, memories from our training with Jerry flooded through me. He had healed me. Jack could heal physical pain.

A more urgent knock pounded on the door again, and Graham's body tensed, his focus turning toward the noise. He placed his hand on my hip and mouthed, "Stay here," before he slipped out of bed and headed toward the door. I pulled the covers up to my neck as I heard the door swing open. Mia's soft voice greeted Graham, and I immediately shoved the covers away and tiptoed around the corner to a welcome sight.

Mia was standing in the front of an eager huddle formation with the rest of the boys at her back.

"Sorry to wake you...we were just wondering if we could give Jack something?" Mia beamed. Suddenly, her eyes grew wide as she stared at my forehead. "Oh my God, you're...healed!" she gasped.

"You are never going to believe what happened," I whispered, shaking my head. There was so much to tell, and I didn't even know where to begin.

"Okay, okay, so you guys are paranormal as shit. So...can we meet Jack? We have literally been waiting for hours," Andrews whined behind her. Mia nudged him in the ribs and plastered on an innocent smile, ignoring Andrews's pained grimace.

"What he means is...we wanted to give Jack some...*things*." Mia lifted her head proudly as the rest of the guys parted behind her. Cooper's hulking form marched forward carrying a large tote bag from Target.

"What's all this?" Graham asked, leaning forward and peering at the treasure trove of items spilling over the top.

"We thought Jack might need some clothes and stuff." Tex clapped Graham on the shoulder with a wide grin. I stared, speechless, with wide watery eyes at the bag and then up at his brothers.

"Guys...this is too much," I whispered, running my hand through my hair. Mia was a teacher, and despite the fact she was probably incredible at what she did, she was still making a teacher's salary. Not to mention, Graham's brothers were practically living in decay and were just scraping by, working at the auto shop. They had already reserved us rooms for the hotel, which I would reimburse them for, but this was just too much.

"Hey, just because he's yours doesn't mean we can't dote on him a little," Reed pointed out with a grin. A resounding echo of agreement rumbled from each of them, a few of them nodding while the others were prodding Davis to show us what was inside the bag.

Davis pulled two items from the top while the others nudged each other excitedly. I gasped as he lifted two gorgeous-looking jerseys and hats from the mix.

"We got him his own St. Louis Cardinals and Blues hockey jerseys. We figured if they're big enough for Tex, they're big enough for Jack," Davis said as the rest of them chuckled.

"Hey, I've never had any complaints about my size," Tex said, crossing his arms with a playful smirk.

Tears burned my eyes as I stared in awe at the brilliant red-and-blue shirts hanging in front of us. I couldn't help but wonder if Jack had ever been to a game or was even familiar with our home teams. He was a boy left to fend for himself at all hours of the day. His priorities were finding out where his next meal would come from. I doubted he could spare any of his energy worrying about sports.

"Each of us picked out a few outfits, but Davis and I approved them for his sake," Mia praised as Davis nodded humbly.

"After I heard about the whole throw-your-entire-life-in-a-trash-bag thing, we..." Davis's face fell as his gaze settled on something behind me.

I jumped as a small hand touched my elbow, and I turned to see Jack push his way in between us with unhinged curiosity.

Jack let out a loud gasp, as his eyes fell on the jerseys in Davis's hands. He stared at them hungrily, like they were the most precious things in the entire world.

"Holy shit, are those...Cardinals and Blues jerseys?" he blurted out as he stepped around me, practically drooling.

"Yeah, we uh...didn't know what your size was...so we guessed, and we hope these fit," Tex said with a grin, as the rest of them pushed Cooper forward, an excited energy buzzing around them.

Cooper dropped to his knee in front of Jack, but somehow, he was still eye level as he took the Blues jersey from Davis and held it up toward him. After a moment of silence, Cooper broke out into one of the biggest grins I'd ever seen him make.

"Yup, blue is definitely your color. You'll fit right in at the game tonight," Cooper's gruff voice boomed as Jack stared at him, his mouth wide open.

"*Game?*" Jack replied breathlessly, his eyes darting from Cooper to the jersey in his hands.

"Yes. We have something very important to ask you," Mia chimed in as she handed him the Blues hat. He peered down at it, his face scrunched up with anticipation before he returned his gaze up at the doting crew before him.

"How would you like to go to a hockey game tonight?" Cooper asked, his deep black eyes glinting with excitement. Bennett reached in his pockets and pulled out a small stack of what looked like tickets. He fanned them out and bounced his eyebrows up and down.

"We got enough for everyone to go!" he gloated as he flashed a grin at us.

"Seriously?" Jack shouted, peering up at them like they weren't real. Out of all the things we'd experienced in the last few days, this was the first time I could tell Jack was fighting the urge to pinch himself.

"Yes...but only if Graham and Georgia say it's okay," Mia urged as everyone turned to look at us. Before I could get any words out, a rush of welcome images rushed through my brain.

Blue sparkly shoes, a roaring crowd...an engagement ring ? 7:47 p.m.

And as soon as the images flashed through my head, they were gone just like that. I fell back from the force of them, but I felt a strong hand wrap around my arm to steady me.

"You okay?" Graham asked his face filled with concern, his fingers still gripping me firmly. I nodded with a nervous smile.

"I think Jack should go...only if he wants to..." I grinned down at him, trying to divert the attention back to him. Jack's eyes were dark as he assessed me. He knew something was up, but he didn't say anything. Instead, he quickly turned back toward Mia and the boys and beamed back at them.

"Hell—" He peered up at me sheepishly. "I mean...heck yes!"

After we all grabbed lunch, I let Jack go with Graham and the boys to get some good bonding time in while Mia and I hung out in her suite. I was grateful to have some time away while I processed everything. Mia rehashed the fun day she'd had shopping with Graham's brothers, and I told her all about everything that happened with Casey, Jack, and our experience with Jerry during our training. I didn't care that I wasn't supposed to tell anyone else; she deserved to know what was going on.

"So, hold on a second. You're trying to tell me that Graham can see the

185

future... Jack can heal people, and you...can see what people would be good at professionally?" Mia asked, her voice lifting at the end. I almost started giggling like an insane person as I replayed her words in my head.

"I know...it sounds ridiculous," I laughed as I nodded toward her and stared at her through my fingers, hiding my face with my hands. Mia's face fell as the sparkle in her eyes dulled. Her gaze dropped to her hands as they knotted in her lap.

"What's wrong, Mia?" I prodded, following her anxious movements. Maybe I needed to cool it with all this paranormal talk.

"So, all you have to do is hold someone's hand and you see images of what they are supposed to do with their life?" she asked, still averting her gaze.

"Yes...why?" I asked, watching her pull her fingers through her hair nervously.

"Can you...tell me what you see when you hold *my* hand?" she whispered. I surveyed her for a second, as every ounce of confidence that had seemed to fill her very being moments before simply vanished right before my eyes. The Mia who was sitting in front of me now seemed unsure, even terrified. Her hands gripped the sheets before she finally lifted her eyes up toward me again, like a lost puppy.

"I mean...I hate to ask you. If it's weird, I totally understand," Mia said before she bit her lip, horror and embarrassment filling her face.

"Of course, Mia! I would do anything for you, but...I thought you loved teaching?" I frowned as her gaze fell back toward her hands again.

I tried to remember our college days as she was finishing her degree in education. She was so excited to have her own classroom and help kids meet their potential. She even had a vision board hanging over her bed of different classroom layouts and activities.

She shook her head at me, locks of golden hair falling over her shoulders, covering her face like a veil of defeat. "The kids are great, but I have a hard time dealing with all the overhead. Sometimes, I feel so boxed in, I might suffocate." I watched her for a second as urgency filled me to help her.

"Give me your hand," I commanded as I reached toward her. She peered up at me, her hair still covering half of her face.

"Seriously? You would really do this for me?" Mia's eyes grew wide, excitement pushing away the defeat.

"Mia, first of all, you have been an incredible friend. I couldn't believe you would just let me live with you without a moment's notice after we hadn't talked in years. Not to mention, you pulled a gun on a man you thought was hurting me. An ex-Marine not to mention," I added, stifling a laugh.

"You also bought my son clothes, which I still intend to pay you back for. But most of all, you know my heart. You *get* me. You are a dear and selfless friend, and I would love nothing more than to give you something back in return." Tears brimmed at her eyes, and her lips trembled as she stared unblinking at me.

"Second of all, I think that I'm supposed to do this for anyone who needs it. I think that's my purpose, to help others who need a guiding hand." I extended my hand out even farther and tilted my head at her. "Well, are you going to give me your hand or not?"

She laughed and reached toward me before panic suddenly filled her eyes. "Does it hurt?" she asked urgently, retracting her hand.

"No, you won't feel a thing!" I assured her as I reached toward her again. She shook her head, her eyes darkening.

"No, Georgia. Will it hurt *you*?"

I took her in as she held her hand away from me. She would refrain from knowing her true destiny, simply so I didn't feel any pain.

"No, it doesn't hurt either one of us. Now give me your damn hand," I demanded. She narrowed her eyes at me, studying me for a few moments before she finally gave in.

As my fingers closed over hers, black onyx wisps drifted around me, and Mia's worried face disappeared right before my eyes. Complete darkness consumed me before I was pulled into an unfamiliar but absolutely beautiful home. Luxury surrounded me. Custom cabinets, hardwood floors, designer furniture, and the soft light of a scented candle that smelled like cinnamon flickered on the center island in the kitchen. I felt a tap on my shoulder as Mia's beautiful glowing face peeked around at me.

"Are you coming? We've still got the second floor to see," she gushed as she headed toward the grand staircase. *Okay, this is new.* In other visions, no one ever interacted with me, except Harlow when I'd seen the farmhouse. I blinked back at her to make sure she was talking to me. Her bright smile twisted into a frown as she waited.

"Georgia?" she asked, concern flashing in her eyes. I jumped at her voice and let out an awkward laugh.

"Um...sorry, I was just...mesmerized by all of this beauty. Mia, where are we?" I asked, as I scanned the beautiful designs all around. The floor plan was stunning, functional, and breathtaking.

"Well, we're in the new floor plan I designed. This is the Platinum layout—do you like it?" She sighed as she perused the great room, admiring her work. I couldn't begin to answer her; I was too busy drooling.

"If this house isn't what you were looking for, I have a few other houses in the neighborhood we could check out." My jaw dropped as I pondered her words. *Other* houses?

"Are you a designer or a real estate agent?" I asked, ignoring her puzzled expression. She crossed her arms and stared over at me like I had lost my mind.

"Well...I dabble in a little bit of everything. I design houses, manage real estate, and assist in reconstructing floor plans. You were there with me when I went to get my Realtor's license, remember?"

"Oh yeah, that's right..." I whispered as I continued to stare around me. The fireplace was roaring, and everything was placed so intentionally. Everything had a purpose, a life to it.

Immediately I was pulled back into the hotel suite as Mia stared at me with wide eyes.

"Georgia? Are you okay? You were starting to scare me," she asked, grabbing my arms and frowning at me nervously.

"Mia! I knew you were creative, but daaayum, girl!" I said as the beautiful images of her artistry and work whirled around in my head. Mia dropped her hands to her sides, her brows drawing together.

"What...what did you see?" she muttered, biting her lip in anticipation.

"You, my dear, are going to be one hell of a real estate guru . I mean, *wow*. You really have an eye for designing a space," I praised as I watched her face light up with brilliant resolve. Mia pulled me into a tight embrace and sighed.

"Seriously? Oh my God, thank you so much, Georgia," she giggled to herself and then pulled away, meeting my eyes again. "You know, I have always wanted to try designing houses...but I was just too scared. I mean I have shelves of sketchbooks with my ideas, and I did some work on my own house. I just didn't see it going anywhere. My practical side kept telling me to play it safe, you know?" Oh, God how I knew. Her face split into a wide grin, and she hopped off the bed, pulling me with her.

"Come on...let's get ready for the game." She led me into the bathroom and turned the curler on.

"You know... I had another vision...but I'm not sure what to make of it," I said as I thought about the strange rush of images that pulsed through me from earlier. The blue sparkly shoes. The roaring crowd.

The engagement ring.

There was a time, a place. Perhaps it was a mission...but Graham and Jack seemed unaffected in the slightest. They didn't see what I saw. Jerry never told us if we received missions as a Reckoning group or individually.

"We were in the arena...and I saw these adorable shoes. They were like these dazzling blue flats. And then there was an engagement ring...or a—"

"Hold on, did you say blue flats?" Mia repeated with wide eyes.

"Yeah they were—"

"Like these...?" She dangled the exact pair from my vision in front of me.

"Where did you get those...?" I whispered breathlessly.

"I was going to wear them, but your feet are so freaking tiny, Georgia! They were in your luggage... I thought you knew."

"Huh." I continued to stare.

"*Georgia!*" she squealed as she ran toward me, the shoes flying to the floor. "What if you saw what you did because...*Graham* is going to propose? To *you!*"

I let out a quiet laugh, shaking my head. "No, Mia. That can't be. We've only known each other for like a day... And those shoes..." I dropped my gaze to the shoes scattered on the floor, gleaming against the light hopefully. "I think those shoes are from my mom's shop. Hundreds, if not thousands of women probably have those exact same shoes. He couldn't—"

"Georgia Lee Scott. He just adopted a *child* with you. You should have heard his friends talking about him last night. They have mad respect for him, and he seems to care a lot about you." She gripped my shoulders as she jumped up and down. "I think he's going to make an honest woman of you.

Tonight!" she squealed as she ran to gather some makeup supplies. "Oh my God, we have to get you ready!"

I felt my knees go weak as the frantic sound of nail polish bottles and compact cases slammed against the counter. A wave of panic and...surprising excitement rushed through me as I contemplated it. Graham Keaton...was going to ask me to be his *wife*? What an idea...

"Mia, stop. This is ridiculous," I insisted nervously.

Mia stopped and turned to stare at me, her face deathly serious. "No, Georgia. You know what's ridiculous? The fact that you've hidden yourself away from the rest of the world for the last few years because of *Braxton*."

I gasped at her harsh accusation.

"Mia..."

"You've shut the whole world out because he broke your heart. A little man-boy hardly worth your time hurt you, and you haven't come back from it." She shook her head as she continued to pull out the entire cosmetology department on the bathroom counter.

"You deserve love again. And seriously, I think you've found it. I know he and I got off on the wrong foot, but listening to his friends talk about him last night..." She shook her head before she turned back toward me.

"Georgia, I've seen the way you are with him. Graham...he *adores* you. The way he looks at you like you're God's greatest gift to him. I mean, for God's sake, you two are *parents*. To me, it sounds like you guys were destined for each other. You've been talking so much about destiny now that you're a Paver...but what about taking a second to consider your own?"

I stared at her in silence as I fought back tears. She was right. I had shut myself away, too afraid to try again. With Graham, I felt secure and loved. I felt protected, and I knew he would treasure Jack and me the way we deserved.

A wave of mixed emotions ran through me. Terror. Joy. Excitement. Disbelief. Certainty. I leaned over on the bed as I thought about the prospect of getting married.

"Mia...I know you're right...but isn't this all too soon? Shouldn't I at least date him for a while to see if we are really compatible? I mean, I dated Braxton for years before I finally realized it wasn't meant to be."

Mia laughed as she watched me. "Georgia...you knew the second you met Braxton that it wasn't meant to be. Remember? It was written all over the way he was with you. Even when you thought it was good, it wasn't really. He was dismissive, and he lied all the time. You just ignored the little things until it finally smacked you in the face. I mean, I'm not going to deny I think you're definitely taking the untraditional route in life. But something beautiful is happening for you. For both of you." She held her hand over the curling iron and smiled, satisfied it had finally reached the right temperature.

"And don't waste your breath comparing this to you and Braxton. You know better than that. Graham would walk through fire for you. Jerry told you to pay attention to your instincts, right? To listen to your heart? Well...what is it telling you?"

I remembered the amazing feeling when I touched his hand. Front porch sunrises, and warm summer rain. Simple and pure love, bravery and honor.

"That he's my...destiny," I whispered. "I can't believe it, but...that's exactly what I feel."

Mia lifted her chin victoriously and pranced over to grab my hand.

"That's what I thought. Now, we'll need to do your nails!" she continued as she rummaged through the polish colors from my bag.

I peered down at my naked ring finger again. Surprisingly, I felt immense joy as I thought about Graham being the one to replace my commitment ring. Except this time, it would be to commit to him, and him alone. I wasn't worried about what happened to my old ring anymore. Graham's unfailing love somehow overpowered that, and now all I could think about was our honeymoon night...

I still wanted to wait until marriage; it was still so important that I didn't give my body away so quickly, especially after my attack. I hoped that he would be able to wait with me and he would understand. I pictured Graham and the respect he had shown me. He watched me sleep in an uncomfortable chair for God's sake. He was a Marine. He was disciplined. *Focused.* I knew in my heart Mia was right about his intentions. He would protect and honor me through it all. He would love us with everything he had.

And in that moment, I knew if he proposed, I would say yes.

18

SOMETHING NEW, SOMETHING BLUE

Mia had picked a gorgeous blue floral top for the game considering I didn't have any Blues apparel in my luggage. She did the full works on me, not leaving one part of me undone. She curled my hair, did my nails, my makeup, and helped me into those gorgeous blue shoes that seemed to wink at me, wishing me luck for the night ahead. I peered in the mirror and smiled back at my reflection, straightening my shirt. I laughed to myself as I pictured my dad's disappointed face if he ever saw me wearing anything but a jersey to a hockey game. I didn't care though. Tonight was about Jack and making this night as memorable and exciting as possible for him. Tonight was about...our future together.

I looked down at the blue sparkly Toms on my feet and could barely contain the excitement bubbling in my chest. I didn't want to think I was jumping feet-first into love so blindly. Deep down, I had a stronger feeling that the joy I felt, the raw excitement that burst through me, was what it felt like to listen to God's plan. In my heart I knew that Jack and Graham were my purpose. My *destiny*. And I hoped to God above that I wasn't just another dumb girl jumping too fast into forever.

While we were waiting for the boys to come get us, I called my parents to update them about everything—to an extent. I told them we were heading to the Blues game tonight with a bunch of Marines. I kindly left any details out about fostering a child—and maybe getting proposed to—out of the discussion.

"Georgia, I was getting so worried, honey. I'm so glad you called, and it's

192

good to hear you're having fun. I just wanted to make sure my baby girl was safe." She let out a long, drawn-out sigh. "Well, how have you been feeling? Has the detective found any leads with your case? Have they found him yet?"

Big fat unfortunate nope.

"No. I haven't heard from her since my interview with her at the hospital. I'm going to see her soon, though. In fact, I have plans to go see her tomorrow." Given that we had tickets to the game tonight, we decided we would make the journey to headquarters in the morning. Hopefully, Scar had learned more about my case since we last spoke. Even though I felt safe with Graham, something in the pit of my stomach remained unsettled, knowing *he* was out there still.

A knock rapped on the door, and I tiptoed over toward it, making it a point to peek in through the peephole. I had sworn to myself after my attack, I would never, *ever* open the door without checking who it was first. Jack, Graham, and the rest of the boys stood huddled together. My heart swelled as I caught Jack's brilliant smile underneath his Blues hat. He was swimming in his jersey, but he was so ridiculously adorable.

And then my gaze fell on Graham. He was so handsome it hurt. He was just so damn hot, and his jaw was still rugged from this morning's stubble. He had a nervous way about him as the rest of the guys crowded around him and Jack. I chuckled to myself as I nodded. *You better be nervous, Graham Keaton. Because I'm* terrified.

"Mom, Dad. I promise, I am safe, and I'm *so* grateful for everything you did for me. But the guys are here to pick us up. Is it okay if I call you tomorrow? A lot has happened...and I need to tell you about...everything."

A long bout of silence followed, and I could practically hear my mom twisting and turning as if she were fighting to say something.

"Okay, Georgia. *Please* be careful out there. Your dad and I love you so much, we just want you safe, okay?" I nodded like she could see me.

"Yes, ma'am. I love you too. I'll talk to you tomorrow, okay?"

"You better. Bye, baby girl," she crooned before she hung up.

I turned toward Mia and shot her the thumbs-up before I gripped the doorknob. As I pulled it open, I grinned at the eight handsome men standing before me. I felt Mia come up behind me, and all of their faces froze as they surveyed us.

"Damn, ladies," Tex drawled as he scanned both of us from head to toe.

My heart fluttered as I caught Graham staring at me hungrily. I felt color rushing to my cheeks as his eyes dipped to my lips. They paused briefly at my neckline before they skirted downward. His jaw tightened as he swallowed, before Jack's sweet voice broke our focus.

"All right, you look good, we look good. We all look good. Can we go now?" Jack asked, peering up at us impatiently.

Our hotel wasn't too far away from the stadium, so we ended up just walking. The snow had kept itself at bay, and we crunched our way through the sidewalk. The streets were lined with fans all dressed in blue as they all filtered in toward the ice rink. The house was packed, and I loved watching Jack's expression as he took the experience in. His eyes were wide with excitement, and everything was new and interesting to him, a permanent smile plastered on his face as we entered the main lobby. Graham kept his hand on my lower back, claiming me, as he led us through the crowd.

"How about we get to our seats, and I'll order you some food," I called through the noise toward Jack. His face lit up even more, and by God, I was going to make it my mission to put some meat on his bones. Even within the last day, I felt like he was looking healthier. His skin seemed more even toned, and his eyes were less sunken in.

We made our way into the ice rink as loud music filtered through, lights pulsating with the beat. I gasped as my eyes fell on the crowd. Hundreds of bright orbs lined the stadium seating. Maybe even thousands of them glinted at us in the mix of disco lights and music.

"Do...you see them?" I whispered to Graham and Jack as I scanned the packed arena.

"Yeah...they're all silver. None of them are gold, like in the training. Does that mean that none of them can be...*paved* tonight?" Graham responded as he took in the sight. I shrugged at them, my mouth drying as I thought about trying to tend to *all* those orbs tonight.

"I guess so," I sighed as I continued to pan the rink.

Ice seemed to freeze in my veins as my eyes settled on a man a few rows back. Unwelcome painful memories surged through me, and the music seemed to muffle and dull into background noise.

It was Braxton.

"Georgia?" Graham's gentle but concerned voice pulled my focus toward him, his hand pressing farther into my back. "What's wrong?" His gray gaze flicked toward the direction I was just staring at.

"Um, nothing. Let's go find our seats," I mumbled, pulling him in the opposite direction and praying that we weren't sitting near him.

I could feel Graham's body tense as I dragged him the other way, but I was grateful he kept his thoughts to himself as we navigated through the arena. Thankfully, our seats were several sections away and had an excellent view of the rink, as the Zamboni prepared the ice for the game. Jack stared in awe as it made its rounds, while Tex kept trying to start the Wave with the people behind him. At this angle, I couldn't see Braxton. All I could see were my family and friends enjoying the sights. I peeked down at my phone.

It was 7:20 p.m. I had twenty-seven minutes to talk to Graham. To make sure we were on the same page before he asked me to be Mrs. Graham Keaton. Another wave of excitement coursed through me as I caught sight of his smile. So carefree, and in the moment.

I leaned toward Graham and shivered as his body heat radiated off him. He leaned in too, sensing I had something to say, and his nose brushed against my neck, sparking a line of fire that blazed all the way down my chest to my belly.

"Will you come with me to get some food for the crew?" I pulled away to see if he'd heard me.

Something about his expression made me want to crumble under that sultry-sexy gaze. If he kept looking at me like that, I was going to need to throw myself on the ice and let the players volley me around to knock some sense into me. Finally, he nodded and stood up, pulling me to my feet.

"Yeah, let's go," he said and leaned over toward the rest of the crew to announce we were going to get some food. After collecting their orders, we headed off toward the concession stands. Once we got in line, which appeared to be a mile long, he leaned toward me again, lowering his voice to a whisper.

"You look beautiful tonight," he said with an appreciative, sweeping glance. A smile crept across my face before I returned the gesture.

"Thank you, Graham. Might I say you look very handsome as well." My God, that was an understatement. The way his jersey was gripping at his muscles and the way his hair was swept back into a perfect mess made it hard to breathe around him. The other women in the lobby seemed to agree with me, as gaggles of them sent him not-so-subtle glances. He didn't seem to notice, though, as his brows drew together, his soft gray gaze boring into me.

"Hey, you okay? You seem...I don't know. You seem...like you have something on your mind."

I drew back in surprise. He was so observant and watchful. He always seemed to be taking in everything around him, almost like a silent inventory of his environment.

"Um, I do want to talk to you about something...but maybe I could talk to you somewhere a little more...private?" I looked around at all the energetic fans.

"Is it about...us?" He tilted his head playfully, a wide grin crossing his face that shot fireworks through me.

I nodded up at him, trying not to melt into a puddle at his feet.

"Good. I've been wanting to talk about us too," he said as he stuffed his hands in his pockets, his eyes slowly falling to my lips again.

It took everything in me not to peek at his pockets. Did...he have the ring in there?

"Can I take your order?" a woman behind the counter called, tearing my focus to her. Her eyes darted between us before her mouth curved up into a knowing smile.

"Do you need a few minutes to think about it?"

I shook my head, almost violently, before I ordered a round of drinks, popcorn, and hot dogs for everyone. After half the order came out and I paid, I left Graham to get the second half and toted myself over to the condiment stand. I carefully placed all the food on the stand and checked the clock on the wall. It was now 7:37.

Ten more minutes.

I swallowed as I glanced over at Graham. He was laughing as the girl behind the counter stacked a few bags of popcorn on a makeshift tray. God, he was so...

"Georgia?" a familiar voice called behind me.

I screwed my eyes shut.

Braxton.

Your timing is perfect, as always. I slowly turned toward the voice, but to my surprise, an unfamiliar man stood before me, his eyebrows raised in surprise. His neatly cut jet-black hair was styled handsomely, as his piercing brown eyes darted from me to the bountiful feast before me.

"Um...hi." I trailed off, trying to jog my memory. Why was he so *familiar?*

He stared for a few more moments in expectant silence. I tucked my hair behind my ear and shook my head embarrassed.

"I'm so sorry...um...who are you?" I stuttered, as I studied his features.

His brows furrowed, and his mouth drooped to an unsettling frown as he regarded me like I had grown a third head.

"I'm uh...your boss. Kurt. Kurt Robinson?" He made his name a question, as if he were hoping I would recognize it. Unfortunately for me, I didn't, and I began to pray that I could maybe have the vanishing Aftereffect instead.

"Human Resources let me know that you'd be out for the next few weeks from a scary hospital stay." He studied me speculatively. "I figured with the length of time you'd be out, that it was pretty bad..."

I stared at him, openmouthed, as I racked my brain for any memories I had of him. Nothing. Color shot across my cheeks as I considered how terrible all of this looked. Here I was, completely healthy-looking, at a hockey game, with a hundred bajillion hot dogs in front of me, when I had notified my work I was bedridden in the hospital.

A stunningly handsome smile brightened his features as he let out a hearty laugh.

"Looks like you've got your healthy appetite back," he said as he scanned the rows of hot dogs and popcorn sitting in front of me. My cheeks deepened to a scarlet shade as I shook my head. *Oh, God, please kill me now.*

"Kurt, right?" I muttered, rubbing my sweaty hands against my jeans. His eyes followed my nervous movements before he squinted back up at me, raising his hands up in surrender.

"Hey, Georgia, you don't have to give me any details about your medical leave. I just...saw you and thought I'd say hi. We were all worried for you at work, so I'm glad to see you're doing better. I'll uh...let you get back to the game, and I'll just see you after the holidays, okay?" he said as he reached his hand out to me. I stared at it for a second before I realized he expected me to shake it. Because that's what professional people do.

Oh, right.

I shot him a weak smile as I reached out to shake it. As his fingers wrapped around mine, the familiar black fog surrounded me. Suddenly, I was somewhere peaceful, tranquil. Brilliant light shone all around me before I realized I was standing in the middle of one of the most gorgeous gardens I'd ever seen. Various types of flowers of every color on the spectrum surrounded me. A babbling brook sounded over in the corner from a nearby pool as birds played, splashing and drinking from the cool fountain. A colorful array of vegetables was gathered in baskets on the ground. I jumped as I spotted Kurt kneeling near a tomato plant, picking the red juicy ones from the vine.

"This one looks perfect!" he announced with pride as he held up a particularly large one and placed it in a basket. He was so gentle with each tomato, as if they were small helpless babies.

"This will be great for the sauce tonight," he muttered to himself.

He proceeded to hum as he brushed his fingers against all the green and yellow ones with reverence. It was as if he were trying to encourage them to grow. Peace and serenity filled me before a loud voice shouted in my ear, pulling me from the vision.

"Georgia, you okay?" Graham was right next to me, his hands gripping my upper arms. I blinked up at him and peered over his shoulder. Kurt was frowning with a bewildered look in his eye as he strained to see if I was okay.

"Y...yeah, why? What happened?" I muttered, as I pulled away from Graham, noticing onlookers and fans staring at me. So much for not being the center of attention...again.

"She looked like she was spazzing out or something," Kurt urged, his frantic eyes trained on me. Graham grabbed the sides of my face, forcing me to look at him and only him.

"You sure you're okay?" His tone was demanding as he searched my eyes.

I nodded as the peace from my vision with Kurt settled over me and calmed me.

"I had a... vision," I whispered up at him, and relief washed over his face.

His jaw clenched before he pulled me into his chest. The thrum of his heart slammed against my face, and I saw Kurt slowly turn away and start walking in the opposite direction. God, this was a complete and total train wreck of an encounter with my boss. I needed to make it right...and try to explain myself. I sucked in a big breath and pulled away from Graham.

"Uh, Kurt! Wait!"

He swiftly turned back toward me, his face pulled into an uncomfortable grimace.

"Kurt, I'm so sorry about how strange I'm being. I'm recovering from a...concussion, and I have some memory loss. Sometimes I get these...dizzy spells." I looked back up at him and almost giggled from the faint memory of him talking to his vegetables in my vision. So deliciously nerdy. He shifted his weight uneasily as he sensed I had something more to say.

"Anyway, I know this is random...but do you like gardening?" I wanted to plant the seed, for lack of better words, like I had at the coffee shop. If he hadn't pursued his passion yet, I was going to make sure it was at least mentioned. Maybe he just needed a little nudge. His eyebrows arched up with intrigue before a slight smile curved at the corner of his mouth.

"It seems you might have a little bit of memory coming back. Yes, I love gardening. I started the gardening club at work, remember?" he laughed, his brown eyes sparkling.

"I guess so..." I said with a grateful shrug. Kurt lifted his gaze over where Graham was standing. His grin faded as if he suddenly remembered that this was still incredibly awkward.

"Well, I'm going to head back to my seat. Good to see you, and hope you feel better." He flashed me another professionally guarded grin and disappeared among a throng of Blues fans.

Thank God he left when he did, because I was seconds away from spouting off random facts about cocoa plants.

"Who was that?" Graham asked behind me, his eyes still trailing the place where Kurt disappeared. I giggled, his cold gray eyes shifting toward me before they softened.

"Are you...jealous, perhaps?" I teased as I grabbed a tray of drinks and a few bags of popcorn still sitting on the condiment stand. He watched me in unnerving silence for a few moments before he grabbed the hot dogs and a tray of drinks.

"I don't know...he just seemed...*off*," he said as he narrowed his eyes in his direction.

I laughed as I replayed the most awkward encounter ever in my head. Not one single part of that interaction made me feel like he was the "off" one. It was most definitely the other way around. I turned to tell him just that, before an eerie feeling overcame me, like someone was watching again.

"Do you feel that?" I asked slowly as I scanned the buzzing hallway filled with excited fans. Suddenly, I caught sight of a bright light surrounding a woman walking briskly toward the women's restroom.

"Graham, do you see that?" I whispered while the light danced around her in electrifying golden waves. I gasped as my gaze caught on the wall hanging just near the bathroom. 7:46 p.m. Graham didn't seem to care as he dug his hands in his pockets. My eyes frantically darted from him to the bathroom entrance where she disappeared. Damn it all to hell!

I turned back toward Graham, taking him in from head to toe, hoping I could etch this into my brain as the moment I chose another's destiny over my own. I turned on my heel, unable to look Graham in the eye as I walked away from him. Away from the man I was falling in love with.

I glided off toward the bathroom, and just before I went in, I peeked back at him. He was watching me, his jaw tight, his eyes made of steel. His hands...still stuffed into his pockets, surely clinging to the ring.

With one last look, I rounded the corner as Graham disappeared behind the wall.

19

RINGS OF FIRE

The bathroom was busy, and most of the stalls were in use. I scanned the small space, but she was nowhere to be seen. A stall opened up toward the back, and something inside me told me to take it. I made my way across the bathroom and snuck into the stall, locking the latch behind me. Soft muffled sobs and sniffles sounded to my right, and the bright light from the orb filtered from underneath the tall walls.

"Hey...are you okay?" I urged, pressing my hands against the stall.

I could feel her energy clam up, but the light grew stronger, flooding into the small space, almost like it was encouraging me to continue.

"Yeah... I'm just..." Another round of sobs echoed against the walls, and my heart broke for her. These sobs were deep-hurt cries. The kind you would expect from someone who just lost someone or found out something devastating.

"Hey, it's okay. Whatever it is, I've heard it all." I shrugged with my lie. *No, ma'am. I haven't heard it all, because I never talk to people. I never ask how strangers are doing in bathrooms, and I rarely have conversations to begin with, so God help me.*

"I'm just frustrated with my boyfriend. We've been together for what feels like forever. Tomorrow is our anniversary, and it's like he just doesn't care to take the next step." She let out another brazen sob that racked the small space with echoes.

"Have you ever told him how you feel? Does he know you want to get married?" I asked hopefully. I could hear her feet tap on the floor like she was in deep thought.

"I mean... I've left hints and stuff. Like pictures of rings in his room, and

I've left my Pinterest page up of my wedding board. Don't you think that should be enough?" Her voice lifted at the end, like she was praying that she wasn't losing her mind. I frowned at that notion. To a woman, I could see how this wasn't just a hint but a very clear message. Leaving a picture of a ring might as well be a smack upside the head. But to a man... Well, I wish I knew what went on in a man's head. Life would be so much easier if I knew.

"And the worst part is..." She trailed off, and I could tell she was holding back a string of cries. "The worst part is I found out I was pregnant last week," she sniffled, her voice shaking nervously. My heart skipped a beat with her news, and I didn't even know her.

"Oh, that's amazing! Congratulations!" I tried to ease her mind, but I could only imagine the fears and worries she had. I of all people could relate to a thing or two about immediate life changes. A soft laugh broke free in the midst of all the crying.

"Thanks, I'm actually really excited," she said, a smile in her voice. "I'm not scared that I'm pregnant. I'm just...scared to tell him because I feel like it will pressure him into marrying me. I want him to ask me on his own time, you know? I mean...he's clearly not asking me because he's just not ready yet." She broke down into another string of inconsolable sobs. The orb grew brighter, begging for me to read it. No matter what she was going through, she still had a purpose to fulfill. I let out a breath and closed my eyes. I slowed my breathing to an even pace and put all of my energy into focusing on her, and her alone.

A beautiful wedding ring filled every thought. Images of it sliding onto her finger and glinting off the light from above consumed me along with the joy and courage that came from choosing to marry someone. The concrete word "Yes" materialized in front of my very own eyes, etching into my brain and setting it on fire.

She *needs to say yes.*

Realization hit me and I came right back to the present, as I stood alone in the stall. Graham was never going to propose to me. Deep disappointment flooded through me. How stupid could I be? I had convinced myself that I was going to be Mrs. Graham Keaton...after only knowing him for just a few days. By far one of the most irrational ideas I'd arrived at in my entire life.

Shame and humiliation coursed through me, and for a moment, I thought about crawling under the stall wall and crying with the mystery woman.

"Hey...are you still there?" she sniffled. "I'm sorry that I threw all of this on you. I mean...you don't even know who I am, and I just..."

"Yes!" I called over to her as I fought back a sob. "Is your...boyfriend here with you tonight?" I asked, trying to gather my wits.

"Yes," she confirmed with a hint of skepticism.

"Good. Okay, this is going to sound weird, but I think that you should go back and enjoy the evening. I have a feeling that your boyfriend will...ask you something very important before the night is through." I prayed that I wasn't reading this wrong. I didn't want to add lying to a pregnant woman crying in the bathroom all alone to the list of things I'd stupidly done tonight.

"Why do you think that all of a sudden?" Her voice was lingering on the I-think-you're-crazy side as I heard her stand up.

"I know you don't know me, but just...trust me, okay?" I encouraged nervously. I heard her stall latch unlock and her door creak open.

"Can I hug you?" she called as she shuffled toward me.

I held back another sob as a pair of blue sparkly shoes appeared in front of my stall. I felt my heart constrict in my chest as the truth settled over me. *Twist that knife, why don't you?*

"Um...I'm actually gonna be in here for a while. I don't feel well," I replied as I sat down on the toilet, clenching my stomach. I watched the light of her orb dance across her shoes mockingly.

"Are you sure? I mean, do you need anything?" she asked, her nurturing motherly spirit already shining strong. *Yes...give me a swift kick in the head so I can get some sense knocked into me.*

"No, I'm fine, but you're gonna be a great mom. I can feel it." I remembered Jerry's words about how sometimes a purpose can be to receive a gift just like the man had received the gift of kindness from the woman in the diner. Her purpose tonight was to be promised to, and to accept the proposal. To receive the gift of unconditional love. I watched her rock back and forth on her heels before her sparkly shoes disappeared. I waited a few more minutes in the stall before I came out and washed my hands. I peered back up at my reflection. My makeup and hair were still perfect. And I tried to remember the good things.

I was alive. I had helped someone else, even if it wasn't me that was getting promised to tonight. I had a small army of friends out there waiting for me. Tonight wasn't ruined...it was still just beginning.

Go and have fun, Georgia. Just go and enjoy the night with your friends. Your family. *If it's meant to be...then it will happen.* My heart sank as I thought about the mystery woman's situation. She had been with her boyfriend for far too long. What if Graham took that long to ask me? Could I wait like her? Especially if I wanted to maintain my vow to wait until marriage. *That is if Graham even agrees to wait with me...*

I let out a sigh as I wiped away a tear and pulled my shoulders back. Once I left the bathroom, I caught sight of Jack, Tex, and Andrews near a table next to the concession stands. But Graham was nowhere to be seen. And I hated how I was grateful about that. I waved at them before my eyes landed on Mia. Her expression was tight and stressed, like she didn't want me to see something. I cocked my head at her and shrugged. I started to head toward her, but before I took another step, I felt a light hand on my shoulder.

"Georgia?"

I turned to find a familiar face from college staring at me with a slight frown adorning her pretty face. I didn't quite recognize her until I saw Braxton's sheepish silhouette behind her. A brilliant orb shone above him too, something that I hadn't noticed before in the stadium. To my surprise, Graham was standing next to Braxton, in mid-conversation. My heart sank as I realized he was helping him. He was *Paving* for Braxton.

"Georgia Scott?" she repeated, her hazel eyes boring into me.

Recognition plagued me as a pang of hurt rushed through my chest. Her name was Grace Sparrow, and she'd lived down the hall from me in college. When Braxton wasn't with me, he was with *her*. Heat colored my cheeks as I gave her a quick once-over. She was stunning. Gorgeous and glowing with chestnut hair that fell down her back and a freaking adorable dimple in her cheek. She wasn't just wearing but *rocking* a Blues jersey, and to my horror, the most adorable sparkly Toms adorned her feet. The sparkles continued to dance against the light from the orb that surrounded her. The orb I had just tended to in the bathroom. Of course it was still surrounding her; she hadn't said yes yet. She hadn't said yes to *Braxton's* proposal.

"Were you the girl in the stall? That helped me?" she demanded.

My heart thudded against my chest as my eyes flitted over to Braxton. He was glaring at me. Graham was watching me too, sensing I was uncomfortable. I quickly turned back toward Grace, whose eyes had started to water. I started to shake my head, wishing I could turn around and lock myself back into my stall away from all of this.

"Thank you," she whispered, as a soft smile met her lips and traveled up to her sweet eyes. A gasp escaped me as she pulled me into a tight embrace, nearly knocking all the air out of my chest. I trailed my eyes back up to Braxton, who was still scowling at me. As if I had ruined *his* night. I started to hate Braxton all over again, not for what he did to me, or the way he was looking at me, but for dragging his feet while his goddess girlfriend and mother of his child waited around. But not for long, because apparently he was going to ask her to marry him tonight.

"Don't mention it, Grace," I whispered back, dropping my gaze, avoiding Braxton's glare.

She pulled back, and a quiet stream of tears ran down her face, which she wiped away before he caught sight of them.

"What have you been up to? I haven't seen you since college…" she pressed, still grasping at my shoulder like we were best friends.

I wanted to cringe at how friendly she was being. But I had never really considered that perhaps Grace didn't know she was also being cheated on. Maybe Braxton made her feel like she was the only one too.

"I mean…given with everything that happened with Brax, I know that it was awkward, but we're all adults now, right?"

Oh, I guess she did know…

"How do you know these guys, Georgia?" Graham interjected. Braxton and Grace both turned their attention toward him as he wrapped his arm around my waist. Braxton's scowl deepened as I leaned into him.

"Graham, this is Grace Sparrow and… Braxton Keller. They're…*friends* from college," I stammered, doing my best to keep it light with the "friends" part. Graham's face broke out into a welcome smile, his eyes crinkling at the corners as he extended his hand out to Grace.

"Ah, it's a pleasure, although I'm sorry to say I haven't heard much about you. I'm Graham, Georgia's boyfriend." I was sure my face turned another shade of pink as I focused on Graham's vocabulary choice. My *boyfriend*.

Though I wished it were my *fiancé*.

"I was just talking with Braxton about some of the goals we've been winning tonight," he said with a meaningful grin. He clapped him on his back, visibly knocking his breath out of his chest.

I winced as I caught his expression. It was a mix of pain and discomfort, but I wasn't sure if it was from the awkwardness or Graham's grip on his shoulder. I tried to hold back a laugh as I realized it was probably a little of both.

"You went to college?" Jack's sweet voice piped up behind me.

I turned to find him snacking on a bag of popcorn as he eyed Braxton and Grace curiously. I nodded at him with a wide smile. He looked like he was having the time of his life. His cheeks were flushed from probably yelling from the stands, and his hat was twisted backward with a thousand percent attitude.

"Oh my *God*, you are adorable. What is *your* name?" Grace asked as she leaned down toward Jack in awe.

He popped another piece of popcorn in his mouth and shot her a lady-killer grin.

"The name's Jack, sweetheart. I'm Georgia's son," he said, shooting her a playful wink that had me rolling. My heart did a thousand and one somersaults as I heard those words come from his mouth. *He's my* son. *Kid, I think I'll keep you.*

I turned back toward them proudly but was quickly set off by Braxton's worried expression. It looked like he was doing the painful math to see if Jack was *his*. I couldn't help but roll my eyes, considering we only broke up a few years ago.

"I'm her foster kid," Jack said with a frown as it seemed he caught Braxton's cringeworthy expression too. I died a little inside from his tone but decided that was a conversation for another day.

"Seems like it's going to be a big night tonight," Graham interjected as he winked over at Braxton. He quickly turned a deep shade of red but then straightened up quickly, shaking off his comment. He knew that she had a proposal coming, and he knew she was to accept the question. Grace's smile widened, her eyes sparkling over at me now.

"Yeah, the Blues are going hard tonight. I think we'll see a big win," she giggled excitedly.

"Yup, the future looks bright...and sparkly," Jack chimed in with a knowing grin. Braxton jumped at his words and reached for Grace's arm, pulling her toward him.

"Georgia, glad to see you're doing well," he mumbled as he threw an arm around Grace's shoulder.

"You too," I said as I lifted my chin confidently.

"I think we're going to go back to our seats now, though. It was...good seeing you."

"Bye, Georgia! By the way, I *love* your shoes!" Grace lifted her hand and waved goodbye as they turned. *Just punch me right in the heart, why don't you?*

Her orb light caught something reflective around her wrist. I gasped as I realized it was the same bracelet that Braxton had tried to give me. Right after he'd begged for forgiveness at my feet. The same one, with both of our initials on it. Sudden emotion shot through me. To my surprise, it wasn't a feeling of hurt, or jealousy, but a peaceful sense of joy. Complete happiness for the both of them and hope that they had found love together. They had managed to stick it out with each other this long, and they were going to have a child together. They were going to get *married.* He was never supposed to be with me. He was always supposed to be with Grace.

Despite his clear discomfort with me, he looked so completely happy with her. The way his arm wrapped around her waist lovingly as they headed back toward their seats. It appeared she was so deeply in love with him too. She craved a future with him, and they were destined for each other. They were each other's purpose.

I felt Graham's loving arm wrap around my own waist. He turned me back toward the table in the distance where the brotherhood and Mia all sat, waving. Mia's face was solemn as we approached, but I shot her a reassuring grin. Immediately, she perked up and threw her arm around my shoulder. Graham's arm remained around my waist, and another concrete realization hit me. Braxton and Grace were meant to be. But Graham, Jack, the brotherhood, and Mia. They were undoubtedly *my* destiny.

208

After the Blues got in an epic win with five goals to one, we watched Braxton's beautiful proposal on the stadium screen. She of course said yes, and the stadium roared as their fulfilled purpose flashed and fizzled with the blaring music. After the game, we headed back to our hotel suite. Mia was dying to ask what happened with Braxton, but she kept her questions to herself. She knew I would tell her when we had some time alone.

Once we got back to the suite, the boys and Mia asked if they could teach Jack how to play poker.

"I already know how to play," Jack replied unimpressed as we all stared at him with wide eyes.

"Well damn, kid. Why don't you teach *us* something, then?" Tex teased as he crossed his arms with a smirk. Jack's eyes lit up, and his mouth turned up into a mischievous grin.

"Okay, but don't say I didn't warn you." He shrugged as he slipped out into the hallway. We all stared at the door he just disappeared from before Mia hopped up and ran after him.

"Come on, guys. I don't know what he's about to teach us, but I know I need to learn it. Let's go!"

Graham and I watched as Mia and the boys chased after Jack. We couldn't help but laugh as Tex wagged a finger over at us.

"No, no, no. You two stay. We'll take care of Keaton Jr., but you two be good, okay?" Tex chided before he shut the door.

Silence fell in the room. The same room we were alone in, except for all the beds that surrounded us. Comfortable, cozy beds, and Graham. I suddenly felt self-conscious again, defaulting to running my fingers over my naked ring finger.

"Do you want me to open the door?" Graham asked as he moved toward it, sensing I felt a little anxious. I felt a laugh bubble in my throat, but it came out as a nervous, jumbled gargle. I cringed as I watched Graham draw back with a deep look of concern. *God, Georgia, please be less awkward.*

"Here, I'll just—"

"No, I'm fine. Sorry... I just have a lot going on in my head." I shrugged as I slumped on the bed, my hands hitting my knees. Graham's eyes flashed from my face to my ring finger I was just twisting, his frown deepening.

"Stop me if I'm wrong, okay?" he asked as he leaned against the wall.

"You ran into...an ex and his now fiancé? But it wasn't an amicable breakup I'm guessing?"

I nodded slowly in surprise. I loved and hated how he was so observant.

"Were you...engaged to him before?" he asked calmly, his eyes dropping to my ring finger again.

I gasped at the thought, before I shook my head with disdain.

"No, we were just dating, until...he cheated on me with...Grace."

His gray eyes softened as he blew out a long breath.

"That must have been hard to see them together," he said as he moved over to sit next to me. I stilled as his heat crept over me, and I slowly turned to look at him, my heart beating faster as his hand innocently brushed against mine.

"Honestly, it wasn't that bad. I mean, sure it was awkward, but it actually helped bring me peace. I'm glad that they're happy together." I was pleased to say that was the God-honest truth.

"So...can I ask what the ring was?" he asked as he pointed at my left hand.

Well, I guess now is a good a time as any to tell the man you're fostering a child with that you're waiting until marriage.

"It was a...commitment ring. Not to Braxton, but to myself. After he cheated on me, I vowed that I would wait until I found someone that cared about my soul. I vowed I would wait to have sex...until marriage." Blood rushed up to my cheeks , and I bit my lip. I peeked down at my hand again, which was temptingly close to his.

"So...you're a virgin?" His question was so simple, unjudging. He knew I had been raped, yet he was asking if I was a virgin. I raised my eyebrows at him as I shook my head.

"Well...no. Braxton and I were together...and..." I nervously peered up at him and was startled by his darkened gaze.

"Georgia, if you're thinking for a second that what happened when you got attacked counts, then you are gravely mistaken. That will *never* count." He turned toward me, his calloused, hard working hand wrapping around mine. The soft scent of warm summer rain filled the room, and romantic front porch sunsets filled my mind.

"Tell me you know that," he commanded, his voice straining like it was the most important thing in the world.

I dropped my eyes from him and finally nodded.

"You know you're safe with me, right? You can tell me anything."

I laughed and shook my head. "Graham, I trust you very much. Otherwise, I would never have agreed to foster a kid with you. I just need to understand what's going on between us. Tonight, you said you were my boyfriend..."

"Was it okay that I said that?" He squeezed my hands tighter, his warmth shooting up my arms with an electrical zing.

I dropped my eyes to my lap and tried to hold back a nervous smile.

"You know, I have a list of requirements that must be met before we can move any further."

I felt him perk up as he leaned forward. He gently put a finger under my chin and lifted it so I could meet his gaze again.

"What are your requirements?" His eyes lit up, but he remained calm, intrigued.

You, Graham Keaton. You're my requirements. I hopped off the bed and paced back and forth in front of him nervously.

"Well, for starters, I need a man that cares about people, like truly cares. Someone who can let me be myself, no matter how awkward I am. Someone who's great with kids, can help me solve problems, and stay with me through the hard stuff, and maybe someone who can cook." I bantered off each item as I marked them with my fingers. I paused briefly to see if he hadn't left the room yet, but he had remained firmly planted on the bed, watching me intently, perhaps even amused.

"Go on, I'm listening," he ushered as he scooted backward, pushing himself against the headboard of the bed.

"Okay... Um, well, I need someone who can remain faithful—that's a biggie. Someone that will...wait to have...sex until we're married." My heart sunk as I caught his solemn expression.

"I'm afraid that's not going to work out, then," he said casually. "The only thing I can cook is a bachelor's soup."

I held back a laugh as the knotting in my stomach settled.

"A bachelor's soup?" I repeated.

"Yeah...pretty much any leftovers that Davis made...and you just mix it up into a soup," he said as his eyes danced over me.

I laughed and tucked my hair behind my ear.

"That actually sounds really good," I said as I climbed back onto the bed, joining him against the headboard. His eyes flicked downward toward my mouth before they slowly, regretfully lifted back upward. I cleared my throat and pulled my knees to my chest, suddenly feeling vulnerable.

"Not that it's any of my business, but have you ever been in a relationship?" I asked curiously. He studied me before shaking his head.

"No. I went right into the military when I turned eighteen, and I've been on tour for most of my twenties. I never really had time to date, you know?" He shifted closer to me. "And I don't know if this will make you feel any better, but...I'm a virgin."

I stared at him, my eyes dropping from his sculpted jaw, right down to his rock-hard body. "But, *why?*" I demanded before I could stop myself. He had been so calm and collected as I explained my sexual history, and here I was being Judgy McJudgerson to his. I bit my lip in horror as he let out a laugh.

"Guess I never found the right one," he replied with a casual shrug.

He peered over at me, his eyes dropping to my lips again, his jaw clenching like he was fighting to say something before he finally gave in to himself.

"Georgia Scott, I want you to listen very carefully. The way you are with Jack, and how my brothers have fallen in love with you and Mia, it's unreal. It has to mean something that you and I were paired together in literal heaven. God knows you're beautiful and..." His eyes dropped to my mouth again, and he leaned in closer. Too close.

Not close enough.

"And the way you're biting your lip like that makes me want you in every way I shouldn't, especially from what you just told me." I immediately released my lip from my teeth and swallowed, as my body tensed with need...and fear. I could feel my heart hammer against my chest as it rose and fell. His gray eyes became steel as he watched me react to him. He slowly grazed his fingers against my throat gently, reassuring me.

"What happened to you...what he did to you. I want to take it away. I've wanted to take it away since Jerry told me about it. I've wanted to show you how a real man loves a woman, and how a woman should feel treasured and adored, and safe in a man's arms. So, I'm going to kiss you now, unless you tell me no loud and clear. Do you understand?"

His gray eyes glowed with a burning fire that I wanted to swallow me whole. Something deep inside me lurched at his words, as warmth spread to every region of my body. How the hell could I say no to that? The only thing I could manage to do was nod before he cupped his hand around the back of my head. He leaned toward me with hungry, hooded eyes and paused briefly, almost painfully, as his eyes scanned my face. He was giving me one more chance to say no. But that word wouldn't come from my mouth. Not to him. Not now. Not...ever. He shook his head in disbelief before his cool breath crashed against my face.

"God you're beautiful."

And before he finished his sentence, his full lips met mine, at first gently and then with an eager, sensual need. His tongue lightly dipped into my mouth, and I gladly parted my lips, letting him in to explore and taste. His movements were firm but gentle all at once, laced with love and patience as he slid his hand down to my waist. A soft whimper escaped my lips, and he quickly responded, pulling me against him, his fingers playing underneath the hem of my shirt. I arched against him, and Graham let out a low moan as his fingers trailed against my neck, his lower body resting just above mine. I could tell he was doing everything he could to not completely devour me whole. I let out a moan, and that was my undoing. Graham growled as he lowered himself onto me and plunged his tongue deep into my mouth, demanding, without reservation. His hips rocked against me as his lips found my throat.

So innocent. So trusting.

His hands explored in a heated frenzy as his tongue worshipped my neck. I froze as his hand slipped upward underneath my shirt and gently cupped my breast.

You know that's not what I came here for, sweetheart.

His hips pushed against me again as the evidence of his arousal pressed into me. To my horror, a terrified cry caught in my chest.

Now be a good girl and let me show you what I really came here for.

His hands wrapped around my wrists, pressing them into the mattress, and panic pulsed through me. The ecstasy quickly transformed into sheer terror as his hand gripped my hip...before I finally let my caged voice free.

"Please, no! Don't hurt me!"

I struggled underneath him, fear constricting me, but he was too strong. Just like *him*. His weight held me down as a sob echoed into the room.

Graham immediately froze above me and pulled away, his wild eyes searching mine.

"Georgia?" he panted, his grip loosening around my wrists. "Did I hurt you?" He pushed himself off me without another word.

Fear and guilt filled his painstakingly handsome face as he watched me shiver uncontrollably.

"Jesus, I'm...so sorry. I shouldn't have..." He threw his hands anxiously through his hair as he watched me, careful not to touch me.

God, this wasn't fair. I wanted Graham so badly. He clearly wanted me...and that *monster* had to creep himself in the middle of all that bliss. All of that *ecstasy*.

"No...Graham, I'm sorry. Y-You didn't hurt me. I just...I don't know..." I shook my head, so embarrassed I couldn't even look at him.

"Georgia, you have no reason to apologize. I should have never gone so hard with you."

I cringed at his words. I hated how fragile I was. *No, Georgia, stop being a victim!*

"I'm so sorry," he repeated as he stood up at the foot of the bed, watching me with pain-filled eyes.

"No, please, I'm fine—"

"I'm...going to give you some space, okay? I'm so, so sorry." And without another word, he slipped into the bathroom and closed the door.

The sound of the water running filtered through the door as sobs rattled through me. *Damn it, Georgia. You found a man who finally makes you feel safe and truly cherished, and you had to go and pull that shit?* That monster wasn't anywhere near here, and yet he was still ruining my life. Tears rolled down my cheeks as I cried into the pillow, wishing I could have been stronger. Wishing I didn't have to ruin one of the best things I'd ever had. Exhaustion rolled through me, and I lifted my tearstained face to check the clock on the end-table.

It was 11:00 p.m. Jack needed to get to bed. I winced as I thought about Graham insisting he sleep on the ground this time. Far away from me. So scared he would hurt me or trigger another flashback. I dragged myself out

214

of the bed and trudged toward the door before I realized I didn't have a key to the hotel suite. Graham had it in his pants pocket. The same pants that were probably sitting on the floor in that bathroom.

Double shit.

Maybe if I just crawl on the ground, he won't see me. I slowly approached the door and pressed my head against it, wondering if I should just wait until Jack came back. No, I was a mom, a full-grown woman. I needed to get Jack to bed, and not even Graham's wet naked body on the other side of the door was going to stop me. I slowly turned the doorknob and inched the door open nervously. I peeked in and caught his handsomely tanned silhouette just barely visible through the foggy shower door. Oh, God, I couldn't believe I freaked. How could I ever recover from this?

I dropped to my hands and knees and tried to shield my eyes from the Adonis bathing to my right as I scouted out his pants crumpled in the corner. I scooted awkwardly, praying he wouldn't find me creepily on the floor while he was showering. It would just make everything about what happened that much worse.

My hands dug into his back pocket, which was empty, before I tried the other back pocket. My fingers wrapped around the plastic card, before I felt something else that was cold, hard, and round. My curiosity got the better of me before I snatched the foreign object out of his pocket.

It was a *ring*.

Insurmountable joy shot through me as I pinched the metal between my fingers. I couldn't believe it! Mia was right. Graham Keaton really was going to propose to me. That warm summer rain, those front porch sunrises...his unconditional love. That would be mine until...

I froze as I caught sight of an inscription inside the silver band, its mocking words cutting a slice right through my heart.

Truth. Love. Honor.

Numbness. Pure and terrifying numbness overcame me as my eyes settled on my commitment ring. The same ring that a monster pried from my finger before he escaped. In Graham Keaton's pocket .

20

GOD'S COUNTRY

"Georgia?"

I yelped with a jump, my back hitting the wall behind me before I caught sight of Graham's face. His brows were drawn together menacingly as steam billowed around him. His steely gaze lowered to the ring in my hand, and his frown deepened, his eyes flashing with something I couldn't read. For a moment, time froze as the photos from my attack flashed before me. His dark, hulking figure rounding the corner to come and ruin me. My blood soaking the hallway leading to my bedroom.

Sometimes sick perps take trophies.

But not Graham. How could it be *Graham*?

"Please..." I pressed myself farther into the wall as he quickly turned the water off and grabbed a towel from the nearby rack.

"Please...don't!" I weakly scrambled to my feet, nearly slipping on the wet tile as I pushed myself toward the door.

"Georgia!" Graham growled as he stepped out of the shower. His hand clawed at my arm, but I narrowly escaped his grip and ran for the hotel door. I could feel him close in on me from behind before I pulled the door open and ran out into the hallway.

I could hardly see as tears welled in my eyes, blurring my vision. I felt like I was running in slow motion; my legs were like lead as I scanned the hallway for anyone to help me.

Damn it, where's Jack and Mia? I flung myself forward, my heart pounding against my chest as I desperately looked for the stairwell. Heavy footfalls sounded behind me, and I veered left into a glass door, praying it was the stairs. I pushed the door open, barely knocking over an elderly woman, who

216

cursed at me as I ran past her. I practically jumped down the flight of stairs, that lead to the hotel lobby, where I hoped to God above that Jack and Mia were waiting. As I pushed the door open again, I spotted Jack's sweet face. His eyes grew wide as he saw me sprint toward him, and he stood up, almost violently. Mia and the brotherhood stood up in alarm as they took in my terrified expression.

"Georgia, what's—"

I cut Mia off as I grabbed her elbow and then Jack's before I pulled them toward the door.

"We have to go!" I panted, not looking back.

Confused shouts and cries sounded behind me from all the men I had trusted. The men who had protected and adored my son, while simultaneously being best friends with my attacker. My *murderer*. We pushed open the front door, and thankfully there were two taxis waiting on the curb next to the entrance. All three of us squeezed into the closest one before I yelled at the driver for dear life.

"Please, drive!" I shouted as my eyes darted back to the front door, praying no one was following us. The driver jumped in alarm, apparently not even noticing we had gotten in his cab. He turned at a glacial pace and stared blankly at me.

"Where are we going?" he asked, clearly not recognizing the urgency of the situation.

I scanned the front door of the hotel, my eyes darting everywhere, hoping Graham or the brotherhood wasn't pursuing us. My heart sank as I saw Tex run out with the rest following close behind. Davis pointed in our direction, and Reed mouthed at me, "What's going on?" I hated leaving them like this, but I wasn't about to explain that their best friend was a murderous rapist. Suddenly, Graham, who was still mostly naked, plowed his way through the huddle. He was clutching a towel that barely covered his lower region, his face crazed with desperation.

"Georgia!" he yelled as he charged his way toward the cab door.

"Just go!" I demanded at the driver before he quickly slammed his foot against the pedal, tailing out for the road. My eyes locked with Graham's and I was taken aback by the way he looked hurt, almost confused. But I should have known better. I should have known to not trust so easily. I watched Graham and his brotherhood disappear as we rounded the corner, and I turned back to face forward, throwing my head into my hands. Why on God's green earth had I thought for a second that I could trust a man I had only known for three days? Who cared if we had this crazy paranormal link that twisted our fates together like some sick joke. And to make things a thousand times worse, I had fallen...hard. For my own attacker.

So innocent. So trusting.

I let out a helpless sob as I thought about Jack. He didn't need all of this drama; he was just getting used to this crazy normal, or whatever this was we were doing for him. I could still feel Graham's tender and loving hands on my body, the way his lips felt against mine. So much for those front porch sunrises. I shuddered away the thought as nausea crept up inside me. Those same hands, that same mouth had tortured me, and had stolen everything from me. But that couldn't be right. Graham's hands were giving, nurturing. He had stopped immediately after I cried out to him. Graham was a protector, a *warrior*. Why would he hurt me the way he did?

"Georgia, for God's sake, what is happening right now? Why was Graham...naked?" Mia demanded as she grabbed my arms shaking me so I would look at her.

I lifted my eyes to her face, and I caught Jack's worried expression behind her as they both stared back at me, dumbfounded. I shakily lifted the ring and held it out for her to see.

"My...r-ring. Graham...h-he had it." I shivered again before she plucked it out of my palm to analyze it.

"He proposed?" Jack asked with an incredulous smile. "Wait, aren't girls supposed to be happy when guys ask them to marry them?"

Mia shushed Jack as she held it up to the light and then handed it back to me forcefully. "Are you sure it's even the same one?"

I swallowed as I slowly slid the ring on, before it landed comfortably at the base of my finger.

"Yes, Mia. I had those words engraved there, and it was in his back pocket," I whispered.

I stared at the ring, disgusted with it and myself. Just days before all of this, I had often twisted it out of habit to keep me grounded. Now, the ring was just a terrible reminder of the things that had happened to me, and the

218

depths of every way I had been betrayed by a man. I quickly tore it off and flung it on the floor of the cab.

"Did he...try anything? I mean...why was he naked?" Mia whispered, dropping her voice so Jack didn't hear. Unfortunately, Jack didn't miss a thing and he grabbed my arm, turning me toward him.

"Did he hurt you?" Jack's eyes darkened as he slowly scanned my face to see if he could mark any bruises. I pulled my lips together in a tight line and turned away from him, looking out as the streetlights flashed by in the night's sky.

"No, nothing like that. He was just taking a shower when I found the ring," I uttered, confusion and hurt suffocating me. I leaned my head against the door, squeezing my eyes shut as tears fell silently down my cheeks.

Mia sighed as she slumped back into her seat, crossing her arms.

"Georgia, this doesn't make any sense. I mean...Graham...he's a good man," Mia said as she seemingly reviewed the last three days in her head. "Do you honestly feel like it was him?"

I shrugged and fell back into the seat with her, feeling completely lost and not knowing what to trust at this point.

"Mia, I don't know... I mean, why would he have the ring in his pocket?"

Mia watched me carefully before she finally frowned with defeat.

"You've got me there, Georgia," she said, shaking her head incredulously. "It just doesn't feel right, though."

Deep down, I agreed with her. Graham and I were alone just moments before, and if he had wanted to finish what he'd started in my apartment, he could easily have done so. But he had made it his mission to make sure I felt safe and comfortable no matter what. He was the one who'd pulled away from me immediately after I'd protested. He listened—he *stopped*. Murderous rapists don't do that.

"So...any idea where we're going yet?" the driver called back to us, keeping his eyes trained on the busy road. God, I had no idea. I'd left all of my luggage back at the hotel, along with Mia and Jack's stuff too.

"We could go to my house? I keep a spare key under my flowerpot," Mia suggested nervously. Instantaneously, a thought crept into my head like it was the most important thing in the world.

Headquarters.

"Take us to 1000 Golden Path Road in O'Fallon, please," I replied calmly to the driver, shooting Mia a reassuring glance.

Mia's eyes filled with worry, but she nodded silently back at me in surrender. I could hear the driver mumble something about how that place doesn't exist, but he seemed satisfied after he typed the address in his GPS.

"Never been there before, so you might have to guide me. The GPS looks like it's leading us into an open field," he said with a shrug.

"No worries, I know how to get there," I said confidently, but it didn't feel like my own words. It almost felt like someone was speaking through me, leading the way. Pale blue eyes seemed to still-frame their way through my thoughts, and suddenly I felt at peace. Jerry was with me, guiding me and keeping me safe.

"So, hold on, Georgia, I don't get it. Superman gave you a ring, but he didn't propose?" Jack asked, his face blank with confusion.

Mia's eyes shot open and watched me nervously, as if she too were waiting for how I would explain all of this. All I could manage to do was shake my head silently and hope that he would take the hint. I wasn't ready to talk about this, because I was still trying to explain this to myself.

"Then what's the problem, Georgia?" Jack's tone was strained, as if he were holding himself back from throwing an all-out fit.

I couldn't blame him, because I was doing the same thing. It was so hard to be strong in front of kids when you felt just as lost as they did. But that's what parenting is. You've got to fake it until you make it, for *them*. I let my silence become his answer, though it wasn't the one he wanted as he let out an aggravated huff and turned toward his own window. We drove the rest of the way in complete silence, despite the fact that each of us was drowning in our own questions and worries. Jack knew what a liar sounded like before they even opened their mouth. Growing up and having to fend for yourself your entire childhood does that to a person. I wouldn't be able to hold him off much longer from the truth, and he didn't deserve that anyway. But for now, this was the only way I knew how to handle this. It was just me, him, and Mia now. I had a job to do, and I was going to protect him for as long as I could.

We traveled through a wide stretch of land, and even in the dead of night, I could tell that there were miles upon miles of rolling fields and plains. We were in God's country now. The stars above were shining so brightly that the streetlights had disappeared. Almost like they were reminding me that whatever was going on in my life, something could still light up the dark. We wound through miles of curvy roads until we turned down a gravel path. After about a mile, his GPS announced that we had arrived to our destination. We all sat in silence and looked around at the vast field around us. In the light of day, I could see how the land could have been magical and enchanting. Maybe even peaceful. But in the dead of this cold winter night, the land was much more sinister and haunting. The black trees in the distance looked like they could swallow us whole.

"Uh, ma'am, it looks like we've arrived." The driver turned back to face us, unimpressed as he scanned our surroundings. I too panned the daunting blackness around us as my palms began to sweat.

"Where the hell are we?" Jack demanded as he turned toward me accusingly.

Before I could answer, a surge of energy passed through me, demanding me to get out of the car. I tried to fight the urge, but the feeling was forceful and insistent.

"We're here," I announced, shooting a consoling look at Jack as I took out my wallet and paid the driver.

"Are you sure, ma'am? There's nothing around here for miles," he pointed out as he looked over at Mia and Jack nervously.

Mia turned toward me with panic filling her face as she watched me open the door.

"Georgia—"

"Yes, thank you. We'll be fine. Jack, Mia? Are you coming?"

Both of them stared with their mouths open like they had finally accepted that I had gone mad. Perhaps I truly had, because my words and actions didn't feel like my own. Nothing about the events from the last hour made any sense to me, and this just put the icing on the cake. I had fled from the only man who made me feel safer than I'd ever felt. And for what? Apparently to find refuge in a dark, open field with no streetlights in the middle of the night.

Oh, and don't forget you're dragging your best friend and a child into the danger zone with you.

Jack and Mia exchanged silent worried looks, but to my surprise, they both slid out and stood with me as the driver watched with disapproval.

"Ladies, are you sure? I really don't feel comfortable—"

"No, sir. Thank you for your concern, but this is where we're supposed to be," I said with a wave as I closed the door.

He gave us all one last nervous glance before he shook his head and shifted his car into drive. We watched in silence as he drove into the night until we were completely alone with nothing but the moon and stars to light our way.

A wet sensation fell on the tip of my nose, and I looked up to see a soft flurry of white surrounding us. Snow began to fall quietly, and the temperatures seemed to have dropped to below freezing. I peered over at Mia and Jack. Of course. None of us had jackets.

Fuck.

"Seriously, Georgia? *This* is your plan?" Jack spat as he kicked a cloud of dust into the frigid winter air.

I watched the dust particles pick up and fly toward a heavily wooded area several yards away. A forceful gust of wind nearly shoved me forward toward the tree line. Were we supposed to go that way? Another bone-chilling rush of air jolted me forward again, answering me.

"This way!" I called as I turned on my heel, running where the wind took me. The cold air on my face felt like knives against my skin, but I didn't care. Something deep inside me pushed me toward the finish line, and I had to get there or we'd be goners by morning light.

"Wait for us!" Mia yelled behind me, and I heard their scattered footsteps against the grass. I slowed slightly to give them some time to catch up, but I wasn't going to stop. The pull was too strong, too hard to fight. We had to get there. I felt Jack and Mia's footfalls in line next to me as we raced through the wilderness, tree branches and snags tearing at us as we treaded through.

"Where—are—we—going?" Mia demanded in between pants as we climbed across a small creek that had frozen over.

"I think we're almost there!" I called back, ignoring her. My face and hands were now completely numb. *God, please let us almost be there.*

A faint hint of spices and delicious scents seemed to waft through the air as we weaved through the trees, almost like it was calling us home. A glow of warm, hazy light flickered in the distance as we approached a small valley. At the edge of the trees, I could just make out the silhouette of a stunning farmhouse standing tall in the dark, like a beacon of light to the lost and weary. Relief flooded through me as I watched a puff of smoke cloud upward from the chimney. The beautiful aromas of food and spices grew stronger by the second.

I sprinted toward it as if nothing could stop me, clinging to the desperate hope that this was really it. I'd seen this farmhouse in my vision when I touched Scar's hand. This was *headquarters*.

As we neared, I could barely make out a figure as they emerged from the front entrance. I watched them gratefully head from the porch down the steps to greet us.

"Georgia, is that you?" a voice called through the night, and excitement and affirmation crumbled any doubt I ever had in myself.

"Yes!" I cried as we rushed toward the voice.

I peered behind me, and Mia and Jack were only a few paces behind. As we approached the front porch, a familiar face welcomed us with open arms. She had stunningly beautiful mocha skin and gorgeous braids that fell down her back. It was Harlow.

"Come on, get yourselves inside before y'all freeze to death!" she demanded as she led us up the stairs and into the front door.

A burst of warm and inviting air mixed with cinnamon and apples greeted us as we filtered in. A fire was roaring toward the back, and a stunning display of red Christmas bows and green ferns lined the walls and stairwell railing. A beautiful Christmas tree decked with lights and candy canes glowed in the corner where a few gorgeously wrapped gifts were placed with intention underneath.

"Good Lord Almighty, I can't believe y'all made it in at this time of night. And without coats—have you lost your minds?" The woman cast an admonishing glare at us. Her expression softened considerably as she spotted Jack. Her deep chestnut eyes snapped over to me, and she clicked her tongue with deep disapproval.

"Georgia, why don't you get your boy into the bath, and I'll put on a pot of coffee for you two. I had a feeling y'all would be in tonight, but I thought..." She paused as if she suddenly remembered something.

"Where's Graham?" she demanded as she fixed her eyes on Mia, her mouth twisting with curiosity. I cleared my throat and stepped forward nervously, knotting my hands at the hem of my shirt.

"Um, maybe I should tell you...while Jack is in the bath?" I pleaded with my eyes, hoping she would get the hint.

"Maybe you should tell her while Jack is standing right here," Jack chided, his dark eyes locked on me. Her knowing gaze snapped back over to him, and she shook her head fervently.

"I think you best do what she tells you, or things won't sit right in this house tonight. Ya hear?" she cautioned, but it was clear she didn't need an answer. She immediately shooed us up the stairs and down a hallway into a beautiful bathroom with a claw-foot bathtub.

"Soap, towels, and shampoo are underneath the sink. There's some nice clean clothes for bed in the closet, and I expect you done and in your bed in twenty minutes. Isn't that right, Momma?" She flicked her eyes toward me, waiting for my confirmation before I suddenly realized she meant me. I was the momma.

I bobbed my head obediently at Jack, who shook his head with a frustrated glare. I could tell the woman was doing her best to not say anything more to him about his attitude, before she ushered us out of the room, leaving Jack alone.

"My name is Harlow, and if you need anything, we'll be downstairs. Otherwise, I'll be sending your momma and her friend up to bed in an hour. We rise early in the mornings around here, so get some sleep!" she called out to him as she shut the door behind her.

Once we got back downstairs, she brewed us a fresh pot of decaf coffee and sat us in front of the bright fire.

"I need to know why you didn't bring Graham," she demanded as she sipped, staring at me over the rim of her cup. Somehow, Harlow was able to make me feel at home and terrified all at the same time. She was gorgeous, and her body seemed young and athletic, but her soul and her demeanor felt so much older. Like she had lived a thousand lives before this.

"I don't know if you know how I died, but—"

"I know exactly how you died. What does that have to do with Graham

224

not being here right now?" Her eyes flashed with impatience as she set her cup down and crossed her arms expectantly.

"I believe...he was my attacker. I used to wear a commitment ring...but the guy who killed me stole it from me. I found it in Graham's pocket." I watched Harlow think about that for an agonizing moment in silence.

"Despite the good things we do for others, Pavers are still merely humans. We are still capable of dark and disturbing things. The problem with your theory, however, is that you, Jack, and Graham died at the same time. Reckonings only link souls that die with the same breath. In Jerry's report, Graham was listed as dying thirty minutes away from your apartment in a bar. The man who attacked you couldn't have been Graham."

"But—"

"Scar has also found some interesting leads that point towards a different man. She was planning on updating you tomorrow morning, first thing."

"Is Scar here?" I jumped up, ready to barge through every room if I had to. I needed to know who my attacker was if it wasn't Graham. But then, why did he have my ring? Even worse, if it wasn't him, how could I face him again with the way I'd left him? I had taken his son away from him. Would he ever forgive me?

"No, Scar won't be in until tomorrow. She's tending to some other business," she said as she snapped her focus toward Mia.

"And *you*." She glowered. "It is a mighty rare thing for an outsider to see this place, let alone come inside. I don't want to say this place is enchanted, but we've got our ways of remaining hidden to the public," she said, leaning forward and giving Mia a skeptical once-over. "Who are you?" she asked, as the light from the Christmas tree shadowed her features, the light flickering dangerously against her skin.

"I'm...uh...Georgia's best friend, Mia." She shrugged as she nervously peered over at me for help. Harlow let that set in for a moment as she chewed on her lip.

"Friendship is a powerful thing, I suppose," she muttered to herself as she eyed Mia speculatively. Harlow's chair scraped against the floor as she stood and let out a defeated sigh. "I suspect Graham won't be far behind now. If he comes tonight, then we'll handle it, but I have my suspicions he won't be in until tomorrow." She clicked her tongue again, shaking her head. "I think it's best that y'all head up to bed now. As I mentioned to Jack, we rise early around here. God's work ain't done without a good night's rest," she warned as she threw the remaining pot of coffee onto the fire, a cloud of smoke puffing around the kitchen. Darkness filtered through the house, except for the glow from the tree in the far corner.

"There are clothes for you in the closet, and don't forget to say your prayers tonight before you go to bed. Tomorrow, we have much to discuss," she nearly threatened as she shot Mia another wary look. "I'll be down the hall if you need anything," she called over her shoulder as she turned and disappeared around the corner.

Mia and I exchanged silent looks before heading back into our room. I was relieved to find Jack sleeping soundly in the bed in the corner. After my head hit the pillow, and I heard Mia start to snore, I cried.

And I refused to pray .

21

SOMEWHERE OVER THE RAINBOW

The heavenly scent of cinnamon and pastries floated up to our room, and my mouth started to water. I slowly opened my eyes as I inhaled and stretched. I froze as I caught someone standing above me.

Mere inches from my face was a pretty girl, no older than thirteen, staring at me with wide, bright green eyes. She immediately gasped and tripped, falling backward onto Jack's bed. Jack woke with a start and flung himself to the floor, dragging her with him in a tangled, scattered mess. She squeaked as he landed on top of her with a loud thud, pinning her beneath him.

Mia was on her feet in a flash and rushed toward Jack and the strange girl.

"Jack, get off of her!" she demanded, lunging forward and grabbing his shirt.

He quickly scrambled off her as she lay there, panting and terrified. Her eyes darted between all three of us as she scooted backward, bumping into a nightstand, and let out another terrified squeal.

"Whoa, hey! It's okay... You just scared us is all," I soothed, raising my hands gently. Her chest heaved as she took us in, studying us.

"I'm Georgia. This is Mia, and that's Jack," I said as I pointed to each us. "Now...who are *you*?" I asked as she seemed to calm down, her eyes settling on Jack.

"I'm Rachel," she whispered as she stood, dusting herself off. "I'm sorry I woke you up, I was just...curious," she admitted as a subtle smile flickered across her face. "Harlow said that the Reckoning trio was upstairs, and I wanted to see for myself."

228

"Is Graham here?" I asked nervously. Rachel shook her head shyly as she peered up at me through long eyelashes. "No... Harlow said he didn't come home yet. Scar will be here soon, though. She just called." She shifted slightly as if she was about to leave but stopped herself.

"Um...Harlow's making breakfast. And there are some people downstairs that you might want to see," she added as she backed toward the door. Then she quickly tiptoed her way past me and slipped out the door without another word.

Jack stared at the door for a moment, before he ran and closed it, turning back to face us.

"I overheard you talking to Harlow last night." He glowered at me as I shrunk before him. Shame and anger coursed through me as I imagined him eavesdropping.

"I know you were doing what you thought was best last night. You were protecting us..." he whispered as he gave me a pointed look.

I just stared at him in quiet fury. Angry that he overheard, and angry at myself for even dreaming that Graham could have been the one to hurt me. No matter if I'd found the ring in his pocket or not.

"I know you thought Graham was the guy who killed you. But you know if he'd ever laid a hand on you, I'd kick his sorry ass." He shook his head with a knowing smirk. "But Superman...he *loves* you. I don't know a lot about love, Georgia. But I know that whatever he feels for you...it's love."

I saw Mia nod in the corner of my eye, but Jack ignored her.

"The way he protected you from my dad...and some of the things he was saying before the Blues game..."

I jumped as the door opened again and Rachel peeked in, her pretty light brown hair glinting off the sun peeking in.

"Hey...um...sorry to bother you guys again, but Harlow wants you to come down for breakfast."

"Thank you, Rachel," Jack said with bright eyes that seemed a little too enthusiastic.

"Yes, thank you, Rachel. We'll be down in a minute." I shot Jack my best mom look, hoping it was as effective as Harlow's. Jack blinked back up at me before the corner of his mouth curved into that infamous half-smile.

"Actually, I'm coming now," Mia said as she headed toward the door, leaving Jack and me alone.

I waited until Mia and Rachel's footsteps disappeared before I continued.

"Jack, I'm sorry you overheard me, and I...honestly didn't know what else to think. He had my ring in his pocket... I just wasn't going to risk anything, especially with you." I tugged his shirt, and he nodded.

"We'll talk about this more later. I want to talk to Scar...and I want *you* fed." I tapped his nose with a grin, and he let out a laugh that made my heart sing.

We headed downstairs to a farm table filled with every breakfast dish and homegrown comfort food you could want. Biscuits and gravy, sausage, pancakes, eggs, bacon, jam and jellies in every flavor, juice, milk, and fruit.

"Good mornin'! You just go head and grab you a plate. It's homestyle around here. The rest will be down in a minute," Harlow called over to us as she whipped something in front of the stove. Before we could start gathering our plates, I heard shuffled footsteps behind me.

"Hi, Gee-Gee," a familiar voice called, and I whirled around to find my parents, their arms interlocked as they both watched me with bright, tearful eyes.

"Mom... Dad?" I cried as I ran toward them, wrapping my arms around them desperately. "Oh my God, what are you guys doing here?"

My mom let out a chuckle as she pulled me away from her, her eyes sweeping me nervously, like she was trying to make sure I was okay. Besides the minor scratches and bumps from the midnight journey through the wilderness, I was of course perfectly fine.

"Your Dad and I are...Pavers, Georgia."

I stared at my mom with wide eyes as I took them in.

"Our headquarters is based out of Illinois, of course, but Harlow was nice enough to invite us to stay with them until you arrived."

"Why am I just now finding this out?" I felt a sense of betrayal and shock as I stared at them, practically two complete strangers. My mom frowned slightly as my dad took a step forward.

"I suppose every parent keeps their secrets," my dad pointed out as he jutted his chin toward Jack. I held back a gasp as I realized they knew who he was and what I had done.

My parents knew that I was fostering him, that I was a mother. That they were practically *grandparents*. That their crazy daughter was not only a Paver like them, but had gone off the deep end and committed herself to two complete strangers. My mom leaned down toward Jack, squinting at him and giving him a quick head-to-toe assessment. She chuckled as she extended her hand out toward him.

"My name is Audrey, but you can call me Grandma, if you wish." She flashed a loving smile down at him as he stared at her outstretched hand. I gasped as I watched him push her hand away and wrap his arms around her, pulling her into a tight embrace.

"Hi, Grandma," he muffled into her shirt. "I'm Jack, but you can call me Jack."

My dad moved next to them and offered his own hand nervously.

"Hi, Jack. I'm your grandpa," he said with a shaky voice.

In all my years, I'd never seen my dad so nervous. He was always so composed and brave. Even when I was in the hospital, he was able to hide his fear with humor. Yet now, he looked vulnerable and young, as his eyes shone with tenderness toward his grandson. Jack slowly pulled away from my mom and peered up at his grandfather, the same worry shining in his own eyes. Together, they were like two deer in the headlights.

"Hi, Grandpa," he whispered before he flung himself into my dad's arms and shuddered with a silent sob. He shook his head in disbelief as he met my tearful gaze.

"A Paver's life is crazy, Georgia. You'd never believe it, but I've met Jack before," he cried as he patted him on the back.

"When?" I quavered as I tried to remain steady from all the shock.

"I was in St. Louis about a month ago, trying to recruit veterans for some local jobs. I was tabling outside when he came up to my booth." He looked down at Jack lovingly as he recalled the moment. "He asked if I had any jobs for him." He let out a hearty laugh as Jack's cheeks reddened.

"Yeah, and you said yes," Jack mumbled as he watched my dad adoringly.

"Yup, I gave him a hundred dollars and asked if he'd get me a sandwich from the shop down the street and to get him one too," he said as he nudged Jack playfully. "I thought for sure you were gonna just take the money and run."

"I almost did." Jack grinned up at him.

"But the kid came back about twenty minutes later with two sandwiches and the change." He shook his head with a wide grin.

"Thanks for letting me keep the change, *Grandpa*." Jack's face broke out into a beautiful boyish grin. "You fed me for the next three weeks." He let out a laugh that quickly died as he watched my dad's face fall. He kneeled before Jack, pulling him into another hug.

"Hey, old man, don't get all sappy with me. We're men—we're supposed to be strong. Remember, that's what you told me?" Jack said, his lip quivering.

"Son, I think you misunderstood. Strength doesn't always mean hiding your emotions; it means being strong enough to show them too."

Before I could cry my eyes out from the endearing reunion, the loud clapping of heels against the hardwood sounded from across the room. The wintry air filled the foyer, and small snowflakes feathered on through from another incoming storm.

"You made it!" A gorgeous brunette wearing a red power suit gushed as she ran toward me.

"Scar!" I practically squealed as she pulled me into a hug. She peered over my shoulder and settled her gaze on Jack and Mia.

"You must be Jack!" She clapped her way toward him as he stared at her with widened eyes. "Jerry told me something very interesting about you, but I suppose we'll get to that later..." She glanced over at Harlow before she peered over at Mia, intrigued.

"And you must be Georgia's very near and dear friend, Mia!" She laughed that gorgeous musical laugh. "It is so nice to finally meet you two!"

"Oh my God, I'm so proud of you! Jerry hasn't stopped talking about your journey, I'm just so..." Her face fell as she scanned the room. "So, it's true, then?" she asked as her espresso eyes flicked back to me. "Graham's not here?"

I let out a sigh before Harlow interrupted us, bringing a hot plate piled with cinnamon rolls to the table.

"How about let's have breakfast before we talk about business?" she demanded as she pulled out a chair and took a seat. Scar thinned her lips, and I felt naked before her, like she was digging through my brain for answers. I avoided eye contact with my parents, as questions were surely churning through their heads too. In the corner of my eye, I saw Rachel slink in from the hallway with a young woman behind her. The woman looked about my age and was the spinning image of Rachel, with beautiful green eyes and sandy-brown hair that cascaded down her shoulders.

"Good morning, everyone," the woman greeted as she eyed me curiously.

"Ah, Taryn, good morning, sweetie. We were just about to have breakfast," Harlow said, almost like she was commanding her to begin the buffet line.

Taryn nodded meekly as she and Rachel grabbed a plate and started to pile on some eggs and biscuits. We all politely followed suit in silence before heading to the table. Even though I was starving, I could barely eat because Harlow's cooking reminded me so much of Davis and the boys.

And Graham.

I wondered what Graham was doing now, what he was thinking...feeling. How did he explain to his brothers that the ring landed in his pocket? How would he explain it to *me*?

"So is Graham one of the Marines you went to the Blues game with?" my mom probed as we all chewed in silence. I nodded as I fought back tears. The last thing I wanted to do was cry in front of all of them. Jack tensed next to me as he swallowed a mouthful of bacon.

"What's a Marine?" he asked as he peered up at me. My dad seemed to sense my sadness, so he cut in.

"Marines fight to defend our country. They *protect* us," he emphasized, and I felt my heart shatter into a thousand pieces as he said the words. I saw Jack shift his gaze to me in the corner of my eye, but I kept mine downward, leaving my plate untouched.

"Harlow, this is really incredible. I'm going to have to get that recipe for those rolls," Mia chimed in, trying to change the subject.

Harlow chuckled and shrugged. "It's not mine. It's actually Jerry's, believe it or not."

I lifted my watery gaze up at her, and suddenly I was aware that Jerry wasn't here.

"Where is he?" I asked, searching the room.

Awkward throat clearing and forks clattering against their plates sounded across the table as silence settled around me. I caught sight of Scar as her eyes flashed dangerously at me.

"It's time," Harlow said, pointing her fork at Scar in a commanding way.

"You sure that's best? Shouldn't we wait until Graham—"

"They've eaten, and they need to know. He doesn't have much time," she replied intently, her eyes snapping over to Jack.

He doesn't have much time.

Jerry? Jerry *doesn't have much time?*

Scar wiped her mouth with her napkin nervously before she pushed her chair back and rose to her feet.

"Jack...Georgia, come with me." Her expression was unreadable as we stood and quickly shuffled into the hall.

The faint whir of a familiar-sounding machine hissed from the end of the corridor, as we approached a closed door. Scar let out a ragged breath before she grabbed the doorknob and twisted it open. As we filed into the room, my heart sunk to the bottom of my stomach as my eyes rested on Jerry. An oxygen mask was taped around his mouth as a tank compressed his chest for him. A nearby computer monitor read all his vitals in a tragic display, a green line bouncing with his heart rate. The man that lay completely comatose on the bed was much thinner than the Jerry I knew. His limbs were bony, and his skin was a sick grayish white.

"What the hell happened?" I shouted before I could stop myself.

Tears prickled at the back of my eyes, and I ran over to his bedside, reaching for his hand. A solemn darkness settled over me, burying me with a sense of nothingness. No images, no feelings, just blackness. I pulled my hand away slowly as fear and sweat beaded at my forehead. I didn't even want to know what that meant.

"He's been in a coma...for about six months," she sighed as her eyes trailed along his pale face. "He's living in the Paving Realm, between life and death. I don't know if you knew this, but he's my Reckoning partner. He's been keeping me updated about everything, but..." She sniffed, straightening his blanket and pulling it up over his chest. "I'm afraid he's deteriorating quickly, especially over the last few weeks. Harlow thinks he's got a few days left—"

"I saw him, though! I saw him outside Trish's Café. He was sitting on a bench ..." I thought back to the moment our eyes locked. A shiver ran through me as I remembered he wasn't even wearing a coat in the middle of a raging blizzard.

"That isn't unheard of. Pavers can materialize, outside the body...but it requires an incredible amount of energy." She peered down at him, her own eyes filling with tears. "He must have felt it essential that you saw him."

"What happened to him?" I whispered, as my fingers trailed down his arm, willing for him to wake, to respond. But nothing. He remained still and lifeless except for the oxygen machine pouring into his chest.

"He refused to come back." She shook her head at him furiously.

"What does that even mean?" Jack demanded, his dark eyes settling on Jerry's body. So lifeless, so empty. So far from the Jerry we knew.

"During his Reckoning, he chose to stay."

I shuddered as I remembered the way Jerry said he'd be forceful if we didn't go back. Maybe he didn't want us to end up like him. He'd even told Graham what happened to me...to give him something to focus on, to return to.

"But why?" I asked softly.

"He didn't want to come back to a world without the love of his life," Scar sighed as she ran the back of her hand against his cheek.

"Six months ago, he was leaving a restaurant with his fiancé when a group of men attacked them." I inhaled a sharp gasp as I thought of the senselessness of such a violent act. Was this much evil always in the world and I had just been blind to it? Or was it because I was so sucked into my own life to care?

"They beat them so brutally that they put Jerry in a coma and..." A tear streaked down Scar's cheek. "His fiancé didn't make it."

Scar gestured toward a photo propped on his nightstand.

"I put his picture next to his bed so he could look at it whenever he feels lonely..."

"Wait...this is Jerry's *fiancé*?" I gasped as I picked the frame up, and Jack and I peered down at it. Two beautiful men beamed back at us. Jerry's familiar pale blue eyes sparkled beneath his peacock-feathered hat, while a handsome man peered over at him with the most captivated, tender look that had "I love you" written all over it

"His name was Ray. They'd been dating for seven years before they finally got engaged this year. They were celebrating their anniversary the night they were attacked."

My stomach dropped as I squinted down at the happy couple. So young and blissfully in love...before it was all taken from them.

"We have a special request to ask from you and your boy," Harlow said as she glanced down at Jack.

"What is it?" I asked timidly as my eyes shot between Harlow and Scar. Both of them had nervous but determined expressions lining their faces. They were desperate.

"We want Jack to heal him."

I felt my chest tighten as I glanced over at Jack. His thin face was tilted up toward me as something flickered behind his eyes.

"*Heal* him?" I repeated, as both shock and anger filled me. "Harlow... I don't know if that's the best idea."

The intense memory of Jack healing me during our first training flashed across my mind. He'd felt my pain and taken it as his own. He'd experienced the same agonizing sting I'd felt from his father's knife against my throat. But that was just a clean cut. Jerry was in a *coma*. A coma he'd been in for *six months*.

"Harlow, do you know what would happen? I mean I've only seen him heal once before. And it hurt him. Healing hurts him!" I shouted as I pulled away from her grasp.

Her lips thinned as she stepped closer to me.

"There are safety precautions we would take to ensure he's protected," she promised.

I let out an incredulous laugh.

"Jerry said he'd only known one other Paver who can heal physically. He said he'd passed on...and I'm getting the feeling it wasn't because of natural causes," I seethed. "How can you be sure he'll be okay if it's so rare? I can't risk his life for the chance we could save Jerry!" I shook my head, backing away from her.

"Georgia, we would like to bring in Dr. Cobbs to monitor Jack before we do anything. He'll keep him hydrated, and safe," Scar reassured. As if that made me feel any better.

"Oh, you mean the man that left Paving so he could survive a normal life? Good God, I understand why he left. There is just way too much pressure on just one human being. How do you guys do it? You have to be exhausted! I mean Scar, you're a detective!" I cried as I pointed at her.

"You see the horrors of humanity. You've probably given my case way too much time already, draining your body of energy and life to bring me justice. I am so grateful for everything you've done for me, but you can't do it all. A full-grown man can't handle it all; why would you think Jack could do it?" I shook my head and crossed my arms. "You can't put all of that on the shoulders of an eleven-year-old boy. He's already been through too much!"

Harlow's eyes flashed dangerously at me as she opened her mouth to speak again. Before she could get a word out, a loud smack crashed against the floor. To my horror, my son's small body was convulsing, writhing at our feet. His face was constricted, his veins bursting out across his neck and temples. His eyes rolled into the back of his head, and he started to make incomprehensible gargling noises.

"*Jack!*"

22

STICKS & STONES

"Call 9-1-1!" I shouted as worried faces peered in from the doorway.

Scar shook her head desperately.

"No, Georgia. The ambulance won't be able to find us—we have to go to the hospital ourselves," she panted as she helped me gather Jack in my arms, pulling me to my feet.

"We'll take my car; it's just right outside. Mia, come with us. We'll need your help!" Scar said as she pushed me toward the front door.

The next few moments were a blur. All I knew was that I had my son cradled against me, and his pulse was weak against my fingers. It was like a movie playing before me as I watched myself from above. Flashes of my feet running against the gravel toward a red SUV. I heard the screech of the tires peel out as we drove toward a dense forest of trees and brush. Scar was driving as Mia brushed Jack's hair tenderly from his face. She was talking, but I didn't know what she was saying as I faded in and out from the terror.

God, please be okay, please be okay.

And then, we were stopped. Had we arrived at the hospital already? I let out a grateful sob as I began to regain my composure. I had to be strong. I could do this. I just needed to carry his tiny body to the front door and trust that the doctors would take care of him. He needed me to be strong, and that was exactly what I was going to do. I rocked him against me, before I heard Scar's distressed voice calling out to me.

"Georgia! *Run!*"

Yes! Run to the hospital! I peered out the window, but we weren't in a parking lot. There was no hospital to run to. We were surrounded by thick brush, the trees overhanging and shadowing, no civilization in sight. I turned back to ask Scar where we were, but she had disappeared from her seat, her car door ajar. Muffled cries sounded from outside the vehicle, before a sickening thud silenced them. A terrified scream shattered through me, before I realized it was my own as thick arms pulled me from the car. I watched helplessly as Jack lay slumped over on the seat. I felt myself being dragged across the cold ground as sticks and rocks tore against my stomach. I searched frantically for Scar and Mia, for anyone who could help. A desperate cry escaped my lips as I caught Mia's blonde hair a few feet away. Both of them lay lifeless, sprawled on the ground.

"*No!*" I sobbed, but no one cared.

Strong hands flipped me onto my back, and sharp, jagged rocks dug into my spine and a scream bubbled in my throat. Before I could let it out, long clammy fingers wrapped around my neck, pinning me to the ground with a terrifying force. Dark penetrating eyes stared back at me with crazed, sickening elation. His jet-black hair, tousled and frayed, went every which way as a chilling smile twisted across his familiar face. I gasped as I remembered the peaceful scene I'd felt when I shook his hand. He was talking to vegetables in his garden for Christ's sake. But now, here in God's country, was my boss. Kurt Robinson. Holding me down with no one to hear me scream.

"Georgia Scott. At last, we're alone...again." He let out a snarl of laughter as his hands wrapped around my wrists, slamming them to the ground above my head. "Tell me something—what was your Reckoning like?"

Terror gripped me as I replayed his words. He just said *Reckoning*.

Another terrified scream caught in my throat as he pried my knees open and shoved himself against me. A satisfying growl escaped from his cracked lips as he dropped his gaze to my abdomen.

"I gotta tell you, Georgia. I wasn't expecting to see you so alive and well after what I did. You were so beautiful, standing there, I thought I was looking at an angel."

He rocked against me as he buried his face into my neck. Bile rose in my throat, and I thought for a moment I was about to heave up my breakfast.

"But what shocked me most of all was the moment we held hands. I saw your eyes change. That's when I knew...you were just like *me*." He slid his hand down my side and dug his fingers painfully into my hip. I whimpered as he wrapped his hand around my throat.

"Tell me, what did you see when you held my hand?" he whispered, his scruffy jawline stabbing against my skin. I bucked against him, but he was too strong, his upper body pushing me into the ground as cold mud sloshed beneath me. His eyes flashed hauntingly with pleasure as he watched me struggle beneath him. I finally stilled as my chest heaved with anger.

"I'm nothing like you, Kurt," I seethed, trying to push myself farther away from him.

A terrifying smile crept across his face before he let out an unhinged, wicked laugh. The familiar stench of his stale, bitter breath crashed over me, and my breakfast drifted upward again. I twisted my face away from him, and my eyes settled on Jack, his poor body still lifeless against the seat of the car. No, this monster could hurt me all he wanted to, but he wasn't going to stop me from saving my son. I had to think, and quick.

I swallowed my breakfast back down again. I turned toward him, my lips brushing against his ear.

"What do you say we take this further into the woods. I...I want this. I...I've always wanted this, but I don't want them to see." I flicked my gaze to Mia, Scar, and Jack. "Maybe they'll wake up and try to...interrupt?"

I fought to keep my voice steady, when all I wanted to do was scream. He pulled away, his dark eyes brightening. Maybe if he would just get off me, I could run. I could find the keys and take Jack to the hospital. At least he would have a fighting chance. Kurt swept his gaze lazily down my body as he shook his head ruefully.

"Georgia Scott, you surprise me every day." He snuck a look over at the clearing near the woods as if he were considering it. Something evil danced in his eyes as he turned back toward me.

"I think everyone deserves a good show, don't you?" He quickly reached down toward my belt line and began to pull my jeans down, over my hips. I let out a muffled sob, unable to hold back my revulsion anymore.

"*No!*" I screamed as I rammed my head against his nose with every ounce of effort I had. A loud crack ripped through the air as a flow of blood rushed down his face.

"*Aaargh!*" he screamed, his hands flying to his nose as he sat up, giving me just enough time to scramble to my feet. I clawed my way up, stumbling against the rocks as I fled toward the car, screaming with all my might. Maybe we hadn't gotten that far away from the farmhouse. Maybe they'd hear. I only got a few paces away before his hand gripped my elbow, jerking me back to the ground. A burst of pain shot across my face as he slapped me. Colors and lights blurred my vision as the metallic taste of blood filled my mouth.

"Now why would you go and do a thing like that, sweetheart?" he growled, slumping forward, forcing my knees open again.

I closed my eyes, as I prepared for another blow. The pain was unbearable as his fist crashed across my cheek, reverberating right through my skull into my brain. This was how I was going to die, and I wouldn't come back this time. This was it. This was how it would all end. I let out a mangled cry as I thought about Jack, how he might die too. That strong, brave boy who'd been through the worst of hells would die at the hands of yet another monster. I felt a trickle of blood flow from my mouth as he drew back his hand again. I squeezed my eyes shut, preparing myself for another blow, and prayed that I could take it. I felt a scramble of movement above me, and suddenly I was free. No, this couldn't be. He was taunting me. He just wanted to watch me squirm before he pounced again. My eyes shot open to find a furious storm of a man flinging Kurt on the ground.

Graham!

His fist pounded into Kurt's face, another loud crack echoing against the forest line. Kurt roared with pain as he clawed at his shirt. Graham was relentless as he threw a lethal-looking punch right into Kurt's eye. Blood spattered across the snow with a sickening crunch. A rustle of movement from the brush behind them tore my focus from the scuffle, and another wave of terror crashed into me at the sight. Several beastly men tore their way through the trees with a brazen savagery that chilled me to my bone. As they pressed forward, I rush of relief filled me as I recognized them. It was Graham's Marine brothers, live and in action.

Bennett ran toward the car and felt for Jack's pulse, while Tex and Andrews tended to Mia and Scar. They were still out cold as I watched Mia's golden hair being lifted from the ground. Andrews effortlessly climbed into the car with her in tow.

Cooper rushed toward Graham and pulled him off Kurt before he got in another devastating blow. He tried to shake himself free from Cooper's grip as he roared with a vengeance, sending tremors right through me. My eyes drifted slowly to my attacker; his violating body lay still and lifeless in the snow. And the shameless thought of revenge crossed my mind.

I hoped he was dead.

Suddenly, I felt two pairs of strong hands wrap around my arms. A bloodcurdling scream ripped from my chest, and their steel grip fell away immediately.

"Georgia, it's just us! It's okay, no one's going to hurt you anymore. You're safe!"

I peered up at a very worried Reed as he knelt next to me. Davis was hunched over, peering down at my throbbing cheek. I let out an anguished cry as I reached for him.

"Keaton!" Davis yelled across the field. I searched for Graham again and was taken aback as his ferocious ready-to-kill glare settled on me. I gasped as he tore away from Cooper and ran toward us, hell-bent like nothing could stop him. He slid into a pile of mud, landing at my feet, as spots of dirt and blood glistened on his hands and clothes.

"Georgia, did he..." He trailed off as he gripped the sides of my face, his desperate eyes searching my body. I shook my head as a sob fell away from me. I quickly peered over his shoulder at the commotion near the car.

"Jack!" I cried.

I couldn't see him anymore. Instead, I watched Tex load Scar into the SUV, her head lolling and jerking with his movements.

God, please be okay.

Before I knew it, Graham had scooped me up, my feet dangling over his arm as he charged full speed toward the car.

"Take us to the hospital!" he yelled as he climbed into the middle row, pulling me into his lap. Tex hopped in the driver's seat while Andrews and Bennett stowed themselves into the back. Reed, Cooper, and Davis nodded as they pulled the doors shut and hit the car, sending us onward. I clung to Graham as I watched the three of them close in on Kurt as we sped away. Dust clouded around them, and I dropped my head on Graham's shoulder, no longer able to keep my eyes open. I couldn't fight anymore. I felt Graham's heart slam against his chest as he grazed my face, the world around me fading in and out until it slowly disappeared.

———

The distant sound of beeping echoed in my head. Voices crowded all around me, like the room was filled with people chanting, whispering. No, *praying*. My eyes fluttered open as warmth spread up my arm. Front porch sunrises and the smell of sweet summer rain poured over me.

"Georgia," Graham breathed, the sound of my name like a prayer on his lips. He rubbed my arm as he stood and leaned over to kiss my forehead. His sweet lips, so loving and giving. A deep pang of guilt rushed through me as I remembered how I had fled from him. How I'd thought he was the one who attacked me. How could I have been so wrong?

I remembered every terrifying moment of the attack. How he had dragged me from the car, pressed himself against me. *How he knew what a Reckoning was...*

And Jack...our sweet son. His limp body, lifeless on the car floor.

"Jack!" I suddenly cried as I shot up, a dizzying pair of lights and stars flying around me in protest. I groaned as Graham pushed me gently back toward my pillow, his fingers brushing against my forehead.

"He's fine, Georgia. Dr. Cobbs did his magic. He'll be sore and dizzy for the next couple of days, but he was just severely dehydrated. Apparently, that's what happens when you overextend your Aftereffects," he said in a low voice. "Scar and Mia are in recovery down the hall too," he continued, his eyes scanning me to make sure I heard him.

A wave of relief washed over me, hearing that they were fine. Graham shot me a small smile, his eyes watering with pride.

"He healed Jerry," he whispered, squeezing my hand again.

"What?" I replied stupidly, still trying to process everything.

Graham's gorgeous face split into that youthful smile I had come to adore. He leaned forward, his arms wrapping around me protectively, fiercely pulling me against him. I could feel his heartbeat race with mine, from the sudden contact. I let out a moan, and he quickly pulled back to make sure he hadn't hurt me before he realized I was just responding to his touch.

"Jack. He healed Jerry."

I gasped as I let that settle in. Of course he had. We were too busy arguing over him that he went and handled it on his own. Just like he always had. Anger and pride washed over me in that instant. Jack had known the risks he was taking. He knew something terrible might happen, but he was willing to sacrifice himself for Jerry.

Graham's brows knitted together, his smile disappearing as something darker seemed to resonate across his mind.

"Georgia... I thought..." He didn't finish his sentence as his eyes swept across me, his jaw tightening. His fingers wrapped around my wrists like he was trying to keep himself grounded.

"I thought I was too late. I thought he had killed Jack, had killed your friends. I thought...he had killed you too." He dropped his gaze, and I felt the sting of tears forming at the corners of my eyes.

"Graham, I—"

"I know you left because you found that ring in my pocket." His hard, steely regard had melted into an achingly somber stare. "I don't know how it got there, but Scar thinks he put it there while we were at the Blues game."

I tried to speak again as guilt began to swallow me whole. What an idiot I had been for running away so quickly. He shook his head, pleading to let him finish.

"I'm so sorry you thought I hurt you like that, Georgia. I understand how hard it must be to trust, with everything you've been through." His gray eyes locked on me, pain spilling out, practically breaking my heart into a million pieces. "I know it might take some time, but I want you to hear it from me first. I would never, *ever* hurt you. The only thing I've ever wanted to do was make sure you were safe and protected. I...I *love* you."

I gasped at his words and let them cradle me, as warmth spread throughout my entire body.

"Graham, I'm so sorry I ran from you like that. You've been nothing but brave and strong...and patient." I dropped my watery gaze to his lips as warmth rushed through me again. "I just saw the ring...and I didn't know what else to think. The way you were looking at me when you were coming out of the shower..." I shuddered as I remembered the menacing look on his face as he ran toward me.

"I was trying to see what you had in your hand. I thought..." He trailed off as he bit back something that seemed to be eating him alive. "I thought you found the ring."

I stared at him for a moment. Something in his expression was so intense, it held me still, urging for me to understand.

"I *did* find the ring, Graham?" I shook my head at him as I continued to watch his puzzling behavior. The way his eyes were dilating and his nostrils were flaring. The way his whole body seemed to tense as he looked at me.

"No, Georgia, I thought you found the ring I bought yesterday."

"I'm sorry, the ring that you *bought*?" I blinked at him, in a daze. I understood his words, but I didn't understand what he was saying.

"Graham—"

I stopped talking as I watched him lean over. He reached down to something at his feet, and to my surprise, he pulled a large book up to the bed. He set it gently in between us and slowly opened it to a page he'd carefully marked.

"This book is really important to me. It's the only thing I have left from my mom since she died. Of all the beautiful words in here, this page was the most worn through. Like she'd read it a thousand times over. I think it brought her comfort, like it brought me yesterday. If I read it, I can almost hear her recite it with me, even now. It's like I can still hear her voice, after all these years."

He craned his neck over the book, placing a finger at a highlighted section, and began to read.

"Love is patient, love is kind. It does not envy, it does not boast…" I felt a tightness pull deep within me as he began to deliver the only passage from the bible I was familiar with.

"It always protects, always trusts, always hopes…" he continued steadily, keeping his eyes trained on the book as he read. I let the weight of the words flow over me as I watched him pour his heart out.

As he finished the verse, he reached for my hand. An overwhelming sense of love and honor filled me again, and his fingers curved around mine. The glory of a new day's sunrise peeked over the horizon as we rocked on our front porch. His strong arms held me tight, protected me, treasured me. His bravery and selflessness held fast against me, as we watched Jack grow into a man, as we loved him through it all. As we loved each other through it all.

"Georgia Lee Scott," he whispered. I started to tremble, even though I wasn't even sure why as he reached toward my face and cupped my chin in his hand. His soft gray eyes searched mine as he leaned in closer.

"I read that verse at least a hundred times yesterday. I read it to Jack so I could try and explain what it feels like to love and be loved. I wanted him to know that's how we feel about him." He licked his lips and swallowed. "I wanted him to know that's how I feel about *you*." He moved closer as the pages of the bible rustled between us.

"And after we read those words together, I asked him for his blessing."

I felt another surge of warmth from his hand shoot through my entire body.

"I asked him for his blessing to marry you. He said yes."

A sound caught in my throat, but he pushed on as his eyes began to glisten.

"I had the honor of talking with your parents this morning. I also asked for their blessing."

I held back a gasp as I squeezed his hand tighter, anticipation eating away at me. His lips parted into a gorgeous smile that set my heart on fire.

"They also said yes."

He slowly stood, and to my surprise he pulled out a white jewelry box.

"Georgia Lee Scott. I just need one more answer from you." He knelt next to the bed, laying everything down for me, for Jack. For our family.

"I know we've only known each other for just a few days, but I feel like I've known you over a thousand different lifetimes. I vow to treasure you, protect you, and love you and Jack for all the days of my life. No matter what comes at us, whether it be parenting or Paving, that I will defend you, care for you, and cherish you through it all. Will you do me the incredible honor of being my wife?"

He opened the box, and a stunning halo-cut ring with diamonds encircling a larger diamond sparkled blindingly under the hospital fluorescents.

A sob escaped my lips as my eyes darted from the ring to Graham's face.

"Graham, are you sure you want...all of this?" I waved toward my battered face and crying eyes. This hot mess of a woman, who struggled to trust, to love, and to open herself up to human connection. All of *that*.

"You mean...the most stunningly beautiful woman I've ever seen? A woman who had faith in a man like me? A woman who would foster a kid with me, just because he needed someone? Hell, if that isn't love, then I don't know what is," he laughed as he brought my hand to his lips. "Hell yeah, I want all of this. I want it all." His eyes shone temptingly as he said those last words. And damn, did I want to give him everything.

"So let me ask you again...do you want... all of *this*?"

I eyed his perfectly sculpted jaw and toned body. The same body that had shielded, protected, and loved me at my worst. The same man who loved Jack and had already proven himself as a dedicated father.

"Yes, Graham Keaton. I think I do."

23

CHRISTMAS LIGHTS

The cold winter days passed until Christmas finally arrived. Casey notified us on Christmas Eve that Max Berkley, Jack's father, had terminated his parental rights, and that Jack was legally available for adoption. Making the decision to make us a legally binding family was as easy as breathing. Harlow reluctantly invited everyone to the farmhouse for a small party to celebrate. I knew privacy was a concern for her, but she seemed to overlook it in honor of the occasion, and I wasn't going to question it. I wanted Mia and the brotherhood there. They were our family now.

I watched excitedly as Davis and Harlow prepped the kitchen and showed each other their favorite recipes and tips. Together, they put out an incredible feast for us. The kitchen was lined with fried chicken, macaroni and cheese, greens, homegrown vegetables from the greenhouse, and an array of desserts.

Jerry and my parents gathered around a table as everyone else piled on their plates. Jerry's healthy glow had returned, and after tonight's meal, he would surely gain a few much-needed pounds. I watched him as I ate, questions burning within me about everything.

"Jerry?" I whispered, barely loud enough for him to hear. His piercing eyes flew toward me as he took a bite of chicken.

"Yes?" he muffled through his chewing.

"Why do you think we were chosen to become Pavers? Dr. Cobbs said that it doesn't happen with every near-death experience...only a fraction of them."

A hint of a smile curved at his mouth as he wiped it with a napkin.

"I don't have all the answers, but I have theories. I know this might seem counterintuitive, but I believe that most Pavers have an unsettling darkness within them. It's not so they can act on it, but so they can handle the things they'll see in the business. We see a lot of horrible things, and we have to be strong enough to take it on, headfirst."

I gawked at him as he took another bite and chewed.

"You see, Pavers are much like a phoenix, crawling through the ashes so they can find new life. The thing is, we've all *died*, and with that comes a significant amount of trauma and grief. But grief shapes you, and tears at you. It can mold you, just like a diamond forms under pressure. However, I imagine your vision is clearer than it has ever been, right? You know what most people don't. You know what's *important*. What makes life beautiful and worth the pain we feel."

We both sat in silence, as I pondered his words. I pictured a phoenix roiling in pain as flames licked and crisped at its feathers. The poor bird is helpless, as it slowly dies an excruciating death until it becomes nothing but a pile of dust. A pile of what was, and never will be again. But maybe not. Maybe Jerry was onto something. Maybe after misery and agony, something beautiful is born from the ashes.

"Georgia, I know you and Graham have your reservations about pursuing Paving," my mom chimed in, "but your dad and I have thrown ourselves into it without regret for the last twenty-eight years. It's one of the most meaningful parts of our lives, besides you of course."

She laughed as she crossed her arms. "If I remember correctly, you had a little something to say about meaningful work in the hospital." She gave me that knowing mom look anytime she had any advice. Usually she was right, so I'd come to trust that look.

I peered over at Jerry again as I contemplated how he must feel. He didn't want to come back, but Scar and Harlow made him.

"Jerry...are you upset that you were brought back?" I whispered.

He sat up straighter as he crossed his leg over his knee and shook his head.

"I'm grateful that I'm back. I regretted the decision to stay as soon as I'd made it, but I didn't know how to override it. No matter how hard I tried,

I couldn't go back." He dropped his gaze, and his brow furrowed as a more pressing topic seemed to come to mind.

"I forgave them, you know," he muttered as he peered back up at me.

"Forgave...who?" I repeated, intrigued.

"The men who killed me and Ray. They hated us for what we were, and they killed us for it. But do you know what I did the moment I realized I couldn't go back?"

I shook my head at him with widened watery eyes.

"I forgave them. Before they assigned me as a Light, I saw God's love. I felt his forgiveness and the grace of a new day. And in all his glory...and all of mine"—he shimmied with a playful grin—"I knew he loved me. He loved them too, even after all that they'd done."

"Jerry...are you trying to tell me I need to...*forgive* Kurt?" My voice broke as a sense of betrayal shot through me. "You know what he did...and even worse, he tried to do it again! He hurt Scar and Mia. He was going to let Jack die!" I seethed through a clenched jaw as the horrifying scene filled my mind. "No, I'm not ready for that. I don't think I'll ever be ready for that."

Jerry shook his head remorsefully as he leaned back in his chair. "Georgia, I'm not suggesting you do anything. I just know that the weight of it all will take a heavy toll if you let it. I know very well what happened, I was there through every second of it which is why I'm even saying anything." He paused and leaned forward, extending his hand. Something played behind his eye that both intrigued and terrified me.

"Why don't you see for yourself...?"

I watched his hand reach farther across the table toward me. I frowned as I peered up at him, angry tears welling in my eyes before I finally surrendered. I reached toward him and let his fingers curl around mine.

No black wisps this time, just love. Pure, honest, undeniable love. Innocence, forgiveness, peace. It was like my whole body was being hugged with a power I couldn't even begin to describe. A universal strength that rained down on me and protected me.

I inhaled a sharp breath as his hand withdrew from mine, a sense of longing filling me. I wanted to feel it again. That glorifying feeling that I was divinely created with intention and grace.

"It's a powerful thing, Georgia. Forgiveness leads to a beautiful release.

Your heart deserves some rest, okay?" Jerry added as he stood. He slowly leaned down and kissed me on my cheek, wiping a tear with incredible tenderness. Then he limped his way over to the buffet again to help himself to seconds.

———

Graham and I agreed to continue and learn more with the condition that Jack never be required to use his healing gifts. Harlow agreed, but something behind her eyes made me feel like she had conditions of her own. Whether that was the case or not, she never listed them. Mia, Scar, and I still had a few lingering bruises from the attack. Jack stewed over the fact we refused to let him heal us. He even tried to bring me a second helping of dessert which I could hardly turn down before I realized he was trying to brush his hand against me so he could heal me.

Scar and Tex seemed to hit it off right away. I could hear her beautiful musical laughter float across the room over the course of the evening as she and Tex sat and talked. I wondered if she was laughing at what he was saying out loud, or what he was thinking. What I wouldn't give to figure out what kinds of thoughts flew through his head. I even caught Andrews and Mia in a spare bedroom to see if they wanted any dessert. I quickly left the room because apparently they were helping themselves just fine.

After dinner, Harlow gently placed three beautifully wrapped boxes in front of me, Jack, and Graham. She stepped back as she folded her arms across her chest with pride.

"Open them," she instructed as she watched on excitedly.

Jerry ambled his way over, his blue eyes ablaze as he stood next to her.

"Oh, I think I know what those are." He beamed as he watched Jack rip open the gorgeous wrapping.

He slowly lifted the top of the box, and his eyes widened as he caught the glint of metal reflecting off the light from above. There, so delicately placed among a pillow of gold tissue paper, sat a watch, a pair of leather gloves, and a leather backpack.

"Are these...?" Jack asked nervously.

Harlow nodded as delight danced across her face. "These are your Paving supplies. We thought you might not want to carry a briefcase. Rachel carries a backpack too."

Jack lifted his gaze over in the corner toward Rachel, who was staring intently at him. Her face immediately tinted a gorgeous shade of pink as she turned away and suddenly seemed captivated with her hands in her lap. Jack smiled down at his backpack, as his own ears reddened.

"I suspect you know what the watch does, but those gloves are to inhibit any healing while you wear them." Harlow glanced up at me as she spoke, to make sure I understood. I thanked her with a silent nod.

"Thanks, Harlow." He grinned brilliantly up at her.

My heart did a few somersaults as I watched his face glow. His thin cheeks had filled out nicely over the course of the last week, especially with Harlow's good cooking. It was beginning to feel so much more natural for him to smile, and less forced. Just like a kid should.

She then flicked her intense stare toward me and Graham and lifted her chin impatiently.

"Go on, open yours too."

I laughed as Graham and I raced to see who could open their gift first. I won, but only because he let me.

"Cheater," I called over at him as I tore the lid off the box. Underneath lay a stunning Cambridge portfolio briefcase in a rich brown leather.

Scar grinned as she pointed out the straps. "You can also attach these straps if you'd like it to be a backpack for when you want to go hands-free!"

"This is incredible, guys. Thank you!"

"Open the front pocket," Harlow said as she nodded toward the bag. I slowly lifted the leather flap. Tucked neatly at the bottom was a stunning gold pocket watch with a unique, intricate design adorning the front. Underneath the timepiece was a pair of elegant gray gloves with a lace underlay.

"They seemed like they were just so...*you*." Scar beamed back at me.

"Did you pick these out for us?" I asked as I slipped the gloves on.

She shook her head.

"Jerry helped too. We thought you might want to wear some gloves too in case you're not feeling in the Paving mood. We wanted to remind you that you always have a choice." Her eyes flashed with the words.

"Thank you, all of you. This is amazing."

Graham shifted in his seat, and I giggled because he was clearly so excited to open his gift, he could hardly stand it.

"Well, go on!" I coaxed, hitting him playfully on the arm. With a wide sloppy grin, he shredded the pretty packaging and threw off the lid shamelessly.

Inside the box, an executive black leather briefcase lay neatly underneath a nest of silver tissue paper. He flipped open the silver latches and gasped at the gorgeous designer watch shining brilliantly under the light. Next to it was a silver pen. Graham carefully picked it up and surveyed it like it was going to throw flames at him.

The words *American Recruiting* were etched into the side, and I furrowed my brow at the name. That was my dad's business.

"Does this pen shoot Jedi mind tricks at people or something?" he asked hopefully, winking up at Harlow. She shook her head with a regretful smile.

"I'm sorry to say, but that is actually from Frank...your future father-in-law." She raised her eyebrows at him as my dad approached the table.

"Graham, I understand you and your men are looking for a job?" my dad asked with a hard-set jaw.

Graham straightened up and studied my dad. "Yes, sir. I believe we would love to learn more about some opportunities if you know of any." Graham glanced over at me nervously.

My dad chuckled and nodded. "I absolutely do. In fact, the chief down at the local fire station said they have a few openings. He was wondering if you and your men would like to join him for an interview next week."

Graham's jaw hardened as the rest of his brothers fell silent. They were listening in, their eyes glistening with earnestness. Graham scanned the room, making eye contact with each of his brothers in a silent regroup. He finally nodded and stood up slowly, stretching his hand out to my dad.

"Sir, that would be...incredible." My dad laughed and took his hand, pulling him into a hug filled with lots of clapping each other on the back. I held back the onset of tears that formed in my eyes from watching him and his brothers. Graham had specifically said they missed the thrill and adventure that came from being in the Marine Corps. Welcome images of Graham dressed head to toe in firefighting gear flooded my mind. I definitely needed a firefighter to come and cool me down after that one.

Later in the evening as Davis surprised us all and started playing a few Christmas carols on the piano, I wandered off down the hall. A quiet room at the end of the corridor caught my attention as it was filled with leather-bound books, an executive desk, and a wall lined top to bottom with paving spatulas. As I stepped closer and peered up at the rows of tools, I noticed each spatula had a name written on it in gorgeous flourished calligraphy. I was shocked to find Graham's, Jack's, and my name in the top row.

"Ah, you found the library," Harlow admired behind me. I whipped around to find her with a book in her hand, skimming through the pages.

"When did you get in here?" I asked timidly.

I swore I had just seen her out on the front porch rocking on the chair with Taryn. She smiled and closed the book, replacing it on its shelf. She pointed at the wall lined with spatulas as she strode over next to me.

"That's the lineage of every Paver that has been assigned to our community in O'Fallon. We've had quite a few talented individuals live here. You're among some of the best, Georgia," she added, running her fingers along the second row. Her hand trailed over one in particular with a familiar name on it.

Dr. Erving Cobbs.

"You know, I was curious, Georgia. You mentioned that Kurt Robinson asked you how your Reckoning was?"

I stared at her a moment, shocked that she felt the need to bring this up now. I shivered as I recalled the terrifying instance he'd asked me as he pinned me to the cold, hard ground. As Jack lay helpless next to Mia and Scar's lifeless bodies...

I nodded silently at her and turned back toward the wall of names, hoping she'd go back to talking about the history of the community again.

"We have never had a security problem here at headquarters. But since your Reckoning, we've had quite a lot of...visitors." I shifted under her gaze. I wasn't sure if she wanted me to apologize or explain myself. "As you've probably discovered, it is essential we remain hidden to the public. It would be mass hysteria if the world found out about us."

"But why not? I mean, Pavers help people anyway—why not allow them to come to us? Wouldn't that save us the trouble from all of this sneaking around, hero-in-the-dark nonsense?" I asked, keeping my eyes trained on the wall.

"I suppose in theory that sounds perfect...until it isn't," she continued, her voice dropping to a whisper. "The problem with that, is that Paving is already an incredible burden, and that's when no one knows about us. Think, if the world knew what we could do, and where we were located...we would never be able to get things done. The point of Paving relies on the freedom of choice. We can't go around and bark orders at the world to tell them to do this or that; we can only encourage. If they knew what they were supposed to do all along, don't you think life would be a little less exciting? There would be no thrill in the chase, the adventure of finding out what they like and what they're supposed to do."

"But what if they knew all along? I would have loved someone to tell me exactly what to do so I could be successful and happy. The chase and adventure only works if you like the thrill of figuring things out. I would much rather be right from the beginning. Don't people deserve that chance? To start off on the right foot...on the right path?"

Harlow seemed to stew on that for a moment before she pulled a spatula from the top row and handed it to me.

"Do you recognize this name?" she asked, her voice dangerously low.

I stared down at the name and shook my head.

Malcolm K. Jenkins.

"No...I'm sorry. Why?" I asked, peering up at her.

She gently took the spatula back and placed it on her desk, leaving an empty hole in the long line of Pavers.

"Because Malcolm Kurt Jenkins is actually Kurt Robinson," she sighed, her intense eyes darkening.

I nearly stumbled as the weight of the truth gripped me. Of course he was a Paver. He had known about my Reckoning when he attacked me for the second time, but it didn't sit right with me for one reason.

"How can he, though? Aren't Pavers hand-picked by God?" I demanded.

A tight-lipped smile flashed across her face as she nodded. "Pavers are capable of evil things because we are still human. We aren't angels, and we certainly aren't perfect. But we still help humanity. Our work is purposeful, divine in nature. Only bad things come from it when Pavers misuse their powers."

"What is Kurt's…Aftereffect?" I asked, as my whole body began to shake.

"He can locate missing persons. He knows exactly where they are, whether they are dead or alive."

I practically choked as I remembered all the times he might have been watching me. Watching my family. He probably knew where I was right now.

"And he left? Like Dr. Cobbs?" A pained grimace shot across her face as I said his name.

"Yes. Several years ago. He couldn't stand the work." She sighed.

"Ah, there you two are! Graham was just—" Scar stopped as she assessed me, her face falling as she flicked her gaze over to Harlow.

"Is she in there?" Graham asked as he peeked in the room with me, his brows knitting together as his steely regard fell on me.

Graham breezed past Scar and was in front of me in two strides across the room, his hands resting on my hips.

"What's wrong?" he demanded before he turned toward Harlow.

"Did you tell her?" Scar asked quietly as she closed the french doors leading into the library.

"Tell her what?" Graham repeated in the same commanding tone.

She let out a long breath as she leaned against the desk. "After Kurt was brought into the authorities, he…escaped while they were processing him," Scar relented uneasily through clenched teeth.

I inhaled a sharp breath at the news as I felt my knees begin to give way.

Graham's hard lines etched across his face as he pulled me behind him. "Are you fucking serious right now? He just *disappeared*?"

Harlow nodded silently, unflinching.

"When did you find this out? Please tell me he actually escaped and not vanished, like some Paving Aftereffect."

Harlow shook her head. "He was able to escape somehow. Pavers can't materialize in their physical bodies. But I hate to say, Kurt has unlimited access to the world in the Paving Realm." My jaw dropped and I shuddered as I pictured Kurt invisible to the eye but able to follow me and my family wherever we went. Not only did he know where I was, but he could watch me anytime he wanted, no matter what I was doing...what I was wearing. I shuddered again as my dinner threatened to come up. We would never be able to escape him. A tear slid down my cheek as I clung to Graham's arm.

"You mean there's no way to...turn off the access once a Paver decides to leave?" I demanded, my voice breaking into a sob.

Harlow lifted her chin, pulling her shoulders back as she stood tall in front of Graham.

"I'm afraid not...which brings me to an important order of business..." She eyed us warily. "Given the fact that our security has been breached, and we have a rogue Paver out on the loose, I was hoping to strike a bargain with you," Harlow said as she stared at the Paving wall again, as if in deep thought.

"A *bargain*?" Graham repeated furiously. As if this were the time.

"On any other occasion, your friends would have their memories retraced so they would forget about this place, along with everything that has happened over the course of the last few days."

I felt Graham's shoulders ripple as he let out a dangerous growl.

Harlow nodded grimly as she watched him. "I understand that would be a monumental loss for you and your friends, so I am willing to make a trade."

"What do you want?" Graham spat, shielding me still from Harlow.

"Your protection," she said with a shrug of her shoulder. "I understand your brothers are well-trained Marines. We will need your careful eye and defense to maintain our security. I will not risk the lives of the other Pavers who reside here, and I do not want a bloodbath on our grounds." She stared him down as he thought it over.

"And Mia?" he asked. She peered over his shoulder at me for a moment, before she nodded at him.

"I won't touch Mia either, but I believe I'll need her to put in some work around here as well. Given that you have a wedding to plan, I suspect you might want to have it here. Perhaps Mia can assist in the matter?" A small smile curved at her lips, and Graham's muscles seemed to relax at her suggestion. Her smile grew as she read his body language.

"Then that settles it. Your protection, for their memories. I will of course need them to sign a nondisclosure agreement." She extended her hand out toward him.

He stared at her for a moment as he considered it. "Does that mean that they can live here? For proper defense, you'll need them as full-time residents. We'll need to have shifts back-to-back."

"There's most certainly room, so that will be fine," she agreed. Graham shifted uneasily before finally grabbing her hand.

"Pleasure doing business with you, *Keaton.*"

Several weeks later...

A woman in a light-gray suit clicked through Trish's Café before her crystal-blue eyes landed on me.

"Georgia?"

I nodded uneasily. "Are you Lacy Stevens? From Whitman's Staffing?" I asked as I studied her designer corporate attire. From the looks of it, she was an executive or someone in upper management. She nodded, her beautifully quaffed hair shining under the light.

"Georgia Scott, you have no idea how glad I am to see you so..." She marveled as she surveyed me. "You look so beautiful—and *happier* might I add."

I lifted my chin with a smile as I took a sip of my mocha latte.

"Thank you. I...apologize I didn't quite recognize you. I still haven't regained any memories from my time at Whitman's." I frowned up at her as she joined me at the table.

"Yes, I understand you've been diagnosed with retrograde amnesia. I'm so sorry to hear that, considering what happened with Kurt..." Her eyes fell as she said his name. "I'm the director of Human Resources at Whitman's."

She pulled her purse to her lap and shuffled through it before pulling out a professional business card. She slid it across the table in front of me, and I smiled as I remembered the moment Scar had given me her business card. No Paving Inc. on this one, though; it had Whitman's Staffing all over it, with a corporate blue design.

"I'm here to discuss your position at Whitman's," she said, squaring her shoulders as if she were preparing herself for something big.

I fought the urge to shrink in front of her. Instead I put my cup down and pulled my shoulders back, mirroring her image.

"Are you...letting me go?" I asked quietly. "I know I've missed a lot of time—"

"No, no, no, Georgia. Oh, God no!" she laughed, shaking her head vehemently. She leaned forward, lowering her voice even though the café was practically empty.

"Given that Kurt was of course terminated, we were hoping that you would...fill his position." She pulled out a notepad from her purse and began scribbling a few things down.

"Your salary will be tripled, and I suspect you'll find some of the perks of his position to be rather noteworthy." She peered up at me as her eyes lit up.

"Lacy...that sounds amazing, truly. But I don't even remember what I do at Whitman's, much less what...Kurt did." I held back a gag as I let his name fall from my lips.

Lacy's face fell as she watched me.

"Georgia, to put it lightly, Kurt did a whole lot of nothing in his role, besides regrettably harass his female employees and..." She trailed off, surely unwilling to finish the sentence. She was probably going to say something like "rape and murder me on the side."

"I was reviewing your recruits in the last year, and I was truly impressed with your work. You've been filling roles left and right it seems. I've had several employers call with excellent remarks regarding the people you've sent their way." She slid the piece of paper she was writing on toward me.

"That is the contact for your office designer and suite manager...if you choose to accept the position."

"Office designer?" I repeated as I took another sip of my latte.

Lacy nodded fervently, her eyes wide with excitement.

"That's correct. We have on-call designers to make your office as stunning as you'd like it. Some of their work—"

"Would I be able to...choose my own personal designer?" I asked. Immediately I thought of Mia and her beautiful work from my vision. Lacy's eyes lit up as she nodded.

"Why, of course you can. In fact, you can choose your entire team of staff if you'd like. Unfortunately, half of the team left since Kurt went MIA."

I shuddered at her words. I didn't want to think about the fact that Kurt was MIA. I wanted him found...among a few other horrible things. She sensed my discomfort and plastered on her beautiful dazzling smile again.

"Georgia, what is it going to take for you to say yes? And don't say beg, because honestly I would."

I thought about the prospect of having Mia come work with me, to help get her foot in the door for designing. I also adored the idea of being able to afford some nice things for Jack...and of course to pay off a wedding.

"Would I still be recruiting out in the field as a director?"

Lacy's eyebrows shot up in surprise at my question, before a look of awe fell over her.

"Is that something you'd like to continue to do?"

And to my own surprise, I nodded at her. I knew the work would be so much more meaningful now that I knew my own destiny. Helping others was always my calling, and in that role, I could truly make a difference. I wanted to make sure I was still going to be able to help people, to make sure that they weren't just bringing food to the table, but that they were nourished every day with what they did. I wanted to make sure my recruits were satisfied and recharged from the labors of the day. That they found meaning in their own work and were using their talents in the right places.

"I'm pleased to hear that, Georgia. Some of our best lead by example in the field. I imagine you'd put some of them to shame with the numbers I'm already seeing in your recruitment log. I don't see why you wouldn't be able to lead and recruit at the same time."

I peeled off my cotton lace gloves and extended my hand out toward her.

"Then, Lacy, I think that sounds like a marvelous opportunity. I have a feeling I won't disappoint you."

"I couldn't agree more, Georgia." She beamed as my fingers curled around her hand.

And I felt my heart race as dark, onyx wisps surrounded me .